NAHLA
WARRIOR OF THE NORTH

OTHER BOOKS BY NICK MARONE

NAHLA

WARRIOR OF THE NORTH

NAHLA CHRONICLES: BOOK 1

NICK MARONE

Delta-V Press
Queanbeyan, New South Wales, Australia

Copyright ©2024 Nick Marone
nickmarone.com

ISBN: 978-0-6488641-6-5

A prepublication catalogue record for this book is available
from the National Library of Australia.

Cover art by Nick Marone

Map by Keir Scott-Schrueder
keirscottschrueder.crd.co

Printed by Lightning Source

Artificial Intelligence Ethical Use Statement
*The first drafts of the epigraphs (quotes at the beginning of chapters)
were written with the help of ChatGPT. The cover art was created in
Midjourney after many hours of refinement. In addition to two human
editors and two human proofreaders, the manuscript was examined by
ProWritingAid to identify errors and suggested improvements.*

This book is dedicated to all Tasmanians and anyone who has migrated across the Bass Strait from the mainland. You are not exiles—I promise.

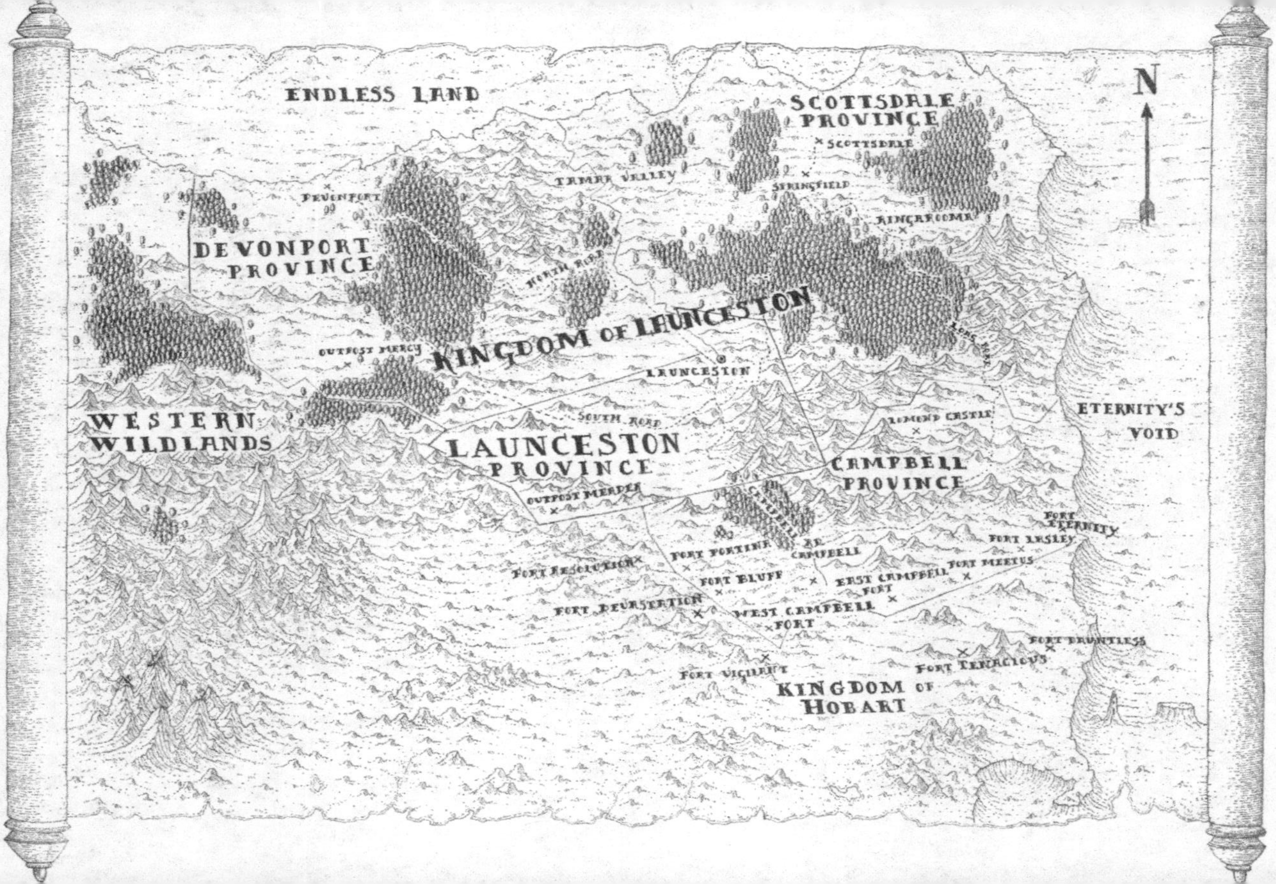
ENDLESS LAND
SCOTTSDALE PROVINCE
N
Scottsdale
Tamar Valley
Springfield
Devonport
Ringaroomra
DEVONPORT PROVINCE
North Road
KINGDOM OF LAUNCESTON
Outpost Mercy
Launceston
WESTERN WILDLANDS
South Road
LAUNCESTON PROVINCE
Lomond Castle
ETERNITY'S VOID
CAMPBELL PROVINCE
Outpost Merder
Fort Eternity
Fort Ansley
Fort Resolution
Fort Bluff
Fort Meetus
East Campbell Fort
Fort Perseration
West Campbell Fort
Fort Dauntless
Fort Vigilant
Fort Tenacious
KINGDOM OF HOBART

1

WARRIOR'S LAMENT

The Endless Land, where sandy earth and dusty sky co-
alesce into one seamless void. The Endless Land, where
undesirables are sent to be forgotten. The Endless Land,
where death itself goes to die.

—Nahla Northborn
Monologues

Nahla TRUDGED THROUGH THE barren wasteland, each lethargic
step punctuating the defeat that ravaged her mind. Her cracked
lips were as dry as the sand that swallowed her feet. The sun
assaulted her entire body, especially the skin that she dared expose
to its harsh rays. Hot winds pummelled her, caking her in dust.

Legends told of a great quantity of water that once covered
the region—water as far as the eye could see. She licked her lips
at the thought, felt the sting and tasted the blood, then chastised
herself for dreaming of myths.

Neither life nor death survived here. Even the bones of previous
exiles had disappeared. Each step brought her that much closer to
realising her own mortality. But she wouldn't stop. Surrender had
brought her to this place. Failure had led to exile, and valour had
chosen her method of execution—her reputation as a fierce warrior
granted her the honour of dying a warrior's death. No hangman's

noose or executioner's axe for Nahla. Instead, her death sentence was exile in the Endless Land, where she would battle and fail against the unconquerable enemy, the sun.

Nobody had returned from the Endless Land. But for her last act of defiance, Nahla resolved to stubbornly walk farther than anyone had ever walked before.

And then I will perish, she thought. *Just as I deserve.*

D<small>AYS LATER</small>, <small>AT THE</small> cusp of exhaustion, the beleaguered Nahla reached a valley flanked by two distant promontories. It occurred to her that she may have inadvertently turned around and ended up back where she'd started, but she knew the entire southern border of her former homeland. This valley was definitely an unfamiliar sight, which meant the Endless Land was not so endless after all.

The sun and the incessant winds had scorned her vision, but she could just see the outline of some ruins on the cliffs. That was a sign. Ruins meant civilisation, even if it was ancient and long forgotten.

It was midmorning, and the sun had not yet reached its zenith. The rocky western promontory was high enough to offer shade. Mercy from the sun was a luxury she would never again take for granted. It was cooler in this hiding spot, but the cliff face still emanated warmth, probably from the previous afternoon. Not even a cold night had drained the rock of its stored heat. She unravelled her head covering and let her dark, curly hair free. Then she opened her water pouch and took a tiny sip, just enough to wet her lips and tongue. It was better than nothing, which would soon be the case if she didn't find a water source.

Now rested and already feeling stronger, she rounded the promontory and pressed on into the valley. At the very least, it would afford her permanent protection from the prevailing winds that had plagued her for most of the trek.

It wasn't long before she started seeing more ruins. In fact, there looked to be a sizeable derelict village on the valley's eastern side, but it was high up an embankment, and she saw no way to access it. Nevertheless, she instinctively kept one hand on the straps of her two travel sacks and the other hand on the pommel of her sword.

She stopped and surveyed the valley ahead. It was quite rocky where she stood, but the ground got sandy up ahead. That was good and bad. She could move more quietly, no longer worrying about her sandals slapping against hard surfaces, but it also meant someone could follow her, or even approach silently for an attack. She would also move slower in the sand, making her a better target for archers. Even in this barren place, having not seen another person since being pushed into the Endless Land at spearpoint, she thought like a warrior—always cautious, always ready to fight.

This situational assessment made her second-guess her decision to enter the valley, but she'd be damned if she returned to the windy plain. She would rather die in battle like a true warrior than be taken by the blazing sun or the relentless wind. So she kept moving. The valley narrowed and opened, twisted this way and that, rising and falling ever so slightly. Nahla progressed carefully and quietly, always scanning above and behind for potential threats.

She walked along the sand, straining her tired legs. Her sweaty feet were gritty and covered in brownish-yellow granules. It was a touch lighter than the dust that had already covered her body. Even her clothes and the armour she hadn't removed were filthy. In fact, the only thing that still shone was her sword, because she had not removed it from its scabbard since before marching across the windswept plain.

Movement!

Nahla froze. Far off on the left side of the valley, where the elevation wasn't much higher than her position, she saw a glint of metal reflect in the harsh sunlight. She stepped slowly to a clump of boulders, trying to blend in with her surroundings. Maybe it was a blessing that her sweaty body was camouflaged in dirt and grime and that her pauldrons had lost their metallic sheen.

She hugged the rock, feeling its uncomfortable warmth, and studied her surroundings more closely. There was no other sign of movement nearby. All the sun-induced fatigue she'd endured earlier faded as a warrior's instinct coursed through her veins. She was ready for a fight if need be.

Her custom-made sword slid out of its leather scabbard in perfect silence. Nahla inspected the blade. The fine point made her smile. This sword was her life, and it imbued her with the energy she needed right now. She had felled many foes with the double-edged weapon. It had saved the lives of innocents and kept royalty on thrones. It was the only possession she would take to her grave. She pushed it back into the sheath and got to work.

One of her travel sacks held the rest of her armour. She pulled the pieces out and went through the age-old ritual of preparing herself for battle. Her main armour piece was a light-grey brigandine—a heavy, sleeveless cloth with armour plates riveted on the inside. The other pieces were vambraces for her wrists and lower arms, greaves for her shins, and a helmet. They still shone in the bright daylight, so she rubbed them on her sweaty arms and legs, then scraped them along the sand, reducing the reflection considerably. Once she had it all sufficiently dirty and dulled, she strapped them firmly in place.

Armed and armoured, Nahla began the quiet advance on her lone target. She needed food, water, and a place to rest, away from the elements. But now that she had entered some strange land she never knew existed, one question burned her mind as intensely as the sun had burned her skin: *Where am I?*

4

Nahla made good progress, moving from cover to cover, not too fast, but not lingering too long in any one spot. If her target had seen her, they were doing nothing about it, which was either worrisome or reassuring. As she advanced, Nahla developed multiple plans, the foremost of which was to make contact and seek assistance. If the reception was aggressive, she could use intimidation. At just over six feet tall, filthy, desperate, angry, clothed in armour, and brandishing a quality sword, she presented a fearsome sight. If there were too many aggressors to take on, she could bargain. She didn't know the social and political situation in this foreign land, but a mercenary could always get work with their skills and talents. And if all those plans failed, she had one last contingency: fight to the death.

She was nearly upon her target. It was a four-wheeled timber cart, covered with a canvas, drawn by a lone horse and what looked to be an even lonelier man. She had approached from behind, giving herself the element of surprise.

"Hey!" Nahla called. She kept a hand close to her sword.

The man looked around and stared wide-eyed. "Please, don't hurt me."

A wimp, Nahla thought.

"I've already given you everything I own," he continued. "The cart is empty."

That said enough. This man was a victim, not a threat. She picked the mercenary card.

"I am not who you think I am," she said. She strode up to the cart and walked alongside it. "Do you have any food? Water?"

The wayfarer's shoulders relaxed, but he didn't stop the horse. "No, they took everything."

She resisted the urge to ask who "they" were. Instead, she asked the next important question. "Where am I?"

The man reined in his horse and the cart stopped. "What?"

"Where am I?" Nahla repeated, suddenly hearing the fatigue in her voice. "What is this land?"

"You're . . . you're in Tasmania."

Nahla squinted. *Tasmania*. The name edged forwards from the recesses of her mind. Tasmania, the land of myth and legend. Nahla's people told stories about it to entertain their children. The seers debated its existence. The oldest written records mentioned it in fables. Adventurers disappeared in search of it. Exiles, criminals, and general good-for-nothings were told to "go to Tasmania"—a euphemism to disappear, out of sight, out of mind, forgotten.

"Tasmania," Nahla repeated, almost to herself.

"Yes." The man studied her. "The Kingdom of Launceston, to be exact. Are you from the Southern Kingdom?"

Nahla had never heard of a Southern Kingdom, or the Kingdom of Launceston, for that matter. Her homeland was north. "I am not from either of those places."

Nahla couldn't imagine what was worse, dying in the Endless Land, or living on the other side of it in a world unknown to her people. She'd barely survived the hot, windswept crossing, and she doubted she could cheat luck again and return. Even if she did, though, she would be slaughtered on sight.

"Where are you heading?" Nahla asked.

"To Launceston," the wayfarer replied. Then, when he noticed Nahla's blank stare, he elaborated. "It's the capital of the Northern Kingdom."

"I'd like to bargain with you. From what you have told me, there are marauders on this road. If you take me to Launceston, I can protect you along the way."

"There is nothing left to steal."

Nahla gestured at the sweating black horse harnessed to the cart. "Your mare would be a worthy prize. I'm surprised she wasn't taken along with your other possessions. And your cart seems in good condition."

"If they keep taking people's horses, there will be nothing left to pull carts, and hence no traders to raid along the deserted roads.

But I accept your offer. You can keep me company for the next few hours."

He slid over and Nahla climbed aboard.

"Thank you. I'm Nahla."

"Deeno. I suggest you make yourself comfortable. The road is bumpy and God's Eye burns bright today."

"I am already more comfortable than I have been in days," Nahla told him.

And so, Nahla travelled with Deeno through the midday sun to a city that he described as "bustling and full of opportunities". She had been exiled, but providence had carried her through the Endless Land to this new world that seemed ripe for a woman of her talents. She rested her left hand on her sword, wondering how often—or how soon—she would need it.

2

OUTSIDER

To be an outsider is to dance on the fringes of normality, daring to step beyond the boundaries of conformity and embracing the untamed winds of individuality.

—Nahla Northborn
Journal of Penance

N<small>AHLA</small> <small>DRIFTED TO SLEEP</small> to the steady swaying of the cart and the peaceful *clip-clop* of the horse. She awoke refreshed, though hungrier and thirstier, but she scolded herself for letting her guard down. She vaguely remembered Deeno speaking in a low, calming voice about Launceston just before she nodded off.

The sun had dipped low enough that the wispy clouds were light pink. A soft breeze caressed them, and Nahla shifted to cool her sticky skin. The movement caught Deeno's attention.

"Was wondering when you'd wake," he said.

"I'm sorry," Nahla said. "I think I fell asleep while you were talking to me."

"I know I can drone on, but I didn't think I was *that* bad." At the sound of Nahla's laughter, Deeno continued. "You said you would protect us on the road to Launceston."

"I have failed you," she admitted. *Like I failed my king.*

"Don't worry about it," Deeno said with a wave of the hand.

8

"I'm teasing you. Your presence alone is enough to ward off any would-be bandits. Where did you get that sword and armour?"

Nahla scanned the horizon and saw that they were approaching civilisation. The fires of streetlamps glowed a few kilometres away. She wondered how much about her past she should tell Deeno. Since he was kind enough to give her passage, and decent enough not to take advantage of her while she slept, she decided it was safe to sprinkle some truths.

"This sword was a gift, custom made as a token of thanks for my service," she said. She raised it so he could see. "The armour was crafted for me too."

"Are you a gladiator?"

"A what?"

"A gladiator. Don't they have gladiators where you come from?"

"I have never heard the word."

"A gladiator fights for entertainment, sometimes to the death."

Nahla's hair bristled at the thought. "My people do not fight to entertain others. Blood is spilled for war, not amusement."

"Hmm." Deeno shifted his grip on the horse's reins and cleared his throat. "Is there much war in your land?"

"Too much."

"Is that why you are here now?"

Nahla frowned, reliving the events of the last few months. "Something like that."

No doubt sensing a wall around the topic, Deeno politely moved on. His talkativeness, perhaps stemming from the lonely hours carting goods across empty roads, kept them going until they reached Launceston. Two large, tall braziers marked the city limits, though a long stretch of dirt road flanked by shorter lamps stood between them and the first buildings. A single tower, high and narrow, sat off the road among some brush. An armoured person with a spear watched them from the upper storey. It was so dark by now that the guard was just a silhouette, barely lit by the nearest brazier. A crescent moon, frequently hidden by fast-moving clouds, made the night even darker. A painter would use the darkest shades, and just a drop of orange, if the scene was on a canvas.

"What's the guard for?" Nahla asked quietly after they'd passed the tower.

"Bandits, marauders, raiders. Whatever they're called, they surround Launceston. The city is safe, but they've stopped patrolling beyond the farmlands."

The road into Launceston was smoother than the roads they had travelled in the previous hours, so Deeno encouraged the horse into a trot. Nahla sheathed her sword.

It was difficult to see much of Launceston with only streetlamps and light overflowing from windows to guide their path, but Nahla could comfortably scan her immediate surroundings. They passed buildings as ancient as those from Nahla's home. Brick, stone, hardened mud, and a patchwork of timber held up roofs of thatch-work or wooden shingles.

People walked here and there, most carrying tools or buckets. Some led packhorses or mules laden with full saddlebags. Many wore ragged and dirty clothes. Some women chatted on a street corner and erupted in laughter. A loud group of children emerged from between two houses and darted across the street, disappearing between more houses on the other side. An elderly man sat under an awning in front of his dwelling, and he waved at Deeno as the cart passed.

The road had been partially laid with smoothed stone and the rest of the exposed earth stamped hard. The cart's wheels glided along with only a few bumps, but the axle screeched. As they went deeper into the city, Nahla noticed that the road became smoother still, with more professional stonework. The buildings were larger, and in better condition, and there were actually trees with green leaves on some street corners. There were also more people bustling around, and more beasts of burden pulling carts with sacks, barrels, passengers, and other cargo.

Deeno stopped by a large stone building that dominated a large intersection. "This is a customer of mine," he said. "One of many taverns in Launceston. I'm going to see if we can get a room for the night. I'm sorry I can't afford two rooms."

"I am comfortable sharing a room if it will save you money."

"Money?"

"Coin. Currency."

Deeno flashed her a puzzled look.

"It's a form of payment where I come from. How do your people pay for goods and services?"

He scratched his head. "Well, I guess we pay for goods and services with goods and services."

"You barter?"

"The term is new to me. Everybody needs something, and everybody else needs some form of service, so we trade possessions, produce, and labour. When you offered to accompany me, you were trading your fighting skill for my transportation."

"I see." It was a new way of economic thinking, certainly different to the power of gold and copper coins that dictated every level of social and political life in her homeland.

"You watch the horse while I talk to the innkeeper," Deeno said, and disappeared inside.

Nahla hopped off the cart and stretched. It had been comfortable to sit down when she'd met Deeno, but the hours on the hard wooden seat had left her stiff. She twisted at the waist and rolled her shoulders. Her armour clanked and rustled. Then, aware that people were eyeing her curiously, she turned her attention to the horse.

The mare was a beautiful creature. Deeno obviously took great care of her. Thickly muscled, with a neatly cut and brushed mane, she was easily seventeen hands tall. It was a Percheron, a breed highly favoured back home for agriculture, cargo, and combat alike.

She had owned one herself, a smoky-grey named Lorelei, and she reminisced about their adventures together as she ran a hand along the neck of Deeno's horse. The mare leaned into her touch. Nahla smiled and sighed. She'd lost Lorelei two weeks ago.

Her throat was dry. She scanned the area for water—a tank, a barrel, a trough, anything that could relieve her dehydration. She only had a few drops left in her water pouch, and her last sip had been when she left the Endless Land and entered the sandy valley.

A wide barrel with a wooden bung sat atop a stand in one corner of the large intersection. Nahla gave the horse another pat before walking to the barrel. Being by the roadside, she felt sure that it belonged to the public. She removed the bung quickly, then replaced it, letting some lukewarm liquid splash into her palm. She licked tentatively.

Water.

Nahla dropped to her knees, opened the bung again and let the water pour into her mouth, gulping it down. She coughed as the dust in her throat cleared. Then she splashed some on her face and felt cleaner and refreshed.

"You dare waste the water!" a voice bellowed behind her.

She plugged the barrel and turned. A crowd had gathered, illuminated by some fiery streetlamps and handheld torches. They stared with wide eyes and open mouths. Some had clenched fists. In front of the crowd was a bearded man in a shiny breastplate featuring a gilded and embossed dog baring its teeth. He wore a dark cape that fluttered in the light breeze, and his tunic, made from a richly woven fabric, went halfway to his knees. He had an ornate helmet with a short black-and-white plume, and he regarded Nahla with a look of utter contempt. Flanking him were two soldiers in matching leather armour and metal helmets, similarly horrified at what they had just witnessed. This man and his entourage were not merely citizens of Launceston. They had uniforms . . . and swords.

12

"I dare to quench my thirst," she replied and stood. They were about the same height. Nahla adopted a guarded stance.

His brow furrowed. "Your minute of drinking could have satisfied an entire family for a day. You have blatantly disregarded the royal decree on water rations." His mouth twitched into a thin smile. "This offence deserves punishment."

"I am an outsider," Nahla said. "I was not aware of your law."

"The law is known throughout this kingdom, and similar laws exist in the territories of the southern kingdom. Ignorance is no defence. Seize her!"

The two soldiers sprung forwards, hands on swords. Nahla whipped out her sword, felt its reassuring weight and familiarity, and a great murmur swept through the crowd. The soldiers responded in kind, but she swung at one of them, slicing her ear off. She yelped and staggered back. Her offsider lunged at Nahla, but Nahla parried. Their swords clanked in the night, and the sudden violence pushed the crowd back. The soldier tried to recover with a riposte, but again Nahla deflected it. He used the momentum of the deflection to bring his sword down on her from above, but she dodged it, grabbed his neck, and brought his head down on her knee, then kicked him to the floor beside his superior.

By this time, the first soldier with the hacked ear moved in for revenge, but the officer held an arm out. "Stay back, Lieutenant Kessia. She's mine."

The officer drew his sword and positioned himself in a well-trained fighting stance. "You have skill," he said, working the sword with his wrist. "Who are you?"

"My name is Nahla," she replied carefully. "And who might you be?"

The crowd had swelled to more than twice its original size. News must have spread that an authority figure was challenging a lawbreaker, and vice versa. They gave the warriors a wide berth as more soldiers trickled through and made a cordon.

The officer started circling, and Nahla mirrored his movements. "You must truly be an outsider if you have not heard of me. I am Lord Johl, governor of this province. Where are you from?"

"From the north."

"From Devonport?"

"Yes." Nahla had never heard of the place.

"So, Lord Vimarr sends his criminals to my province? If you've come here to make a new home, then I shall grant it. Your home is now Launceston Prison. Will you continue to resist?"

"I shall." She readied herself and scanned for other threats. The soldiers stayed away from her.

"Then you will die tonight."

Johl advanced at lightning speed. His sandalled foot slapped the ground and his sword whipped at Nahla's torso. She did an empty fade, jumping back and then quickly springing forwards for an attack. Johl parried, then feinted. Nahla fell for the deception and caught the point of Johl's sword square in her chest. It pierced the canvas of her brigandine, but the metal plates beneath stopped the blade before it reached her belly. It angered her that she had been fooled, because she felt it was a continuation of the series of mistakes that had led her to this very situation.

She batted away Johl's sword, closed the distance between them with a long step, and twisted his arm upwards so his sword was out of harm's way. Then she elbowed him in the nose. The metallic cheek guards of his helmet rattled as he staggered. In his momentary daze, she struck hard at the side of his torso, but his breastplate curved around his body and her sword bounced off. She had rarely encountered armour of that quality before.

Now bleeding from the nose, Johl no longer played the gentleman. He gripped his sword with two hands and attacked in a dizzying rage of precision strikes. They were strong, but he moved slower than before. Nevertheless, a second after Nahla parried one

14

attack, Johl had already started another. Hungry and tired, her arms ached and her head pounded from the sudden onslaught of sword fighting. She held out, though Johl was gradually pushing her back. The crowd cheered for Johl, egging him on.

One of Johl's strikes bounced off her sword and hit one of her pauldrons. The shock went right up her neck, but she ignored it and knocked his sword downwards and then brought her hilt up to his chin. Johl shrieked, swore, and deflected Nahla's next attack, then swung in from the right. Nahla ducked under it and rolled on the cobbled road. Johl's sword embedded itself in the wooden water barrel. Seeing her chance, she grabbed his leg and pulled him to the ground. While on his back, he produced a dagger from within his cloak and swiped at Nahla's exposed thigh. The tip scratched her skin. He raised himself on one knee, but before he could strike again, she kicked the dagger out of his hand and then punched him in the face, sending him back to the ground.

Nahla raised her sword to deliver the final blow, but powerful arms enveloped her from behind. She shouted as Johl's soldiers wrenched her sword from her hand and pinned her arms behind her back. There were at least ten of them in the circle now, and one was helping Johl to his feet. He heaved his sword out of the barrel and pointed it at Nahla's neck. Bloodied sweat ran down his mouth and into his beard, and he huffed to catch his breath.

"I was going to assign you to the labour crew in Launceston Prison," he said between breaths, "but I think a more severe punishment is in order." He checked his sword, frowned that it was bereft of blood, and sheathed it. Then he spat blood out of his mouth. "Take her to the prison. She'll get her punishment tomorrow."

Nahla went cold as one soldier handed Johl her sword, her most prized possession. Then they led her away through the crowd, who jostled and hurled verbal abuse. She wondered what punishment Johl had in store for her, and if she could fight her way out of it.

3

CASS THE BLASPHEMER

I, Lord Johl, Governor of Launceston Province, hereby officially condemn the woman known as Cass the Blasphemer
for seven counts of blasphemy and one count of sedition.
The prisoner is to be kept in Launceston Prison until such
time that a suitable public execution can be organised.

—Lord Johl
Judgement of Cass the Blasphemer

THE SOLDIERS MARCHED NAHLA through the city. Two held her
arms tight against her back, while two more followed close
behind. In front, a large man carrying a flaming torch yelled at
passersby who blocked their path. Leading the pack was the one
they called Lieutenant Kessia. She held a clump of bandages
where Nahla took off her ear.

Nahla protested against her situation, but Kessia struck out
with a ferocious backhand across Nahla's cheek. When Nahla
squirmed in silence, the soldiers simply tightened their grip.

Launceston Prison loomed in the distance despite the dark night.
Its walls stood higher than any of the surrounding buildings. Bright
braziers on the walls marked the prison's perimeter. Larger fires
burned higher at the tops of towers, and she could see beams of light
shining inside the walls.

Some more walking took them through another run-down residential neighbourhood, which then morphed into an industrial area. Nahla could tell by the layout of the buildings and artistic signs swinging from awnings or fastened above front doors. Along the main road, they passed a blacksmith's workshop, an armoury, a fletcher, another tavern, and a butchery. A sign advertising a tannery pointed out of town along a well-worn path. Nahla scrunched her nose. Tanneries stunk, so it was right to have it far away.

The main road led to a big wooden portcullis at the entrance of the prison. Towers flanked the gatehouse, all structures built entirely of rough-hewn stone. Nahla watched as a guard in one of the towers did something she had never seen before. He put his hands against a long rod and manoeuvred a huge, shiny metal disk around the outside of a brazier. The fire reflected off the metallic surface and illuminated Nahla and her escort on the road.

"Who goes there?" a voice called from the gatehouse.

Nahla couldn't see because the reflection from the fiery tower was too bright. She felt her handlers tense at the disembodied voice.

Kessia stepped forwards. "Lieutenant Kessia of the Provincial Garrison. We bring you a prisoner from the Governor himself."

"Open the gate!"

Through the shadows beyond the portcullis, Nahla saw a sturdy timber double-door opening. Some prison guards marched through the gatehouse. The portcullis rose, screeching on metal chains. Armour clanked as Johl's soldiers pushed Nahla into the custody of the guards. There were salutes, some overly stiff and polite verbal exchanges that were nothing short of professional.

Kessia faced Nahla. "I hope you get murdered or raped tonight. Preferably both." She spat at Nahla's feet, checked the bloody bandage from her ear wound, then marched off with the rest of her soldiers.

"So," one of the prison guards began, "what did you do?"

They walked Nahla through the gatehouse.

"I drank water," she said.

"That all? The lieutenant's injuries wouldn't be your handiwork too?"

"It was water I did not own. And, yes, I chopped off the lieutenant's ear."

One of the other guards chuckled. "Remind me never to say 'Listen 'ere' to that one."

All four guards laughed as they moved across the entrance courtyard.

"And I fought Lord Johl."

Their merriment ceased.

"Don't be telling lies like that," the first guard warned.

"I fought him, and I defeated him."

"Lord Johl's dead?"

The first guard bashed a fist against the junior warden's arm. "Don't be ridiculous. His Lordship is the kingdom's best swordsman. This gutter rat is lying. Aren't you?"

Nahla regarded the superior blankly. "Lord Johl is not dead," Nahla said.

"There, see? Now, no more of that talk, or you'll have inmates harassing you." He waved a finger at her. "Now let's get inside. The prison is crowded, and I still don't know where I will put you."

THEY THREW HER INTO a large cell and slammed the door shut. Crowded was an understatement, and it reeked of unwashed bodies and unsanitary conditions. At least forty people lined the stone walls—men and women in dirty, torn clothes. They scooped runny food out of wooden bowls, and the sight reminded Nahla of just how hungry she was.

"Hey!" she called out to the guards who had locked her inside. One of them returned, hand on the hilt of his short sword. "How can I get some food?"

The guard scoffed. "Ask someone in there, because I won't be bringing you any. Supper's already been delivered tonight." Then he walked off.

When Nahla faced the prisoners again, some averted their eyes back to their bowls. They looked just as hungry as she felt. She wondered what they had done to end up in this dark, smelly place. At least the cell was a few degrees cooler than the night outside. She remembered descending stairs, so perhaps the cell blocks were half-submerged into the ground.

Nahla walked between the prisoners, eyeing them left and right, hoping that one would share food. But they kept their heads low and their mouths full. She must have looked a strange sight—a brooding, dusty woman kitted out in armour.

A commotion started at the far end of the cell. A tall, powerfully built man with a mass of black, frizzy hair was harassing a short, pale woman for her food. Her long blonde hair was so light it was nearly silver, and the man had a firm grip on it, pulling her head back and demanding that she relinquish her bowl. To her credit, she refused adamantly, but the brute was not hearing it.

"I'll throw you across the cell if you don't give it to me," he said coldly.

"Nobody is throwing anyone," Nahla said. She stood in the middle of the cell, hands on her hips. Spoons stopped scraping in bowls. All eyes were on her.

"Oh, it's the fresh meat," he said. "Tell you what: I'll let her go if you give me your armour. I can trade it for something."

Nahla smiled. "How about you come over here and take it from me?" She ignored the hunger in her belly.

The brute shook the blonde one last time before releasing her hair. Then he stood at his full height and approached Nahla. As he neared, she got a better look at him and wondered if she had bitten off more than she could chew. He was taller and wider than Nahla, with biceps as big as her face and a hairy, muscled chest that was caked in sweat and grime. He wore only shorts, revealing equally strong legs that could kick the life out of her. He stopped a few paces away, and the other prisoners cleared the area. Perhaps they had seen him fight before.

"I will give you one last chance to surrender your armour to me," he said. His voice was deep, menacing, intimidating.

"How honourable," Nahla said. "I give *you* the first chance to strike me."

He cracked his knuckles and rolled his thick neck. Regardless of how big and frightening as was, his size worked against him. He lunged forwards with a guttural roar, but Nahla quickly sidestepped him. As he passed, she jumped and whacked her metal vambrace against the back of his head. He groaned at the impact, but he spun around faster than Nahla anticipated and used the momentum to whip the back of his hand at her face. His fingertips caught her cheek, which was enough to sting.

"Who taught you how to fight?" he growled, then charged her. His arms stretched wide and collected Nahla in a deadly hold, pulling her off her feet and slamming her against the cold stone wall. He pinned her there, trying to squash her chest.

"I taught myself," she said, and bashed a fist into the side of his neck, hitting a nerve. He released his grip and stumbled backwards in a daze.

Nahla followed with a firm palm up into the brute's stubby nose. She felt the soft tissue bend and cartilage break. By the time he stepped back in shock, he already had blood covering his mouth and chin. His eyes bore into her with a mix of rage and embarrassment, but Nahla didn't give him a chance to act on it. She swung her leg and hit the side of his knee hard with her armoured shin. The move dropped the big guy. Then Nahla quickly smashed the side of his head, aiming for the temple.

20

The brute's eyes closed before he hit the floor. He landed with a thud and stayed there. Nahla watched and waited, panting. Nothing happened. One of the other prisoners crept over to the motionless brute and nudged him with a dirty foot. Still no response. The prisoner spat on the motionless body, offered a half-toothed grin, and shook Nahla's hand, then chuckled as he went back to his fellow inmates. The others applauded, clapping, whistling, or banging their empty wooden bowls on the hay-covered floor.

Nahla walked shaky-legged to the end of the cell and sat next to the diminutive blonde woman. She closed her eyes and rested her head on the cool wall, letting her heart rate return to normal. When she reopened them, she found the blonde woman holding a half-full bowl in front of her.

"You keep it," Nahla told her, again ignoring her hunger pains.

Nahla searched nearby for the brute's food, but there was nothing. Either he had already eaten it, or another prisoner had stolen it during the scuffle.

The blonde put the bowl in Nahla's lap and whispered, "Eat it. I can hear your stomach growling."

"Thank you. What's your name?"

"I'm Cass," she said quietly.

"The *Blasphemer*," one of the nearby prisoners added.

"Cass the Blasphemer," Cass confirmed.

Nahla shovelled a spoonful of tasteless muck into her mouth. "What are you doing here? You don't look like a criminal."

"And they do?" Cass gestured at the dirty, ragged occupants of their cell.

"Point taken. But you haven't answered my question. Why are you here?"

"I am here for publicly accusing the real criminals—the king and his lords. That makes me a seditionist. I am here for treason, to be punished by execution, but I've managed to hide by jumping from one cell to another. I think I'll be here in perpetuity."

Nahla had never heard of words like *seditionist* and *perpetuity*. "Of what could your king be accused?"

"*My* king?"

"He is not mine. I've come from a northern land."

"I see." Cass shuffled around to face Nahla better. She sat cross-legged, barefoot, her pale skin covered in dirt. "I have never heard of a land to the north of Launceston."

"People keep telling me that."

"Then you do not know about the longstanding mandate about water?"

This Nahla knew only too well. She told Cass how she came to be a guest at Launceston Prison.

"You fought Lord Johl?" Cass asked, wide-eyed. "He's the worst of the lot. Did you kill him?"

"No."

"That's a shame."

The brute regained consciousness and rolled onto his back, grumbled, then sat upright. He gave Nahla a nasty look, then nodded—one warrior begrudgingly acknowledging another. Nahla nodded back, hoping there wouldn't be any bad blood between them thereafter.

"That's Jugg," Cass explained. "You're the first to challenge him."

"Why is Jugg here?" Nahla asked.

"Ask him."

Nahla sighed. "Hey, Jugg!"

The brute had crawled to a corner to lick his wounds. "What?"

"Why are you here?"

Jugg looked away. "I stole a loaf of bread. And what petty crime have they accused you of?"

"I drank some water, and then fought Lord Johl and nearly killed him."

The prisoners stared at her again. Then they assaulted her with questions. How did it happen? Why did she fight him? Where?

How did she defeat him? Is he wounded? Did she kill any of his soldiers?

Nahla held her hands up to quieten them. "It seems Johl has a reputation in this cell," she said to Cass, loud enough that everyone else could hear.

"Raise your hand if Lord Johl is the reason you are imprisoned," Cass said. All raised their hand. "Corruption runs strong with the king and his lords, and Johl is the worst."

"You were saying something about water?"

"Ah, yes. God blesses us with sufficient water to survive. We sometimes have enough to drink, the right amount for industry, not enough to bathe, and nothing for pleasure. But the king has more than his fair share. I publicly accused him of contravening the water mandate that his own ancient predecessor enacted—a law that has governed this land for as long as recorded history. This angered the priestesses, who dole out the water as God supplies it. By accusing the king of having more than his needs, I was also accusing the priestesses of giving more than what was allowed, and therefore challenging God Herself. Hence, my epithet."

"Epithet?"

"Cass *the Blasphemer.*"

Footsteps echoed outside the cell, hushing Cass. A few guards appeared at the cell door.

"Which one is Nahla?" one guard called.

"I am here," Nahla replied.

"Stand up when I speak to you!"

Nahla stood. She felt the mushy food working its way through her empty gut.

"Lord Johl has decided your punishment," the guard continued. "You are to fight in the gladiatorial arena tomorrow. I hear the king himself will be in attendance."

Nahla said nothing, just stared at the guard in the dimly lit corridor.

"Well, don't just stand there," the guard said. "Be happy you won't be rotting in here for long. It is a privilege to die entertaining the king."

Nahla smiled thinly and nodded. "I look forward to entertaining the king tomorrow."

"That's better. Now get your rest, and everyone else shut up. I don't want to hear any talking."

The guard left, and the cell went quiet. Nahla sat down. Cass lay on some hay-stuffed bedding on the floor, eyes already closed.

Nahla stayed awake longer, pondering her situation and the events of the day. This time last night, she had been resting in the torturous Endless Land. Now she was imprisoned in a foreign kingdom and condemned to death for a second time in as many weeks.

She caught Jugg staring at her before she finally decided to sleep.

4

ROYAL ENTERTAINMENT

Come one, come all! Watch the latest battle for survival as Launceston's most fearless and savage inmates fight for your entertainment and for the favour of the king.

—**Anonymous**
Advertisement for a gladiatorial contest

THE GUARDS FETCHED NAHLA early in the morning and manhandled her through the cool corridors of the prison. The sun was just beginning to shine through the high eastern windows, which were narrow and open to the air, but thickly barred. They passed a prisoner who was leaning against his cell door, hands hanging outside the bars. He whistled at the procession, and one guard whipped a truncheon across his exposed wrists. Nahla tried to ignore the painful yelp.

She was told to wash herself and clean her armour, because it was "fit and proper to be presentable for the king".

"How will I fight?" she asked. "What weapons are available?"

"You will be given weapons. More than enough."

Nahla only needed one weapon, but she'd lost it to Lord Johl. She wondered if he'd be watching the gladiatorial contest. Her blood boiled at the thought.

She was handed over to two female guards, who took her into a dark room and locked the door. Inside was a washbasin, a table, a bucket of water, and some rags. They ordered her to strip.

Nahla stared expectantly, then understood that she would not have privacy. With the care of a veteran warrior, she untied her armour and laid the pieces neatly on the table. The extra freedom of movement was a relief, but she felt exposed without the protective layer. As she removed her brigandine, one guard approached the table to inspect the armour pieces.

"You touch them, you die," she told her. She'd already lost her sword, and she'd be damned if these wardens stole her armour too.

The guard straightened, looked at her counterpart incredulously, and stepped back to her original position by the door. Nahla then removed the last of her clothes—some light undergarments and her sandals—and stood on display for the guards. She stared them down until they were so uncomfortable that they looked away, then she got busy washing herself.

Under the rags on the table was some tallow soap made from animal fat. She poured the water into the basin and lathered up. At first, she recoiled at the water's coolness, but then splashed it freely on her body, welcoming the refreshment. She actually smiled as the dirt and grime washed off her tanned skin. The water was already dark by the time she'd done her face and shoulders, so she emptied the basin. A pipe fed into an empty bucket. Perhaps the dirty water was used elsewhere.

Her thigh stung slightly where Johl had cut her the night before. She inspected the wound: a red line that hadn't healed as quickly as she would have liked. She patted it softly with a damp cloth, then continued down her leg. Her hair was caked in dust. She'd saved some water to rinse it, though there was not enough to wash it thoroughly. At least she felt cleaner.

Finally, Nahla gave her armour a wipe with a damp cloth, saturated her undergarments, and then suited up again. The wet clothes would keep her cooler during the impending fight.

She was now clean, as requested, and ready to die for the king in the gladiatorial arena. She gave her wardens a wave of the hand as if to hasten the slaughter.

UNDERGROUND CORRIDORS CONNECTED THE prison to the arena. She heard the buzz of an excited crowd as four guards escorted her towards the bright morning light. One of them opened a heavy gate, then they pushed her unceremoniously into the sunshine.

"Go to the centre podium," one told her.

The crowd cheered as she entered. The scorching sun struck her cool skin, and her eyes took a moment to adjust to the daylight. After she'd blinked a few times, she saw that the arena was a huge oval with multitiered seating filled with people. The crowd roared louder as more gladiators entered the arena from other dark corridors. A deep, rhythmic drumbeat rose above the cheering and chatter. Nahla's heart thumped in time with the drums as she realised regular town and country folk had come to witness a slaughter, and she could soon be one of the victims.

The guards yelled at her from behind and she hurried towards the centre, which sported a long, low podium, on which were several armour-clad people already waiting. Standing tall among her would-be opponents was a large man with a big mat of frizzy black hair.

Jugg.

Nahla stepped up on one of the podium's corners and kept herself hidden behind the other gladiators. There must have been at least twenty others, and more were coming. As the podium grew ever more crowded, Nahla studied her surroundings, preparing herself for whatever trials might come her way. The arena's ground was sandy, but it must have been a thin layer, because it had been comfortable to walk on. In front of the podium was a half-circle of tables with many weapons ready for the taking—swords of varying sizes, spears, polearms of intricate designs, axes, maces, flails, and clubs, just to name a few. She saw some shields too. Since none of the gladiators looked armed, she felt certain that all the contestants would madly rush to the weapons. Now she regretted hiding in the back.

Trumpets blasted a long, monotonous tune, and the crowd quietened. Directly ahead, red banners unfurled either side of a decorative royal box. It was sheltered from the sun and stood higher than all the seating tiers. The gladiators nudged and pushed each other to get to the front row of the podium. Then a group of resplendent people entered the royal box—a collection of colourfully dressed men and women, and a chubby, bearded man wearing a gold crown and loose white garb.

The king surveyed the silent audience and the gladiators below as his followers took their places either side of him. Nahla noticed the difference between those in the royal box and the scores of people sitting under the hot morning sun. The king and his advisors—or family members, or other wealthy socialites, or whoever they were—looked extravagant in their fine clothes and neat grooming, whereas the common people were dirty, unkempt, and ragged. And yet, they all seemed happy to be here. Perhaps the thrill of the contest was a welcome distraction from their simple lives.

A man in a black cape arrived and stood next to the king.

Johl!

Nahla saw red when she focused on the nobleman. Johl regarded the gladiators with an air of disinterest until he spotted Nahla. They locked eyes for a moment, then Johl grinned ever so slightly, turned his chin up, and looked away. Nahla controlled her breathing. There was no use in getting worked up now. She would need all her wits as soon as the fight started.

The king raised his hands. His huge sleeves slid down his pale arms. The trumpets suddenly played a quick introductory tune, then stopped as sharply as they began.

"People of Launceston!" the king shouted into a speaking horn. His voice boomed and echoed throughout the arena. "I present to you another fine selection of gladiators who have graciously volunteered to entertain you today. Gladiators, as always, a reward awaits the last remaining fighter. May you fight well, may you please the crowd with your skill and prowess, and may the best warrior win!"

The king raised a hand. A drumroll started. Nahla tensed. Then his hand dropped, and the drums ceased. "Begin!"

Jugg immediately pushed two gladiators aside and kicked the one in front of him off the podium. Nahla didn't stick around to see the rest. She darted to the nearest table, fighting off the fist of another woman who tried to slow her progress. They reached the same table and both grabbed the same sword—the only sword. The other woman scratched Nahla's hand. Nahla let her have the sword and picked up a small, round shield instead. Then they battled.

The woman swung madly. She didn't seem trained or experienced in combat, and Nahla felt a trace of regret as she battered the sword away and smashed the shield into the woman's face. The manoeuvre knocked her opponent out cold. Nahla didn't want to kill her, so she took the sword and left her lying on the sandy ground with a bloodied face.

Now armed with sword and shield, Nahla entered the fray. At the other end of the free-for-all, Jugg was fending off two opponents with a triple-headed flail. She had no more time to assess for other risks because a heavily scarred man bounded up to her with a polearm, jabbing at her midriff. She deflected each attack with her shield or sword, but the man was using the polearm to its advantage—he was too far away for Nahla to launch a successful counterattack. The man growled as Nahla bested him every time. He seemed like a seasoned fighter, but perhaps the polearm was not his weapon of choice. Each attack was well timed and forceful. In fact, they were too well timed, and always aimed at the same spot on Nahla's body.

Nahla waited for another attack. As the sharp tip of the polearm neared her belly, she bashed it away with her shield. Then she dropped her shield, grabbed the polearm by its wooden shaft, twisted her body down its length, and used the momentum to drive her sword into the man's gut. She did it so fast that he was still holding the polearm with two hands. The last thing she saw as she reefed her sword out and retrieved her shield was the man's eyes bulging in shock. She whispered an apology, but by this time, he was already on one knee, using the polearm to keep himself upright. Nahla moved deeper into the slaughter.

And slaughter it was. There were at least ten others lying motionless on the sandy ground, and those who were still alive fought ferociously. Nahla spotted Jugg skewering two gladiators with a spear before her attention turned towards two well-armoured women brandishing swords. They were obviously working together, and Nahla must have seemed an easy target. She readied herself for the first lunge.

The woman on the left, whom Nahla named Shorty, stomped forwards and thrust her sword high, aiming for Nahla's face. As Nahla defended it with her shield, Shorty's compatriot, Blondie, made her move. Blondie aimed low, coming in from the side, and Nahla parried with her sword. Now, with her shield arm and sword arm out at wide angles, Nahla's torso was dangerously exposed. She trusted her brigandine, but a well-aimed strike under the arms could spell disaster.

Nahla stepped back rapidly, colliding with another gladiator who was having enough of his own troubles in a one-on-one against a curly-haired, curly-bearded redhead. The collision with Nahla distracted him, and his foe drove him through with a sword, then ran off to fight someone else. By this time, Nahla had spun away and was already sizing up Shorty and Blondie again. The duo moved like experts, and Nahla was certain they were ex-soldiers or captured mercenaries, maybe even veterans of the arena. She recognised their footwork, their stance, and identified ways to exploit them. Sometimes, the well-trained fighters were easier to fight. It was the wild amateurs who were more unpredictable.

This time, Shorty and Blondie attacked together, swinging at Nahla's sides. Shorty's sword banged against Nahla's shield, but Nahla had no time to follow through, because her sword clashed with Blondie's with such force that it made Nahla's ears ring. A few more rounds of unsuccessful thrusts, jabs, and lunges, and Nahla decided enough was enough. She gave one heavy sweep of her shield and used the moment of surprise to quickly retreat to one of the weapons tables. Shorty and Blondie were soon in hot pursuit.

A spear leaned against one table, and Nahla dropped her shield and grabbed it. She had received only brief training with spears and hadn't bothered to use one in years, but she knew the basics and had the strength. She spun around and launched it at one of her pursuers. The spearpoint found purchase in Blondie's leather cuirass. She stopped in her tracks and fell to the ground. The attack happened so fast that Shorty was stunned into inactivity. She gave one last look at her dying friend before turning back to Nahla, but by this time, it was too late. Nahla was upon her, slashing wildly. Before too long, Shorty fell beside Blondie and Nahla was once again free to assess the larger situation.

There were but a few gladiators left now, and they all focused on Jugg. Nahla didn't know where she stood with Jugg—she'd challenged and bested him in the prison cell, and he hadn't done anything to her after that. But he also gave no sign of friendship either. So she approached slowly and cautiously across the body-strewn arena. In these seconds of unspoiled observance, Nahla noticed the crowd's cheers. They were going berserk in the final moments of the contest, and Jugg was putting on perhaps the best show they'd seen. But surely he couldn't survive against the four men who surrounded him!

Nahla saw how the fight would unfold. The red-haired man sliced at Jugg's muscled arm, but Jugg batted him away with a fist, then buried an axe into the man's back. Jugg took the redhead's sword and made short work of another warrior who tried to sneak up from behind. It was as if Jugg had some extra sense, like he knew where all his enemies were, despite not having eyes on them all the time. Thus, in a few seconds, he'd halved his odds. Though it was a free-for-all, the remaining two gladiators nodded at each other, determined to bring down this dangerous beast.

They attacked, lunging in unison, and Jugg countered. Jugg's sword looked like a toy compared to his hulking frame, but he wielded it with the skill of an expert fighter and the strength of a behemoth. His first defensive countermove shattered his opponent's low-quality sword. Then he quickly whipped it in the other direction and severed the other attacker's hand at the wrist. The crowd cheered with delight, and Nahla wondered if she should have joined the fight when she had the chance. She swallowed hard at the spectacle, disgusted at the wanton disregard for human life and her own part in it. She risked a glance at the royal box. The king watched with keen interest, as did the courtiers, but Lord Johl focused on Nahla. Again, they stared at each other, but the cries of pain and fear brought her attention back to the fight at hand.

The now one-handed man dropped to his knees in shock, and Jugg gave him a backhander to the face, knocking him to the ground. Now, alone and utterly defenceless, the final gladiator threw his broken sword away and reached for another held by a dead man. But he couldn't prise the weapon from the dead fingers quickly enough. Jugg cut him down mercilessly.

Now just Nahla and Jugg stood in the arena.

Jugg looked sideways, seeming to notice Nahla for the first time, though she imagined he had been aware of her presence all along. They faced off with nothing but sand and bodies between them. The crowd murmured softly, then Jugg pointed his sword at Nahla.

"You die today," he shouted.

Nahla readied herself as Jugg walked menacingly towards her. His bare chest had a sheen of sweat and blood spatters under the morning sun, and his left arm was tinged red from the slice he'd sustained moments earlier. He moved like a bull before a charge, slightly hunched, eyes on his target. As he neared, Nahla saw the fire in his eyes, saw the crimson on his sword, and she gripped her sword with two hands. She'd left the shield behind—a mistake she hoped would not prove fatal.

Jugg growled and swung when he was within reach. Nahla parried, but the force of Jugg's attack reverberated through her sword and up her arm. He attacked high next time, and she ducked. While lowered, she hacked at Jugg's calf, but did no damage. When she rolled away, she quickly checked her sword and noticed that even though it was double-edged, one side was completely dull. At most, Jugg would get a nasty purple bruise.

She backed away as Jugg advanced. Thinking about the dull blade reminded her of how Jugg broke the other gladiator's sword. If these weapons were so inferior, she'd need a backup weapon, or else Jugg would chop her to pieces. But his sword was probably the same.

Nahla saw a sword lying on the ground, covered in sand that had glued itself to the blood on its shaft. She rolled again and picked it up in one movement. It felt risky wielding two swords—she'd never done it before and would have preferred a dagger instead. But the extra weapon didn't deter Jugg. He slashed downwards at Nahla's head, perhaps wanting to crack her helmet and head at the same time. Nahla crossed the two swords and held his attack at bay. With their swords locked high above their heads, Jugg picked up a massive foot and stomped at Nahla's knee, but he landed on her thigh instead. She lost her balance and dropped to her other knee. Jugg followed through with another kick, this time into the centre of her torso. Her brigandine spread the kick's energy, but she had the wind knocked out of her and fell back-wards, losing one of her swords as well.

Her immediate response was to roll away, and she was glad she did, because Jugg's sword came down exactly where she had landed. Jugg yelled in anger and exasperation. Nahla kept rolling until she hit something solid—a dead body. Then she heard Jugg laugh and saw the glint of his sword as he raised it again. But he brought it down so fast that it hit the armour of the dead man beside Nahla, which sat higher than Nahla's body. She was safe, with only millimetres to spare between her face and the sharp edge of Jugg's sword.

Nahla sliced again at Jugg's calf, this time with the correct edge of her sword. He cried out, more in annoyance than pain, but he raised his leg instinctively. Nahla then swept her armoured shin against his ankle and the large man toppled over. Same tactic, same result. Seeing her opening, she tried to pin him to the ground and angled her sword towards his chest, readying to strike, but he countered her position and flung her sword out of her grip. Then he used his powerful limbs to push her body off his and plant her into the sand.

He straddled her. One side of his mouth twisted upward in a victorious smile. Armour protected her chest and neck, so he brought his sword down lengthways towards her face. As he did so, Nahla frantically grasped a leather-wrapped handle from the belt on the waist of the dead body next to her. She raised her vambrace next to her face, and Jugg's sword stopped with an ear-splitting metal-on-metal shriek. Then she pulled a dagger from the dead body and brought its tip up to Jugg's throat.

And just like that, they were at an impasse. She could not say why she didn't thrust the dagger into his throat. Maybe she had done enough senseless killing for the day. Maybe she subcon-sciously admired his warrior spirit. Whatever the case, it was enough for Jugg to cease all movement. They held each other's gaze as if acknowledging that they were at a draw and unsure of how to escape it.

Someone clapped, but Nahla and Jugg were too focused on each other to risk looking at who it was.

"Arise, warriors," came the king's voice through the speaker horn. "The fight is over."

Jugg stared at Nahla for a moment longer, then nodded slightly, accepting the draw. He threw his sword away and Nahla dropped the dagger. They stood and faced the royal box, but kept their distance from each other.

"You have fought admirably," the king continued. "I am sure the people will agree."

A great cheer erupted from the commoners.

The king smiled, said something to his advisors, then raised his hands to silence the arena once more. "I would like to meet both of you in person. You will come to my court for a midday feast, which is the first half of your reward. There, we shall discuss the second half. Please go with the prison wardens. They will make the necessary arrangements. Once again, well done!"

The crowd cheered again as the king left the royal box and the prison guards flooded the arena. Several approached Nahla and Jugg, though they treated them differently now, almost as if they were no longer prisoners. Other guards stabbed the dead and dying gladiators and dragged the bodies to waiting carts.

Nahla felt dizzy with a mix of emotions—rage, relief, surprise, and the usual post-battle jitters. Jugg gave her one last look before following his escort. Nahla watched him leave, thanking her lucky stars that she'd survived yet another fight with such a brutish man. It seemed their time together was not over, because she would have to share his company with the king himself and, hopefully, Lord Johl.

Nahla looked forward to meeting the governor again.

5

KING EERO

In a realm of excess, a king so round. He feasts on riches, with no care unbound. As his people toil, burdened by his decree, the king indulges, blind to their plea.

—**Cass the Blasphemer**
The Truth

Nahla was no stranger to the filth of battle and was glad to have another wash. The guards let her bathe privately this time. They gave her three buckets of water, sweet-smelling soap, and proper cleaning products for her armour. To top it all off, someone handed her a deep-green cloak. When she held the thin material up to the sunlight that poured into her washroom, she could see through the delicate material. After her wash, she suited up for the second time that day, feeling dignified in her freshly shined armour. The cape hooked around her neck with a polished chain and clasp.

She admired herself in a tall mirror. With her armour shined, her skin cleaned, her hair washed, her stately cloak, and her helmet under her arm, she almost—almost—looked like the important woman she had been only a few weeks before. The thought left a weight on her chest. She turned away from her reflection in shame and regret.

Someone knocked and entered.

They respect me now, Nahla noted, *but not enough to wait for permission to enter.*

It was one of the guards, a freckled woman who must have spent too much time in the prison, for her skin was neither tanned nor sunburned. "If you are ready, gladiator, we will take you to the royal palace. The one they call Jugg is already waiting."

Nahla frowned. She didn't expect a man like Jugg to take much care in his appearance. Then again, he had barely any armour to clean.

"Lead the way," she said.

She beckoned her outside, and a retinue of guards took her out of the prison into the main courtyard. The heat was impressive, and Nahla felt her body warming in a matter of seconds. Two carriages, a few guards, and one giant man waited. Jugg also wore a green cloak, but it was only just wide enough to cover his shoulders, and it looked rather tight around his neck. He probably knew how ill-fitting it was, but he stood with a mix of pride and impatience. He had oiled his leather loincloth and had procured two tassets—metal plates for the upper thighs—which he secured from his belt. Even his hair had been thoroughly washed, combed, and tied back into a ponytail.

"Is it customary for your kind to make people wait for you, Outsider?" Jugg asked. "I hear the king is an impatient man."

Nahla stopped a few paces away. "It is customary for every man to wait for a woman. Besides, we have been invited for lunch and it is not yet the eleventh hour." She had checked the sundial back in the courtyard.

Jugg grumbled and went to the first carriage without another word. Several armed guards mounted the carriage inside and out as if it held a priceless treasure. The driver of the second carriage motioned Nahla inside, and more guards piled into and around hers as well.

"You are celebrities now," explained a wide-eyed guard. The horses trotted across the courtyard and the carriage swayed.

"Why?" Nahla asked.

"That was one of the biggest and bloodiest gladiatorial fights I have ever seen," another guard said. "You and the big fella did well to survive until the end. But that last duel . . . wow."

"The crowd loved it."

"So did the king."

"And you won the prison governor a lot of meat. He had a bet with one of the local butchers."

Nahla listened to the guards heap praise on Jugg and herself, but the real adoration came just outside the prison walls. The carriages passed through the gatehouse and between a throng of people lining the roadside. Nahla pulled back the curtain on the carriage window and waved. The people waved back and shouted. They were all drugged on euphoria. She wondered how long it would last. Probably not long enough. Then she imagined Jugg and her having to fight again for the amusement of these common folk, and the thought disgusted her. She closed the curtain and sat back for the ride. Is this what had become of her? Nahla, a decorated military commander, reduced to a king's toy to keep his subjects happy?

The carriages made good time along the cobbled roads. Before too long, they were clattering down a tree-lined avenue. Now they were away from the clamouring crowd, and Nahla had opened the curtain again. She had seen precious little of Launceston, and most of that had been at night, so this was her first chance to examine her surroundings properly. The city looked like every other city from her homeland. Maybe this kingdom wasn't so foreign after all.

They halted by a bridge. Someone exchanged words with the lead carriage driver, and then the horses moved again. The bridge—which was actually a drawbridge, now that Nahla could scrutinise it—spanned a rocky ravine. Thick chains led to a gatehouse on the other side, which itself was part of a solid wall of stone. Soldiers in uniforms she had never seen before protected the gatehouse and patrolled the walls. They wore a mix of fine brown leather, polished armour, red-and-yellow plumed helmets, round red shields with a yellow crest, and yellow-gold accents.

The horses trotted through the gatehouse and wound their way through spacious roads lined with buildings. Having visited similar places back home, Nahla had a rough idea of what these buildings were. It made sense for a king to have his own self-sufficient mini village within his walls. They were the usual tradespeople—blacksmith, armourer, fletcher, baker, butcher, and so on. The carriage passed a tavern, which was large enough to be an inn as well. One building had a wooden sign with a quill and an inkpot, so that was most likely a scribe. There were some residences, though the tradespeople probably lived above their place of work. A barracks and training ground would have been somewhere within the walls as well, or just outside.

Then Nahla saw the palace—a gorgeous facade of dressed stone with a wide portico supported by circular columns. The building itself was symmetrical, three storeys, with glass windows, a testament to the king's wealth. Nahla had seen few buildings with glass windows in her lifetime. Plants grew along some walls, partially covering a few windows. The windows themselves had adjustable cloth awnings at a variety of angles.

The carriages travelled on a round driveway and parked. The passengers disgorged and assembled at the foot of some steps that led to the palace's huge front doors. A collection of soldiers waited at the top, chief among them being a man in a red cape and plumed helmet in a style different from the rest. His plume went sideways, whereas the other plumes ran from front to back.

"I am Lieutenant Killo of Launceston Prison. We bring the gladiator champions from this morning's event."

"The king thanks you for this service," the soldier with the sideways plume said. "I am Lieutenant Barrin of the King's Legion. We will take them from here. Come, gladiators, the king awaits." He was a rather handsome man with a smooth, steady voice well-suited to command.

Jugg was the first up the stairs, taking them two at a time. Nahla followed. As she climbed the steps, she could feel the cool air from the palace's interior wafting out of the entrance. But the change in temperature once inside was remarkable. In fact, it was so cool that she was thankful to have the cloak around her arms, thin as it was.

The foyer was a large, stone-floored room with a wide staircase leading up to the palace's upper levels. Lieutenant Barrin veered left towards an open doorway. Two soldiers on either side of the doorway held spears against the floor and stomped to attention in perfect unison as Barrin passed. He kept a brisk pace, his cape twirling behind him.

Jugg drank in every detail of the palace. It was clear he had been nowhere near such opulence, and never in his wildest dreams would he have imagined being here, of all places. Nahla had seen better. Her old king had a palace twice this size. But now someone else lived there.

Lieutenant Barrin stopped by a wide double door. "Forgive me, but I was not present at the arena when you fought. What are your names?"

"I am Jugg Torsen. Of Launceston."

"I am Nahla."

"*Nahla* what?" Barrin asked.

"Just Nahla. My people have no other names."

Barrin straightened and squinted at her. "Your people? Where are you from?"

"The Kingdom of Melbourne."

"I have never heard of such a place. You, Jugg Torsen, have you heard of the Kingdom of Melbourne?"

Jugg shook his head.

Barrin, still unsatisfied, faced one of the soldiers flanking the double doors. "You there, have you ever heard of the Kingdom of Melbourne?"

The soldier tensed. "No, sir. First I've heard of it, sir."

"I cannot tell the king you are from a kingdom that does not exist," Barrin said to Nahla. "It would cause all manner of problems. Tell me the truth. Where are you from?"

Nahla was proud of her birthplace, and proud of her kingdom, but she recognised the need to compromise. Moreover, she understood the so-called "problems" Barrin mentioned. If she admitted she was from another kingdom, perhaps the king would want to investigate. Or, worse, perhaps he would suspect Nahla of being a spy and deal with her accordingly.

"I am from the north," was all Nahla said.

"From Devonport province?"

There was that name again. Johl had asked the same. Nahla nodded. She decided then and there to stop mentioning Melbourne.

Barrin sighed and raised his eyebrows, apparently finished with the matter. He opened the double doors and rushed in.

"Ah, Barrin!" a white-bearded man called from the other end of a spacious throne room. Large windows threw light into the room, and Nahla noticed for the first time how thick the walls were by the depth of the windowsills. They were easily as thick as her arm was long. "You have arrived with my guests—my champions."

The ruler sat smiling on a throne that looked like it had been carved out of a solid mass of rock. He wore the same light-fitting clothes from the arena earlier that morning, and a gold crown nestled in his curly hair. Now that Nahla was much closer to him, she could see how pale and clear his skin was—he looked like he had never done a day of hard work in his life, and spent most of his time away from the sun's harsh heat. He had a belly, and Nahla assumed the beard hid a plump neck. His eyes darted back and forth between Nahla and Jugg, sizing them up.

"I have, indeed, Your Majesty," Barrin said. When they were but a few paces away from the throne's dais, Barrin gestured to the sovereign. "His Majesty, King Eero of Launceston."

Nahla bowed deeply, no stranger to being in the presence of royalty. She glanced at Jugg, who quickly did the same.

"Your Majesty," Barrin continued, "I present Jugg Torsen of Launceston and Nahla Northborn of Devonport."

"Two fine warriors if I ever saw them," Eero said. He hopped off his throne and slipped on some sandals that were at the bottom of the dais. Then he moved closer to Jugg and Nahla, inspecting their form. He grinned at Jugg. "Oh, take that ridiculous cape off. It doesn't even fit you."

Jugg did so, and Nahla could see the relief on his face. His shoulder and back muscles were now on full display, as were the numerous cuts and bruises he'd sustained during the gladiatorial contest.

"Tell me, how does one get as tall and muscular as you?" he asked Jugg.

Jugg opened his mouth as if to speak, then closed it and clamped his lips together.

"Well, spit it out," Eero insisted.

"Fighting and food theft," Jugg finally said. His deep voice echoed in the room. Barrin cleared his throat. "Uh, Your Majesty, sir."

Eero chuckled. "Oh, I know the perfect job for you, then. Oh, yes." He chuckled some more. "You will fit in well. Now, why do you fight with so little armour?"

"I have never had armour that fits me, Your Majesty."

"Hmm, I see. Well, you *are* a giant of a man. Is he not a giant of a man, Barrin?"

"A giant of a man, Your Majesty."

"Yes." King Eero circled Jugg again. "Lord Johl will have armour custom made for you. Hmm, but that ponytail will need to go. Johl won't like it."

42

Jugg breathed heavily, and his intimidating barrel chest rose and fell in a growl. "Lord Johl can cut my ponytail from my cold, dead body."

Eero stared at the beast, then threw his head back in laughter. "Such fire! I hope Johl knows how to harness it." He laughed some more before turning his attention to Nahla. "And you, your fighting spirit, your skill with weapons, your ability to fend off this . . . monster. Where did you learn to fight?"

Nahla took a deep breath, wondering how much of the truth she should let on. "Your Majesty, I was trained from a young age." She used her most courtly voice, honed from years of experience.

It impressed Eero. "My dear, only an exceptional soldier could train you to your skill level. Who trained you?"

"You are right, Your Majesty. He was a soldier." She fought the feelings of sadness rising within her. "But he is dead now."

"I see," Eero nodded. "I see. Well, I have a job for you too. I cannot let such talent go to waste."

He returned to his throne and waved for a court official, who brought a wooden tablet with some paper, a quill, and an inkwell.

"Your name again?" Eero asked Jugg.

"Jugg Torsen," Jugg replied. The court official wrote it on some paper.

The king grinned. "Jugg Torsen, I am assigning you to the Launceston Provincial Garrison under Lord Johl."

"Uh, thank you, Your Majesty."

"Don't thank me. Thank Johl. He specifically requested it." Eero now faced Nahla again.

"Nahla Northborn," Nahla said, remembering just in time the silly name Lieutenant Barrin had invented for her. It felt unnecessary having a second name.

"An odd name, but I am not one to judge," Eero said as the court official inscribed Nahla's name onto another sheet of paper. "I am employing you in my King's Legion in a special role. To be a

43

legionary is the greatest military honour someone like you can hope to achieve. But first, I need a test of loyalty—I have a mission for you. Lieutenant Barrin will discuss the particulars after the feast."

"I am honoured, Your Majesty." She had never heard the word *legionary*, but she put two-and-two together and figured a legionary served in the Legion. A special soldier, then, like Nahla used to be.

The court official rested his writing board on the armrest of King Eero's throne and dripped two circles of a vibrant red wax on each page. Then Eero pressed a metal stamp into the wax and nodded at the results.

"Your official induction papers," he said.

Jugg accepted his page without studying it. Perhaps he couldn't read. Nahla inspected the text and admired the penmanship. The wax seal bore the design of two crossed swords with the words EERO, KING OF LAUNCESTON arranged around the seal's outer edge.

"Jugg, you must get yours sealed by Lord Johl as well," Eero said. "But I imagine that will be the first thing Johl does."

"Understood, Your Majesty."

"Very good! Now that this boring official business is out of the way, let us eat. I have a feast prepared for you, the likes of which you have probably never seen before!"

Nahla, who had attended many royal feasts, had probably seen better than what Eero could offer, but she feigned surprise and delight as she followed the king to the dining hall. She thought back on the whirlwind that had been the last week: exiled, cheating death in the Endless Land, convicted of a crime, imprisoned, fighting for her life as a gladiator, and now being inducted into the King's Legion, a unit that sounded much like the one she had known for most of her life. She wondered what "special role" Eero had in mind for her. That and the so-called "test of loyalty" clung to her mind as she walked the palace's corridors to the feast.

44

6

A FEAST OF LORDS

They gather in their privileged circles, ensconced within the lofty echelons of power and prestige. They entwine themselves in webs of influence, weaving the threads of a curtain that separates them from the masses. This aristocratic cabal, blinded by their entitlement, preserves a cycle of inequality and perpetually neglects the lives of those beyond their elitist enclaves.

—Cass the Blasphemer
The Truth

T HE FEAST WAS WELL and truly underway as Nahla followed King Eero into the dining hall. She heard the laughter and the stringed instruments as they approached a massive double door carved with detailed reliefs of wild parties. Perhaps this artwork was a record of historic banquets, or an artistic impression of what mattered most to the king. Two legionaries snapped to attention and pushed the doors open. Eero strode in without thanking them.

"Our gladiators have arrived!" Eero announced in a booming voice.

Richly dressed men and women around a long table erupted in cheers and applause. Nahla bowed, happy that they had broken from their merriment and the piles of food on their plates to honour two convicted criminals. Then she quickly eyed the variety of meats, vegetables, fruits, and cakes on the table. The glasses were filled with a deep-red liquid, most likely wine, and there were casks along one wall to keep the glasses topped up. A cool breeze swept through from a deep veranda that wrapped around three faces of the room. It was shaded and partially walled with a vine-covered lattice. A small band of musicians played stringed instruments, adjusting their volume to suit the highs and lows of the chatter around the table.

A man wearing the finest military uniform Nahla had seen in Launceston stood with a toothy smile and greeted them. He wore a gleaming cuirass embossed with innumerable depictions of battle. He gave Nahla and Jugg a firm handshake as the others returned to their meals and conversations.

"Some of the best fighting I've seen in years," he said. "Truly a pleasure to watch."

"This is Captain Vox of the King's Legion," King Eero said. "Nahla is your latest recruit, Vox."

"Ah!" Vox shook Nahla's hand again. His breath smelled of fruity wine, and she caught a whiff of some flowery cologne. "If you continue to fight as well as you did today, I will be glad to have you under my command." He scoffed. "If a thousand of my legionaries fought as well as you, we could wreak havoc all over the Kingdom of Hobart."

Nahla, who had never heard of such a kingdom, took the compliment with a smile. "I thank you for your kind words, Captain."

"And you," Vox said to Jugg, sizing up the man's height and muscular frame, "you have the strength, skill, and stamina of an entire section of my Legion."

"Alas, I have assigned him to Lord Johl's company," Eero said.

"I'm glad you granted my wish, Your Majesty."

The new voice made the hair on Nahla's neck bristle. She and Jugg turned. Before them was Lord Johl, seated at the corner of the table, grinning over a wine glass. Here was the man who had condemned both of them to prison, just a few paces away.

"Thank you, *my lord*," Jugg said in his deep voice.

Johl held their gaze.

Eero extended an arm towards Johl. "I present Lord Johl, Governor of Launceston Province, first among the Lords of Launceston."

Johl remained seated.

"We've met," Nahla said. She calmed herself and remembered to adopt a professional demeanour.

"Excellent!" Eero said. "Then you can catch up over lunch. Come, your seats are waiting."

Eero took the giant chair at the head of the table and gestured for Nahla and Jugg to join him adjacent to his right . . . directly across from Johl. The governor sipped his wine and regarded Nahla with feigned disinterest. The bridge of his nose was bruised blue and purple where she had smashed it during their scuffle the previous night. *Good*, she thought. *I hope it's broken.*

The feast was a help-yourself affair, so Nahla did just that. Now more than ever, she realised the extent of her hunger. She collected a large chicken breast, some sausages, mashed potatoes, boiled peas and carrots, a full corn cob, and a salad of six or seven fresh ingredients. Every bite was a burst of flavour that Nahla hadn't experienced in weeks, and she savoured every mouthful.

A clean-cut man sitting next to Johl watched her with interest. "Nahla, right? I'm Vimarr. Have some of this wine. I promise that you have tasted nothing like it before. The grapes were grown in my vineyard and produced in Jaruk Easton's wineries."

Nahla swallowed her food. She'd heard his name before and had to quickly search the recesses of her mind. "Ah, Lord Vimarr."

The recognition brought a self-loving smile to the Governor of Devonport's devilishly handsome face.

"Tell me about Jaruk," Nahla said. She hoped her statement wouldn't reveal her ignorance. After all, several people had already assumed that she was from Vimarr's province.

"You know him? Oh, what am I saying? Of course you don't. But you know of him, right?"

"A little."

Vimarr pulled a face as if Nahla should have known *everything* already. That was bad. She had to convince Vimarr that she was, in fact, one of his subjects, especially now that they called her Nahla Northborn. "Jaruk is the kingdom's leading wine merchant, and I am privileged to have him based in my province."

Nahla nodded her approval at the fortuitous business arrangement and made a mental note to remember the importance of Jaruk. Then, unfortunately adding insult to injury, she declined when Vimarr raised a wine jug and offered to pour her some. She had never been a big drinker back home, and she wanted to be fully alert for Eero's test of loyalty. Johl watched this exchange with his dark eyes and ever-present smirk. He also watched Jugg, who was wolfing down food and making all sorts of guttural sounds. The giant man downed a full glass of wine and let out a satisfying burp.

With half her plate finished already, Nahla looked down the table to see how many other women were present. She could count them on one hand, and they sat way down the other end. She wondered what position they held—what made them important enough to attend the gladiatorial contest in the royal box and then feast with the king, but not important enough to sit at the king's end of the table. A slender lady with milky white skin and a sheet of perfectly straight black hair sat at the far end in a high-backed chair. Perhaps she was Eero's queen, but Nahla was too wise to ask. Surely a citizen of the kingdom would know if the king had a queen.

She spotted a large jug of water and asked if she could have some. There were chuckles around the table as the jug went from hand to hand before it reached Nahla. She filled her glass.

"Still a lover of water, I see," Johl said, testing her.

Nahla took a big gulp and smiled her most courtly smile. The water was cool and refreshing, and it helped her think of a suitable reply. "Of course, my lord. Water is life."

"Well said," someone called from down the table.

Nahla had to lean forwards to see who it was—a woman with voluminous grey-white hair and lavish blue robes decorated with white-and-gold etchings. She raised her glass of water at Nahla, and Nahla returned the gesture.

"Have you met Matriarch Anurak before?" King Eero asked. He held a greasy chicken leg and spoke with a full mouth.

"I have not," Nahla said. "But it is my pleasure." She tried to place the title with an occupation, but was drawing a blank. The only time she had heard the word *matriarch* was in reference to a widely respected mother of a large, successful family. There were plenty of such women back home. She doubted whether the definition had the same meaning in this context, unless Anurak was somehow related to the king. So Nahla tried to politely dig for more information. "I wish to give you the respect befitting your position. What is your honorific?"

The woman smiled. "You may call me 'Your Eminence'."

"Very well, Your Eminence," Nahla said and raised her glass again. She was none the wiser and would have to do some more research later. But her first impression was that Anurak spoke with reverential authority and was certainly not out of place at the king's table.

At this point, Captain Vox raised his voice above the other loud conversations. "Barrin, come over here, lad. Eat something."

The legionary had been casually patrolling on the veranda, away from his superiors. He came over at his captain's beckoning.

"Please forgive me," Barrin said, "but I must be on my way. I was delaying for Nahla's sake, but it seems she may be here somewhat longer than I initially expected."

"Nonsense!" Eero said. "Join us, Lieutenant."

"My sincerest apologies, but I really must make preparations. Nahla, if you could please find me when you are ready. I will be near the stables."

Before Barrin could leave, the king ripped out a large chicken wing from the cooked bird on a platter and handed it to him. Barrin accepted it gracefully, bowed, then marched away.

"He's a good officer, that one," Vox said once the dining hall doors had closed.

"Damn fine," Eero agreed. "You're in excellent hands, Nahla. I hope you live up to my expectations." He swallowed and leaned forwards. "Otherwise, it will be back to the arena for you."

The king and the nobles within earshot laughed at the unpleasant joke.

Even Jugg laughed. "I'll have to join you," he said, "just to finish what we started." He nudged her a bit too hard in the arm. The comment brought the laughter to a new height.

Johl didn't laugh, though. Instead, he watched Nahla with a smirk for a few menacing seconds, then returned to his meal.

The king gave the impression of someone who was easy to speak to if one chose the right topics, so Nahla tested him for information. "Your Majesty," she began, "may I ask about the assignment you have given me?"

"Of course," Eero said. He shoved the rest of a sausage into his mouth and chomped loudly. "Old Garyd is having trouble with a bandit leader." He pointed to a grey-haired man further down the table, who looked up at the mention of his name. "Garyd's province is large, and his forces are stretched thin. How long have you been hunting this bandit leader?

"More than a year," Garyd said. "He eludes me every time."

"I want you and Lieutenant Barrin to scope out a suspected bandit enclave not far from Garyd's capital," Eero said.

"And how will I manifest my loyalty?" Nahla asked.

"I need you to prove to me that you will obey Barrin's command, that you will fight courageously if necessary, and that you will not betray your privilege of service by defecting to the bandits. You were a prisoner, after all, which presumably means you committed a crime."

Nahla nodded, eager to hear what else he had to say, but Johl weaselled his way into the conversation.

"She did, indeed, Your Majesty," Johl said a little too loudly. "A water thief." He smiled.

The laughter and chatter hushed at the table and all eyes turned towards Nahla. The fieriest expression came from Matriarch Anurak. In the background, the musicians still strummed and plucked their instruments, maybe oblivious to Johl's accusation, or too frightened to stop.

"Hmm," Eero began. "A serious crime. But these are desperate times. We are being pressed from three sides—bandit and marauder bands from the north, the Kingdom of Hobart from the south, and the wild tribes from the west—so we need all the good fighters we can muster. I will overlook your crime if you have served your sentence and understand the severity of what you did."

"Have you performed your penance?" Matriarch Anurak asked.

Unsure of the meaning of the term, Nahla responded as truthfully as she could. "No, I was imprisoned for less than a day before the gladiatorial contest."

Some were visibly stunned by the comment.

"Not even one day in prison?" Anurak asked, wide-eyed. "Your Majesty, this woman needs to perform penance before she can serve in your Legion. She is tainted with sin—and water theft, one of the worst sins at that!"

"She will do her penance when she returns from the task I have assigned her. Only then will she be formally admitted into my Legion. She hasn't even taken the oath yet."

"Please send her to me the moment she returns from her assignment," Anurak said forcefully. "I will see to her penance personally."

Now Nahla had another task to do, which she knew nothing about. However, she understood the word *sin*, and recognised its religious connotations. She connected some dots and realised that Matriarch Anurak must be from a religious order. Her own kingdom was not overly religious, but some surrounding allies and enemies were, and they often waged war on the grounds of religious differences. Did Anurak hold so much religious power that she could make demands of the king?

Eero, for all his profound authority, bowed to Anurak's request. "You have my word, Matriarch. Now, as I was saying, Nahla, I have graciously elevated you from the gutter, and I have offered you the best life someone of your talents could hope for. You will have food, shelter, the adoration of the king, and above all, no more want for water. I keep my legionaries well supplied."

Nahla bowed her head slightly. Though the words stung as she prepared them in her mind, she knew she had to say them. "Then I owe you my eternal loyalty and devotion, Your Majesty. I will not fail you."

The last sentence, which she added on a whim, hurt her more than the first. Only one king truly held her loyalty, but she had failed him. To add insult to injury, it was now well beyond her means to reconcile the mistakes of the past.

"Careful!" Eero said. He chuckled. "Don't make your oath now, or else Matriarch Anurak will drag you to your penance immediately." Then he laughed heartily, and everyone joined him.

Nahla offered a courtesy laugh because she still didn't know what a penance was. "There is one more matter that troubles me," she said once the laughter had subsided.

52

"Speak."

"I had a sword. It has been in my service for a long time." She paused, wondering if she should include more details. What whirlwind of noble rage would she unleash if she openly accused Johl of taking her most prized possession? "I believe it has been confiscated."

"By whom?" Eero asked. He furrowed his brow. "We shall have it returned to you."

Nahla glanced at Johl ever so quickly, but the king was alert enough to see it.

"Lord Johl, do you know the whereabouts of Nahla's sword?" Eero asked.

"I would not know, Your Majesty," he said calmly. Then he drank some wine, hiding his face behind the large glass.

Nahla made up her mind. "The last I saw of it, it was in your hands when you sent me to prison."

Again, the table went quiet, though not as quiet as before. People still held their conversations, but they all seemed to turn an ear to the more interesting one developing at Nahla's end.

Out of the corner of Nahla's eye, she saw Jugg staring at her, so she faced him. He looked like he was bursting to ask the question, but he knew his place at the table and hence kept his mouth shut. She knew exactly what was on his mind, though: *You really fought him, didn't you?*

Eero put his elbows on the table and rubbed his hands together. "Well, this is interesting. Tell me, Johl, is Nahla speaking the truth?"

Johl's smirk remained as he eyed the king. He spoke with perfect, practiced skill. "She is, Your Majesty. The sword is in my possession, but I will need to ask my chamberlain where he put it."

And in so few words, Nahla noted, Johl acknowledged that he had her sword, but also reinforced his earlier, "truthful" statement about not knowing of its exact whereabouts. He was a cunning man, and she would have to tread carefully and mind every word she said.

"Then we have a simple solution to a simple problem," Eero said. "Johl, upon your return to your castle, ask your chamberlain to locate Nahla's sword and have it sent here."

"I'm afraid it's not so simple, Your Majesty. You see, Nahla and I had a duel, and I was the victor, so I took her sword."

Eero was about ready to give in, but Nahla bit back as politely as possible. "If I remember correctly, Lord Johl, you were on the ground with a bloodied face—with my sword about to crash down on you—when your soldiers took me captive. Correct me if I am wrong, but it would seem that I was the victor in our little duel."

Eero slammed a fist playfully on the table. "Ha! I was going to ask where you got that nasty wound on your nose."

Now, with his pride also wounded, Johl lost his smirk and his lips went thin. "Nevertheless, Your Majesty, I was arresting her for water theft when she refused to submit. For this refusal, and for attacking me and my soldiers—and cutting of Lieutenant Kessia's ear—I gave her a sufficient punishment: an immediate prison sentence. I consider the sword not only a spoil of victory but also compensation for injuring my escort."

Several people had shifted their attention to this conversation now, listening attentively.

"Hmm," Eero said. "Nahla, it seems you were making quite a bad name for yourself. Strange that we have never heard of you before."

"Yes," Johl said, fiery eyes burning at her, "very strange. What were you telling me earlier, Vimarr?"

"That I had never known the likes of Nahla in my province," Vimarr said. "You were either a very cunning criminal, or you came to Launceston to begin your criminal career."

Nahla eyed both governors. "We all make mistakes."

"Indeed," Eero said. "Unfortunately for you, I will rule in Lord Johl's favour on this matter. Don't worry, I'll have Barrin supply you with another sword."

The words were like a punch in the gut, like he had torn away another piece from her already-dying past. "As you wish, Your Majesty," she forced out.

"And try not to attack any of my lords from now on." Then he turned to Johl and spoke quieter. "You must show me this sword when I visit you next. I think . . ."

Nahla ignored the rest of the conversation, since it was no longer directed towards her. Eero and Johl chatted among themselves while Nahla examined the others to take her mind off her sword. Lord Vimarr shifted his gaze when Nahla looked at him. The others had all returned to their own discussions once the king swiftly ended the matter. They would probably whisper about the exchange between Nahla the ex-criminal and the great Lord Johl, and news would spread to every corner of the kingdom that Johl had a dirty run-in with a feisty warrior woman.

Jugg was looking down at her. He leaned closer and whispered, "You are more courageous than you seem. Either courageous or stupid. You'll die either way." Then he turned away and bit into a sizeable chunk of bread.

Courageous. Nahla digested the word. Was she courageous for fighting Johl? Was she courageous for challenging him in front of the kingdom's leaders? Whether it was courage or stupidity, the fact remained that she had lost her sword to someone who clearly despised her, and she could not recover it.

She glanced at Jugg. He was the only one she knew who could get even remotely close to her sword in Johl's castle, but her relationship with him was tenuous. No, she wouldn't risk asking for Jugg's help. She would have to bide her time until she could retrieve it herself. One way or another, she would have her sword again.

Nahla soon finished her meal and decided that she could not stand to be in Johl's presence any longer, so she thanked King Eero for the feast and excused herself to find Lieutenant Barrin. Eero called for a legionary to escort her. Either he didn't want her to get lost, or he didn't yet trust her to make her own way there. Probably the latter.

She gave Johl one last intense glare before leaving with her escort.

7

LIEUTENANT BARRIN

Professional and efficient. Inspires loyalty. Destined for high rank.

—Primus Marcle, CO, 2C, King's Legion
*Performance Appraisal for Lieutenant Barrin,
CO, 3P, 2C, King's Legion*

T HE LONE LEGIONARY NEVER said a word as he escorted Nahla through the palace. Like Lieutenant Barrin before him, he kept a quick pace, which Nahla appreciated. The sooner she could begin her task, the better. Being idle was not her strong suit, especially when she was thinking about how to reclaim her sword from Lord Johl.

On the way, she took in as much passive information about the palace as her eyes and ears could handle. It was larger on the inside than initially expected, but it had all the features of a royal home, at least in the public areas where Nahla walked. Artworks, sculptures, quality furniture, and richly woven carpet adorned the rooms.

They reached a spiral staircase made of stone. Nahla suspected this was one of the circular towers in one corner of the building. It was wide, so it hadn't been designed with defence in mind. The palace designers must have been confident that it would never come under attack.

They descended and emerged at a barracks. It was a long, narrow room lined with beds, with doorways at regular intervals on each wall, possibly leading to other sleeping quarters, an armoury, or a kitchen and dining area. Most barracks looked the same. The room smelled faintly of body odour, taking Nahla back to her raw recruit days when she was a young soldier. A barracks reeked then as it reeked now, but she eventually climbed out of that and ended up in the much-nicer officers' quarters. Now it seemed like she was back where she had started, only in a new army under a new king.

"Have you seen Lieutenant Barrin?" her escort asked anyone within earshot.

One soldier who was cleaning some leather vambraces looked up from his bed. "Last I saw, he was out by the stables."

The escort thanked his colleague and moved on, Nahla in tow. Nahla could have said the same if she had been asked, but the soldier seemed hesitant to speak to her. Maybe he looked down on her status as a gladiator. Or maybe he did not know that she would soon join his ranks—though in that case, he still might look down on her, thanks to her past.

Whoever designed the palace had wisely built the stables close to the barracks. A door opened to a tidy walkway that bordered a spacious arena where some cavalry troops practiced their equestrian skills. Some fought one-on-one with other riders, whereas a different group put their horses through the rigours of stamina and manoeuvre training. All around the arena were sturdy shelters where more horses rested. One huge shed, its doors wide open, housed an immense pile of hay.

Barrin stood ramrod straight with a cluster of other legionaries under a sheltered viewing platform. They watched the juniors training—pointing, nodding, shaking their heads. One or two even shouted words of encouragement or harsh reprimands and warnings.

"Lieutenant Barrin, sir," the escort said and stood to attention, bringing his fist to his chest in salute. He kept himself and Nahla out of the protective shade under which the officers stood.

"Ah, there you are, Nahla," Barrin said. He left the group of officers and joined them in the sunlight. "I thought you might have stayed with the king for longer. You are dismissed, Private."

The legionary again punched a fist against his armoured chest, then about-faced and marched away.

"I wanted to get started on my special assignment," Nahla explained. "Should I salute you?"

"Not yet. Not until you take the oath of service."

He put his hands behind his back and studied her from head to toe. He kept his brow furrowed and eyes narrow in the sun's glare as he examined Nahla's armour, her stance, her form. Then he strolled around her. It was a professional inspection, one which she had experienced on both the giving and receiving end in her years as a soldier back home. When he made a full circle and stood in front of her again, he nodded his approval.

"Who made your armour?" he asked.

"An armourer from my homeland."

"Ah, yes, your homeland," he said with raised eyebrows. "Sticking with that story, are we, Nahla *Northborn*? Where did you say you were from?"

"Devonport."

"Don't toy with me," he said sternly.

The tone in his voice made her heart thump. He said it with the perfectly crisp voice of command and just a sprinkle of threat.

"What did you really tell me?" Barrin asked.

"That I'm from Melbourne, on the northern edge of the Endless Land."

Barrin glanced at the other officers behind him, then aimed his head towards the stables. "Walk with me."

He led Nahla away from prying ears into a big opening in one of the stable buildings. It smelled of manure, chaff, and horse sweat, which Nahla preferred any day to the usual body odour of a barracks.

Barrin stopped near two horses. "Why do you insist on saying you are from a land that does not exist?"

"Because it does exist, and that is where I was born."

He regarded her with a frown. "Be careful who you say that to. You already have a reputation as a good fighter. News of your prowess as a gladiator has already reached the Legion. The lower ranks will latch onto the myth of a foreigner with superb skill. But the officers will take it more seriously, especially Captain Vox. Launceston is already facing enemies on three sides. We don't need a mysterious fourth enemy that may or may not exist to our north."

Nahla understood the implications. Even if she could not prove that there was a kingdom to the north, the mere mention of it might cause a wave of unrest within the Launceston elite, drawing soldiers away from other vital fronts to protect the northern border. No army could ever hope to cross the Endless Land and strike at Launceston—Nahla herself was incredibly lucky to survive the journey alone—but King Eero and Captain Vox might not believe that. Then there was another issue that Nahla had already thought of, but Barrin had either neglected to consider or politely left unmentioned: Nahla could be a spy. If Launceston was anything like Melbourne, enemy spies did not live long after they were discovered.

"Then I shall give up on building my personal legend," Nahla said, hoping the new lie might be enough.

"Everyone has a past they are not happy about. But faking one is never the answer. Build your future, not your past." Apparently done with the subject, he bent down to a haystack and fetched a sword that was resting within its scabbard. "This is for you—a standard issue."

Nahla felt its weight. "Better than the rubbish I had to use this morning."

"Most likely."

She unsheathed the sword and studied the blade. It looked brand new, recently sharpened and oiled. The craftsmanship was good. It wasn't the best she'd seen, but it was a lot better than the inferior weapons she used against the gladiators earlier in the morning. Satisfied, she slid it back into the scabbard and fastened it around her waist.

"Now we ride," Barrin said. "Do you know how to ride?"

"I do."

Barrin directed her to a chestnut Arabian quietly tied to one of the stable bays.

"This is Ajax," Barrin said, "a four-year-old gelding with a good record. He's been riderless for a few weeks, but he's yours once you take the oath."

Ajax was shorter and slimmer than Nahla's old horse, Lorelei, but that was the difference between an Arabian and a Percheron. He had a narrow, angled head with big nostrils and a shining black mane.

"Why is he riderless?" Nahla asked. "Is he unwanted?"

"His rider was killed. Shot in the back with an arrow." When Nahla flashed a concerned face, Barrin waved it away. "A minor border skirmish. Now, lead Ajax out there and saddle up. We're going for a ride." He walked off.

Nahla ran a hand along Ajax's neck and spoke softly. The horse responded well to her voice, but it was still nervous. He would have to grow accustomed to his new owner. She untied his lead rope and walked him out of the stable to where Barrin had directed, parking herself under the shade of a tree. Then she hoisted herself into the saddle, which Ajax allowed with only a small grunt. She petted him again and waited.

Barrin emerged from a different stable with a black Friesian—a tall, solid beast with a wavy mane and tail. He looked positively glorious with his shiny armour and plumed helmet. If he rode through town, he'd attract attention for all the right reasons. "Follow me," he said.

He led Nahla through the palace grounds to a small gateway in the perimeter wall hidden behind some buildings. A legionary unlocked the heavy wooden door, then walked through the wall tunnel and unlocked the second door on the outer wall face. Barrin trotted through.

They were now outside the palace and took a narrow, winding track down to the dry moat and then crossed a small footbridge. Legionaries patrolled the area on both sides of the moat. They took one look at Barrin on his mighty steed, saluted, then went about their business.

Barrin halted and surveyed the fields of brown grass before them. He pointed. "You see that windmill? Ride to it as fast as you can. Don't let me catch you."

"Shouldn't be a problem on this," Nahla said, scratching Ajax behind the ear.

"Don't get cocky," Barrin replied. He drew his sword. "If you feel my sword tap your back, you know you've lost. Now go!"

Nahla kicked Ajax into a gallop. The hot wind felt great against her skin. Ajax's hooves pummelled the ground as he charged towards the windmill. She could hear the thumping of a second horse close behind her—Barrin, despite riding a slower horse, was nearly keeping pace. He held his sword high like a cavalry trooper, its sharp tip aimed at her, poised to strike. Nahla kicked again and the energy and enthusiasm she felt somehow transferred into Ajax, for the horse increased speed with renewed vigour. It had been a while since she'd ridden an Arabian, and she'd almost forgotten the thrill of going at full gallop.

The windmill loomed ahead. It was a stout structure with large canvas sails rotating smoothly in the breeze. A few workers stopped to watch the two riders galloping towards them. They grabbed pitchforks and other farming implements, perhaps believing that

Nahla was a criminal being chased by the King's Legion. When she arrived, they thrust their farming implements at her so vehemently that she had to keep Ajax away.

Barrin shouted as he approached. "Stand down! We are training! Drop your weapons!" His voice carried the firm tone of a confident military officer, Nahla noted with approval.

The workers complied. Nahla admired their courage to arm themselves on the spur of the moment. She supposed that living outside of the palace walls—out in the open and at risk of bandit raids—had made them ready and willing to defend themselves.

Barrin sheathed his sword. "Well done," he said. "Let's go to that empty field."

They trotted down a slope and stopped in a relatively flat field bordered by shrubs and some trees. A low stone wall marked a boundary line. Barrin wheeled his horse so that he faced Nahla head on.

He drew his sword again. "Now we fight."

Nahla shifted in her saddle. "I thought we were scouting a bandit camp."

"That's tomorrow. For now, I want to test your skill. I haven't seen you fight yet, and I want to know if the rumours are true."

Nahla smirked. They were several kilometres away from the palace and its purpose-built training grounds. "And you want to test my skill far away from the rest of the Legion? Are you afraid I will beat you?"

Barrin allowed himself a smile. "Your sword, Nahla." She did as commanded, then Barrin continued. "The bandits fight mostly on horseback. Hit-and-run tactics. I don't know if they taught you how to fight on horseback in your fantasy kingdom, but if we run into trouble tomorrow, I want to make sure that you know how to handle yourself."

As a former high-ranking officer in Melbourne's own Royal Guard unit, she knew how to fight in a saddle. "How do I win?"

"Unhorse or disarm me. Of course, in the field, you are well within your rights to kill a bandit. But for this practice, no strikes against the neck, head, or legs. Keep your sword away from my horse, or else I'll bury you here. Now, attack when ready."

"Yes, sir!" Nahla shouted and drew her sword, kicking Ajax into action at the same time.

She struck out at Barrin. His horse was easily two hands taller than hers, so her attack came at him from below. In a real fight, she would have aimed at his armpit, but she angled the attack towards his armoured torso instead. Barrin easily parried it, but that was Nahla's intention. As Ajax moved her forwards, she whipped her sword around and struck against Barrin's back. Her sword clanged against the rear of his shiny cuirass.

"A neat trick," Barrin mumbled.

He spun his Friesian around and charged in pursuit. Nahla turned as well and met his advance. Their swords clashed in a dizzying succession of strikes. Nahla and Barrin knew they were practicing, but Ajax and Barrin's horse could not tell the difference. Caught up in the heat of the fake skirmish, their nostrils flared, ears turned back, and eyes opened wide. They snorted and squealed as their bodies invaded each other's personal space. Nahla and Barrin came so close to each other that Nahla had to fight the natural urge to crack him in the face with her sword pommel.

The riders struggled to keep their horses apart and they spun on the spot in a cavalry dance. Nahla held the rein with her left hand and wielded the sword with her right. She pushed Barrin's sword arm backwards with such force that she saw her opening to unhorse him. She leaned forward and grabbed him around the waist, then beckoned Ajax to pull away. The horse reacted to the movement of its bridle, but she lost her grip on Barrin's slippery metal cuirass.

"Not as easy as it looks, eh?" Barrin taunted.

Apart now, their swords had more freedom of movement, and they both used that to their advantage. Their strikes were heavier and more varied. Barrin even tried some lunges. Nahla realised that if the bandits had such high-quality metal armour as Barrin's, then hitting them with a sword wouldn't work. She'd have to slice at their legs, strike their heads, or, as horrible as it sounded, go for their horses.

"How are bandits usually equipped?" she asked during a lull in the fight.

"Fairly standard swords," Barrin replied. Sweat dripped down his face. It must have been terrifically hot under his helmet and expensive armour. He put his hand up to pause their skirmish. "Some have maces or axes. The axes are quite simple, but even a simple axe can kill. I've also seen a few archers, but they usually fire on foot. Nasty buggers, those archers. We'll bring shields with us tomorrow."

"And armour?"

"Mostly leather. You can tell who a higher-ranked bandit is if they wear plate or chain mail. It's usually stolen and ill fitting. But the ones we're scouting tomorrow may be better equipped than most. We think they have their own forge. That's why Lord Garyd is so alarmed."

"Tell me more."

"This bandit group is making strategic raids throughout Garyd's province. They're almost acting like a small illegitimate kingdom. They've seized an iron mine and have enough manpower to ward off Garyd's troops. Garyd fears that they will become too strong for him to deal with alone, and so he has appealed for help."

"Hence our little scouting party."

Barrin took a deep breath and looked as though he were weighing his words. "Something like that."

"Is there more to the story?"

He nodded, clenched his lips, then spoke as if he'd decided it was okay to tell Nahla the truth. "Ordinarily, a neighbouring lord would send troops to assist. Garyd's neighbours are Johl to the south and Vimarr to the northwest, but neither will help militarily. So the king is investigating personally."

It sounded like provincial power plays to Nahla. Evidently, the younger lords were delighting in the struggles of Old Garyd. She digested the information with a nod. "Hopefully, our reconnaissance is worthwhile."

"Yes. But it will be for nothing if we get ambushed and killed. You still need to unhorse or disarm me. Come on, keep trying."

They charged at each other again and swung their swords wildly. Barrin used techniques Nahla had never seen before, and Nahla countered them with defensive moves that were probably never used in Launceston. It was clear their different schools of training were proving a match for both of them. Fighting on horseback was not really Nahla's strength, though. If she could only get him off his horse and finish the fight on foot . . .

She saw her chance. Ajax had spun around so that Barrin and Nahla fought on their left sides, meaning they had to stretch their sword arms over their rein arms. Nahla bashed away Barrin's last attack, looped her rein arm through his, and quickly smacked his horse's rump with the flat face of her sword. His Friesian shrieked and took off, but Nahla held Barrin tight. His feet left their stirrups and he tumbled back off his horse, crashing to the ground with a grunt of pain and embarrassment.

He stood in a huff. "You struck my horse!"

Nahla sheathed her sword. "I merely startled it."

"The rule was not to touch each other's horses." He looked away and shook his head at how far his horse had run. It had slowed some distance away and trotted along the low-lying stone wall.

"I interpreted that as not *attacking* each other's horses. And besides, by doing the unexpected, I gained the upper hand. I was taught never to give my enemies reason to trust me."

Barrin narrowed his eyes. "That kind of thinking will make you loved and hated in the Legion, depending on which officer sees it. You have a fresh perspective, and your fighting technique is . . . different." He grinned, and a boyish spark came to his eyes.

"Come down here. I want to play some more."

She hopped off Ajax, and the two of them walked away from the horse. Nahla drew her sword again and stood in her typical fighting stance, which differed from Barrin's. She stood at an angle, her forward leg slightly bent at the knee. Barrin faced her more squarely and had his legs spaced further apart. Both held their swords double-handed.

They fought for at least another half an hour before Barrin reluctantly agreed that he could not best her. He got so frustrated that he even threw off his helmet, letting his wavy, sandy blonde hair dry off in the hot breeze. By the end of their tussle, both breathed heavily and wiped sweat from their brows, but Nahla was clearly the victor. She had scored more hits and knocked him away more often than he'd done to her. She had even playfully slapped him across the cheek once, which had stunned him into inactivity, leaving him open for yet another strike to his torso.

"I hope we do not need to fight like this tomorrow," he said. "But if we do, I don't think you'll have a problem."

They gathered their horses and rode back to the palace, after which he helped Nahla secure a bed in the barracks and organised other necessities, including a travel sack and waterskin for their journey the next day. They would set out before dawn with a few other legionaries, so he encouraged her to get her equipment in order, have a hearty meal for supper, and get sufficient rest. It would be a long day, and if they encountered any bandit resistance, a long day might stretch to a long few days.

Nahla was thankful for the rest. After the rough sleep in Launceston Prison the previous night, the hectic gladiatorial contest in the morning, and her friendly scuffle with Barrin during the hottest part of the day, she was drained of energy. But now she had a half-decent bed to sleep in, a full belly, and the favour of a king. She met sleep's warm embrace quickly and peacefully. It was her first night with no bad dreams of the bloody and fiery loss of her homeland.

8

SCOUTING PARTY

A portrait of fiery hues, kissed by God's Eye. I know of no other place that is at once beautiful and unforgiving. Such is the blessing of God—She gives us a burned and difficult land so that we may more fully appreciate Her life-giving water.

—**Anatol, Royal Surveyor**
Commentaries on the Lands of Launceston

THEY LEFT BEFORE SUNRISE the next morning—Nahla, Barrin, and two junior legionaries named Ragh and Rhos, twins with messy curls of red hair under their helmets. Together, this scouting party, plus two riderless donkeys strapped with water bags, left Launceston heading northeast, guided only by stars and well-known roads. Barrin took the lead.

Before too long, the stars winked out and the sky turned purple-blue. Cloud formations glowed pink as a slowly rising sun hit them from behind the horizon. Nahla felt a chill just before sunrise and was glad for the red military cape Barrin had given her before they set off. It was thicker than the green one she'd received from the prison.

Later, when Launceston had disappeared behind them and nothing but hills, plains, and a dirt road lay ahead, Barrin ordered

Ragh and Rhos to disperse. Nahla recognised the fairly standard marching order—Ragh rode on ahead about a hundred metres and Rhos brought up the rear by about fifty metres. With the twins sufficiently out of earshot, Barrin struck up a personal conversation with Nahla.

"Tell me about your homeland," he said bluntly.

They rode side-by-side, their horses kicking up dust on the narrow road. The sun had peeked over the horizon about two hours ago, and Nahla could already feel her legs getting sweaty against Ajax's belly.

"My fake past?" Nahla asked.

"Call me curious. Does it really exist?"

Two parts of Nahla's mind fought for her next words. A good officer was duty bound to report suspicious news. An even better officer investigated it. All Barrin had to do was snoop around Devonport—wherever that was—and he would soon find that Nahla had not come from there. So she told the truth. "Of course it exists. Do you continue to doubt me?"

Barrin straightened in his saddle and sighed. "I do still doubt you. But we have a long journey and I'd rather not do it in silence. Suppose your land was real. Is it very different from Launceston?"

"Not that much." No sense in spilling too many details.

"And what did you do there?"

"I was a soldier."

"That explains your fighting skill." Barrin went quiet, then cleared his throat. "And who did you serve?"

It felt like an interrogation, but Nahla couldn't tell whether he'd been ordered to do so, or was simply asking to satisfy his own curiosity.

"I served a king. Other soldiers served other kings. And still more soldiers served warlords."

"Sounds like a lot of soldiers."

"The political situation was . . . strained."

Terrible memories flashed in her mind, but she pushed them aside. She didn't want to talk about her past, but she feared Barrin would open those wounds eventually.

"How was it strained?" Barrin asked. "Like Launceston, with enemies on all fronts? Or in a different way?"

"We were a warlike people. If we weren't fighting over land or resources, we fought over grudges or jealousies. We often battled the warlords, but I lost count of the times we took the sword to other kings as well."

"So, you have plenty of experience?"

"I guess I have a talent for war," Nahla admitted with embarrassment. She didn't feel proud about it.

"Did you ever fight for water?" Barrin asked.

"Rarely. Our water system was good. You have a different system here."

"How so?"

"I don't know where or how your people get water." Nahla shot him an interrogative glance and then gestured at the water bags on the donkeys. "Back home, we had wells."

"Wells? What is *wells*?"

Nahla furrowed her brow. If Barrin didn't know what a well was, then that left bigger questions about how Launceston stayed hydrated. She told him about wells, that they were just holes in the ground where people could draw water using a bucket and rope.

"Preposterous!" Barrin waved a hand dismissively. "Now I *know* you're telling me a fairytale."

Far ahead, Ragh must have heard Barrin's brusque voice, for he quickly twisted in his saddle. On seeing that the officer was not in any danger, he refocused on the land ahead.

They rode on in silence for the better part of an hour after that. Nahla took a sip from her water pouch and wondered why water was such a touchy subject in Launceston. Was it the same across all of Tasmania? Lord Johl had said another kingdom in the south, the Kingdom of Hobart, also had strict rules about water supply and consumption.

She thought of Cass, whom she'd met in Launceston Prison. What had they called her? *Cass the Blasphemer.* She questioned the royal decree about water. Nahla wanted to ask what that decree said, but doing so would poke a vast hole in her story. Whatever it said, water was such a serious topic that simply questioning the royal decree led to imprisonment and executions. Nahla started brainstorming the right way to word her questions for whoever had the right answers. She didn't want to appear rebellious, just inquisitive.

Barrin broke her train of thought. "If you *are* from a faraway land, why have you come here?"

The fires of recent memories ignited once more in Nahla's mind. She saw blood-drenched swords, saw the clouds of arrows crossing battlefields, heard the wails of horses run through with polearms, and felt the searing heat of burning buildings. Her heart thumped as she remembered the enemy pressing in against her slowly dwindling force—stone battlements collapsing by the relentless onslaught of siege weapons, enemy soldiers pouring over castle walls, a blazing belfry tower disintegrating by the gatehouse, the cries and screams of frightened villagers . . . the expression of loss and defeat in her king's eyes.

"Nahla?" Barrin asked. "Did you hear me?"

She snapped out of the memory. "Uh, yes. Yes, I heard you."

Nahla took a deep breath and wondered how much of the story she should tell. She opened her mouth to speak, but something caught Barrin's eye. He held out a hand to keep her silent. Ragh had dismounted at the crest of a hill and was waving at them.

"Follow me," Barrin said. His voice had an edge of alertness. "Ride on the dry grass."

They galloped up the hill, jumped off their horses, and lay down on the warm earth next to Ragh.

"Two unknown travellers, sir," Ragh said, pointing.

"Good job," Barrin said. "Head back to the donkeys and refill your water pouch."

Nahla spotted two riders in the distance. They skirted a steep line of erosion in the terrain. Barrin watched them through a long wooden tube.

"I think they may be bandits," he said.

Barrin handed Nahla the tube. It had glass at each end. "What is this?"

"It's a telescope. Look through it."

Nahla put her eye against the end Barrin pointed to, and her view of the bandits magnified noticeably. Such a marvellous device! She could see the men's dirty faces, the good condition of their armour, and the swords dangling from their waists. Their saddlebags were full too.

"What are your orders?" Nahla asked. She returned the telescope, now secretly wanting one for herself.

"We can take them, but I fear they will see us approaching."

"Let me go alone."

Barrin disapproved. "That is precisely what I was told not to do. You need to show that you will fight *with* us and *for* us, not run off with a bandit clan."

"No. I have a plan."

"Spill it."

Nahla walked over the crest of the hill, leading one of the water donkeys. The placid beast happily moved to Nahla's beckoning. She hoped it would move faster when necessary.

Barrin and the twins stayed hidden on the other side of the hill, but Barrin said he would watch her closely with his telescope. She trudged loudly down the dirt road to attract the bandits' attention, but they were far away and had their backs to her.

She started singing. She hated doing so because she thought she sounded more like a crow than a songbird. But the sound would carry down the hill across the open terrain and hopefully catch the bandits' ears.

Nahla kept singing with her head down until she heard galloping horses. Then she looked up and froze, feigning surprise, then quickly turned and fled back up the hill with the donkey. The animal hee-hawed as it ran, and water sloshed around in the saddlebags. The bandits moved quickly, and she gasped when she saw how close they were.

She ran over the hill and kept running past Barrin, who was getting up from his hiding spot, and past Ragh and Rhos, who were already mounted and waiting. The yelling and cursing and horses neighing made her stop. Her plan had worked! The bandits took the bait and fell right into her trap.

The twins had already grappled the bandits, pulled them from their horses, and were roughing them up on the ground. By the time Nahla ran back to join them, the fight was over. The bandits lay beaten and swordless.

Barrin interrogated them while the twins inspected their saddlebags. Nothing but food.

"Where are you taking the food?" Barrin asked. "That's a lot for two skinny bastards like you." They remained tight-lipped. So Barrin drew his sword and pressed it against the throat of the taller one. "Must I ask again?"

"We were taking it to our camp," one of them said.

The tall bandit smacked his friend angrily. "Shut up!"

"That's better," Barrin said. "And where would this camp be?"

The bandits eyed each other.

"Briseis Hole."

The tall one swore and told off his friend, but quietened when Barrin pressed his sword harder and drew blood.

"Show me on my map. I will let you go free if you cooperate."

The talkative one nodded.

"Excellent!" Barrin said, then drove his sword into the angry bandit, who collapsed with one last gurgled curse. Barrin cleaned his sword on the dead man's clothes. "I have preserved your life because you've been helpful. Keep it up, and you have nothing to fear."

Nahla rather liked the way Barrin carried himself. He had an iron voice and knew how to use it to get results. She guessed bandits valued little to the King's Legion, and perhaps even less to these specific legionaries, because they had to do the work that provincial soldiers should have done already. But Barrin was conducting himself professionally, and Nahla was happy to watch.

Barrin had unfurled a detailed map inscribed on a large rectangular parchment. The bandit pointed.

"It's about a five-hour ride from Scottsdale," the bandit said, "but we don't need to go near Scottsdale from here. There is a more direct route." He traced a line on the map with his finger.

"Still a long way," Barrin said. "It will be night or probably dusk when we arrive."

"Time is of the essence," Nahla said, eager to get moving.

"Yes." Barrin rolled up his map. "You will come with us, bandit. If you are telling me the truth and we arrive at a bandit camp, you will live."

The bandit bowed slightly. "What will happen to my clan?"

"Nothing." Barrin smiled. "But tell me, is your clan the one terrorising Lord Garyd of Scottsdale?"

The bandit looked away.

"Do you want to end up like your friend?" Nahla asked.

"Fine! Yes, I belong to Clan Daxton. We control everything east of Scottsdale."

"Hmm. Okay, you ride with us now. Show us the way, and no funny business. I want to know everything about this camp and your clan. And I mean *everything*."

They trotted off. The bandit took them to a narrow track through a forest. His horse was tethered to Ragh's, and Barrin questioned him for hours. Nahla listened and digested all the information, building a mental picture of the camp and tallying up the clan's size and structure in her mind.

Barrin wanted accurate military intelligence. Nahla wanted something else.

9

DISOBEYING ORDERS

Loyalty binds us, but unquestioned obedience shackles our potential. One must always dare to seize opportunities within the bounds of loyalty.

—**Nahla Northborn**
Monologues

Nᴀʜʟᴀ ᴘᴇʀᴄʜᴇᴅ ʜᴇʀsᴇʟғ ᴀɢᴀɪɴsᴛ a dead tree trunk and watched the fires in the sleepy camp below. The bandit guide had fulfilled his end of the bargain, taking Lieutenant Barrin's scouting party to a high, forested hill overlooking a sandy depression dotted with tents. True to Barrin's estimation, they had arrived just after the sun disappeared below the horizon, and they managed a long, silent study of the camp before the light of dusk finally faded to black. Barrin wanted more information, so he set up camp and ordered Ragh to patrol between him and the bandits. The young legionary would be relieved in a few hours by his sister, Rhos.

Since she was still not completely trusted, Nahla could not go on picket duty with Ragh and Rhos. Instead, she stayed near Barrin while he interrogated the captured bandit. He intended to learn everything he could about the camp and its leader, Daxton. How many lived in the camp? How many other camps belonged to Clan Daxton? Which one was nearest? How often did the other bandits travel between camps or around the countryside? How often did Daxton visit? Was he there at the moment? How did he become the bandit leader? Did he have deputies and a command structure?

So many questions, Nahla thought. When the bandit gave half-answers, Barrin pushed and pressed for more. If a question was met with silence or an outright refusal to answer, Barrin threatened and demanded. And when the bandit expressed concern for the welfare of his clan, Barrin reassured him with a gentle tone.

Nahla winced at the reassurances. Back home, people who formed marauder bands to rob and pillage the land were dealt with severely. It was hard enough to run a society in a hot dust bowl of a world. Nobody needed opportunistic criminals undoing everybody's hard work. People had to labour for their food and drink, shelter and clothing. To threaten someone's fields and produce was to threaten their livelihood, not to mention the flow-on effects to the rest of society.

But maybe the situation was different in Tasmania. Nahla watched the bandit as he stammered out his answers for Barrin. Perhaps maltreatment or the risk of starvation forced bandits into their criminal ways. From what Nahla had seen, while the people of Launceston worked hard, they also needed to be "bribed" to distract them from the drudgery of everyday life. King Eero used the gladiators to this effect, and who knew what other tricks he played to keep his subjects in line?

She licked her lips and sipped at her water pouch. Barrin wanted to stay on this hill at least until noon the following day, watching the surrounding roads, spying on the camp with that fantastic thing he called a telescope. Meanwhile, the five of them had to share the water that the donkeys carried.

She didn't intend to stay until noon, however. Her purpose on this mission was to prove her worth, and prove it she would, for she had a big, bold plan brewing in her mind. Now that she had seen the camp with her own eyes and overheard vital details about it from the captured bandit, her plan was taking shape. She just needed to wait until daylight.

Nahla heard the crunch of dry bark. She slept lightly, as she often did out in the wild, and so became fully alert at the sound. She opened her eyelids a little and saw Ragh treading back to their camp.

Silly boy, she thought.

Barrin was already awake, for he and Nahla had taken turns watching their prisoner throughout the night. The dawn shift was his turn. She stood and stretched, enjoying the cool shade of the forest. Barrin offered her some food, which she gratefully accepted.

"May I use your telescope?" she asked while chewing. Then she remembered her manners and covered her mouth, but it was too late. Barrin had seen the masticated clump of her breakfast and simply handed her the contraption without a word.

She trained the telescope on the bandit camp and watched the early morning routines. Barrin asked their captive about what normally happened of a morning. The bandit explained that everybody had a job. A foraging party would head out to prey on unsuspecting travellers or surrounding farms. Guards would be changed, fires snuffed out, breakfasts prepared. If messengers had arrived overnight, they would head back to their home camps, perhaps carrying news, other orders, or even supplies.

Nahla listened to everything and tried to see all of those activities through the telescope. Two guards stood lazily by the camp's entrance, and two others were snaking their way between the tents. Another bandit went around the camp extinguishing the torches, but a big fire in the centre kept blazing. Several bandits gathered around it, drawing food from a large cauldron. A few horse riders trotted out of the camp and headed north. They were most likely the foragers, or a troop of scouts.

A large tent dominated the camp's rear. Nahla couldn't decide if it was an armoury, a storehouse, or a command tent. She asked the captive bandit, and he confirmed that was Daxton's quarters.

"He was there when I went foraging," the bandit said. "But he may have left by now. He moves around a lot."

Nahla kept the telescope on that tent. Her whole plan rested on Daxton's presence.

The tent flaps opened and out came a man with a thick black beard and a fully bald head. He wore a loose-fitting, dirty white shirt and patchy brown shorts. Apparently, he felt safe in his den of thieves, for he wore no armour, nor did he have any weapons.

"Bandit," Nahla said, "tell us again what Daxton looks like."

"Tall, bald, tanned, with a neat black beard. Most of the fingers on his left hand are missing."

Nahla lowered the telescope and adjusted the zoom. Sure enough, this bandit had only two fingers on his left hand.

"Daxton is here," she announced.

"Good," Barrin said. "We watch him."

Nahla returned the telescope. "May I have a word with you?"

Her tone caught Barrin off guard, but he assented. After ordering Rhos to watch the prisoner, he motioned for her to join him a few paces away by a large tree.

"I have a plan," Nahla said.

"I'm beginning to think you always have a plan. Go on."

She spoke, outlining her simple plan and highlighting why it would work. Halfway through, she could already see Barrin's expression changing. When she finished, Barrin shook his head.

"No," he said sternly, "absolutely not. Our mission is to scout. Understood?"

She understood many things, like why their mission was to gather intelligence and why she was tagging along. But what she couldn't fathom was why Barrin wouldn't pounce when a glorious opportunity presented itself.

"Is that understood, Nahla?" Barrin repeated.

"Yes."

He glared at her.

"Yes, *sir.*"

With that, he left her by the big tree to brood. She crossed her arms and leaned against it, watching the camp. The way she saw it, there was one high authority in this land, and that was King Eero. The king himself had assigned her this task, and it was the king who told her what Daxton was doing in Lord Garyd's province. Now Nahla saw a way to strike a fatal blow to the bandit clan. *Forget about Barrin!*

Instead of returning to the lieutenant, she marched straight to her horse. Ajax stood where she'd left him the night before, and he greeted her with a wave of the head.

"Eager for some action, boy?" she whispered. She wondered if horses ever felt the same mischief she was feeling right then.

Nahla borrowed a rope from Rhos' saddle and made a knot. Then she checked her sword and armour, packed her red military cape in her knapsack, mounted Ajax, and trotted off through the forest.

"Hey!" Barrin called in a sort of growling whisper. She heard his footsteps as he ran to his own horse. Within seconds, he had caught her. "You disobey my order!"

"Look, Barrin, when I see an opportunity, I take it," she told him. They trotted side by side. "Trust me—I have enough experience. More than you, actually."

That last comment made him stumble on his words. "I'm still your commanding officer."

"Back home, I was a lot more senior than you."

"We're not in your fantasy land," Barrin snapped, "which means here in Tasmania, *I* outrank *you*, and *I* give *you* the orders. Now, turn around before you get us all killed."

"You're a soldier, just like me, Barrin. But I'm thinking you legionaries are just for show. Follow me or stay here. But I'm going in there, and when I come back, you and Ragh and Rhos better be ready to hightail it out of here."

"What—?"

Nahla galloped down the hill, leaving him behind. She didn't hear him pursue. They had the element of surprise, eyes on the clan leader, and all the intelligence they could possibly need. In a military operation, the only thing worse than not having intelligence was having it and not using it. Now Nahla would use the knowledge they had gained and take matters into her own hands.

She reached the bottom of the hill and turned onto a dirt road. The bandit camp lay below in the depression. An odd place to build a camp, she thought, but that was Daxton's problem.

Around the corner, the two guards by the entrance did a double-take when they saw the lone madwoman charging towards them. Nahla had not yet drawn her sword, hoping they would think of her as a rushing messenger. Since she wore no royal or provincial colours, they may mistake her for one of their own.

Her gambit must have worked, because she sped past them and suddenly found herself in the middle of the clan. Everyone stepped out of her way. Surely they would question this stranger galloping through their morning routines. If they suspected her, maybe her audacity had them stunned into inactivity.

She grabbed a torch that had not yet been extinguished and held it out against the tents as she passed them. Now she heard yelling and shouting. She wanted to draw her sword too, but holding both sword and torch meant it would be difficult to use the horse's reins, so she opted to burn her way to the camp's centre.

By the time she reached the large central campfire, several bandits had fetched weapons, but they were still wearing their bed clothes or undergarments. She spotted Daxton. In his eyes was the realisation that some lunatic mercenary had come for him. He bellowed orders to his people and ran for his tent. Nahla threw the torch at an advancing wall of underdressed men and women and darted for Daxton, but he made it to his tent before she could catch him.

Then she was surrounded. Her sword made quick work of the defenders, but they tried to pull her out of the saddle. She bashed them away and kicked one or two, but she needed to keep her feet in the stirrups. When it became too difficult, she spurred Ajax and he barrelled through them to safety. When she turned around, she saw the bandits following her undeterred. But behind them came Barrin, Ragh, and Rhos. The line of bandits heard the rumble of hooves, but by then it was too late. Barrin and the twins crashed through in an expertly timed cavalry charge, which decimated and demoralised the bandit ranks.

"Go get him!" Barrin barked at Nahla. He sounded angry, but his face spelled victory.

Daxton ran towards a horse. Nahla chased him down, leaving Barrin and the twins to deal with the other bandits who were joining the fight. Now mounted, Daxton drew his sword and galloped through the camp, Nahla in hot pursuit. On the path to the camp's entrance, Nahla passed bodies of dead and dying criminals who were cut down when Barrin charged through.

She didn't want Daxton to escape, which was why she brought the rope. It was a hard trick to pull off, but she'd been taught how to do it back home. She twirled the rope above her head as she rode, then swung it at Daxton. The noose went around his neck and she pulled hard. He yelped and fell back off his horse, dropping his sword.

Within seconds, the bandits converged on her to protect their leader. She swung at them with her sword, especially at the few who had halberds—a dangerous pole weapon with a pike end and a razor-sharp axe. They aimed at Ajax, the easiest target, but she desperately blocked them. Most of her attention was on the bandits, but she felt the tug on the rope as Daxton tried to get up.

Then Barrin came storming through to provide much-needed relief. Nahla could have taken them all by herself, but she would have come out of the fight bloodied, bruised, and most likely horse-less. Ragh hopped off his horse and punched Daxton in the face, then took Nahla's rope and bound the bandit leader's hands and tied the rope to the horn of his saddle.

"This is going to hurt," Ragh said, then mounted and rode off, dragging Daxton close behind. The bandit leader screamed.

"Let's go!" Barrin yelled. "Rhos, Nahla, follow Ragh!"

They fled the camp, leaving behind a mess of burning tents and bleeding enemies. Ragh had stopped up the road where it was quiet and properly strapped a now unconscious Daxton to his horse. A nasty wound on Daxton's face showed where Ragh had probably smashed him with the hilt of his sword.

They rode off victorious, back to fetch their water donkeys and the bandit forager they'd tied to a tree before coming to Nahla's aid. On the long journey home, Barrin said very little, and Nahla wondered what praise—or wrath—awaited her when they arrived in Launceston.

10

DIVISIONS

A network weakened by cracks can only withstand the
weight of its purpose for so long before collapsing under
the strain.

—Cass the Blasphemer
Proverbs of Change

Barrin set an uncomfortable pace. They rode as hard as the horses
could go, slowing only for the roughest terrain. Several hours into
their return journey, Barrin barked his first words, an order to stop
and rest. The team moved to the side of the dusty road and climbed
off their horses to stretch. Nahla's thighs hurt from the hours of
friction in the unfamiliar saddle. Rhos nibbled on some fruit and
offered Nahla an apple. Ragh gave their captives a small drink. The
talkative youth complained, but Ragh told him to shut up. Daxton,
the clan leader, had said nothing except for the few curses when
the ride became too bumpy. Barrin kept his distance and sat on his
steed. He stared off towards Launceston, perhaps contemplating
how his king would react to Nahla's impetuous act at the bandit
camp.

Nahla wondered the same.

After twenty minutes, Barrin ordered everyone on the road
again, and they trotted the rest of the way. At some point, Barrin

84

must have recognised they were nearing the city, for he sent Rhos ahead. She galloped away, leaving a trail of dust behind her.

When they arrived at Launceston, a guard in a tower jeered at the captured bandits.

"You will stay silent!" Barrin growled at him, and the guard stiffened.

Nahla frowned. Evidently, the long journey had done nothing to lighten Barrin's foul mood. She hoped King Eero would feel differently.

They rode through the busy streets of Launceston. Passersby understood that the men tied to the horses were criminals, and they struck out with fists and spat at their faces. Ragh let them do it, but Barrin threatened to lop off the hands of anyone who didn't stay away.

Rhos waited outside the palace with a woman dressed in a stunning red robe. She wore a white hood to protect her head from the sun. Her face bore the subtle lines of healthy middle age, though she was pale and taut, as if she had never needed to suffer the sun's interminable heat. Barrin greeted her politely, but Nahla could still hear the edge in his voice.

"That's the king's chamberlain," Ragh whispered. "She's a nasty one. Have you met her before?"

"No."

Nahla couldn't remember seeing her at the feast. A chamberlain rarely leaves a king's side when he is in public, but perhaps she had been busy elsewhere.

"Bring them in," the chamberlain said to Barrin. "The king awaits with his lords."

Nahla hopped off Ajax and tied him to a nearby post under a tree. Ragh and Rhos handled Daxton and the young bandit, who grunted and grumbled in protest. Since they had it under control, and since Barrin had not given her any orders, Nahla watched with her hand on her sword pommel. But out of the corner of her eye, she noticed the chamberlain studying her. The woman stood with her arms crossed, her hands fed into the drooping sleeves of her robe, perhaps to hide the delicate skin from the sun.

They marched Daxton through the palace, and Nahla got the sense that they were giving this criminal a special honour. She couldn't imagine many criminals being brought to a king in his own home.

When they reached Eero's throne room, the chamberlain announced them in a booming voice.

"Lieutenant Barrin, Your Majesty," she said. Her voice echoed in the hall, and Nahla knew she was using the acoustics to her advantage. "And with him, bandits from Scottsdale Province."

Barrin tucked his helmet under one arm and bowed before King Eero. All the lords stood beside the king, and they regarded Daxton with curled lips and narrowed eyes.

"Your Majesty," Barrin said, "we have returned from our reconnaissance."

"I can see that, Lieutenant," Eero said with a grin. "But you have done more than reconnoitre."

"Our mission was to scout the lands of Scottsdale for known bandit activity," Barrin continued. Nahla got the sense that he had rehearsed this little speech on the long journey home. "We happened upon this bandit, who was part of a two-man foraging party. His counterpart was not cooperative, so we killed him. In exchange for his life, this one led us to Daxton's bandit camp."

"You saw his camp?" Lord Garyd asked, wide-eyed.

"We did." Barrin paused.

Eero leaned forwards. "And?"

"The camp was set alight, and many inhabitants were killed. I cannot say for sure, but it may be destroyed."

Nahla watched everyone's expression. She could not doubt the joy on Garyd's face, for Daxton had been a thorn in his side for a long time. Johl, however, did not look pleased. His face was flushed red, though that could have been another heavy lunch of good food and wine, or simply that he was in Nahla's presence again.

"What I don't understand," Johl said, "is how a simple reconnaissance mission led to the destruction of a bandit camp and the capture of its leader. Surely the King's Legion is capable of following orders?"

"Yes, Barrin," Eero said. "Please explain."

Not wanting Barrin to take the brunt of the windstorm that was certainly brewing before him, Nahla stepped forwards. "Your Majesty, I can explain."

"The question was asked for Lieutenant Barrin to answer," Johl snapped.

Eero eyed her suspiciously. "Go on."

Nahla explained how they had camped in the forest overlooking Daxton's camp, and that they had the perfect opportunity to strike. With one fatal blow, they could sever the bandit clan's brain and sow chaos throughout its ranks, so she had pounced, despite Barrin's objections. As she spoke, she remembered just how dirty her skin and armour were. Since Barrin had not allowed them to rest for long on the way home, she was still covered in the blood and grime of battle, a testament to the ferocity of the fight within the camp. No wonder the chamberlain had been staring at her.

The king leaned back in his throne as Nahla finished, but it was Johl who spoke first.

"So the filthy water thief disobeyed a direct order from the *king*?"

"Nahla did the right thing," Garyd piped up. He moved closer to Nahla and faced his noble counterparts. "I wish more were like her. We need more action around here. Too much talk and not enough action. How many times did I ask for your help, Johl? Huh? And you always said no. Well, now someone who is not even fully inducted into the King's Legion has taken the initiative and delivered us a victory. Your Majesty, Nahla did the right thing."

"Oh, please," Johl said. "If your troops were under a firmer command, you would have swept away this bandit scourge by now."

"How dare you!" Garyd, grey and wrinkly, bristled with anger at the younger lord's blatant disrespect. "My province is more than twice the size of yours, poorer, and has fewer soldiers. Do not lecture me on waging battle with bandits when you have not left the comforts of Launceston in years."

The last words bounced angrily off the stone walls. Nahla started to see the cracks between Eero's subordinates. Johl and Garyd clearly didn't like each other. The clean-cut Lord Vimarr of Devonport stood close to Johl in a defensive stance. Meanwhile, a short, portly man covered in jewellery watched the argument from the sideline. Nahla didn't know his name, but he had been sitting with the lords at the feast and was probably a governor as well. She couldn't tell what side he supported.

"Gentlemen," Eero said calmly. "Please, let us not argue among ourselves in the presence of guests. This is a joyous occasion." He gestured at the bandits. "Here we have the source of your woes, Garyd. I hand him to you for interrogation. And his friend too."

"His friend is particularly talkative," Barrin said.

Daxton cast a disapproving stare at the youthful bandit, who slouched guiltily.

"Allow me to be the first to thank you, Nahla, for your quick thinking," Garyd said. He went to shake her hand, but on seeing that it was bloodied and dirty, retracted his hand with an awkward chuckle. Then he glared at Daxton with pure hatred.

"Too right," Eero said. "Nahla, once again you have done the unexpected, and for that I thank you. I gave you a test of loyalty, not a test of *obedience*." As he said the last word, he looked purposefully at Johl. "You have proved your loyalty to my kingdom by helping to secure our northern province. As your reward, I am officially inducting you into the King's Legion. Hayla!"

"Your Majesty?" The chamberlain stepped out from the shadows behind the king's throne.

"Fetch Captain Vox. We will need him to induct Nahla."

"At once, Your Majesty." Hayla relayed the order with a swift finger at one of the guards by the door. The soldier left to find his captain.

"And I think a reward is in order for Lieutenant Barrin and his legionaries here," Garyd said.

"What would be appropriate, Hayla?" Eero asked.

"I think double water rations for seven days should suffice."

"I agree. Well done, legionaries!" Eero clapped. "Perhaps your attack on the bandit camp will go down in history as the beginning of the end of our troubles in Scottsdale Province. See to their rewards, Hayla. Now,"—he addressed Ragh and Rhos—"take these criminals to Launceston Prison."

The twins straightened, saluted, and dragged the bandits away.

"This is not the end of us," came a slow, deep voice.

"What did you say?" Eero asked.

Daxton, his arm twisted by Ragh, looked over his shoulder. "This is not the end of us," he repeated. "Your tyranny will end, Eero, and yours too, Garyd."

Eero's lips went thin and pale. "You are lucky my friend wants to interrogate you, else you would be headless already. Take them away!"

After they'd left, Garyd said, "If I am not needed here, Eero, I shall go to the prison to begin the interrogations."

The king nodded. "Very well, old friend."

"My lord," Barrin said, "I will also supply you with a report of everything the younger bandit told me. I just need to write it down first."

"Excellent! Thank you, Lieutenant."

"Perhaps you should write that report while the information is still fresh in your mind," Eero said. "You are no longer needed here, Barrin."

"Your Majesty." Barrin bowed and left with Lord Garyd.

"I think our business here is at an end," Eero said to the remaining lords. "You may join me later tonight for dinner. Usual time."

Johl scowled at Nahla before answering. "Unfortunately, Your Majesty, Vimarr and I have some business to discuss before he leaves for his province. We will dine at my castle tonight."

"Uh, yes," Vimarr said. "A shame, but duty calls."

They made to leave, but Johl cast a burning glance at Nahla as he passed. His absence sent a chill down her spine.

"So it is just us tonight, Alden?"

The round lord laughed, his cheeks stretching happily. "Indeed, Your Majesty. I will savour your evening feast once more before departing in the morning. The southern borders are not quiet, and I want to be there. See you in a few hours." He waddled out, but not before sharing a loud greeting and jolly laughter with Captain Vox as the Legion commander entered.

"Captain Vox," Eero began, "you have a new legionary in your ranks."

"Nahla!" Vox said. He looked her up and down. "You look like you've been fighting gladiators again."

"Something like that, sir." She knew to keep her comments short when dealing with superiors.

"Well, then, I will give you the Oath. Put your right hand over your heart and repeat after me."

Nahla pledged her everlasting loyalty to the king and her enduring service to the King's Legion. She vowed to defend the kingdom with every drop of blood coursing through her veins, to ensure the borders were secure, to safeguard the king and his household, and to protect his subjects.

"Congratulations, Nahla!" Eero said. He grinned as if he knew he was winning a card game. "I am glad to have a soldier of your talents in my service. And it is because of those talents that I have a special job for you. Have you ever *trained* soldiers before?"

"Yes, Your Majesty."

"Good. You have exceptional skill in tactical warfare. I want you to train the King's Legion. Captain Vox will help you."

She looked at Vox, who nodded as if to say that he and the king had already discussed and agreed on the topic.

"Also, I am giving you a special assignment," Eero continued. He gestured for her to come closer. "I want you to train my son. He is sorely lacking in military skills."

Until this point, nobody had mentioned that Eero had a son. "How old is he, Your Majesty?"

"He is thirty at the end of the year."

Nahla struggled to hide the shock on her face. A thirty-year-old prince with no military training? Being just a year older, Nahla had probably seen enough fighting to last a lifetime. She imagined a plump, lazy, spoiled brat who had never used a sword but loved to boss around his shiny legionaries.

"How hard am I allowed to push him?" Nahla asked bluntly.

Eero laughed. "Push him as hard as you like! He'll be king after me, and he needs to know how to fight. There will be war with the south soon enough—if not in my lifetime, then definitely in his. Do you know strategy, or just tactics?"

"I know both reasonably well."

"Hmm. I think you know more than you let on. But I trust you to get the job done."

"It shall be done, Your Majesty," she said with a little bow.

"Good. You will meet him tomorrow, but right now you need to see Matriarch Anurak for your penance. I promised I would send you to her as soon as you returned. I know you may be tired and are dirty from your fighting, but if you don't go right away, I will never hear the end of it. So, please, go do your penance. It's a necessary evil."

While Eero had been speaking, Hayla had quietly organised a damp cloth for Nahla. Nahla thanked her and started scrubbing the dirt and blood from her face.

"Where shall I meet the matriarch?"

"Hayla will show you. Be on your way." Eero waved her off, and Hayla started walking. Nahla hurried after the chamberlain.

11

PENANCE

Through the humble act of penance, we find redemption for the sins that weigh us down. It is in acknowledging our faults, seeking forgiveness, and embracing the path of self-reflection that we embark on a journey towards spiritual healing and inner transformation. This is what sets us apart from the barbarians of the west and the heathens of the south.

—**Elspet, Sixty-Seventh Matriarch**
A Treatise on Penance

COURT OFFICIALS WALKING THE esteemed halls of royalty usually did so with haste. This was true of Chamberlain Hayla when she escorted Nahla, Barrin, and the others to show off the bandit leader to King Eero. Now, however, as Hayla took Nahla to meet Matriarch Anurak, the distinguished woman slowed to a more comfortable pace, almost leisurely.

Nahla remembered how serious Anurak was about penance. The old woman had ordered Eero to send Nahla to her the moment she returned to Launceston. Anyone who could freely and publicly make such demands of a king certainly warranted Nahla's attention. But Hayla seemed to be in no rush.

"You are a peculiar woman," Hayla said. Her voice oozed

control and calmness, and she spoke at such a low pitch and volume that her words failed to echo along the stone corridor.

The statement caught Nahla off guard, and she did not reply immediately. After a few steps, she finally asked, "Why do you say that, Chamberlain?"

"I watched you fight in the arena, and then I watched you at the feast later that day. You are at ease behind a sword *and* before kings and nobles."

"I see both as swordplay—one using metal, the other using the tongue." The chamberlain was not present at the feast, so she must have been watching from a hidden room.

Hayla chuckled. She wore her white hood, which obscured her face as she walked beside Nahla. "You speak as though you have experience at court. Tell me, whom have you served?"

And just like that, the smooth-talking chamberlain had put Nahla into a corner in a matter of minutes. Every second that Nahla remained silent would convince Hayla that she was on to something.

"I served a faraway ruler," Nahla said.

Hayla sighed and slowed her pace even more. "The only faraway ruler is Queen Zula of Hobart." Now Hayla turned and studied Nahla as they walked together. "Are you from the Southern Kingdom?"

"I am not."

Hayla faced forwards again. "Hmm. Well, there are no royal or noble courts in the west—the barbarians are not like us. The only other courts belonged to King Eero and his lords, and none of them were familiar with you. So, I ask again, whom have you served?"

Nahla stopped and took a deep breath. She rested a hand on the pommel of her sword and the thought of ending Hayla's life fleeted across her mind. Something about this woman was unsettling. But to attempt murder against the chamberlain would admit guilt. Technically, she had nothing to be guilty of. She had not come from the land of Eero's enemy, nor was she a spy from her homeland.

"I served under King Vasylis of Melbourne, though I am now an exile."

They had stopped in a corridor with no guards in sight. Hayla stared at Nahla with a completely unreadable face, then turned and continued walking. Nahla followed.

"I have not heard of Melbourne," the chamberlain said. "Where is it?"

"Far to the north. I walked for many days through a desolate plain to get here."

Hayla digested the information silently. If she dismissed it as a lie, she gave no indication. "And why were you exiled?"

The question made Nahla's heart skip a beat. Memories of failure flooded back to her mind. "Civil war."

"Did you fight against your king?"

"No. I fought with undivided loyalty."

"I see. Your king lost, and you were exiled. What became of Vasylis?"

Nahla's hands sweated, and she could feel her body warming under Hayla's quiet interrogation. "He was killed in battle."

They reached an unguarded door. It was devoid of any decorations. Hayla regarded Nahla with a thin-lipped smile. "How fortuitous. Your former liege is now dead, which means you no longer owe your loyalty to him. Now you belong to King Eero." She fished out a ring of keys from a deep pocket in her robe.

"You believe my story?"

"I don't believe anything I hear. Of course, it warrants more investigation. Even from a cursory glance, you don't look Tasmanian. You are not like us—your skin, your eyes, your hair, they are all much darker than ours."

Nahla had noticed that her complexion, though tanned like many others, was noticeably darker than most people in Tasmania, but she had never thought it would be a defining characteristic. Obviously, she was different enough for Hayla to take note. She decided she wouldn't tell Hayla about how Barrin did not believe she was from Melbourne. The lieutenant would probably get reprimanded for not reporting it to his superiors.

Hayla opened the door to the dwindling light of dusk. Outside was a colonnaded courtyard with a lush green garden and a magnificent fountain as the centrepiece. The trickling water was music to Nahla's ears. A lone guard patrolled the perimeter.

"This way," Hayla said.

They walked along a path through the garden to another locked door on the other side. This one had a guard posted, and he straightened when he saw the chamberlain's red robe. Hayla opened the door and beckoned Nahla through.

On the other side was a wide, paved square, bereft of gardens or fountains, but lined with water carts. They were simple four-wheeled carts, each with a large leather water container. But something else caught Nahla's attention. A massive, tiered building dominated one end of the courtyard. It rose in five levels, each level getting smaller, culminating in a tall rod at its top. Actually, as Nahla looked more closely at the dim building against the darkening sky, she saw that small rods lined the edges of each level. The structure was unlike anything she had ever seen before.

"The Royal Temple," Hayla said, breaking Nahla's trance. "Only servicing the king, his extended household, and his Legion." She started walking towards a smaller building that looked more like a large residence.

Nahla pretended like she knew that already. "Always an impressive sight."

Hayla said nothing. They came to a simple two-storey building, the entry of which was on the shady side. It was a sturdy edifice with high, narrow windows. A tall bell tower rose from one corner. The front door, easily twice Nahla's height, had a metal coat of arms depicting a blue shield criss-crossed with a white X. In each blue quadrant was a golden water droplet. Flanking the door were two women dressed in fine armour, with deep blue pelerine capes over their shoulders and matching hoods. So far, this was the third uniform Nahla had seen in the kingdom—the black of the Launceston Provincial Garrison, the red of the King's Legion, and now this very dignified blue of the Divine Guard.

"Our conversation has been most enlightening," Hayla said. Her tone was unreadable. "This is the headquarters of the Guardians of Life. Anurak should be here. When she releases you, ask for someone to take you back to your barracks."

"And then I will receive further orders?"

Hayla smiled. "You won't be needing orders for the time being." Then she departed.

Nahla watched the chamberlain cross the courtyard, wondering what would become of their conversation. She decided almost immediately that it would be safer not to speak to Hayla ever again.

The two guards by the door made no attempt to hide the fact that they were watching her. They had the same teardrop herald on their breastplates, like the one on the door. These women were tall and strong, with a fierce gaze to match their impressive weapons. Both held razor-sharp halberds, and each had a sword and dagger strapped to their waist. Two kite shields leaned against the building, also bearing the teardrop emblem.

What had Hayla called them? Nahla asked herself. *The Guardians of Life.* As far as she could tell, this was a heavily religious military order.

She approached the door carefully and banged the heavy knocker. The guards watched her from the corners of their eyes.

A woman in a white robe answered. She looked Nahla up and down and raised her eyebrows at the blood still on Nahla's armour. "How may I help you, daughter? Do you require medical attention?"

"I am Nahla, here to see Matriarch Anurak."

The priestess nodded once, slowly and deliberately. "Follow me."

Nahla entered and immediately felt the change in temperature. The square outside, fully paved with stone, radiated heat from a full day of sun, but the administration building's thick walls kept it cool and refreshing. The priestess glided along the foyer, her robes hiding her footsteps. Wherever she looked, Nahla could see at least two of the blue-garbed soldiers.

The priestess ascended a wide staircase. She made no sound, nor checked to see if Nahla followed. Along the wall beside the stairs was a colourful fresco that wrapped around the entire staircase. The image was pure fantasy. It depicted fields of green grass and fruit-bearing trees, fat animals, and clean and healthy people. A huge body of water dominated one end of the painting.

"We all long for heaven," the priestess said from several steps above Nahla, "but for the moment, we must endure in this world. Please follow."

Other priestesses walked about on the next floor, moving slowly and silently. They kept their heads low, as if in deep thought, and gave Nahla no attention.

Nahla's guide turned down a long hallway lined with canvas paintings of distinguished women. They all wore the same blue robes with white-and-gold etchings that Matriarch Anurak had worn to King Eero's feast. The priestess knocked on a door at the end of the hallway. An abrupt voice admitted them from the other side.

The priestess entered. "Nahla to see you, Matriarch," she said in the softest voice.

Matriarch Anurak looked up from her desk. A single candle cast a yellow glow against her face. "Thank you, Tish. You may go."

The priestess bowed and left. Nahla, having never reported to a religious leader before, did what naturally came to her as a soldier and stood at attention, back straight, arms at her side. Her stomach growled and Anurak smirked.

"I see Eero was true to his word and sent you here quickly," Anurak said. "You've not had time to eat."

It sounded like a statement, so Nahla didn't reply. She'd learned that it was better not to speak to superiors unless explicitly requested to do so. All the lessons from her younger soldiering days were returning.

"Lord Johl and I had a long conversation about you while you were away," Anurak continued. "He told me about your crimes— how you assaulted his soldiers, how you attempted to kill him, but worst of all, how you *stole* water." She shook her head. "Such crimes demand the harshest punishment, but Eero is tempering my hand. Do you feel any remorse?"

No, Nahla thought, for she felt no crimes had been committed. However, she felt sorry for chopping off Lieutenant Kessia's ear. Denying any remorse would only make matters worse, so Nahla played into Anurak's hand. "I am ashamed of my actions, Matriarch."

"Good. That is the first step. Did you reflect on your actions during your time in prison?"

"No, Matriarch. There was no time."

"No time? *No time?*" Anurak's face went red, no longer the calm and collected woman she had been at the feast. "Do you understand the gravity of your sins? Do you not respect the divine gift of water or the age-old law against its misuse? What about during your long trek with Lieutenant Barrin? Did you contemplate the mark against your name during any of those hours?"

"No."

Anurak slammed a fist on her desk and stood. "You admit shame, but that shame has not spurred you to action. Johl said you were a duplicitous one, and a rebel."

Nahla held her tongue. No doubt Johl had exaggerated many things about her.

The matriarch rounded her desk. "You are on dangerous ground, Nahla. Have you done anything whatsoever to mend your reputation before God? Have you even expressed your sorrow towards Her?"

The events of the past few days flashed before Nahla's eyes. She'd beaten a criminal into submission at Launceston Prison, killed gladiators and bandits, burned a bandit camp, and . . .

"I ensured a fellow inmate had enough to eat when I was detained."

Anurak rolled her eyes. "Criminals are imprisoned for a reason, Nahla. They are degenerates who must be removed from society. Johl was right to send you there, though he could have had you executed on the spot. Still, an act of benevolence shows that you are not completely lost. Of what crime was this inmate accused?"

"Blasphemy."

"You . . ." Anurak's eyes widened. "You showed kindness to a *blasphemer*!"

Anurak drew a dagger from her robe and held it high with righteous anger. Nahla acted on instinct, putting her left arm in the path of the attack and grabbing her sword hilt with her right hand, leaving the weapon sheathed.

A bell boomed loudly from the nearby tower. The two women froze. Anurak glanced down at Nahla's sword arm. The bell continued, finally ending on the sixth beat. Nahla's heart thumped. Here she had induced the kingdom's religious leader into a fury and had signalled that she was ready to fight back.

Anurak lowered the dagger, her chest rising and falling with heavy breaths. For an elderly woman, she had a feisty energy. "Your contempt for what is holy cannot continue, but I will not kill you today." She returned the dagger to its hiding spot beneath the rich blue robe. A few cautious seconds later, Nahla took her hand off her sword hilt.

"There is obviously something wrong with your mind, Nahla. You are a killer, and you have no regard for life. You butchered gladiators in quick succession, you were ready to kill Johl and me, and you stole life-giving water from the people of Launceston. As the Matriarch of the Guardians of Life, I cannot allow an aberrant person such as yourself to roam the kingdom. You must change your mindset. You must learn to understand and appreciate the sanctity of life and the role water plays in it. I am putting you on half-rations of water for six months. Do you know how to write?"

"Yes."

"Good. For those six months, you will keep a daily journal. You will reflect on life—yours and those around you, including that of plants and animals. Put those reflections in your journal. Write about how you feel. Show how you are sacrificing comforts and putting the needs of others first. After six months, I will review your actions and your innermost thoughts. If your attitude has not improved, your penance will evolve into more drastic measures."

A strange punishment, Nahla thought. A strange little speech too. For all the talk about respect for life, Nahla certainly hadn't seen it. The wanton, state-sanctioned bloodshed in the gladiatorial arena? The readiness to strike her down with a dagger? The tendency towards executing blasphemers?

"We must also do something promptly and more public, something to kickstart your penitential reflections," Anurak said, returning to her chair. She rang a handbell. The priestess who had escorted Nahla entered the room. "Tish, make preparations for the Ceremony of Divine Discipline. It is to be held immediately in the courtyard of the Launceston Temple."

"At once, Matriarch." Tish bowed and ran off.

Anurak smiled darkly. "The Divine Discipline is reserved only for the worst cases that do not receive execution orders. It is short but forceful. Let this be the beginning of a successful penance."

Nahla didn't like the sound of whatever discipline Anurak had in mind. She was beginning to see what a dangerous mix of people dominated the upper echelons of Launceston's society: a self-centred and vengeful lord, an all-powerful king, a mysterious and manipulative chamberlain, and now a fanatical religious leader. Perhaps being in the king's good graces was not enough to save her from Anurak's ire.

A bell sounded again, this time ringing a different tune: the signal for punishment.

Aline of black carriages ferried them to the city's second temple. The Launceston Temple was smaller than the Royal Temple, but still impressive with its tiered design towering over the surrounding buildings. Nahla studied it as her carriage approached. Now that night had descended on Launceston, the temple glowed with unearthly light. The tips of the rods along the edges of each tier shone bright white. Even from far away, Nahla could tell that the lights were not the same as fire. These lights did not flicker. What power had the people of Launceston harnessed? Or did they really serve a God that kept Her buildings illuminated all day and night, like a beacon of hope?

When the carriages parked, Nahla was ushered out and six priestesses wearing solemn black robes led the way to the centre of the courtyard. A line of blue-uniformed soldiers marched on either side of Nahla. Her heart skipped a beat when she saw what awaited her—a platform with a simple pole at its centre. More priestesses waited at the bottom of the platform. One held a book, while another had something coiled in her hands. Burning torches surrounded the pole, providing plenty of light for the gathered crowd to witness the night-time ceremony. A nearby bell tower mimicked the tune from the Guardians' headquarters, which drew more people to the event.

When they reached the platform, the bell stopped, and Anurak raised her arms. "Tonight, I give you a violent warrior convicted of water theft, assault, and attempted murder. She will undergo the Divine Discipline. Let the ceremony begin!"

The crowd cheered. It was the same cheer Nahla had heard in the gladiatorial arena, except now they weren't cheering for her. She realised then that they hadn't really been cheering for her in the first place—instead, they were rejoicing at the sight of bloodshed. That perception confirmed what was about to happen. Nahla would suffer pain in the name of so-called penance, and the crowd would love it. After all, why else would they have left their houses and taverns to stand outside in the early night hours?

Two priestesses started to remove Nahla's armour, but struggled with the ties and latches. Nahla wanted to get the whole affair over with, so she did it for them. She stripped to the waist, as instructed, and heard the priestesses gasp in shock from behind her. She allowed herself a wry smile.

The scars.

She had three long scars on her back, gifted to her long ago by an enemy warlord. They were difficult to see without a mirror.

Anurak stood next to her. "It seems you have already endured a similar punishment, Nahla," she said over the din of the crowd. "It's a shame that you have not learned from it. May this be your last."

Nahla couldn't tell if that meant this should be the flogging that would turn her life around, or the flogging that would end her life altogether.

"Come to the post," Anurak said.

Before Nahla turned, she glimpsed someone sitting on horseback behind the crowd. A torch lit up his face. She squinted, and Lord Johl smiled back at her. She turned away from him and spotted a priestess unfurling a rope with several thinner threads peeling off the end. She had never seen such a rope before.

Two priestesses tied her to the pole, her arms held high above her head. They tied her feet too. The timber was warm and rough against her bare chest. Another priestess walked in front of her and sat a large book on a pedestal, opened it to a two-page spread with six lines of text, then weighted each page with shiny golden chains. The pages were spattered with a few drops of dried blood.

"Is the book close enough to read, Nahla?" Anurak asked from behind her.

"Yes."

102

"Very well." The crowd quietened. "Read the first line. Loud voice."

Nahla took a deep breath. *"Tenet One: Water is Life, for without it, we die."*

She heard the whip before she felt it—a high-pitched rush as the priestess swung it. The whip's multiple ends slapped her back. She grunted, refusing to cry out.

"The next line," Anurak prompted.

"Tenet Two: Water is a Gift, for we do not create it. It is given to us, if only we ask for it first."

She tensed as the next strike hit her back. For the moment, she still stood upright, defiant.

"Tenet Three: Water is Union, for by it, we stand as one."

The third whipping dug into existing wounds, adding to the pain. This time, Nahla let out a short, shrill cry. Then she clenched her teeth and focused on the book.

"Tenet Four: Water is Judge, for it defines our laws."

She shouted for longer after the fourth strike. She wanted to curse everybody. Curse Johl, curse Anurak, curse Launceston.

"Continue!" Anurak barked.

"Tenet Five: Water is Power, for it alone determines our future."

The fifth strike sent such a shock of pain through her body that she sagged against the pole, letting the ropes hold her in place. The whip the priestess used was harsher than the one she had endured so many years ago back home. But she survived then, and she would survive now. She would not give them the satisfaction of losing consciousness, either.

Last one. *"Tenet Six: Water is a Healing, for it cleanses the body and mind."*

The priestess wielding the whip must have put all her might into the last strike, because she gave a guttural roar as she swung. When the threads made contact, Nahla felt like she had been stabbed with a thousand daggers. She let out a whimper and put the full weight of her body against the pole. She heard footsteps climbing the platform, then somebody doused her wounds with water. She shrieked at the burning sensation.

Through bleary eyes, Nahla saw a priestess slowly retrieve the book from the pedestal. Her face was neutral, as if the gory punishment and Nahla's screams had not fazed her. Then, as the other priestesses untied her, Nahla heard Anurak's voice.

"The Ceremony of Divine Discipline has concluded. Let this be a reminder to all that water *must* be respected. A valiant gladiator, a provincial soldier, or one of the king's legionaries will all be punished for breaking the royal decree on the misuse of water. Even the members of the Divine Guard are not immune to such punishments. Go home and think about the blessings that sustain your lives."

The crowd dispersed. Nahla slumped when the ropes no longer held her weight, but the priestesses caught her and placed a thin white shawl over her shoulders. Her legs shook. She felt like hitting someone.

"Let the wounds heal," one of them said. "They will serve as a reminder of your sins and as a mark of your penitence."

They helped Nahla down the platform and across the courtyard. Every movement sent a streak of pain through her entire body. The shawl clung to her back as blood and sweat soaked through. She glanced up at Johl to find him smiling at her again. He threw a grape into his mouth and spurred his horse, disappearing into the night. She wanted to be angry, but all the pain was overpowering.

How quickly the Guardians of Life had changed from torturous madwomen to kind healers! As they helped her into one of the black carriages, all Nahla could think about was how the Kingdom of Launceston was so terribly backwards. And now, as a legionary and a sinner, she was definitely a part of it.

12

FOILED PLANS

To make plans is to dance with fate, yet the final steps remain shrouded in mystery.

—Unknown
Tasmanian proverb

O<small>N THE WESTERN SIDE</small> of Launceston, perched on a hill and surrounded by thick walls, was the imposing Castle Trevallyn. Lord Johl stared out a narrow open window at the city that was his domain. Launceston was the capital of his province, as well as the capital of the kingdom. His control was firm and unchallenged since the day he received his golden chain of office.

Until Nahla showed up.

Johl clenched his fists. *Nahla*. Even her name left a foul taste in his mouth. The bruise on his nose had healed since their scuffle, but the wound to his ego still festered. He'd tried to have her killed in the gladiatorial arena, but her unnatural fighting ability had saved her skin. Then, behind closed doors and away from prying ears, he'd sternly warned King Eero about letting someone like her into the Legion.

But worst of all—what really made Johl's blood boil—was that she had dashed his plans in Scottsdale Province. For that, he tried to convince Matriarch Anurak to execute her, but the king had already demanded clemency. When Johl heard the bells signalling the Divine Discipline, he knew he'd failed yet again. Despite not getting his way, he rather enjoyed the spectacle of her succumbing to the whip, knowing that she could be broken and scarred forever. Nobody went unpunished when they attacked Johl, and in Nahla's case, there was plenty more punishment to come.

"Well?" Vimarr asked. The Governor of Devonport had extended his visit to help Johl with pressing matters.

Johl turned around and let out a grumpy sigh. "Everything we've worked for has been ruined."

Vimarr, who sat with his feet up on the dining table, paused before he took another sip of wine. "What do you mean, *everything*?"

"I mean, every plan we made, every litre of water and cartload of food paid in bribes, every sword, spear, shield, bow, arrow, and horse we gave to those miscreants has been for nothing. My spies returned to me today. Daxton Clan is in disarray—Garyd's soldiers will finish the job if they act fast. That means all the gains we made in recent months will be completely reversed."

Vimarr sat upright and slammed his wine goblet on the table. "That's ridiculous. All because Nahla captured Daxton?"

"Yes. She severed the head of our little proxy war."

"Jaruk won't be happy."

"To hell with Jaruk!" Johl stomped forwards to his longtime co-conspirator. "That filthy wine merchant only cares about business. What about us? Scottsdale Province still stands. It was supposed to be ours for the taking!"

Lord Vimarr raised his chin in noble deference to his friend. "You're right. We waited too long."

Johl grumbled and sat at the head of the table. "We didn't have a choice. Daxton kept delaying. Damn that bandit scum!"

He should have known not to place too much trust in a bandit leader. The cretin knew nothing about politics and war. Johl and

Vimarr prodded him into all kinds of plans. After months of surreptitious planning, misinformation, and materiel support, they had finally manoeuvred Daxton into his most favourable position yet—flanks secured, well supplied, and within striking distance of Scottsdale. All he had to do was follow Johl's and Vimarr's instructions. In another month, he could have crushed Garyd's troops to such an extent that Johl and Vimarr would be *obliged* to lend military support. In doing so, they would have the *unfortunate* luck of being too late to stop Daxton from assaulting Scottsdale and killing Garyd. Then, unbeknown to Daxton, the provincial lords would spring their trap on him, eliminate his clan, retake Scottsdale, and convince King Eero to divide Scottsdale Province between them under the guise of *keeping the peace*. Jaruk Easton—the wealthy wine merchant from Devonport—would expand his wine empire into Vimarr's half of the province, and Johl and Vimarr together would reap the benefits of Scottsdale's underdeveloped mines.

But Nahla had destroyed that plan, and it would be next to impossible to resurrect it without some serious adjustments.

"We need to murder Daxton while we have the chance," Vimarr said. "And that other bandit they caught?"

"That other one is already dead," Johl said with a sadistic smile. "Little runt didn't last the first night in prison. But they've put Daxton in isolation under special Legion protection. My people haven't reached him yet."

"What if he talks?"

"He won't talk. He's too well rewarded."

"He knows too much about us." Vimarr rubbed his temples. "I'd be more comfortable once he's gone. If your people can't do it, I'll send mine."

"Don't be absurd," Johl snapped. He aimed a finger at Vimarr. "You have no business in Launceston Prison."

"Then what do you propose we do about it? He's in isolation. How will you get to him? You can't bribe a legionary."

Johl leaned back in his chair. Vimarr was right. The King's Legion was notoriously honourable. If Eero had commanded them to watch Daxton, Johl had zero chance of bribing them to let one of his spies in. Besides, any failed attempt on Daxton's life might push the bandit leader to turn against him. Sometimes, there was only one way to ensure a plan succeeded. "I'll do it myself."

Vimarr regarded Johl thoughtfully. "Is that wise?"

"It needs to be done, and done right. The sooner the better."

"How will you do it? Poisoned food?"

"No. That will raise too much suspicion."

"Then how?"

Johl smiled. He might actually like this mission. "I'll argue with him. Get him angry. Then I'll bury my sword in his gut in 'self-defence'."

Vimarr nodded. "Then our troubles will be gone."

"Not quite."

"Nahla?"

"Nahla."

Johl felt the rage building within his chest. Nahla was a problem that needed squashing. Someone like her in the king's service was an obstacle to Johl's plans, and he needed to remove that obstacle now before it became insurmountable.

"Nahla has already caused us too much grief," Johl said. "But we need to be cautious when we remove her."

"She's in tight with Eero, and will soon be so with his son."

Johl nodded slowly. He had many ideas, but none were foolproof. "Let me think longer about Nahla. Killing her won't be as simple as killing Daxton." He poured himself another cup of wine. "But she'll die regardless."

13

PRINCE MYEL

His very essence promotes tranquility as his words, adorned with empathy, cascade upon wounded hearts, soothing their afflictions with the delicate touch of understanding. Through his noble bearing and benevolent acts, he becomes the embodiment of respite, an unwavering beacon of solace in a world yearning for grace amid the throes of anguish.

—Cass the Blasphemer
Myel: The People's Prince

WHEN NAHLA RETURNED TO the barracks after her whipping, the King's Legion stared in awe at her bloodstained shawl. It was wholly inadequate for the wounds she had sustained. Her blue-clothed Divine Guard escort received scornful looks and comments as they delivered the bleeding legionary to her comrades. One of them dropped Nahla's armour in a heap by the door. Several legionaries rushed to Nahla's aid when the Divine Guards left. One man—one of the oldest soldiers in the barracks—took control of the situation and barked orders at the others.

"Get some water and food," he said to one legionary, who stared at Nahla's back. "And find some proper bandages. We need to patch up the preceptor. Go!"

Preceptor, Nahla thought as they sat her on her bed. Such a strange word. It was even written on her official induction paper from the king, but she didn't know what it meant.

The old soldier sat on the opposite bed and gave her a cup of water that a junior had brought. "Not often I see a new legionary whipped on their second day," he said. "And certainly not one of your rank." He handed her the cup.

Nahla sipped. "I'm on half-rations for water."

"Forget that. Keep drinking. You need it for your wounds."

"Thank you." She took a longer swig. "I'm afraid I don't know your name."

He stood and planted a fist against his chest in proper salute. "I'm Jaymen. Private Jaymen."

"Aren't you a little too old to be a private?"

"I would be a preceptor like you, but I keep getting in trouble." He pulled off his loose shirt and showed his back. Scars went every which way, indicating several whippings. He sat down shirtless and scratched his hairy chest. "Looks like they gave you a good thrashing."

"The Divine Discipline for me."

Jaymen's eyes went wide and he swore. "I've never had that one. You've done well to remain conscious. They use a special whip for that ceremony." He twisted and looked back up the length of the barracks. "Where are those bandages?" he shouted. A legionary carrying a wooden box scurried into the barracks through a side door.

"I'm sorry, Preceptor," Jaymen said. "Would you like to dress your wounds in private?"

"We are all brothers and sisters in arms here, and our bodies should not embarrass each other. We should all be willing to fight in the nude if need be."

Jaymen chuckled. "Already done it." When Nahla smirked, he waved it away. "I'll tell you another time."

Jaymen helped Nahla onto a stool and began slowly peeling back the shawl.

Nahla winced at the stinging pain as the cloth separated from her still-raw wounds. When Jaymen had removed the entire shawl and she was once again topless, Jaymen threw the bloodied clothing on the floor.

"You've been whipped before?" Jaymen asked.

"Yes, many years ago." She still remembered the laughter of the pig who had ordered her torture.

"Maybe when I tell you about my butt-naked skirmish, you can tell me about your previous whippings."

He dabbed her wounds with a wet rag, and she clenched at the stinging pain. "We'll see. I'd like to hear about your punishments too."

"Deal."

He was a burly man with age lines on his face and strands of greying hair. Despite his calloused hands and gruff voice, he had a gentleness and technique that showed years of battlefield medical experience. Nahla questioned him.

"I was training to be a medic," he said softly. Then he started wrapping a bandage around her body, working his way down her torso. "I was good at it too, but then I did some stupid stuff, and they banished me to the lower ranks for the rest of my service. Can you lift your breasts, please?"

Nahla did so, and he continued wrapping down her body, but left her breasts free.

"It's not too tight, is it?"

"No, it's just right." She felt the slight pressure of the bandage against the open wounds, but experience had taught her that this was the right way to dress large cuts.

As Jaymen finished, he told a much younger legionary to find Nahla's undershirt in the pile of armour that the Divine Guards left. She returned in seconds.

"Does the Preceptor not have a sword?" the young woman asked.

"I do." Nahla replied. "It is not there?"

"No. Just clothing."

"Bastards must have kept it," Jaymen said. "Wouldn't be the first time they've done it." He helped Nahla into the undershirt.

"The Legion and the Divine Guard do not get along?"

"Not getting along is an understatement. Those women hate us, and we hate them. Don't we, legionaries?"

A chorus of vulgar support rang out in the barracks.

"If I were you," Jaymen continued, "I'd stay away from them. The only thing they hate more than a legionary is a female legionary. To them, it only means that you weren't good enough to be one of them."

"Noted."

Jaymen encouraged Nahla to sleep on her belly. Then he told the other private to attend to Nahla throughout the night. He promised to change the dressings every day until the wounds had sufficiently healed.

"Oh, and give her all the water she needs. Screw the Guardians."

The comment elicited some quiet laughter from nearby legionaries.

"Thank you, Jaymen," Nahla said. "You're an asset to the Legion."

"Thank *you*, Preceptor. I hear you are our new battle instructor. We look after our preceptors . . . if they look after us."

He smirked, and she smirked back. "I'll keep that in mind."

"Get some rest. We'll talk more tomorrow."

He left and barked at the other legionaries to mind their own business. Nahla got up from the stool and grumbled at how much her back hurt. *If I ever see that matriarch again—*

"Is there anything I can do for you, Preceptor?" the young legionary asked.

112

"I'm starving. Do we have any food?"

"I'll get you some from the kitchen."

Nahla lay facedown on the bed and let her entire body relax. She hadn't felt so tired or so sore in a long time. Well, that wasn't entirely true. She fought hard during the civil war, endured many sleepless nights, and suffered countless cuts and bruises. But she expected many rough days to come, for she was still learning the rules of this foreign land.

She sighed. The following day, she was supposed to meet Prince Myel, King Eero's son. As well as training the King's Legion, she was also to give the prince private lessons. Soldiers she could handle; a spoiled, lazy prince was something else. She imagined the red raw cuts on her back and decided the prince could wait. She didn't want to appear weak at their first meeting.

She fell asleep before her attendant returned.

A week later, Nahla's wounds had healed enough to remove the bandages. Jaymen held a mirror for her and she glimpsed the horrifying scars on her back. She'd been struck six times, but the whips had several ends, so there were innumerable scars criss-crossing her back, almost covering the three she already carried from years ago.

Welcome to Launceston, she thought sourly. She'd started writing her penitential journal while she rested and actually wrote those words, but then she erased them with a wet cloth.

Despite Jaymen's protests, Nahla put on all of her armour and announced she was meeting Prince Myel. But before she left, Jaymen made her promise not to do anything strenuous. That was fine, because she knew she couldn't.

During her convalescence, the prince had sent a servant to inquire of Nahla's whereabouts, since she had missed their scheduled meeting without sending word. In truth, she had been too angry to show such politeness. But after Jaymen sent the messenger away with news of Nahla's whipping, the prince began sending her daily baskets of fresh fruit to aid the healing process. That made Nahla reconsider her preconceptions about him.

Coordinating via a daily messenger, Nahla and the prince set a new time to meet. Now the messenger had arrived again to show Nahla the way. They went to a private section of the palace complex, an area reserved for the king's family. The prince lived in a modest two-storey residence attached to the castle keep. They approached from a courtyard, but Nahla suspected there would be an entrance from the keep as well. The King's Legion, on seeing Nahla's plumed preceptor helmet, saluted and admitted them to the prince's home.

Nahla's back ached with every step she took, but the pain was nowhere near as severe as a week ago. However, in between grimaces during the short walk from the barracks, she imagined what Prince Myel would be like. Everyone said he had no interest or respectable skills in warfare, and that he rarely participated in political ceremonies or military events. But he had been kind enough to send Nahla food and, she noted, it had been the tastiest fruit she'd eaten in years. Maybe he was just a comfort-loving brat who avoided civic duties.

The prince's messenger walked through the house's luxurious ground floor to a large garden that bordered the castle wall on one face and the keep on another. Most of the yard was filled with fruit-bearing trees and vegetable patches. A shirtless, sweating man in dirt-covered shorts toiled hard in the garden, digging up rich, dark earth to prepare it for seeds.

"Preceptor Nahla, Your Highness," the messenger announced.

The shirtless man dropped his pickaxe and faced them. Nahla's eyes widened for several reasons. First, she had thought this hard-working man was just a common labourer. Second, the prince was incredibly handsome and fit, the total opposite of what she had imagined over the past week. He smiled at her, then realised he was not ready for their meeting.

"Time got away from me," he said as he stepped out of the garden. His voice carried high tones of culture—it sounded like slow, gentle music on a warm summer's night. He brushed the dirt from his hands and pointed back to where he'd left his pickaxe. "I wanted to get cleaned up before you arrived, but I had a spur-of-the-moment idea for that patch."

"It is I who must apologise, Your Highness," Nahla said. She removed her helmet. "I was the one who delayed our meeting."

"Oh, please, call me Myel." He looked at the messenger. "Thank you for bringing the preceptor. Please prepare us some cranberry juice." The messenger disappeared. "How are your wounds healing?"

"The bleeding has stopped. Thank you for the fruit too. Did they come from this garden?"

"They did!" Myel spun around and spread his arms wide. "This is my labour of love."

"It's impressive."

And indeed it was. It was uncommon to see so many varieties of plant life thriving together in a little green ecosystem. From what Nahla had seen, most people in Launceston didn't have gardens of their own because they did not have enough water to keep them healthy. Food grew on farms, which received a special dispensation of water, and the produce was then distributed according to need.

Myel gestured to a vine-covered pergola at one end of the garden. "Come, let's sit. I am in no rush to begin my training, and I am sure you would like more time to recover."

Nahla sat at an ornate table under the pergola. The warm breeze cooled as it slipped through the vine leaves, and it was a blessing to have the sun off her face. "I appreciate your concern for me, Myel, but I would rather not delay your training much longer."

"I have little interest in war."

"Respectfully, while you may have little interest, there are many around you who *are* interested, and not all for good intentions. Your father worries that when it is time for you to take the throne, you will be unprepared for the risks of war with the Southern Kingdom."

"Ah, yes, dear old Dad," Myel said with an eye roll.

A servant brought a tray with glasses and a jug of deep-red cranberry juice. Myel dismissed her and poured Nahla a glass. "The cranberries are my own."

Nahla sipped. "Delicious." But she would not let the tasty food and Myel's pleasant hosting distract her. "How much experience have you had with swords or other weapons?"

He shrugged. "I know how to swing and stab."

"Horsemanship?"

"Excellent."

"Archery?"

"Also excellent."

"So you could probably teach me a thing or two about using a bow?"

"I suppose I could. But *you* are the teacher. I'm the student."

"Learning goes both ways. What do you know of battlefield tactics? Or military strategy?"

"Is there a difference?"

"Yes, there's a huge difference."

"Then I don't know. I keep myself busy with more important things, like building, planting, and growing. I don't see the point of killing and destroying."

Nahla bit her lip. She didn't want to offend the prince, but he needed to understand that if he didn't know how to fight, everything he built and planted could be taken from him.

"It's more about perceived power and the ability to protect those in need," she said. "Your people don't know how to fight. Not properly anyway. When the time comes for you to defend them, you need to know how to do it properly. A lifetime of success and progress can be undone by failing to prepare for known risks." She dropped her eyes, knowing the truth of that statement all too well.

"You speak with experience," Myel noted.

Nahla nodded.

"What makes you qualified to train the son of a king? What is your background?"

Careful, Nahla, she thought. *Don't reveal too much . . . at least not too soon.* "I have been a soldier since I was thirteen. I've seen enough fighting to last several lifetimes, and I've probably killed more people than you've even met. I can fight with any weapon, with shield or without, on foot or on horseback. Your father has seen me in combat, albeit briefly, and my skills convinced him I was the right one to train you."

Myel furrowed his brow. "Where has my father seen you?"

"At the last gladiatorial fight."

"Oh." He pulled a face as if several puzzle pieces suddenly fit together. "*You're* the one everybody's talking about! So you are a longtime soldier, fallen from grace, sentenced to be a gladiator, but since redeemed from your condemnation to join the King's Legion and train the Prince of Launceston."

"Something like that." She smiled thinly.

"So why were you whipped?"

"For water theft."

"Aha." The puzzle in Myel's mind seemed complete now. He sighed and finished his glass of cranberry juice. Then he folded his arms across his muscular chest and surveyed the garden. "I plan on doing great things for my people when I become king, but some of my plans won't sit well with the elite. I'll need the support of the Legion to keep everybody in check. You're a soldier—what would the Legion think of a king who doesn't know how to command them?"

"They will obey you because it's their duty, but they will not respect you. If you make too many blunders, that disrespect could evolve into disobedience or, worse, mutiny. Your officers must respect you as well, because their attitude towards the king will trickle down to the lower ranks. But you are worrying about internal affairs. Do not forget the external problems as well: the Southern Kingdom, the tribes of the west, and the roving bandit clans."

Already, despite only being in Launceston a short while, Nahla was assessing the situation as if this kingdom was her own. Prince Myel, however, looked displeased with the topic.

"Well," Myel began, "how do we proceed?"

Sensing that she had won, Nahla leaned forwards to outline her plan. "The way I see it, you have four areas for improvement, and I can help with all of them. First, you need to associate yourself with the Legion. They need to see you as their patron, their benefactor. Second, I will train you in a weapon of your choice."

"I own a broadsword."

"That's a good start. We can try a few different weapons to see what feels right for you. In the end, we will have one custom made. And while I'm training you for combat, I will also train you in the other two areas I mentioned: tactics and strategy."

"You still haven't told me the difference between the two."

"Tactics are using your troops to win battles. They're about facing the enemy and coming off victorious. Strategy is larger scale. It's the overall plan for a war and how you hope to achieve your end goal."

"I see." Myel scratched his chin. "And will you teach me politics as well?"

Nahla shook her head. "I'm not a politician. I don't know how to run a kingdom. My business is war, and how war affects the politics of your kingdom. I suggest you seek other advisors to teach you about government. Maybe spending more time with your father might help?"

He rolled his eyes. "I'd rather read a book."

"If all I did was read a book before my first battle, I would have been killed in the first few minutes."

"Point taken." He stood and poured her another glass of cranberry juice. "You don't mind being direct with me, do you?"

She laughed. "I'm sorry. It must be the cosy setting, the first-name basis, and the—" she pointed at him "—relaxed attire."

Still standing, Myel grinned. "Yes, well, I was never one for stuffy royal protocols. That's why I live here, away from the others in the keep." He paused, and his eyes studied her. "I don't think we'll start my training straight away. You still need time to recover from your, uh, barbaric whipping. Let's wait another week."

Nahla raised her glass. "You are too kind."

"I'd rather get to know you first. You're welcome to stay here and chat with me, but I need to get back into the garden. This new bed of tomatoes won't plant itself."

Nahla certainly had no objections to that—sipping delicious cranberry juice under a cool vine-covered pergola, watching an enchanting prince work shirtless in a garden. It was the most pleasant experience she'd had since leaving her homeland. Maybe she was finally settling in. But she knew there was much to do in the months ahead: training Myel, training the Legion, staying in the king's good books, and keeping at least one step ahead of Lord Johl.

For the moment, however, she put all those thoughts aside and tried to enjoy the present. Myel was talking to her in between swings of his pickaxe, and she tried to listen to his words instead of watching his rippling muscles under the scorching sun.

14

THE KING'S LEGION

I solemnly swear, with unwavering devotion, my everlasting loyalty to the king. I pledge myself to the King's Legion, ready to serve with enduring dedication. I vow to protect our noble kingdom with every drop of blood coursing through my veins, to defend our borders and keep them secure. I shall be a stalwart guardian, safeguarding the king and his household, and standing as a shield for his subjects. With this oath, I bind myself to the sacred duty of preserving our realm and upholding the honour and prosperity of our beloved kingdom.

—Legion Recruits
Oath of the King's Legion

THE KING'S LEGION MARCHED in perfect unison. Sandals stomped on the earthy parade ground, shiny armour clanked, flags fluttered in the warm breeze, and sergeants yelled even when it was completely unnecessary to do so. The Legion paraded with all the impressive formality expected of an elite unit.

It dawned on Nahla just how far she had fallen from her lofty position in the Kingdom of Melbourne. Back then, she would have been an observer of such a parade; or, if it was a large event, leading it from the front rank. Now, though, Nahla marched like a common soldier, herded in the middle of the Legion's company of specialists—all the engineers, surveyors, medics, Guardians, instructors, quartermasters, armourers, smiths, and the like. She'd learned that the rank of preceptor meant a trainer in a particular field of speciality. Hers was warfare.

The bell tower across the palace complex rang midday, barely discernible over the sound of the marching companies. The entire Legion, minus most of the platoon currently on guard duty, strutted into the parade ground during the hottest part of the day. Even the Legion's full cavalry force was present, outfitted with their tall, red-feathered helmets and red sashes across their cuirasses.

This was no ordinary parade. Nahla had quickly learned the Legion's palace schedule. Every day at midday, one platoon—a contingent of a company of approximately five hundred legionaries—would march into the central courtyard of the palace complex. The incoming platoon commander, a lieutenant, would exchange responsibility for the new twelve-hour palace guard shift from the outgoing platoon commander. The cavalry was never involved.

Today was different. Nahla marched with about 6,500 legionaries, cavalry troopers, and officers. King Eero wanted to see his whole elite military force before some left to help Lord Garyd in Scottsdale Province.

"Company, halt!" The order echoed along the entire line of the Legion as company commanders barked at their underlings. Nahla's company commander, an old lieutenant with one eye and one hand, had the most distinct voice of all. Her loud voice carried higher than the rest. Nahla liked Lieutenant Dehra. Her battle injuries rendered her unfit for combat, but she was well respected and more than suitable for overseeing the company of specialists.

Nahla stopped. It had been a long time since she marched, and longer still since she had received marching orders from anyone. But old habits die hard.

"Company, right turn!"

As one, foot soldiers and horses turned on the spot. King Eero and Prince Myel watched from a palace balcony. Eero had been delighted in his son's newfound interest in the Legion and wanted him to be present for this marvellous display of strength. While smaller than any of the provincial armies, the King's Legion was still a formidable force, and Myel would be a part of it. Nahla kept her face neutral, but as she watched Myel on the balcony, she couldn't help but think how impressive he looked in his new King's Legion uniform. A silver-and-gold cuirass glistened even in the shade, and his red-and-white double-plumed helmet was the only one of its kind in all of Tasmania.

Mounted on a sturdy horse in front of the Legion, Captain Vox drew his heavy cavalry sabre and held it high. It was a formal salute to the kingdom's highest authority, an acknowledgement that the troops he commanded were forever in the king's service, and that they were ready and waiting to hear the king's voice.

Eero put his hands on the balcony's balustrade. "Legionaries! I thank you for coming to stand before me in the hot sun. I have gathered you here to express my appreciation for your service. This unit has a long and illustrious history, spanning many generations. But now I call upon you again to serve your king's interests abroad. A bandit clan roams throughout Scottsdale Province. Our very own Preceptor Nahla captured their leader, but we must finish them before they can recover. I am dispatching one infantry company and one cavalry wing to assist Lord Garyd. May you fight ferociously, may you find glory, and may you bring honour and praise upon the Legion!"

The legionaries stayed silent, true to their discipline. Vox, apparently sensing that the king wished for some kind of reply, called up to the balcony, "The Legion accepts your kind praise and worthy mission, Your Majesty. Hail to the King!"

The soldiers shouted in one thunderous burst, "Hail, Eero, hail!" Nahla missed the cue and only managed the last word, but nobody noticed.

The cheer put a smile on Eero's face. "I am also announcing a new royal patron of the Legion—my son, Prince Myel." Myel stepped forwards. He certainly looked the part. "You will see much more of Myel from now on. He will be the vital link between the Legion and the royal house. You are my fist, but Myel is the heart that pumps the blood between us. He will be your king someday. Show him what you're made of!"

Captain Vox raised his sabre again. "All hail Prince Myel!"

This time, Nahla joined in. "Hail, Myel, hail!"

When Eero had learned that Myel would take more of an interest in the Legion, he'd responded jubilantly. He'd created the figurehead role of Patron of the Legion. It had all the glory and stature, but none of the rank. He could involve himself in military matters, but Captain Vox and the company commanders would always outrank him until his father elevated him further. It was a start.

"Salute!" Vox yelled.

Fists and gloves clashed against metal breastplates and cuirasses. The sound echoed off the stone walls. Nahla felt completely at home among the soldiers. For so long, she knew that someday she would die alongside her comrades, which was why the thought of perishing in the Endless Land was so upsetting—to be taken by the sun, alone and leaderless, was the worst death a warrior could face. But now she had somewhere to live, something to fight for, and people to protect. Although she had fallen from her high station in life, at least she was doing something she enjoyed, something she was born to do.

"We have a murderous bandit clan on the loose," Eero continued, "and the soldiers of Scottsdale Province need our assistance. It's time for the King's Legion to step in and solve the problem once and for all. May you find swift victory, and may God watch over you. Captain Vox?"

"Your Majesty?"

"See to the deployment." With that, Eero was done with his soldiers and turned away. Before he left, he put a hand on Myel's shoulder and spoke a few words. Myel nodded and stayed on the balcony.

Vox sheathed his sabre and faced his troops. "Primus Carro?"

"Sir!"

"Take First Company to the temple for the Litany of Water. The rest of the Guard will resume normal duties."

What followed was music to Nahla's ears—commanders yelling crisp orders, units peeling off and marching away, horses trotting in unified gaits on the courtyard's smooth ground. Lieutenant Dehra told her company of specialists to get back to work, though she said it in such a relaxed tone that Nahla almost forgot to salute as she departed. Since the specialists were not really combatants, they didn't have regularly scheduled guard duty or weapons training. Instead, they all went separate ways—some to their barracks, others to workshops, while those who were formally attached to First Company followed them to the temple. They would go to Scottsdale Province to support the soldiers and cavalry in a variety of ways, such as repairing weapons and equipment, providing medical care, and provisioning supplies.

A hot breeze stung Nahla's cheeks. The desire for shade prompted a search for a covered vantage point overlooking the temple courtyard. Despite now making Launceston her home, Nahla still knew very little about the Guardians of Life and their ziggurat temples. She'd only seen two temples, and apparently each of the kingdom's provinces had one as well.

Bordering one side of the temple courtyard was a crenellated wall, effectively dividing the inner palace grounds from the outer section. It had a wooden roof, which provided enough shade to observe the Litany of Water in the courtyard below. The Legion's First Company formed ranks in front of the temple. Between them was a column of water carriages, some of which had wooden barrels, others with leather bladders. Nahla leaned on the warm stonework, watching every movement, listening to every sound.

Facing the assembled First Company was an impressive double line of Divine Guards. From what Nahla had been told, the Divine Guards were ferocious fighters, but their sole purpose was to protect the Guardians of Life and the kingdom's religious property. She wondered who might win between eight guards and eight legionaries, but decided not to play that game. Everyone was technically on the same team, despite the valley of animosity separating them.

The temple doors opened with nothing but blackness inside. Three priestesses emerged—the blue-robed Matriarch Anurak and two white-clad juniors a few steps behind. The company commander, Primus Carro, approached the waiting matriarch and knelt. Their conversation resonated off the stone courtyard and surrounding buildings.

"Much venerated Matriarch, my troops require sustenance for their journey north. We come to you for the Litany of Water."

"Arise, Primus," Anurak said. "The Guardians of Life will administer the Litany of Water and convene with God for Her blessing. Are your troops prepared?"

"They are ready, Your Eminence."

"Then let us begin."

Nahla watched the ceremony and scrutinised every moment. Matriarch Anurak stepped closer to the waiting soldiers. She thanked the unnamed God for Her reliable supply of water, then continued with a solemn oath of respect for water, acknowledging its divine source and the sacredness of its use. First Company echoed as one, "*Fiat.*" Nahla had never heard the word, but it sounded like a collective agreement.

Anurak then petitioned the still unnamed God to provide life-sustaining water to King Eero's troops. The water, she said, would keep the legionaries hydrated in their fight against the lawless bandits who dared to disrupt the kingdom's internal peace. She condemned the bandits as murderers, water criminals, and blasphemers—barely a step above the barbarians of the west—who deserved nothing less than to be vanquished.

After her petition, Anurak called her two priestesses. They took the first water carriage and led the horses into the temple. The yellow-white stones of the courtyard were bright under the midday sun. Nahla squinted as the temple doors opened, trying to get a glimpse of the interior, but all she saw was darkness. She figured as much, though, since the temple had no windows. Anurak followed the priestesses inside, and the doors closed.

First Company stood like statues, completely silent. Nahla swept her eyes over the thousand-plus legionaries, cavalry troopers, and specialists. She could see their sweat, but she admired their discipline. She'd already trained some of them in her limited time as their preceptor. Perhaps if they knew she was observing them, they'd straighten their backs and sweat a little more.

A short while later, the temple doors opened again, and the two white-robed priestesses walked the water carriage out. The horses pulled more slowly, and the tops of the six wooden barrels glistened wet.

Empty barrels go in, Nahla thought, *and the same barrels come out full.*

The priestesses handed the full carriage to a waiting driver, then fetched the next one in the column. Nahla stayed on the wall as they repeated the process until all carriages were full. When the last carriage left the temple, Anurak re-emerged.

Carro bowed in front of her. "First Company thanks our benevolent God and appreciates the selfless work of the Guardians of Life."

"Godspeed, Primus Carro," Anurak replied, though she sounded uninterested.

Carro bowed again and faced his troops. "We march for Scottsdale!" Then he mounted his horse as lieutenants and sergeants organised their units into marching columns.

Nahla frowned. Such pomp and ceremony. She wondered if this spectacle happened every time a military unit left Launceston. If she were back home, her soldiers would have been marching already. Then again, if she was back home, they would have started the march in the early morning hours when it was much cooler.

First Company stomped through a gateway below. One lieutenant, a tough one Nahla had met only once before, looked up and tapped her helmet to say hello. Nahla waved back, hoping to see her again. She didn't know how many bandits roamed Scottsdale Province, or if they were part of one clan or many. But she knew that there would be death and destruction, and some legionaries would not return. Such was life when one lived by the sword.

On that note, Nahla returned to her barracks. She had an afternoon training session scheduled with one of Third Company's platoons, but she needed to see Prince Myel before that. On the way, she reflected on the Litany of Water. The ceremony taught her something about the Guardians of Life and their venerated temples, but not enough to quench her thirst. The pun made her grin. She vowed to uncover more answers, but the scars on her back were a powerful deterrent.

Careful steps, Nahla. Careful steps.

15

MORE QUESTIONS THAN ANSWERS

Answers, though elusive at times, can be sought and discovered with persistence and diligence. Yet, it is often the questions that bear the weight of uncertainty. For within the enigmatic depths of a question lies the uncharted territory of curiosity. It is in the act of questioning that we embark on the path of truth. Sometimes, the quest itself holds the key to our deepest understanding.

—**Nahla Northborn**
Journal of Penance

THE FIRST TIME NAHLA set foot in Launceston Prison, she was an outsider, a nobody, and a criminal. Now she rode in a royal chariot and walked alongside a prince. Guards stood at attention and saluted, and though such respect was given to Prince Myel, Nahla felt just a little of it seeped her way by association.

"If I am to help secure the northern province," Myel had said the day before, "then I must learn about the bandits. We should speak to that bandit chief you captured."

Nahla could not argue with that logic. It was excellent to see Myel taking an interest in the affairs of the kingdom, in addition to his military studies. Unfortunately, Lord Garyd had failed to pry anything out of Daxton, despite long days of interrogation, so maybe Myel could approach the bandit with a fresh perspective.

Early in the morning, Myel donned his new King's Legion uniform and sent for Nahla at the barracks. They chatted over a breakfast of fruits and vegetables grown in Myel's garden. Then they took Myel's royal chariot and, with an escort in tow, set off for Launceston Prison.

The prison guards at the gates were understandably surprised when they saw the king's son. Someone must have sent word to the governor of the prison, because by the time Myel and Nahla crossed the prison courtyard to the main building, the governor was waiting for them.

"Your Highness," the governor said and bowed. He had crumbs in his beard, and his breath smelled like the citrus-flavoured water people often drank at breakfast. "I am Governor Ibeza. What brings you to Launceston's house of intractable lowlifes?"

Myel leaned in and shook Ibeza's hand. "You have a bandit leader by the name of Daxton. I wish to speak with him."

"Of course, Your Highness," Ibeza said with another bow. "I shall take you to him myself. We keep him in isolation, in the eastern tower. Nobody is allowed to visit without my express permission."

"Good," Myel said.

The prison was as cold as Nahla remembered it. She wondered if Cass was still alive and felt a pang of guilt. Such a fragile creature was so out of place in this den of criminals, yet she had somehow escaped her state-sanctioned execution.

"How is Daxton faring?" Myel asked.

They moved at a steady pace along one of the prison's many stone corridors. "He is quiet," Ibeza replied. "I haven't spoken to him since the day he arrived, but the king's interrogators are regular visitors. I think Lord Garyd has given up, though. Haven't seen him in days."

"I would like to read their reports."

"Not much to report, Your Highness. Daxton is tight-lipped, so I'm told. In fact, I'm not sure how he will take to your presence. He may not speak at all. Or he may refuse to see you altogether."

"He is a criminal. He has no right to refuse an audience with a prince."

They reached the stairwell of the eastern tower. As they ascended, Nahla noted how the temperature gradually increased. The stonework still retained heat from the previous day. All the thermal energy released overnight still hung thick in the poorly ventilated space. The isolation cells, which occupied the tower's centre, were probably stifling hot. Nahla was sure they'd find out as soon as they reached Daxton's cell.

The top floor had more openings in the stonework, but with minimal effect. Governor Ibeza's face was glazed with sweat as he stopped at Daxton's cell door. Two legionaries ceased their chatter abruptly and stood red-faced at attention. One of them was Rhos, the copper-haired twin of Ragh, both of whom helped capture Daxton.

Ibeza pointed to the legionaries. "Your guard detail, rotated every four hours, as requested." King Eero had ordered a day-and-night guard at Daxton's cell, as well as other provisions not usually afforded to prisoners. So far, it was a cheap bribe that hadn't paid off.

Myel turned to his escort. "You and you, stay out here. Nahla, come with me." Then he pointed at the cell door. Ibeza opened it and excused himself—he had to start his daily business. He closed the cell door behind them.

The heat smacked Nahla as soon as she walked in, but the smell of fresh, warm bread and the pungent odour of an unclean body quickly overtook the sensation. Daxton sat against the round stone wall eating a slice of buttered bread, not the vile slop Nahla had eaten during her single night in the common cell block. He had a half-eaten loaf on a tray next to him. Daxton's tan wasn't as dark as Nahla remembered, and his black beard was longer, but he still had the same fiery eyes.

Daxton stopped chewing the moment he saw Nahla. "You!"

"Happy to see me?" Nahla asked.

"Our friend seems to have fond memories of you," Myel said.

Daxton propped himself up when he heard Myel's polished voice. "And you're the king's son. Malt? Milk?"

"Myel," came the stern correction. Nahla saw Myel's chest rise confrontationally from the corner of her eye. He wore light leather armour, which creaked with his body's movements.

"You look like a milk-drinker," Daxton said. "Just as I would expect from the pampered son of a king."

"Mind your tongue, bandit!" Nahla snapped. "Or I'll have it cut out."

"Seems to me that you need my tongue intact, judging by all the visitors I get. But if you're here to ask me questions, I suggest you give up before you begin."

With her bluff called, Nahla rested her hand on her sword pommel and let Myel do the talking. The prince sat on a small stool, bringing himself closer to Daxton's level. Nahla readied herself in case the bandit chief tried something stupid.

"You're right, you know," Myel said. "I am a pampered prince. I never had to worry about anything—water, food, shelter. But over the years, I've seen how my father and his cronies live in extravagance, usually to the detriment of their subjects. I aim to take a different approach when I'm king. Tell me, why did you become a bandit? What pushed you out of normal society to a life of crime?"

Perhaps it was Myel's honesty. Or perhaps it was his calm demeanour. Whatever the case, Daxton's hostility melted just a fraction.

"Mismanagement," he said, then took another bite of his buttered bread.

Myel sat upright and glanced at Nahla. "What do you mean?"

"I cannot speak for the other provinces, but Lord Garyd is a hopeless governor. While he sits pretty in his castle, his people starve, despite there being enough food grown locally. The water rations are never enough, the mines are underdeveloped, the roads are terrible, the local garrisons are too strict . . . should I go on?"

"Why didn't you petition the king?"

"We did. Several times. But we received no reply, and our messengers never returned. We offered countless prayers too. Seems like God only supports the wealthy."

"So you became—" Myel stopped before saying the last word, and Nahla knew exactly why. Suddenly, the word "bandit" didn't seem right.

"A bandit?" Daxton said and laughed, the sort of laugh tinged with disgust and self-pity. "That is what *you* call me. No, I'm a *rebel*, which is much more than a bandit. By calling us bandits, Garyd delegitimised my reasons for fighting and kept the rebellion contained within Scottsdale Province. What's another bandit clan in the kingdom? Nothing. But a rebellion . . ." He didn't need to say the rest.

Nahla was learning something today. But it didn't make sense for Garyd to keep Daxton's rebellion a secret. Was he embarrassed?

It was news to Myel, too, and Nahla noticed the subtle change in his questioning. "If you are a rebel, you've been quite successful, at least in disrupting Garyd's governorship," Myel continued. "Why were you targeting economic centres in the province?"

Daxton kept eating as if he hadn't heard the question.

"How did you defeat Garyd's troops on so many occasions?"

Still, Daxton ignored Myel.

"Something else I've been wondering: How did a group of untrained and unarmed rebels get so well armed?"

Daxton grinned, but he remained silent.

Nahla glared at the rebel. It was no wonder that King Eero had been so jubilant over Daxton's capture. It all made sense now. Nahla had unwittingly severed the head of a problematic rebellion! But

Daxton was hiding something, and she'd be damned if she let him stay silent on the matter. Getting Daxton to talk would be the best way to boost Myel's credibility in the royal court. It might even save a few legionaries before they tried to pacify Scottsdale Province. And where there was victory and spoil, Nahla would benefit too.

She heard voices outside and a key turning in Daxton's cell door. Rhos entered. "Lord Johl to see the prisoner."

Johl stepped in and froze as soon as he saw Nahla and Myel. Jugg, easily a head taller, stopped behind his master in the narrow doorway.

"Your Highness," Johl said, "what a pleasant surprise." He'd recovered fast, Nahla noticed. She also saw that Johl and Jugg were outfitted with their high-quality black-and-silver armour, and each had a sword and a shiny dagger at their waist. Johl offered a slight bow in the presence of royalty. Jugg ignored the prince altogether, sneering at Nahla instead.

Myel stood. "Lord Johl, what business do you have here?" Nahla sensed a nervous tension between them.

"I have come to see the man who is responsible for Lord Garyd's headaches." Johl looked past Myel. "I sent many resources to Garyd at the request of your father, and it was all for nothing. I want to know how this man was so successful against the might of a provincial garrison, and if there is any way I can recover my losses."

Johl stepped further into the room and Jugg followed. Rhos, small in stature and rank compared to the others, closed the cell door but stayed inside. Nahla gave her an approving nod.

"Then we seek the same answers," Myel said. "But he is reluctant to speak."

"I have ways of making people talk." Johl looked over at Jugg, who cracked his knuckles.

Jugg had taken a position close to Nahla, making her feel small and cornered in the cramped cell. But she had defeated him in this very prison before, and she would do it again if necessary.

"Torture won't be necessary, Johl," Myel told him. "Besides, he is not your prisoner. He belongs to my father and therefore comes under royal jurisdiction."

"Perhaps we should move Daxton to the palace dungeon, Your Highness," Nahla suggested.

Johl's eyes blazed with searing hatred. Daxton sat and watched his captors play the careful game of polite politics.

"I'll think about that, Preceptor."

"I would still like to question him," Johl insisted. "Maybe when you are finished?"

"The answer is no, Johl."

"I would hate to miss any opportunity to get information out of this criminal."

Myel faced him. "At what point does a prince's 'no' mean 'no'?"

Johl eyed Myel. "Understood, Your Highness." Then he gave Daxton a long, hard stare. "Let's go, Jugg."

Jugg looked down at Nahla and grumbled before following his master. Rhos let them out. Once their footsteps were no longer audible, Myel raised his eyebrow suspiciously at Nahla and turned back to Daxton.

"It seems we may have saved your life today," Myel said. "Or at least some bones."

"Perhaps."

"Are you going to answer my questions now?"

Daxton sighed heavily, as if the prince's presence was an inconvenience. "No."

Myel nodded. "We'll leave you alone for now, but I want you to remember that you are much better off if you cooperate."

"Am I staying here or moving to the palace?"

"I'll think about that. When you want to speak, ask Governor Ibeza to send for me."

Daxton's face was unreadable. Myel and Nahla left him to ruminate over his situation and the strange episode with Johl.

When they were out in the stairwell again and Rhos locked the cell door, Myel addressed Rhos and the other legionary.

"From now on, *nobody* is allowed in that cell unless they have signed permission from me," Myel said. "Nobody. Not Governor Ibeza, not Lord Johl, not even the king's interrogators. If they don't have a warrant from me, with my signature, wax seal, and dated on the same day, you turn them away. Understood?"

"Yes, Your Highness."

With that, Myel and Nahla descended the tower along with their escort. Nahla didn't speak on the way down because she was waiting for Myel to say something first. The circular stairwell echoed, so she assumed he was waiting for a more private opportunity to speak.

They informed Governor Ibeza that Daxton was still uncooperative, and that Lord Johl's visit was inappropriate.

"Lord Johl was here?" Ibeza asked.

"Yes. He did not come to you first?"

"No." He scratched his beard. "This is highly irregular."

Nahla tried to figure out why Johl had visited the prison armed to the teeth. What business did the Governor of Launceston Province have with a Scottsdale rebel? There was definitely a connection, and it did not look good.

"In that case," Myel began, "I want you to keep Johl and anyone from his court and his garrison out of this prison. He has no business seeing any of the prisoners anyway, and especially not Daxton. They don't come past the prison walls."

"And if he threatens me?" Ibeza asked. "After all, this prison belongs to his province, and I am appointed by him."

"If he threatens you, then we will move Daxton to the palace dungeon. I don't know why my father put him here. I'll speak to him about that."

Nahla could think of several reasons. Maybe Eero also knew that Daxton was a rebel, and it was to keep up the pretence that

Daxton was just a common bandit. Why would a king lock up a mere bandit in the palace? Maybe Johl had insisted that Daxton go to Launceston Prison. Or maybe Eero didn't want to taint his pristine palace with a prisoner, even the dungeon. Or, for all Nahla and Myel knew, Eero might use his dungeons for some other purpose, such as storerooms. It was clear that Eero liked to pretend that everything was perfect in his corner of the world. He surrounded himself with fineries and tried to be an optimist, and he would conveniently forget about the troubles of governance unless it was necessary to get something done. Putting Daxton in Launceston Prison meant he was kept out of sight, out of mind. But if Daxton really was a rebel, surely Eero would want to do something about him, and fast.

"I'll send more legionaries," Myel said. "You can keep some at the front gate, and others posted indoors. Maybe put some at your office door, and some more at the bottom of the eastern tower."

"That would be most appreciated, Your Highness."

"Thank you for handling this delicate matter for me, Governor." Myel also told Ibeza about the new warrant arrangement for visiting Daxton. Ibeza agreed that it was a good idea. They shook hands.

Later, on the ride back to the palace in the royal chariot, Myel began a debrief. "I think there is more going on behind the scenes than I've been told," he said.

Nahla gripped the chariot's handrail as Myel turned a corner. "That is often the case in war and politics."

"What is your assessment?"

"I felt you handled the entire situation very well. You were calm, yet firm, and quick to set up additional safeguards."

"Thank you, but I meant your assessment of Daxton and Johl."

The wind was refreshing as the open-air chariot sped through Launceston. Nahla could see why Myel favoured it, though it was a security risk. "That's trickier. My professional opinion is that there is something happening between Daxton and Johl. I truly believe Johl came here to kill Daxton, or severely maim him."

"Yes, I thought the same."

They didn't speak for some time. Nahla mulled over the ramifications of Johl's involvement with Daxton, though just how they were linked was still a mystery.

"We were there at just the right moment," Nahla said.

"Sometimes fortune smiles on us. Today, I think it smiled on Daxton. I just hope he opens his mouth soon. It would be better for all of us."

The chariot rolled over the palace's drawbridge. Nahla always liked the rhythmic sound of the wheels and horseshoes against the wooden planks. "If Johl is mixed up with Daxton, then it won't be good for him if Daxton talks. We might have more internal strife than we bargained for."

Myel slowed the chariot once they were inside the palace grounds, lest he suffer the ire of his father. "I think you're right. We need to be careful."

It seemed like being careful was all Nahla did nowadays.

Myel parked the chariot outside his house and servants bustled out. He let them untether the horses and wipe the dust off the chariot's colourful body and spoked wheels. They led the horses to a water trough.

"I need to organise these new guards for the prison and the visitation warrants," Myel said. "But I want to visit Scottsdale in a few days, and I want you to come with me."

"You want to get some battle experience?"

"No, not at all. I just want to see for myself how organised the rebels are, how much they have taken from Garyd, and visit the Legion. Might try to talk to Garyd as well. Just a quick tour. I'll have your schedule reorganised so you can accompany me."

"Sounds like a good idea. In the meantime, Your Highness, remember we have a training session this evening."

Myel grinned. "You know you can call me Myel."

Nahla, aware that servants and legionaries were nearby, bowed politely and tried to hide her embarrassment. A mere soldier, even a preceptor, should not be so familiar with a prince. Maybe she would call him Myel in private. "Until this evening, Your Highness."

Myel waved her away in a purposefully comical dismissal, because she technically couldn't leave his presence until he said so.

Walking back to her barracks, she now considered the added mystery that needed solving—a rebel leader with a potential link to a provincial lord. She hoped she and Myel could get answers soon, because it sounded like the kingdom was about to get a lot less peaceful.

16

A LORD'S REVENGE

In the tempestuous realm of retribution, where emotions
wield their harrowing might, the pursuit of vengeance be-
gets nothing but a bleak symphony of anguish. As the hand
grasps the sword of retaliation, the heart, once radiant,
withers beneath the weight of resentment, destroying the
very essence of humanity.

—Cass the Blasphemer
The Truth

THE DAGGER FLEW ACROSS the room and slammed into a painted
ceramic vase, shattering it into a mosaic of pieces. Lord Johl didn't
even look at the damage he'd caused. He felt like trashing his entire
office. He clenched his fists and scanned the room. All at once, he
wanted to sweep everything off his desk, toss some chairs aside,
and rip the paintings off the walls. But such an outburst would
achieve nothing. Instead, he put his hand high on the window
frame behind his desk and stared down at Launceston.

Breathe, he thought to himself. *Breathe.*

In the distance, he could see the towers and walls of Launceston
Prison. The sight made his heart race again. In that tower were three
people who could completely undo his master plan. He ground his
teeth and looked away.

Waiting by the closed office door was a soldier who had already established himself as the most vicious in Johl's army. Jugg stood like a rock, his bulk almost hiding the door behind him. Together, they shared the scar of their failed mission to assassinate Daxton. If Jugg was concerned about Johl's temper, he hid it well.

Good, Johl thought. *I need soldiers with a backbone.*

"Once again, Nahla has thwarted my plans," Johl said quietly, seething with anger at the mention of her name. "But this time she had help."

"I would crush her if I had the chance," came Jugg's deep-voiced reply, as much a subtle request for permission as it was a firm statement of support.

Johl looked across the room and saw the pieces of the vase. If he didn't do something soon, his plan would fall to pieces exactly like that vase and the damage would be too great to piece together. The analogy spurred him to a flurry of thoughts and actions. He tugged on a rope protruding from the wall next to his desk. It rang a bell in the room below, requesting his chamberlain's presence.

Next, Johl fetched some expensive paper from a drawer and sat down to write. He preferred not to send written messages, but this was an exceptional circumstance. Using his best wooden pen with a decorative feather and fine metal tip, he scratched out a brief letter:

> Potential compromise. Be ready for political and/or military retaliation. Will send updates when more information is available.

He folded it without signing and sealed it with a blob of wax, but didn't use his personal seal. Instead, he pressed it with a flat stamp.

The chamberlain burst in—the only person in the castle who could enter any room without knocking. His eyes briefly scanned the broken vase before focusing on the governor.

Johl didn't greet him. He had no time for pleasantries. "Find the fastest rider in my garrison and have them deliver this to Lord

Vimarr." He handed the chamberlain the letter. "Tell them to leave immediately. If Vimarr sends a reply, I want to receive it as soon as it arrives, day or night, even if I'm asleep."

"Understood, my lord," the chamberlain said.

"Go now."

When the chamberlain left, Johl pointed at Jugg. "You know about our spy in Eero's palace?"

Jugg nodded.

"We need to send a message. I want to know Myel's movements. I want to know who he speaks to. I want to know what he knows. And I especially want to know if Daxton has told him anything about me. If he has . . ."

Jugg ran a finger across his neck.

Favourite governor or not, if Eero knew about Johl wanting to kill his son, there would be legionaries swarming Castle Trevallyn within half an hour. But killing Myel would be just one part of a much larger plan.

"Nahla," Johl said. His face twitched when he said the name. "When the opportunity strikes, I want her captured."

Jugg's face dropped. "Not killed?"

"She will die eventually. I'll take sweet pleasure in that."

"My lord, will you allow me the honour of dealing the death blow?"

Johl studied the beast of a man standing before him. He'd watched Nahla defeat Jugg in the gladiatorial arena, which seemed an impossible feat. He tried to forget the fact that Nahla had beaten him, too, and was only seconds away from ending his life. No, Nahla would fall by *his* hand.

"Nahla fought me before she fought you," Johl told him. "She's mine."

For the first time since they'd met, Johl noticed a glimmer of rebelliousness in Jugg's eyes, but only for a second. At that moment, he wondered whether Jugg would kill Nahla on sight just to satisfy his own revenge. In the grand scheme of things, Johl supposed, at least he would have one less nuisance to worry about, but he would be terribly upset about not doing it himself. He'd make sure Jugg understood that.

Jugg's barrel chest rose and fell as he took a deep breath. The man never smiled, but now his frown appeared more menacing than ever. "So be it, my lord."

"Of course, if she came to me with broken bones, I would not complain."

The beast's eyes brightened. "Thank you, my lord."

"Good."

Johl whipped out another sheet of paper and wrote some terse instructions.

Watch the fox. Learn everything. Report daily.

"Fox" was Johl's code word for Prince Myel. Again, he left it unsigned and unsealed. He gave the letter to Jugg.

"Add this to the correspondence for the palace. I think there's an agricultural delivery scheduled this afternoon, with correspondence going in with it. Make sure our spy gets this letter."

The letter looked tiny in Jugg's hands.

"Also, I need a constant watch over Launceston Prison. Set up shifts with our own people to watch the prison gate. Now this is important: they must not be dressed in our uniforms. Have them looking like civilians. I want to know if Myel, Nahla, or any royal official enters the prison. Understood?" When Jugg nodded, Johl dismissed him. The burly man saluted and stomped away in his big sandals.

Now that Johl was alone, he turned his attention to the most pressing issue at hand. He had to kill Daxton, and he had to kill him yesterday. Everything hinged on whether Daxton would talk. Johl hoped he hadn't spoken already. It would complicate matters—resources would need to be rerouted, schedules changed, and people assassinated earlier than planned. Going back to the prison was out of the question. Disguising one of his own provincial soldiers as a legionary also came with its own risks.

Then he remembered Nahla's suggestion to move Daxton to the dungeon underneath the palace. He cursed her, but realised that it might not be such a bad idea. After all, Johl had relative freedom of movement in the palace. But he'd rather keep his distance, especially now that Myel was on the case. He wondered if his palace spy would carry out an assassination, or at least help to facilitate it.

Either way, he would kill Daxton, no matter where he was. The hardest part was getting to him. He put his mind to it, and eventually an idea blossomed.

Sequestered in a private corner of Castle Trevallyn's grounds was a nondescript, single-storey building that few people visited. Johl approached it alone and knocked. He cradled two wine bottles in his arm and they clinked against each other. He scanned his surroundings. Apart from a soldier patrolling on the nearby castle wall, nobody was within line-of-sight. A wrinkly old woman with leathery skin answered the door.

"My lord," she said, "good to see you." She curtsied as far as her aged bones could manage.

"We must speak in private," Johl said.

She beckoned him inside, and he was immediately hit with a mix of organic scents. Sweet and pungent flowers, leaves, and liquids filled the room. A cauldron bubbled and steamed in the corner, making the room nearly as warm as the morning outside.

The old lady locked the door. "What brings you to me, my lord? Are you ill? Is someone hurt?"

"I need a poison, Ermi. A strong one."

Ermi gave a knowing nod. "You make use of my services more for evil than for good, but I am not one to judge. You pay well."

Johl stifled a grin. Ermi had been the physician at Castle Trevallyn since before he assumed the governorship. But it wasn't until he started concocting secret plans that he discovered a more devious side to Ermi's skill set.

"I assume the wine is for me," Ermi said.

"Yes and no." Johl handed them to her. Her arms sagged despite the feeble weight of the glass bottles. "They're not for drinking."

"I figured as much." She set them down on a nearby table. "A powerful poison, you say? How powerful?"

"Powerful meaning fatal."

"I know that. I meant, do you want the death to be quick, or does it need to be delayed?"

"The quicker the better. Instantaneously, if possible."

"Not easy to do." At that, Ermi went to the back door and picked up a pair of gloves and a bucket. "Follow me, your lordship."

Johl was not accustomed to taking orders from others, but Ermi was one of the few people who were indispensable in his life, so he let it slide. Outside was Ermi's private garden, but it was far from ornamental. This garden was not for sustenance or beauty. Rather, it provided her with all the ingredients she needed for creating medical treatments. Everything grew in neat rows, categorised according to a system that only she understood. Her knowledge came from her young traineeship as a Guardian of Life, before they ejected her for fraternising with a legionary.

The plants were healthy and full, thanks to daily watering. Johl made sure she had enough water. However, the plants that Ermi wanted were not in this garden. Instead, she went to a locked timber gate hinged on a brick wall taller than Johl. Ermi spent some time finding the right key, but she opened the door soon enough.

"Please stay by the gate, my lord," she warned. "These are rare and dangerous specimens. Some are toxic even to the touch."

Johl had never seen this garden before, but he knew it existed. Usually, he requested a poison, and she told him when it was ready. Like the other garden, this one was also organised neatly by rows. Some plants were small and grew in pots against Ermi's house, or against the castle wall opposite the building. He watched her pick flowers and leaves with gloved hands—pink flowers here, some thin green leaves there, tiny purple-blue flowers from another patch, and so on.

"You want it strong, and I need enough for two wine bottles," she explained.

Johl preferred to use wine when dealing with poisons. The flavour and smell masked the sickness and death in every drop. It would be a shame to waste the Devonport vintage, but it was a small price to pay.

When Ermi had filled her bucket, she waved Johl back and locked the secret garden, then rushed inside. "Are you going to stay?"

"How long will it take?"

"Half an hour at most."

Curious to see the professional in action, Johl said he would watch.

"You'll make yourself useful, my lord," Ermi said, careful to add the respectful title on the end. "Please open both doors and all windows, and put on that mask and gown over there."

To think, a provincial lord being bossed around by an old physician! But when someone had knowledge and experience like Ermi's, Johl could make exceptions. While he fulfilled her commands, Ermi emptied the cauldron into jars, scrubbed it, and refilled it with water. They had to wait for it to boil first.

"Would you like the labels removed from the wine bottles?" Ermi asked.

Johl considered it. If Eero discovered that Daxton ingested poisoned wine from Devonport, it would cause a kingdom-wide scare. He imagined nobles and court officials destroying their supply of Jaruk's bottles, fearing that if one had been tainted, others may be too. Jaruk's reputation would suffer, but he'd be handsomely recompensated when everyone restocked their cellars with a new batch. The rich and powerful could not live off water forever—only the "commoners" did that. If anything, the debacle would redirect attention to Vimarr's province, which should give Johl some room to manoeuvre. Plus, he never liked Jaruk.

"No, leave the labels on."

"As you wish, my lord."

Ermi blew on the fire under the cauldron and busied herself with the rest of her apothecary equipment—glass tubes, metal tongs, and a stone mortar and pestle. Johl picked up one of the wine bottles and had a smart idea. He scratched out three small corners of the label, then did the same to the other bottle. They would be easier to identify that way. He also made a mental note not to drink any wine until the bottles were outside of Castle Trevallyn. Better safe than sorry.

Eventually, the cauldron bubbled and Ermi finished preparing the ingredients. She faced Johl. "Now we make the most potent poison Launceston has ever seen."

17

THE SPIDER'S WEB

Beware the delicate strands of the spider's web, for within its gossamer beauty lies a treacherous trap.

—Unknown
Tasmanian proverb

N<small>AHLA SAT ON HER</small> horse during the early morning ceremony. The sun was only just rising over the Launceston skyline, but already her thighs sweated against her saddle. Ajax, her chestnut Arabian steed, moved his head lazily, perhaps already aware of the long ride that awaited him.

A priestess had just taken a mule laden with water bags into the temple. Prince Myel figured they could make good time and reach the Legion's First Company in Scottsdale later that evening or early the next day, so they didn't need a big water carriage. Myel glanced at Nahla when the temple doors closed. His face said everything that Nahla felt about the ceremony. She couldn't understand how a vital part of Launceston society could be shrouded in so much mystery and protected by the threat of death. The Divine Guards watched them.

For their journey north, Myel had chosen Nahla as his primary travelling companion, as well as four highly regarded legionaries. They knew roughly where First Company had gone in Scottsdale, but that was two days ago. The unit could have moved in any direction in response to rebel activity. Primus Carro hadn't sent a messenger so far, but King Eero expected one at least every week. Still, Myel felt confident he could find Carro and apprise himself of the situation.

The journey promised to be an excellent learning opportunity for Myel. Finally, he would get out of the city and experience the activities he should have done from the moment he came of age— long-distance travel, time with his soldiers in the field, assessing military strategy and political headaches. He had privately admitted to Nahla that he didn't feel ready for such responsibilities.

"There is no time like the present," Nahla had told him. "I'm here to help." He took some comfort in that.

Nahla resolved within herself to never leave the prince's side and to support him in any way possible. She'd already lost a king, so she'd be damned if she lost a prince as well, especially one as likeable as Myel.

The priestess returned with their mule. Myel went through the perfunctory thanks and received the priestess' equally disinterested well-wishes. Nahla wondered why it wasn't Matriarch Anurak herself out here blessing the prince. Surely that would have been more appropriate.

With the Litany of Water complete, Myel's small band headed out.

SEVERAL HOURS INTO THEIR journey, when the so-called "God's Eye" had risen and cast its repressive rays upon them, Myel took a sudden break from discussing politics and soldiering.

"What do you think is inside?"

"Inside what, Your Highness?" Nahla asked.

"Inside the temple."

Nahla, aware that this sort of talk should never be overheard, ordered their escort to spread out. Safely out of earshot, Nahla indulged Myel's curiosity.

"I've been sceptical about the temples," she said. "I don't understand how they work."

"Yes, I'm the same. I don't see how water can miraculously appear when they take containers inside. Yet that is exactly what the people believe. If that really does happen, why can't people do the Litany of Water at their homes? Why is that power vested in the Guardians?"

"That sort of talk will get you into trouble. You've seen the scars on my back."

"And that is precisely why I feel safe talking to you about it. There is no love between Anurak and myself, and I'm fairly certain you feel the same way."

"You're very perceptive, Your Highness."

"Please, they can't hear us," Myel said, pointing to the legionaries travelling in front and behind them. "Call me Myel."

Nahla had lost count of how many times he'd made that request. She grinned. "Myel, you'll get us in trouble if we're overheard."

Myel frowned. "Tullius!" he shouted. "Can you hear our conversation?"

One of the soldiers ahead shouted back. "Not a word, Your Highness."

"Good. Keep it that way."

Nahla looked away and stymied a laugh.

"Satisfied?" Myel said. When Nahla faced him again, he raised his eyebrows and smiled victoriously. "You've seen my garden, how healthy and productive it is. I receive more water than the average Launceston citizen by virtue of my royal blood. Imagine if everyone was so privileged. Imagine what they could do. Industries would prosper. People would have an abundance of fresh food grown in their own backyard. We could rejuvenate the soil and plant more trees. Can you imagine that?"

"It sounds impossible."

"But it *is* possible, because I've done it already, only on a small scale. Think about it. When you visit me in my garden, do you feel the difference in temperature?"

"It's cooler in your garden," she said. But for Nahla, Tasmania in general was slightly cooler than her homeland, though she couldn't understand why. The difference was negligible, though. She still felt the heat.

"That's right. There's something special about plants. They change the climate. If we had trees everywhere and healthy gardens in every home, the kingdom would be a very different place. But that will never happen while the Guardians have control of the water supply."

He gazed off into the distance, and Nahla imagined he was picturing his ideal world. What Myel described was similar to the painting she had seen in the Guardians' administration building— green grass, vibrant trees, an overflow of fresh food. Did Myel believe he could make Tasmanian heaven a reality? She hadn't studied the local religion much, but she wondered if the rolling fields of green grass helped to keep the populace in a permanent state of subservience. There were similar religious beliefs back home—endure the current world and be rewarded in the next.

Nahla licked her lips, choosing her words carefully. "Does this mean you don't believe water comes from God?"

Myel scoffed. "I can tell from your tone that even you don't believe that."

She bit her tongue. Of course, she didn't believe it, because she had seen otherwise. Myel still didn't know the truth about her past. He only knew the basics—that she was a soldier, that she disliked politics, that she was damned good with a sword, and that she wasn't from Launceston. "Like I said before, I'm sceptical."

They carried on in silence for a short while. The only sound was the steady clomping of horse hooves on the dirt road.

"I have plans and ideas for the future, Nahla. You'll see. Launceston will be different."

Myel called for his escort to close in again, ending their blasphemous conversation. But Nahla knew it wouldn't be the last time they discussed the future.

SINCE THE DISTRESSING EPISODE at Launceston Prison, Johl went into full damage control. Besides sending half a dozen messages to co-conspirators, he also ordered his provincial army to double down on its training schedule. He had to be prepared for anything.

Johl stood on a balcony eating grapes and watching some of his soldiers train in the field below. They were divided into two teams. Team A had to storm a barricaded Team B and seize the red flag. The clashing of their wooden swords and the shouts of sergeants carried upwards to Johl's vantage point. One by one, the forces thinned as sword tips or dull blades struck limbs and torsos. The war game had rules, but in real life Johl would rather his troops fight with unbridled ferocity. He'd have to tell his officers to train more realistically from now on.

He heard quick footsteps and reached for his dagger, but it was only his chamberlain coming to join him on the balcony. He let his heart rate settle before speaking.

"What is it?"

"A message from the palace, my lord," the chamberlain said, handing over a note. If he'd seen Johl's fearful clutch of the dagger, he was smart enough not to let it show on his face.

Johl tossed a few more grapes into his mouth and read it, instantly recognising his spy's handwriting. He smiled. *So Myel and Nahla have left for Scottsdale? With any luck, they'll be killed by stray arrows.*

A thought came to him. It was irrational, but it spoke to his true feelings. He turned to the chamberlain. "Find Jugg. Tell him to come to me."

He had seen little of Jugg in the past couple of days. The beast was too busy being a target in his soldiers' training sessions. Anyone who could beat Jugg one-to-one was promised a reward. Triple rations of water for a week, unlimited food, and a free run of any brothel in town. There were no winners yet.

Johl raced through the implications of Myel and Nahla being away. It meant he had some freedom to act without worrying about the prince's scrutiny. He could avoid Eero, but Myel was a bit too enthusiastic. If he played his cards right, he might even get away with the most heinous plan that was formulating in his mind.

Jugg stomped across the room and stood at attention on the balcony. "You requested my presence, my lord?"

"I did." Johl regarded the giant, noting that he was slippery with sweat. He'd probably been fetched from some sword practice or strength training. "I have two jobs for you. On my desk in my study are two bottles of wine. Take one—just one—and slip it into the next food delivery for Daxton. I hear they come in special boxes every few days. Don't take one for yourself, and don't taste them, or you'll be dead before I can kill you for defying my order." Johl would keep the other poisoned wine bottle as a backup.

Jugg nodded and smiled. He understood the wine was tainted.

"I have something else as well. East of Launceston, about four hours away, is a . . ." Johl explained his plan almost in a whisper, and Jugg nodded eagerly at every main point. "Take Penna. She's been there before."

"At once, my lord." Jugg saluted and left.

If Johl had more people like Jugg, he would be invincible. But as fortune had given him only one, he had to make plans within plans and use Jugg wisely. He thanked his luck that Nahla hadn't killed him when they fought as gladiators. He now had a menacing weapon to unleash on his enemies, and Jugg happily did his master's bidding. The man had no compunction with the sort of plans Johl often envisaged, plans which would have made most other soldiers pale with fear.

A DAY LATER, A CART driver named Deeno arrived at the storehouse of Launceston Prison. The afternoon was hot and dry and he was thirsty, despite it being only a short journey through town. Thankfully, he didn't need to unload his cargo. The prison guards did that for him. Deeno found a shady spot against the prison wall and sipped lukewarm water from a pouch that a guard had given him.

The prison was routinely supplied with fresh fruit and vegetables, cuts of meat, bread baked only a day earlier, and, of course, water. But lately there had been some special deliveries on the manifest, and always in a box with the royal seal painted on all sides. The guards placed bets over what goodies these boxes contained.

Occasionally, Governor Ibeza would inspect the deliveries personally, and he usually took a keen interest in the royal provisions. The governor ignored Deeno as he watched his guards unload.

"Is our special box in there today?" Ibeza asked, hands on hips. He frowned and squinted, apparently in a sullen mood.

"Here it is, sir," one of the guards replied from atop the cart. He handed it to a colleague on the ground, who held it up for Ibeza.

Ibeza grumbled and scratched his beard. Then he shook his head. "King Eero goes too far this time." He pulled out a wine bottle. "No prisoner deserves alcohol. Make sure Daxton knows his wine was confiscated." Then he carried the bottle to his governor's cottage.

Deeno saw the whole brief episode. As a lowly cart driver recently hired by the prison, he took another sip of water and purged the memory from his mind.

18

A PRINCE ABROAD

A conflict brews on the horizon. It will be a short, bloody battle. Soon, the Legion will strike and crush these vagrants once and for all. The odds are in our favour.

—Primus Carro, CO, 1C, King's Legion
First Company Diary

THE JOURNEY WAS LONG, but Prince Myel rode with such a steady speed that they didn't need to camp overnight. They made only a few stops to rest the horses and air out sweaty thighs. Nahla was growing more impressed with the way Myel had taken to his new responsibilities. He was seizing the nuances of politics, management, and military theory. In time, he would no longer need her teachings in the art of war, but Nahla would gladly stay on as his advisor, especially if Myel would try to change the very social structure of the kingdom. He would need all the help he could get at that point.

As they travelled through Scottsdale Province, they passed pairs of King's Legion cavalry troopers who informed them of Primus Carro's last known position. This way, Myel could track First Company's movements. They found the unit's rear guard as the sun was setting. A lieutenant directed them to Carro's camp several kilometres ahead.

Nahla had been scrutinising everything the moment she entered the province. She would quiz Myel when they had a chance. The cavalry watching the entrance to Scottsdale met her approval—they would help secure the supply and communication lines to and from Launceston. However, she didn't know how many bandits or rebels First Company had to contend with. Were there so many that they could harass the company's rear area? Or only enough to defend their own positions against the royal attacks? Whatever the case, it seemed Carro was taking no chances until he knew more about the enemy. Leaving an entire platoon—nearly a third of his force—as a rear guard meant he was being cautious. She would ask Myel what he thought of that.

They found Carro's tent perched on a low hill of dry grass. It stood larger and higher than the rest of the encampment. Myel dismounted and beckoned Nahla to follow him inside.

"Are you decent, Primus Carro?" Myel called, and Nahla pressed her lips together to stifle a smile.

"Who asked that?" Carro bellowed from inside. "What fool bothers me with such a ridiculous question?" He whipped open the tent flap. "Oh, my goodness, Your Highness! I'm terribly sorry. I—"

"It's all right, Carro. I didn't want to barge in unannounced."

"Please, come in. I see you've brought along Preceptor Nahla." He slammed the tent flap shut, and Nahla thought he might have been cross with himself, or just frustrated about his situation in Scottsdale.

"Yes," Myel said. "She is as much *my* trainer as she is the Legion's preceptor of combat."

Carro's tent was large, as befitting a commanding officer, but it was bereft of decorations, which was exactly how Nahla preferred the quarters of such a rank. What an officer brought on a campaign said a lot about their character. A narrow bed with a straw-filled mattress lay on the floor at one end, a medium-sized wooden chest lay perpendicular to it and doubled as a nightstand, and a small table stood against another tent wall, on which was a map. Myel inspected the map.

"My troops speak highly of the preceptor," Carro said. Then, with a bow, "It is a welcome surprise and a morale boost to have you here, Nahla."

News of Nahla's fighting spirit had spread to the soldiers even before she was inducted into the King's Legion. When she endured the intense flogging by the Guardians, her reputation soared to greater heights. No doubt the Guardians hated that. And now that she was the Legion's wise and firm trainer, the soldiers respected and appreciated her even more.

"You are too kind, Primus," Nahla said, and left it at that. This was Myel's visit, and she didn't want to detract from its purpose. But she was too inferior in rank to steer the conversation onto the correct course without appearing to overstep her position. Thankfully, Myel knew that moving swiftly was the key to success, and he wasted no time getting down to business.

"What do you know about the enemy's movements?" he asked.

Carro frowned. "Not much. I've sent my cavalry scouts ahead and they've reported on small groups of bandit activity to the east. I'm expecting a liaison officer from Lord Garyd to arrive tonight or tomorrow to fill me in on the rest of the province, but I suspect that information would be out of date. Still, I have a feeling we'll be moving east soon."

Myel and Nahla studied the map. Nahla had heard from various legionaries that there was technically no official eastern border to Scottsdale Province. Unofficially, it stopped at the edge of a forest that ran nearly the full length of the province from north to south. Beyond the forest was an unimaginably large, empty expanse which cartographers and explorers believed was the end of the world. They called it Eternity's Void. The histories briefly mentioned exploration parties sent east, only to return after days of trekking without seeing other life or significant landmarks, if they returned at all. It reminded Nahla of her journey through the Endless Land, except in that case she had travelled far enough to find another civilisation. The odds of that happening again in another direction were not worth mentioning.

"We are visiting Garyd tomorrow," Myel told him. "I need the Legion and Garyd's forces to work together."

"They haven't been very successful against the bandits, Your Highness."

Nahla detected some apprehension in Carro's voice, perhaps even some disdain. A well-trained provincial army that couldn't handle a bandit clan? She had to admit, it sounded impossible, but she suspected there was much more to the story. If only that damned Daxton would talk!

"Yes, I know about their failures," Myel said. "But with the Legion to bolster their numbers, we can envelop the enemy. Speaking of which . . ." Myel paused, and Nahla knew he was debating the bandit–rebel dichotomy. "We may be against more than just a bandit clan."

Carro narrowed his eyes. "How so, Your Highness?"

"I have reason to believe that these bandits are actually a growing rebel force."

"Hmm." Carro paced the tent, scratching his chin. "That means we're fighting more than just criminals. We're fighting something much worse—*ideas.*"

"Ideas are not all that bad. It's how ideas are turned into reality that is usually the problem. That, and the amount of resistance to them. I would like to learn exactly what these rebels want. We may end this fight without more bloodshed."

"A legionary is not afraid to spill blood—theirs or someone else's," Carro said. "These rebels need to respect the rightful rulers of the land. Compromise will only weaken your father's authority."

Myel backed off. "We shall see."

To Nahla, this showed that Myel would have a hard time with Carro. There were five primuses in the King's Legion, four of which commanded a regular company and one in charge of the cavalry. That was five high-ranking officers whose respect Myel had to earn, and it was clear he hadn't earned Carro's just yet. But it was early days. Myel still had to prove himself.

"In the meantime," Carro said, "we already know of some key locations where the bandits—or rebels—centre their activity." He tapped on the map with a silver-ringed finger. "We've already scouted the camp that Nahla raided. It's completely destroyed and abandoned. Other locations include a string of mines in the far east, and a fortified town called Ringarooma, which is surrounded by fertile land and woodcutters' camps. I have a feeling that town is their headquarters, but it is quite close to Scottsdale."

"How close?" Nahla asked.

Carro drew an invisible line with his finger. "The easiest route is about five hours on foot. But to approach either Scottsdale or Ringarooma along a more concealed route, which is preferred, would take nearly twice as long."

Nahla quietly commended Carro's assessment of direct and concealed travel in both directions. He was clearly developing both offensive and defensive plans. "And how far is Ringarooma from here?"

Carro pointed to an area south of Scottsdale called Springfield, which was surrounded on three sides by hills and mountains. "We are here. To go directly to Ringarooma, we'll have to cross this mountain range. It will take over ten hours."

"And to the mines in the east?" Myel asked.

"Nearly a full day's trek."

Myel exhaled. Scottsdale was the kingdom's largest province, and he was just now realising its true extent. That much was plain on his face. Nahla shared his concerns and also acknowledged the difficulty in stamping out rebel activity across such a large area.

No wonder Garyd struggled to contain the growth of Daxton's territory.

"What's your plan?" Myel asked.

"I'd like to assault Ringarooma. Strike a blow at their heart. With their leader captured and their headquarters destroyed, they will realise that their days are numbered. A swift attack will bring a swift victory."

Myel faced the primus and looked him square in the eyes. "I'd like to resolve this peacefully."

Carro straightened his back and raised his chin. "Your Highness, I have the utmost respect for you as our new patron and as the son of my king, but you are not my military superior. I take orders from your father, and his orders are to destroy Daxton's clan."

Prince and primus faced off. The tension was so thick, Nahla could cut it like butter. Standing before her were two blatantly opposite people—an officer of war and a prince of peace. Nahla had endured many years of fighting and had seen enough bloodshed and burning buildings. She, like Myel, wanted a peaceful solution too. But Carro's stubbornness did not bode well for Myel's future. If Myel made an enemy now, it would only lead to difficulties when he became king.

"At least wait until I have returned from Scottsdale," Myel pleaded. "I must speak with Garyd."

Carro cleared his throat. "That suits me, Your Highness. I cannot move until Garyd's envoy arrives, and even then I need to coordinate with the captain of the Scottsdale Garrison."

"Then our plans have aligned. My team will make camp here and leave for Scottsdale before sunrise."

"Please, Your Highness, take my tent for your lodgings tonight, unless you have brought something more comfortable."

"Nonsense! I'll sleep with my escort."

Could've worded that better, Nahla thought. But she admired Myel's willingness to tough it out like everyone else.

"In that case," Carro said, "you can share this hill with me. There is plenty of room beside my tent."

"Thank you, Primus Carro. You are most accommodating."

With that, they engaged in a busy series of bows, handshakes, and well-wishing. Nahla and Myel left the tent to find that the sun had already set. First Company had lit torches throughout the camp. They walked to their horses.

"See that our tents are set up, but far enough away that we cannot be overheard. I have some things to discuss with you before bed."

"Of course," Nahla said.

"I'm going to mingle with the legionaries. Come find me when you're ready so we can eat together."

Myel trudged down the hill. Nahla watched him in the waning dusk, a prince among his soldiers. Legionaries bowed in awe as he approached and then stood gobsmacked when he stopped to speak to them. And not only that, but he also stayed to carry on a conversation! She smiled, glad to see him interacting with the legionaries. He was their patron, after all, and they loved having a member of the royal family so close by. However, Primus Carro and the company's lieutenants were a different story. He'd have to work harder to win their hearts, but Nahla believed he could do it. He had the charisma, and soon he would have the military experience. She only wished that it wouldn't be forged in an unjust war.

Nahla found Sergeant Tullius under a tree, feeding his horse a carrot. She liked the man as soon as he presented himself as one of Myel's escorts for the Scottsdale expedition. He was strong, rugged, and took orders without question. "Tullius! Let's set up camp."

"At once, Preceptor!" He called his fellow escorts and followed Nahla to a flat section of the hill at a reasonable distance from Carro's command tent.

She and Myel had a big day of strategy and negotiations ahead. She wondered if Lord Garyd would be as stiff-necked as Carro.

19

A WINE WITH SUPPER

When the end is achieved through whatever means necessary—what price victory?

—**Nahla Northborn**
Monologues

GOVERNOR IBEZA RARELY LEFT Launceston Prison. As overseer of the city's convicted criminals, he was given a residence within the prison's walls, with all the amenities and supplies he needed. Sometimes, he would venture out to spend time in the city proper, but he had few friends and his job prevented him from wandering too far, so he mostly stayed on site.

Every day was mostly the same. He ate a hearty breakfast, which he cooked himself, then toured the prison's wings and towers. If there were any pressing issues that had developed overnight—such as a disturbance or an inmate's death—he organised a clean-up and a half-hearted investigation, followed by reports. Then came more administrative work, which he did from his office, preferring to remain undisturbed during those hours.

Since the bandit leader had arrived, he usually visited him just before lunch and tried in vain to coax him to talk. Then, during the hottest part of the day, Ibeza would have a cool lunch of vegetables and refreshing juices. His afternoons kept him busy with more administrative work—organising labour teams, selecting appropriate prisoners for gladiatorial contests, reviewing his guards' performance, or managing the prison's supplies.

In the late afternoons, he made another inspection of every wing and tower, and then walked the perimeter wall with his most senior guards. While on the wall, he often gazed at Launceston sprawling in every direction. So many houses, so many people. In one direction, the king's palace stood tall and proud. In the other direction, Lord Johl's residence, Castle Trevallyn, sat dark and imposing atop a hill. He sometimes marvelled at how he lived in his own little world within the prison, though recent events were becoming more entangled with his daily life. After completing the perimeter inspection, Ibeza ended his day by giving the night watch commander some instructions, and then headed home.

Ibeza's home was built into one corner of the prison's wall. He had a watchtower above his roof, which he liked to call Tower One. He only assigned the most capable guards to that tower, and the quietest, because he didn't feel like hearing the echoes of chatter throughout the night. It was bad enough living alone—he didn't need to be reminded that he had no one to talk to at night.

The home was enough for his needs. If he had a family, a larger house in the city would have been better, but he had given up on that dream. Now he was content to live out his years in this governor's house, inside his little domain, without the joys of a wife and children.

When Ibeza arrived home in the evening, he grumbled because he'd forgotten to close the shutters. The hot daytime air had significantly warmed the interior, despite the home being in the prison wall's shadow. He shook his head and entered the small kitchen. At least there would be a cool breeze overnight.

Since the house was so warm, Ibeza decided on a cold salad for dinner. He went to his underground pantry to fetch some ingredients. The room was delightfully cool, and he wondered why more homes weren't simply built into the ground to enjoy the same passive cooling effect. Perhaps it was too labour intensive. He didn't dwell on it, though, because it was not his problem to raise the living standards of the kingdom's subjects. Instead, he filled a basket with some food and turned to leave. As he reached for the door, he spotted the wine bottle that King Eero had sent to Daxton. He didn't usually drink wine with salads, but he was curious to try the Easton vintage. The stuff was normally reserved for the rich and powerful. He chuckled. Was it too much to live like a king for one night?

After lots of peeling and cutting, Ibeza had his salad ready. He took it to his dining room, which was nothing more than an alcove with a two-seated table built into the wall. A cooling breeze already streamed in from the shade outside. He poured himself a tall glass of wine and drank it with his eyes first. Such a deep red! He downed it like water—half the glass to wet his palate. Delicious! Then he shovelled some salad into his mouth, washed it down with the other half of the wine, and poured some more.

He swallowed hard and frowned. The initial sweet flavour of the wine soon left a foul taste. He studied the bottle, looking for signs of age. The bottle was only dated a year ago. Even with his limited knowledge of winemaking, he knew that Easton's high-quality products lasted decades. He likened it to owning an ugly artwork made purely of gold. Just because it wasn't pleasing to his eyes, it didn't mean it wasn't valuable. So he poured another glass, taste be damned. He'd finish the bottle tonight and never try another.

How could the nobles like this stuff? Ibeza wondered.

He continued eating and drinking, grimacing at every gulp. But towards the end of his meal, his heart raced and his breathing quickened. It was indiscernible at first, but then he couldn't mistake the difference. His muscles ached too, and a pain spread in his chest. He thought he might have been eating too fast, so he downed the rest of his wine to force the masticated food along its natural path. But the pain continued.

Soon, he was gasping for air. He broke out in a sweat, and he clawed at his clothes to cool down. His heart beat harder than ever before, and the pain in his chest worsened. He grunted, trying to resist the sharp pangs that were tormenting his body, but he knew that something was terribly wrong. He pushed his chair back, scraping it along the stone floor.

He tried to stand, lost his balance, swore under his breath, and everything went black.

D AXTON AWOKE TO THE sound of heavy footsteps outside his cell door. A key clattered in the lock and the door burst open. In came four legionaries. They locked the door behind them, and Daxton feared for the worst.

So this is how I go? Slaughtered in my cell by the kingdom's finest warriors.

But the legionaries did not attack. Two took up positions either side of the door. The third searched frantically through Daxton's food, while the fourth inspected random items in the circular cell.

"If you're searching for a weapon, I have none," Daxton said. He rubbed his eyes.

"No wine, Sergeant," said the one searching the food hamper. He had a mop of red-headed curls. Daxton had heard his name before, but could not remember it.

"I've never had wine here," Daxton said.

The crouching sergeant threw down some dirty clothes before standing at an impressive height. "And you'll be glad for it. You had a bottle of wine in your latest food delivery, but Governor Ibeza took it. He was found dead this morning. The wine was poisoned."

That news woke Daxton properly. He blinked hurriedly a few times. "He's dead?"

"As dead as dead can be. But that wine was meant for you. Somebody wants you dead."

"I'm posting more guards here," the sergeant said. "And I'm having your food taste tested by other prisoners first. From now on, you'll get your food a day after it arrives."

But Daxton heard none of the sergeant's words. His heart thumped as a torrent of concerning thoughts filled his mind. It didn't take long to decide what to do. "I want to speak to Prince Myel right away."

"His Royal Highness is in another province."

"Please, you must send word to him. Tell him I am ready to speak. I'll tell him everything he wants to know. You must hurry."

The sergeant gave him a stony stare, then nodded and told the redhead to ride immediately to Scottsdale with Daxton's request.

20

THE OLD GOVERNOR

With grey hair comes wisdom. However, such wisdom can become entangled with apathy, obstinance, and stagnation.

—Cass the Blasphemer
The Lords of Launceston

Lord Garyd's castle occupied a low hill in the centre of the mostly flat city of Scottsdale. As Nahla and Myel approached early in the morning, the city looked more like an oversized fort. In reality, Scottsdale was just like any other city in the kingdom, but roving bandits in the region had put the populace on high alert.

On the path to the castle, the people were so fearful of a bandit attack that they had built defences upon defences. A deep ditch several paces wide surrounded the entire city, with sharp logs dug into the ground just waiting to skewer anyone foolish enough to fall in. A drawbridge was the only way in or out, because they had also constructed a stockade on the inner side of the ditch. Wooden towers were spaced at irregular intervals, and a sturdy gatehouse protected the drawbridge. Just these defences alone made Scottsdale more protected than Launceston, but it didn't stop there.

As Ajax trotted along the cobblestone street, Nahla felt the fear in the populace. Men, women, and children carried swords or daggers, and every corner had a handful of armoured provincial soldiers. Four contraptions that Nahla had never seen sat in a public square. Myel kept moving, but she studied them as she passed. They looked like giant longbows mounted on a support structure. A team of soldiers oiled metal mechanisms that allowed the bows to swivel. Lined up next to each contraption were barrels filled with arrows. She assumed they were some kind of multi-arrow weapon and made a mental note to see them in action if they were ever used.

Myel, Nahla, and their small escort trotted along another draw-bridge into Lord Garyd's castle. The old governor now had royalty in his domain who, together with a company of the King's Legion, would be demanding that he send his troops out of this well-defended city, but for a very specific reason. Nahla silently admitted that their day might involve a lot of persuasion and compromise.

A tanned, muscular woman in blue-and-silver armour and a plumed helmet met them even before they had dismounted. At first, Nahla thought she was a Divine Guard, but then she saluted Myel.

"Your Highness," she said, still standing with a stiff back. "This is a surprise."

Myel climbed off his horse. "If I had announced my arrival, it would not be unexpected or surprising. You have me at a disadvantage . . ."

"I am Captain Ziva, commander of the Scottsdale Garrison."

"Well met, Captain," Myel said. "I present Preceptor Nahla Northborn of the King's Legion." He gestured at Nahla as she also dismounted.

The two women looked each other up and down, and Nahla knew she had a seasoned soldier inspecting her. Nahla guessed she and Ziva were about the same age. She fought the instinct to salute because legionaries did not salute provincial officers of any rank.

"A pleasure to meet you, Preceptor," Ziva said. "Your reputation precedes you. If we had ten of you in Scottsdale, I think our bandit problem would be over before too long."

Nahla offered a slight bow. "Thank you for your vote of confidence, Captain."

"We must speak with Lord Garyd immediately," Myel said.

"He is *still* eating breakfast at the moment," Ziva said with just a subtle hint of apology. Nahla suspected there was some head-butting between Ziva and Garyd. She imagined Ziva wanting to take the fight to Daxton's forces, while Garyd was in full defensive mode.

"Then we shall join him," Myel said. He had only eaten breakfast about two hours ago, but the man could certainly eat again. "Come, Nahla! This morning, we feast with my father's longest-serving lord and oldest friend."

SEVERAL HOURS, A LUNCH break, and many words later, Myel and Garyd had not come to an agreement. Captain Ziva had opted to stay and contribute to the discussion instead of meeting Primus Carro out in the field. That would have angered Carro, who now had to contend with a more junior representative from Garyd's court. Without Ziva to negotiate the larger military decisions between primus and governor, Carro was effectively stuck in Springfield, unless he moved his company eastwards alone. This was entirely possible, given Carro's eagerness to take the fight to the rebels.

Garyd proved to be a perfect host, supplying his noble guest and Nahla with the finest foods and wines, all the while offering the politest arguments Nahla had ever heard. The old man, while an unlucky military strategist, discussed matters of court with an air of dignity.

"Daxton has thrashed us in every engagement," Garyd said, "and when we finally have the advantage, his forces are nowhere to be found. I'm convinced he has a spy in our midst. I've had Ziva shake up our entire command structure, but that only resulted in desertions and mutiny. We've withdrawn to the safety of Scottsdale. My people have been flocking here for protection, leaving entire villages empty."

"The situation is different now," Myel told him. He leaned forwards on the plush couch. Garyd grabbed a biscuit and chewed while Myel spoke. "Daxton is locked up in Launceston. His people are headless, and you now have a whole company of the King's Legion in the province. We have the upper hand."

Garyd swallowed and frowned. "Removing Daxton won't change anything."

Nahla, standing behind Myel, pursed her lips and looked at Captain Ziva. The provincial officer sighed inaudibly, clearly exasperated. They'd listened to hours of rebuttals and excuses. Granted, some of his reasons were valid. It was undeniable that Daxton had some help. Nahla had a suspicion who was responsible, but she had no proof, nor any plausible motive. Despite that, Garyd now seemed afraid to take his forces out of the safety of Scottsdale.

"My lord," Nahla said. "Primus Carro is at this very moment preparing to move against what he thinks is Daxton's headquarters. Daxton's troops are demoralised and headless, as Prince Myel said. We must strike while the iron is hot."

Ziva narrowed her eyes at Nahla, as if questioning how a mere preceptor could comprehend the strategic situation. But she nodded nonetheless, for Nahla's comment was indeed the right one militarily.

Still, Garyd hesitated. "And if we are defeated, my people will be the ones who are demoralised—more demoralised than they already are."

"I don't think Nahla finished her thought," Myel said. He twisted around and shot her a disappointed, lopsided smile, and Nahla gave him apologetic eyes. She had lapsed into her old ways from Melbourne—swift and aggressive military action. "We must strike while the iron is hot, but not with violence. Use our forces to move in and pressure them to surrender and relinquish the land and resources they have stolen."

Garyd shifted his aged bulk on the soft cushions. "Your Highness, I appreciate your interest in this struggle and your goal of achieving a favourable outcome. However, you were absent from the beginning, and you have not seen what my people have suffered. Nobody from Launceston understands the full extent of what has transpired here. The only right thing to do is to crush these bandits once and for all. My people demand it. My *dead* people demand it!" His face went red and his hands shook. To hide the raw emotion, he shovelled another biscuit into his mouth and looked away.

"Then we must advance on this bandit stronghold as Preceptor Nahla suggested," Ziva said quietly.

Garyd sighed. "And leave Scottsdale undefended?"

"Scottsdale is well defended, my lord," Ziva said. "We can leave a rear guard and advance with Primus Carro in a pincer movement."

"To force a *peaceful* resolution," Myel reminded.

"To bring about *utter annihilation*, Your Highness," Ziva replied.

Myel sipped at a glass of wine. It was now nearing sunset and about time to eat dinner, but Nahla would not think about food. Not while Myel grappled with the tenuous situation in Scottsdale Province. She figured the time had come to play their last card, the crucial piece of knowledge they had held close to their chest. She cleared her throat and prompted Myel by subtly and quietly introducing the topic.

"A peaceful resolution and a violent resolution will each have far-reaching effects in their own way," Nahla said. "We must think beyond Scottsdale Province."

In front of her, Myel nodded. He got the message, and it was now his turn to do the rest. "Garyd, do you still believe you are facing bandits?"

The question caught the old governor off guard. "Yes, of course! Who else?"

Standing next to Garyd, Captain Ziva narrowed her eyes again and looked back and forth at Nahla and Myel. Nahla knew her mind must be ticking. In fact, she'd probably come to the correct conclusion already.

Myel continued. "I have a strong testimonial from Daxton himself that they are not bandits. Garyd, you've been fighting a *rebellion* for a long time."

Garyd sat upright. "Impossible. Nobody rebels against the Kingdom of Launceston."

Myel raised his eyebrows. "What bandit clan could be so organised, armed, resourced, trained, and informed of your movements?"

"My lord, I'm inclined to believe the prince," Ziva said. "I've fought Daxton's forces. They don't fight like criminals. They fight like soldiers."

"But how have farmers and labourers turned themselves into soldiers?" Garyd asked. "It doesn't make any sense. And why would they rebel?"

"These are questions I'm still trying to answer," Myel told him. "But I suspect foul play."

"Foul play?"

"Like you've suspected, someone is feeding them information—vital information that has helped them become a force to be reckoned with. Now they control more than half your province and pose a real threat to you and the kingdom as a whole. Their fight could spread to the other provinces."

"All the more reason to crush them," Ziva said and as she planted a fist into her hand.

Myel shook his head. "If we crush them, it could have the opposite effect. It could be like throwing oil on a fire."

Garyd frowned and went into deep thought. But it did not last long. They heard heavy footsteps from the hallway before a

Scottsdale soldier thrust the sitting room door open. Following him was Ragh.

"Apologies for the intrusion, my lord," the soldier announced. "A legionary has arrived from Launceston with urgent news."

"What is it, Private Ragh?" Nahla asked. The man was sweaty and flushed red.

Ragh did a quick salute. "My apologies for disturbing your meal, Your Highness, my lord, Captain, Preceptor." He nodded at each person. "I have come from Launceston Prison. Governor Ibeza died last night after drinking poisoned wine. He had confiscated the wine from a delivery bound for the prisoner Daxton, and now Daxton wants to speak with the prince as quickly as possible."

"Someone tried to assassinate Daxton?" Garyd said and laughed. "Bastard deserves it! Shame about Ibeza, though."

"No, Garyd," Myel said. "Don't you see? Why would someone want to kill a rebel leader already in custody? Someone is tying up a loose end, and Daxton is ready to tell us everything." He faced Ragh. "Have you posted more legionaries?"

Ragh nodded. "The order went out to tighten security as I was leaving. I rode here immediately after being sent to notify you."

"You must be starving and thirsty," Myel said. "Here, have something to eat and drink."

Garyd's eyes went wide at the idea of a legionary pilfering his exquisite snacks and wine, but was powerless to defy the prince's offer. Ragh approached the table in halting steps until Myel waved at him to hurry.

"Lord Garyd," Myel said and stood. "I must leave for Launceston at once. What Daxton tells me may end your troubles here for good."

The words hung thick in the air. Garyd scratched his chin. "I don't know what to do now."

"Hold off on your attack and convince Carro to wait. I'll send a message as soon as I can with whatever information Daxton gives us." Then he turned to Ragh, who was stuffing his face with biscuits and washing them down with expensive wine. "You, legionary, when you've had your full, ride to Primus Carro and tell him everything that has happened just now. He *must* wait . . ." He paused and glanced at Nahla, thinking. "Somebody give me some paper. I'll write my order instead, and I'll have you co-sign it, Garyd."

Reluctantly, Garyd added his signature at the end of the brief message and gave it to Ragh.

"Deliver that to Primus Carro at Springfield," Myel said. "You would have passed through their camp to get here. Then return to Launceston and find me."

"It shall be done, Your Highness." Ragh swallowed the last of the snacks. Then he saluted and left.

As terrible as Ibeza's death sounded, the assassination attempt and Daxton's sudden willingness to talk was a breakthrough that Myel could not miss. Nahla couldn't wait to leave, even if it meant a long, tiring journey home.

"Lord Garyd," Myel began, "thank you for your hospitality. I plead with you to refrain from any attacks until you hear from me again. If Carro disobeys my order, he will answer to me. This is our best chance to avoid further bloodshed."

Garyd stood and clasped Myel's hand. "As you wish, Your Highness. I dearly hope you are right, and I hope you can reach Launceston before some other incident befalls Daxton. Or else his rebels here might be out for vengeance, and then I will have no choice but to spill blood again."

With that ominous warning, the prince and governor shook hands again, then Myel and Nahla darted out of the room. They had to ride to Launceston at a gallop. Every second counted.

21

A RIDE BY MOONLIGHT

The rhythmic dance of hooves underneath an ethereal glow—it has been, and always will be, the music of timeless grace.

—**Royal Stable Master**
In conversation with Prince Myel

Nahla followed Myel at breakneck speed through the camp of First Company. Legionaries stepped out of the way to let the charging horses pass in the quickly dimming evening light. Some didn't salute, because Myel was too fast or the evening was too dark for them to identify this hurtling madman. Nahla did her best to keep up, spurring Ajax with her heels.

After exiting the camp, when just the road to Launceston lay before them, Nahla firmly suggested that Myel allow two of their escorts to ride in front. It was still prudent to travel in the correct formation.

Myel agreed and ordered two legionaries to take point. "Ride like you've never ridden before. Don't let me overtake you."

Tullius and another sergeant named Garrus rode ahead, while the other two stayed behind. By this time, the evening sky had changed from pink to almost black. Stars pricked through the dark canvas of the cloudless heavens. Off to one side, a full moon illuminated the road enough for Nahla to easily see every bump. It meant that they could travel faster, but Nahla knew they would have to slow down eventually. It was over sixty kilometres to Launceston, and the horses couldn't gallop nonstop for that long.

She settled in for an arduous ride and considered herself lucky that they weren't doing it under a blazing sun.

SEVERAL HOURS INTO THE journey, after Myel had reluctantly slowed their pace, they emerged from a tight, winding portion of the road with trees on both sides. The field beyond opened up wide, its natural features discernible in the moonlight. She watched Tullius and Garrus bouncing and swaying with the movement of their horses. The road ahead was wide and curved gently to the right. Now that they had cleared the twisting trail, Nahla was about to suggest going for another sprint, but some movement in the trees ahead caught her attention.

Tullius and Garrus saw it a moment later and reared their horses to a sudden stop. Nahla and Myel did the same. Several riders emerged from the edge of a thickly forested area and cut in front of Myel's group. A sword glinted in the moonlight. Garrus growled an order to back down. More swords were drawn. In a matter of seconds, Nahla, Prince Myel, and their four escorts were outnumbered two-to-one and embroiled in a skirmish. Whoever these aggressors were—bandits, mercenaries, rebels—some split off from the fight with Tullius and Garrus and charged for Myel.

"Stay back, Your Highness!" Nahla shouted. "You and you," she said, pointing at the other two legionaries, "protect the prince!"

Nahla drew her new sword and grimaced at how unbalanced it felt in her grip. How she longed for her original weapon! She charged to meet the onrushing fighters and barred their approach to Myel. Swinging madly, she cut down one of the six enemies before they swiped at her. But she wasn't their target. Nahla spared a glance at Tullius and Garrus. They were surrounded and fighting for dear life, but Nahla couldn't help them. Her primary concern was Myel.

The two legionaries protecting Myel held their ground in front of the royal target, but were quickly encircled. Myel drew his blade, but being on horseback made him noticeably unsteady. As Nahla raced into the fray, she saw one legionary, Lemmi, pulled from his horse and trampled to death. Nahla swung heavily at the exposed neck of one attacker, killing him instantly.

Nahla shouted to draw attention to herself and swung at the next attacker. He blocked it, but at least it bought Myel some valuable seconds to re-position his horse. He jabbed at the man, but the attack was poorly aimed and the tip of his blade scraped off the hard, rounded edge of a leather tunic.

Through the sound of clashing metal, Nahla bellowed angrily at her student, "You have a sabre! Swing and chop! Don't stab!"

"Thanks!" Myel yelled. She could hear the strain in his voice. Maybe fear too. This was his first real skirmish, and Nahla knew he lacked confidence.

Myel slashed at the attacker between him and Nahla. His brute strength, hidden beneath shiny regal armour and a mild-mannered demeanour, forced the sabre through the attacker's shoulder. The man let out a guttural moan and swore. Myel had chopped off his left arm. It dangled alongside his horse as the fingers still clutched the rein. He still held a sword in the other hand, but with little control of his steed and the excruciating pain from exposed flesh, bone, and nerves, Nahla could quickly dispatch him with a sharp jab into the side of his torso.

At the same time, the other legionary in their midst, Ripli, screamed in horror as a blade found one of the small gaps in her segmented armour plates. The sword must have pierced through to her spine and lodged itself, because the attacker couldn't pull it out. As Ripli fell backwards off her horse, she dragged the man down with her. Their horses went skittish at the unexpected transfer of weight on their backs.

For a split second, Nahla debated taking the few steps over to finish the man while he tried to dislodge his blade, but a shout from behind caught her attention. Two remaining enemies were now within striking distance of Myel. The prince cut heavily across one man's face and chest, quickly ending his life. The last enemy battered Myel's sabre to the ground with a mace, then lifted the mace high to start another strike. Nahla was too far away to deflect the blow. The mace crashed into the side of Myel's helmet and he slipped off his horse. One foot stayed in the stirrup, and the horse gently dragged him a few paces away.

As the attacker admired his savage handiwork, revelling at being the one to defeat the prince, Nahla went into a blind rage and charged at him, yanking him out of his stirrups with an outstretched arm and dropping him to the grass below. Then she spun Ajax around and cut downwards towards the man's face, but he blocked it. The force of his mace against Nahla's pitiful sword momentarily jarred her arm and she couldn't raise it in time to defend against his attack. Knowing she was too late to react, she watched as the mace rose and came down at her hip. She was ready to endure the blow, trusting in her legionary armour. But maces were designed for destroying armour plating. She braced for the impact.

The man's eyes went wide and he stopped mid-swing, then dropped to the ground with an arrow in his back. Nahla breathed heavily and scanned her moonlit surroundings. A short distance away, at the bend in the road they had just travelled, Ragh was returning his bow to its saddle case and drawing his sword. Then he kicked his horse into action and charged to assist Tullius and Garrus.

Nahla jumped off Ajax and went to Myel's motionless body. The side of his helmet was still intact, but it had a nasty dent. Blood trickled down his cheek. She removed his foot from the stirrup and glanced over at the last stage of the skirmish. Garrus was on horseback, wrestling unarmed with the final enemy horseman, holding the attacker's sword up out of harm's way. Tullius, on foot, pushed his sword deep into the attacker's back before Ragh arrived.

Silence descended on the road just as suddenly as the fight had begun.

"Legionaries," Nahla called. "To me!" She gently removed Myel's helmet and gasped at the bloody, matted hair above his ear. "Garrus, water and bandages. Tullius, check on Lemmi and Ripli."

"What can I do?" Ragh asked.

"Get your bow and keep watch. There may be more coming. While you're at it, round up all the horses. We'll bring them with us." Nahla cradled Myel's head in her hands. *Please be alive*, she thought. *Please*. Thankfully, he was breathing. At this moment, Nahla cared about Myel the person more than Myel the prince. He had proved to be a wonderful student and an endearing friend. She just wanted him to be alive.

"Preceptor," Tullius said. "Lemmi and Ripli are dead."

Her heart sank. She hadn't lost soldiers since before she was exiled from Melbourne. Though losing Lemmi and Ripli paled compared to the deaths she had witnessed back home, their sacrifice still hurt. "Strap them to their horses. We'll take them to Launceston."

Garrus poured water on Myel's wound, the last drops from his canteen. He parted hair and searched for the source of the blood, dabbed the area with bandages, then wrapped Myel's head. There wasn't anything Nahla could do, so while the legionaries fulfilled their tasks, she inspected the lifeless attackers.

As she studied all twelve dead bodies, it was difficult to ascertain who they were. They wore mix-matched armour, some of it inadequate, and none had any markings to signify allegiances. As far as she knew, they could have been Daxton's rebels patrolling the

Scottsdale–Launceston border. Or perhaps they were a bandit clan separate from Daxton's followers, or even a roving mercenary band, which presented its own worrying questions. She knew criminals often lurked along major roads to prey on unprotected travellers, but to attack the King's Legion was ludicrous. No, something about this situation put Nahla on edge.

"His Highness is bandaged," Garrus said. "But we should get him proper medical attention as soon as possible."

"Agreed," Nahla said. Ideally, she would have constructed a litter to carry Myel home, but they didn't have time for that. "Tether his horse to mine." They would have to ride slower, but at least she could bring Myel and the dead legionaries home.

When everyone was ready, Nahla gazed down the country road. The starry sky met the tops of grey, moonlit trees in the distance. She knew there were more sections of road that bordered a forest or cut right through another. They weren't just copses of trees either, but full wooded areas that stretched for several kilometres. Though they were out of Scottsdale Province, she was now more wary of being attacked again.

"Tullius and Garrus," she said, "who of you has the best eyes?"

The legionaries grinned at each other as if they knew the answer, but it was Tullius who spoke. "Mine are as sharp as any eagle's."

"Excellent. You'll take point. Garrus will follow a few paces behind, leading the horses carrying Lemmi and Ripli. I'll take the middle with Prince Myel and the riderless horses, and Ragh will bring up the rear." She faced Ragh. "Stay back, but within earshot. You have a good aim with that bow. It might come in handy again if we run into more trouble."

"Will do, Preceptor," Ragh said.

"Let's move out!"

Leaving the dead attackers sprawled on the road and in the field, Nahla and her smaller team continued their journey to

179

Launceston, though at a painfully slower pace. She wondered how King Eero would react to his wounded son—whether she and the surviving legionaries would be rewarded for keeping him alive, or severely reprimanded for letting him come close to death.

Nahla had seen countless head wounds before, and most did not end well. Her stomach churned at the thought of Myel dying. She prayed that he'd regain consciousness before they arrived in Launceston, and that there would be no lasting side effects. It would be such a horrible twist of fate for the prince's life to be cut short after his first skirmish.

Whether or not he woke, Nahla would speak to Daxton alone. There was no way Myel would be in any condition to interrogate the rebel if he were conscious, so now it was all up to Nahla. What Daxton had to say would determine the fate of Scottsdale Province, and maybe even the fate of the kingdom.

22

DOORS AND ROADBLOCKS

Opportunities emerge like gleaming jewels. Yet, behind the shimmering facade, hidden obstacles await. It is in the delicate dance between opportunities and setbacks that we find the true essence of growth and progress, for it is through overcoming these hurdles that our triumphs become all the more rewarding.

—**Nahla Northborn**
Monologues

N\ahla marched through the halls of Launceston Palace. She didn't much care about the noise her sandals made on the stone floor, or the clanking and squeaking of her armour. The first legionary she saw received a curt order to fetch the king for a meeting in the throne room.

"But, Preceptor," the legionary had said, "it is the middle of the night. The king is asleep."

"Then wake him!" Nahla had bellowed, her voice echoing inside the palace foyer.

She didn't know how the sovereign would feel about being woken to meet a mere preceptor, even one as popular as Nahla, but at this point, she didn't care. Eero had to know about his son, the rebellion, and the threats from the shadows of the kingdom.

Myel, still unconscious, had been placed under the care of the Guardians at the Royal Infirmary, which Nahla was none too happy about. She'd left Ragh, Tullius, and Garrus to guard the prince until she returned. As soon as he had received full medical attention, she'd have him moved to his own residence for ongoing care and recuperation. She didn't trust the Guardians. The sooner Myel was out of their hands, the better.

Alone in the dark throne room, Nahla paced slowly at a respectable distance from the empty dais. Two legionaries patrolled on night watch, but they paid the preceptor no heed once they determined her identity. While Nahla was deep in thought, she heard one of the heavy doors open.

"Preceptor!" A woman's voice. "What is the meaning of this?"

She looked up to see Chamberlain Hayla in a dark-green cloak, though without her usual hood. Her hair was perfectly combed and silky smooth. *Does this woman never sleep?* Nahla wondered. She carried a lamp, which lit up her intense, glowering eyes.

"Chamberlain, I must speak urgently with the king," Nahla said.

"He is on his way. What news do you have that you must rouse him during the darkest and quietest part of the night?"

"It concerns Myel and Scottsdale."

Hayla's eyes widened for half a second and her mouth opened as if to speak, but she quickly shut it. Nahla's statement hung in the air, echoing in the voluminous chamber.

"Then the king *must* hear." She lit a nearby brazier with her lamp.

Moments later, King Eero arrived with four guards in tow. He wore a thin red robe and his normally unruly hair was even more tousled. He rubbed an eye. "What is it, Nahla?" He yawned as he sat on his throne, while his escort fanned out behind him.

Nahla bowed. "Your Majesty, I bring grave news. The worst is that we were ambushed on our ride home from Scottsdale, and your son suffered a head wound."

All sleep disappeared from Eero's wrinkly face. "Is he okay? What happened?" The legionaries behind him broke their statue-like appearance and shared furtive glances.

"He's unconscious and with the Guardians now. They assure me he will be fine. We were rushing back to Launceston because we received word that Daxton wanted to speak with Myel. Partway into our journey, an unidentified group attacked us on the road. They outnumbered us two-to-one."

"What do you mean 'unidentified group'?" Hayla asked with just a hint of derision in her voice.

"They did not announce themselves and made no attempt to converse with us. Instead, they shot out from a nearby forest and attacked. They wore no insignia that might indicate a clan or group. They fought to the death, so there are none alive for questioning. Two legionaries were killed, but we brought their bodies back, along with their horses, and the attackers' horses."

"And how did Myel receive his wound?" Eero asked.

"A mace to the head."

Eero propped an elbow on an armrest and scratched his chin. "This is most distressing. Most distressing. To add insult to literal injury, your journey home was also a waste of time."

Nahla's heart skipped a few beats, and she had to force herself to breathe again. "Your Majesty?"

Eero sighed, as if he hated being involved in such a hot mess. "Daxton was attacked in his cell. Yesterday, well after sundown, one of the prison's gong farmers arrived to empty Daxton's chamber pot. The legionaries on duty heard a scuffle in the cell and discovered Daxton in a pool of blood, his throat badly cut. The legionaries fought with the gong farmer and took him into custody, but I am not sure what has happened since then."

"And what of Daxton? Is he alive?"

Eero waved a dismissive hand. "They brought him to the palace and the Guardians inspected him. But it was late in the night, and I went to bed. He's probably dead now."

Again, Nahla had to control her breathing to think straight. While Nahla grappled with the fallout of losing the primary lead in her investigation, Hayla spoke in a quiet, measured voice. "A shame Daxton did not speak to us earlier."

Nahla squared her jaw and studied the chamberlain's unreadable face. "I will visit Daxton," Nahla said. "He had something to tell Myel."

"You are wasting your time," Eero said. "Even if he hasn't died yet, the man's probably unconscious, like my son." He paused. "Of course, I won't stop you. I need an update as much as you do. But I am sure it will be fruitless."

"Still, I will go as soon as I am dismissed from this meeting." Nahla felt like the situation was slipping from her fingers. She was glad Myel couldn't be here. "Where is the gong farmer in custody?"

Eero raised his eyebrows and turned to Hayla.

"In Launceston Prison," the chamberlain replied. "In general population, I believe. No more room in isolation."

Nahla frowned. "I would like to speak with him as soon as possible. I'd like him moved to the palace dungeon."

Eero shrugged. "I guess that can be arranged. Hayla, organise for the prisoner to be transported here."

"As you wish, Your Majesty. We have a new group of low-security inmates coming here for labour duties tomorrow. I'll add him to the passenger list."

"Now to another matter," Eero said. He leaned forwards on his throne. "While I am greatly alarmed over the attack on my son, I think you performed admirably—outnumbered two-to-one, the victim of an ambush, and still victorious. I am creating a personal guard retinue for my son and promoting you to lieutenant to lead it. Select eight legionaries whom you feel are most suited to the task."

"A wise decision, Your Majesty, and I am most grateful," Nahla said. "Might I suggest you have your own personal guard as well? These are dangerous times."

"The entire Legion is the king's personal guard," Chamberlain Hayla said. "He does not need a guard within a guard."

"Hayla is right," Eero said with a nod. "I have thousands of guards already. Although those guards also protect my son, I see the benefits of him having a dedicated subgroup with him at all times, since he will now travel throughout the kingdom. Hayla, get the necessary paperwork in order by midday tomorrow."

Hayla cleared her throat. "Midday tomorrow, Your Majesty, or midday *today*?"

"Goodness, is it morning?"

"It is."

"Well, by midday *today*, then, Nahla will be adjusted on the roster. No more official training responsibilities for the Legion as a whole, since she will no longer be a preceptor, though Myel may allow her some ad hoc training opportunities. Despite her small command, she will have the same seniority as the other lieutenants. And organise for a new helmet, cuirass, and sword befitting her new rank."

"It shall be done, Your Majesty."

Hayla gave Nahla a deep stare, her eyes bright under the flames of the nearby brazier. This woman was so powerful, yet so quiet. When she spoke, she used honeyed words and impressive powers of perception. Nahla couldn't be sure whether she had an ally or an enemy in the chamberlain. Time would tell.

"What news do you bring me from Scottsdale?" Eero asked, changing topics.

Nahla took a deep breath to deliver the damaging news. "His Highness and I believe Scottsdale is facing a growing rebellion in what is misunderstood as a large bandit clan."

"A rebellion?" Eero and Hayla asked simultaneously.

"Yes. Daxton hinted as much during our first visit with him. But when we pressed him, he refused to speak. We raced back to Launceston as soon as we heard he was willing to talk."

"None of my investigators were told that," Eero said.

"Did Daxton say anything at all to your investigators?"

"Well . . . no."

"Your Majesty, something terrible is brewing in Scottsdale." Nahla needed to get this point across as delicately as possible. "For so long, Lord Garyd believed he had an uncontrollable bandit clan on the loose, but there is mounting evidence to suggest that Daxton's people are more of an 'army' than a 'clan'. They are too well organised and equipped, and they have been successful in fighting back Scottsdale's forces. *Too* successful."

Eero furrowed his brow. "I don't take your meaning, Nahla."

Of course you don't. "There is no way a group of civilians could be so successful without help. Prince Myel and I believe Daxton was just a proxy leader. Someone else is behind the troubles in Scottsdale."

The king leaned back and scratched his chin again. "What do you make of this assertion, Hayla?"

"An interesting theory," Hayla said softly. Her voice barely echoed in the empty room. "But it is completely unsubstantiated. How have the so-called rebels behaved since Daxton's capture?"

"No significant gains, but they have avoided major conflict with the Scottsdale Garrison." At that, Nahla remembered an enlightening point. "However, that could be because of Garyd recently concentrating his forces around the capital city, giving relative freedom of movement to the rebels throughout the province."

"Coward," Hayla spat.

"The fool will bring his defeat upon himself if he does that," Eero growled.

"Nevertheless, Your Majesty," Hayla said, "the fact that Daxton's clan has evaded Scottsdale troops since their leader's capture does not suggest that they are receiving information from an outside source. Rather, they are simply taking advantage of the lack of opposition. A flock of sheep will roam freely wherever there are no fences or foxes."

Eero grunted and rubbed his eyes. "Then it's good that we have a company of the Legion in the province. Nahla, did you have time to speak to Primus Carro?"

"We did," Nahla said. Now she was stepping as lightly as possible, because Hayla had put a big dent in her argument.

"And what did he say?" Hayla asked slowly.

"He agrees with the rebellion theory. He wants to target what he thinks is the rebel headquarters."

"With Garyd's support?"

"Yes," Nahla said. Before Eero or Hayla could reply, she added, "But Prince Myel was advocating a different approach. A peaceful resolution."

Immediately, Eero shook his head. "We are past that now. They attacked my son in cold blood. There can be no peaceful resolution now."

Nahla felt Myel's goal slipping away with every word. "Your Majesty, with all due respect, we don't know if it was Daxton's people who attacked us."

"Who else?" Hayla barked. "Where did this attack happen?"

"On the Scottsdale–Launceston border."

Hayla scoffed. "Then you were attacked by Daxton's border force, which suggests that they are in charge of their own reconnaissance and strategic intelligence."

Nahla did not know how to counter that argument, because with Daxton incapacitated, she had no testimony with which to fire back. *Why is Hayla arguing so aggressively?*

"Your Majesty, the evidence speaks for itself," Hayla continued. "This clan has grown too troublesome and needs to be crushed."

Eero dropped a fist on his throne's wide armrest. "Yes, I agree.

Draft a letter for Lord Garyd and Primus Carro. Tell them I am sending another company of the King's Legion. When the new company arrives, Garyd will relinquish command of his provincial troops to Carro, and the combined forces will march against Daxton's rebels, or clan members, or whatever they are. There will be no mercy, no parley, no peaceful resolution."

Nahla swallowed hard. She felt dead inside, and Myel would feel even worse.

"Excellent, Your Majesty!" Hayla exclaimed. "Before year's end, this rabble will no longer exist, and Scottsdale will have reclaimed its territory."

"Indeed. And then we can focus more fully on matters in the south. Nahla, will you allow me to return to my bed before sunrise, or do you have more to report?"

Eero and Hayla watched her. The king had bags under glossy eyes, and the chamberlain looked wiry and ready to pounce.

"Nothing more, Your Majesty. If I am dismissed, I will visit Daxton. Where may I find him?"

"In the Royal Infirmary," Eero replied. "Odds are, you may have walked right past his room when you took Myel to the Guardians."

That was probably true, though the information was as unhelpful as Daxton's assassination attempt. She bowed and thanked Eero for granting her an audience, then promptly left, defeated and gutted.

She took a different route back to the Royal Infirmary, choosing quiet passages through the palace. Windows were left open to take advantage of nightly breezes, cooling the palace before the sun reheated it again the next day, a never-ending cycle. She welcomed the cool air. It helped clear her mind.

As she walked along a top-floor hallway that overlooked one of the palace courtyards, she saw movement in the garden below. A cloaked figure with a black hood scurried along the pebbled pathways, crossing the courtyard. She could have been mistaken, but it looked like Chamberlain Hayla's green cloak. The best chamberlains fulfilled their duties quickly and quietly. Perhaps Hayla was rushing to Launceston Prison to prepare the assassin's transport to the palace, or going to the barracks to organise Nahla's new equipment.

Hayla's performance in the throne room puzzled Nahla. She certainly felt comfortable offering her unbidden opinions, and she displayed marvellous insight on political and military matters. But she had squashed Nahla's attempt to work towards a peaceful resolution in Scottsdale. More death and destruction awaited the province, and Nahla felt partly responsible for failing to prevent it, thanks to Hayla.

At the Royal Infirmary, the Guardians on the night shift were surprised to see Nahla again. When she requested to visit Daxton, they were doubly surprised.

"He is in no condition for visitors," one of the priestesses said. She was a plain young woman, but her bright blue eyes were a defining feature.

"Is he conscious?" Nahla asked.

"No."

Nahla bit her lip. "I'd like to see him. Please lead the way."

Young and alone with the tall, armed, bloodstained preceptor, the priestess quickly acquiesced and beckoned Nahla to follow. She led Nahla to a room near to Myel's, in a hallway teaming with legionaries and Divine Guards. The tension between the warriors was apparent by the way they ignored each other on either side of an imaginary line. The legionaries stomped to attention when they saw the preceptor.

Inside Daxton's room, Nahla understood the full import of the rebel leader's situation. He had a thick set of bloodstained bandages around his neck. His pallid face made him look like he had knocked on death's door already. Next to his bed was

189

a bucket filled with bloody cloths. A Divine Guard stood at a nearby window and watched Nahla with a scowl.

Another Guardian washed her hands at a basin near the bed. "He had his throat cut," the priestess said once she'd dried her hands. "Lost a lot of blood."

"He's alive?" Nahla asked.

"Barely."

"Will he survive?" As soon as she asked it, she feared the worst.

"I cannot say."

Nahla frowned. "Please notify me if he wakes. I must speak with him immediately." She went for the door.

"He should not have visitors until his wounds are sufficiently healed," the priestess said.

Nahla gave both Guardians a long, hard glare. "You *will* inform me when he wakes, and he *will* speak to me."

"Care to rephrase that command, Preceptor?" the Divine Guard asked. She stepped forwards, hands on her hips.

"No, I don't," Nahla replied. "This is *my* prisoner, not yours."

"As a medical patient, the prisoner is now under the protection of the Guardians. Therefore, you will accord the priestesses every civility that their righteous position deserves."

Nahla stepped closer to the challenger. She stood taller than the Divine Guard, but that didn't bother the other woman at all. They were two warriors facing off, arguing over a man who could be dead in the next few hours.

"Don't speak to me about civility. Or would you rather see the scars on my back?"

"Those scarred by God have received the most sublime discipline."

Nahla's lips curled. "God did not scar me. A mere woman scarred me."

"Matriarch Anurak is no mere woman!" the Divine Guard barked. Her hard grey eyes stared at Nahla. "She is the kingdom's spiritual leader, appointed by God Herself."

Without breaking the staring contest, Nahla repeated her command to the priestess with more force. "Inform me immediately if Daxton's condition changes, for better or for worse. If you fail to do this, I will mete out discipline myself, God and God-appointed women be damned."

The Divine Guard squinted and winced but did not respond to the challenge. Sensing that she had won, Nahla left the priestesses and their stubborn guard. Outside, she ordered the strongest legionary to stand in Daxton's room, just to level the playing field. Then she went to Myel's room.

They had sequestered Myel at the other end of the narrow building, in the same L-shaped hallway. Ragh stood outside. Nahla paused before entering the room.

"Preceptor?" Ragh asked upon seeing Nahla's tight lips.

"Not good, Ragh," she said without looking at him. "Not good." Then she stepped inside.

Tullius and Garrus stood when she entered.

"How is he?" she asked.

"The priestess said he's stable," Garrus said. "Whatever that means. He's no different from when we loaded him on his horse and brought him here."

Nahla gazed at the young prince, his head bandaged, a peaceful expression on his lips. At least he didn't look pale and half-dead, like Daxton.

She sighed deeply and felt the weight of fatigue finally set in. A prince knocked unconscious, a rebel leader lying on his deathbed, two legionaries lost to the sword, a province about to erupt in all-out war, and an insidious influence behind it all. How had she ever become entangled in such a web?

She called Ragh into the room. When all three legionaries gave her their attention, she delivered the disastrous information. "Daxton is fighting for his life down the hallway. An assassin attacked him earlier tonight."

The soldiers parted their lips and sucked in breaths of shock.

"King Eero has approved an attack on Daxton's rebels in Scottsdale," she continued. "There will be no peace."

"What of Prince Myel's plans?" Ragh asked.

Nahla shook her head. "No peace." She paused. "Look, I'm certain you can see that something isn't right here. A rebellion. Assassinations. Ambushes. There is something happening behind the scenes, and we're caught up in the middle of it."

"Pawns in a king's game," Tullius said, rather poetically.

But again, Nahla shook her head. "King Eero is not the major player here. He thinks he is. But there is someone else pulling the strings."

"Sedition?" Garrus asked. She could see righteous indignation boiling within him.

"Perhaps," she said. "Who knows the purpose? But the kingdom has changed, even in the short time I've . . . been among you." She caught herself just in time, for she was about to say, *even in the short time I've been in Launceston.* "The king has instituted a new permanent personal guard for Prince Myel, with me as the lieutenant commanding. I'd like you three on my team."

They straightened their tired backs. Though their body language gave the appearance of weariness after a long day—Ragh must have been awake over twenty-four hours—their eyes were aglow with zeal.

"You have my heart and my sword arm, Lieutenant," Tullius said passionately.

Nahla stifled a grin. "Thank you, Tullius. My promotion hasn't been formalised yet, but thank you for your support."

The others echoed Tullius' remark.

"I know you three must be exhausted. I'll send replacements when I get to the barracks. In the meantime, keep watch over the prince."

There was nothing more she could do. So, after a final sad glance at Myel, she finally gave her head a pillow to sleep on.

She knew, however, that in organising replacements for Tullius, Garrus, and Ragh, she'd have to explain to the barracks what had happened to Prince Myel. In doing so, sleep would not come as soon as she wanted, but when it did, it would be a welcome reprieve from a horrible day, and a necessity to handle the long day ahead.

23

ALONE IN THE SNAKE PIT

Woe to the one who fights for truth. Your battle is difficult, and your enemies are numerous. Take courage, however, for your struggle is righteous.

—Cass the Blasphemer
The Truth

T HE NEXT MORNING, BLEARY-EYED after a fitful sleep, Nahla stood in front of eight hand-picked legionaries—Privates Brande, Jaymen, Marston, and Sheph; the twin corporals, Ragh and Rhos; and the mature sergeants, Garrus and Tullius. These chosen few were Prince Myel's personal guard detachment. Nahla studied their tanned faces and well-kept armour. She had trained all of them during her short tenure as preceptor, and they had stood out from the rest, both in skill and in their ability to obey a command promptly and loyally.

"I have chosen you for a special assignment," Nahla said. She paced up and down the line. "King Eero, in his far-sighted wisdom, has allowed for a select group of legionaries to protect his son, the prince. You eight legionaries have the honour and privilege of this permanent assignment, and I am now your lieutenant. Above me, there is only the prince."

She stopped to let that sink in. No longer would they be subordinated to a platoon lieutenant or a company primus. Now they answered to Nahla.

"You may have heard that the prince was attacked on his journey home from Scottsdale, and that he sustained a head injury." The briefest murmur swept through the line of soldiers. "Your comrades, Lemmi and Ripli, died defending their royal charge. They fought valiantly against a larger enemy force. Our goal as Protectors is to ensure that no weapon—no arrow, no hand, no poison, and no devious plan—touches Prince Myel. From now on, we will live at the prince's home, and we follow him wherever he goes. He is the future of this kingdom, which makes him a high-value target for our enemies. His very life depends on our vigilance."

She took her position in front of the assembled group again, eyeing each legionary one at a time. They were a mixed bunch, drawn from the companies still in Launceston. She selected her team quickly, before the next company left for Scottsdale. There was one legionary she'd wanted from First Company, but it would have taken too long to send for him.

"Rhos, Brande, and Jaymen, there are legionaries guarding Prince Myel's room at the Royal Infirmary. Relieve them of their duties and stay there until further notice."

The three privates stomped to attention and marched off. Nahla watched them. They walked in a line, feet moving in perfect unison despite their varying heights. Jaymen, the older fellow who had patched up Nahla after she'd returned from her whipping, led the trio. Since they first met, Nahla appreciated Jaymen's wisdom in the ways of the Legion and the kingdom in general. Though he was the oldest private in the Legion, he was still strong, quick with a blade, and sharp of mind. The younger legionaries looked up to him as a father figure and mentor, but the officers did not respect him because of some "stupid stuff" he'd done while training as a medic. That didn't stop her from recruiting him, though.

"The rest of you, grab your possessions and transfer them to Prince Myel's home. His servants will get you settled in."

Those legionaries marched off in a different direction, leaving Nahla alone at the barracks. Now she had an assassin to interrogate, and he was expected to arrive at any moment.

✕

Nahla waited in the shade in front of Launceston Palace. She wanted to oversee the transfer of the assassin from the prison carriage to the dungeon the moment he arrived.

A team of brown horses pulled the carriage across the wooden drawbridge. Chamberlain Hayla emerged from the palace, but Nahla stepped out from the shade to stop the carriage driver. She held up a hand, deliberately presenting an imposing figure with her King's Legion uniform and menacing face. The driver stopped. Out of the corner of her eye, she saw Hayla quicken her pace, but she was still out of earshot.

"Nahla?" the driver asked.

It took a moment, but then a genuine smile crept across her lips. "Deeno?"

"Look at you, all fancy in your armour," Deeno said. "Last time I saw you, you were minding my cart while I inquired about lodgings."

"Yes, a lot has happened since then."

"I'll say." He leaned down and whispered, "These are difficult times. You've done well to be where you are now."

By this time, Hayla had arrived at the carriage. "Lieutenant Nahla, what is the meaning of this?"

"I am here to escort my prisoner to the dungeon," Nahla replied sternly.

But Hayla wasn't so easily intimidated. "Hardly a task for an officer. But we're all here now, so let's get this over with."

Nahla looked up at Deeno again. "You have a prisoner who is not here for labour. He is to come with me."

"Of course," Deeno replied. He jumped out of his seat and jingled a keyring as he went to the rear of the carriage.

"How come you're driving for the prison?" Nahla asked him as he picked the right key.

"Plying a merchant cart on the roads between provinces was getting too dangerous and less profitable. I work for the prison now, moving supplies and inmates."

As soon as the key clicked, the door burst open and a man filled with animalistic rage burst out, growling like a dog. His hands were chained together, but he held a makeshift knife. The first person he saw was Nahla, since the swinging door had battered Deeno away. Hayla stepped deftly to one side, out of view.

Nahla drew her sword as the man lunged for her. He must not have had any military training, nor any experience with swordsmanship, because he left himself open and Nahla sliced at his hand. She sidestepped as he growled in pain. When he spun around, he was foaming at the mouth and mumbling gibberish like a man possessed.

"Stand down," Nahla ordered.

He took a tentative step forward, flaring his nostrils, pointing this knife at her.

"I said stand down!"

Hayla advanced slowly with a dagger, while legionaries ran from the palace entrance to assist.

Nahla's words weren't registering—that much was clear. As he breathed heavily and inched closer, Nahla noticed he had blood all over his hands, up his arms, and all over his chest. She risked a glance at the open prison carriage, fearing the worst.

The prisoner pounced again before she got a good look inside. This time, she sidestepped and shouldered him off his feet. He tumbled onto the stone drive and legionaries rushed to contain him, but he was on his feet before they arrived, swinging madly with the knife.

"Kill him!" Hayla shouted.

Sometimes, warriors needed to hear nothing more. They converged on the raging animal, deflected his blows, and ran him through with their swords. He went down with a guttural scream. Nahla wiped a crimson stain from her blade and slid it back into its scabbard. Then she inspected the prison carriage, and her worst fears were realised.

Every prisoner lay slumped in their seats, still chained to the hooks on the floor. The whole scene was a bloody mess, in some ways more gruesome than even the worst battle. Throats were cut, chests punctured, bellies slit open, and the carriage floor was slick with everything that had poured out. Nahla checked the palace driveway and saw for the first time the red footprints that the insane prisoner had tracked all over the stonework.

She faced Hayla and spoke through her teeth. "This was supposed to be a low-risk carriage. How did that *thing* get on board?" Before Hayla could respond, she searched for Deeno, spotting him standing at a safe distance. "And you! How could you not hear the murders of—" she checked again "—*five* inmates?"

"It's loud when driving two horses and a wooden-wheeled carriage through cobblestone streets," Deeno replied, but he sounded dejected, as if it was his fault. "And prisoners are always shouting like idiots."

Nahla couldn't blame him, though. A maniacal prisoner had been added to a low-risk transport—no mere driver could be responsible for that. She eyed Hayla again. Was it too much of a coincidence that the gong farmer had been slaughtered along with the other prisoners?

"I will investigate this at once," Hayla said, regaining her composure and raising her chin. She frowned, tightening the silky white skin around her mouth. She pointed at the nearby legionaries. "You, throw that prisoner into the carriage." Then, to Deeno, "And you, take these bodies back to the prison and bring six new ones."

"Six new bodies?" Deeno asked.

"Six *live prisoners*, you halfwit!" Hayla looked up at Nahla, her eyes just visible under her yellow cowl. "If you will excuse me, Nahla, I have much work to do."

Hayla stormed off before Nahla could respond. She felt like yelling at Hayla's back, but that would have been inappropriate. She remembered her courtly manners despite recent setbacks.

"You had an important prisoner in here?" Deeno asked. He locked the carriage as the legionaries loaded the bloody body of the murderer inside.

"Yes," she replied. "An assassin who was a critical lead in a very serious investigation."

Deeno nodded. "I see. I'm—"

The rattle of wooden wheels on wooden logs shifted their attention to the drawbridge. A team of black horses emerged, pulling an ornate black carriage. Nahla had seen that carriage many times already.

Johl.

The wicked man stepped out alone and surveyed the blood-stained stonework. His eyes drifted to the legionaries, their armour stained red after they'd hauled the insane prisoner back to the prison carriage. Then he rested his gaze on Nahla.

"Lord Johl," Nahla said, bowing to the absolute minimum required to publicly respect his lofty station.

"Preceptor," he replied before turning towards the palace.

"It's Lieutenant now," Nahla corrected.

Johl paused and faced her, his expression unreadable. "*Lieutenant* Nahla. An officer now? Well then, if the king has left you in charge of receiving his guests, then you have failed abysmally. I am not accustomed to seeing his palace sullied with blood, his front doors unguarded, and nobody saluting me upon arrival."

Nahla bit her tongue. She had many retorts, but none were polite. "You must not keep the king waiting, my lord."

He smiled, perhaps aware that he had failed to draw her into an argument. "Indeed." Then he swooshed his thin black cape and trudged into the palace.

Deeno raised his eyebrows and mounted the driver's seat. He waved goodbye before lightly goading his horses into movement. As he left the driveway, fresh legionaries entered the scene to replace the ones who had helped Nahla subdue the recalcitrant criminal. A cleaner also arrived with a mop and a large bucket. Hayla was already responding to the morning's problems, but Nahla couldn't believe that she had run off so quickly just to organise replacement legionaries and a cleaner.

I‍T SEEMED LIKE ALL Johl did lately was respond to problems. He had been in damage control for far too long, and he was growing impatient.

News had arrived about the attack on Myel, but not through the channel he had originally set up. No, his contact in Launceston Palace had informed him of the situation, rather than the leader of the mercenary gang he'd contracted to ambush the prince. The palace contact said that all the mercenaries were dead, and that the prince had suffered a head wound.

Good, he had thought. On the one hand, he needn't worry about a loose end from the mercenaries—he had planned on having them all killed anyway, since they were technically criminals in his home province. But on the other hand, their mission had failed. Myel still lived. Nahla had escaped without a scratch and had been promoted too! And to make matters worse, Myel now had his very own personal guard, with Nahla in charge. His two most troublesome enemies were now even more closely intertwined.

Some news that certainly warmed his heart was the assassination of Daxton, along with the elimination of the man's killer. He knew

Daxton still lived, but his wounds were so severe that there was no way he could recover. He'd be dead in a matter of days, if not hours.

He held a tight grip on his plan, but it was a constant struggle to prevent it from loosening. If he didn't act soon, he feared the seams of his machinations would unravel and he'd be exposed. Many people would die if that happened. But he was willing to kill many more to ensure it didn't.

Legionaries at the door of King Eero's office opened the door, allowing him to enter without even breaking stride. It felt good to have such authority.

"Johl," Eero said without looking up from his desk. He had his head buried in some correspondence. "Johl, what has become of this kingdom?" He stamped his signet ring in some wax and regarded the governor standing before him.

Johl sat in a chair opposite the king. "These are not times for weak men, Your Majesty." The words carried a subtle hint, but Eero would not understand. *And yet, it is weak men who create times like this*, he thought wryly. "How is your son?"

"He is recovering, and you're absolutely right about weak men. Garyd has been a weak influence in Scottsdale, and look at the state of his domain now." He paused. "My son believes Garyd is facing a *rebellion*."

"Rebellion, Your Majesty?" Johl squinted at the word. "Nobody rebels against the kingdom."

"There is a convincing argument for it, and Garyd's weak-willed governorship hasn't helped." Eero leaned back and sighed, then rubbed his eyes. "I'm dispatching another company of the King's Legion to help pacify the rebels."

Johl had to consider his words. Eero was playing his game perfectly, though unwittingly. "Are you sure that's wise, Your Majesty?"

"What do you mean?"

"The King's Legion is an elite force, hardly necessary to quell a bunch of peasants."

Eero chuckled like a tutor. "I forget you are not involved in all the discussions. The rebels are incredibly organised, so I'm told, and armed to the teeth. I deem it necessary to end them with overwhelming force, quickly and efficiently."

Johl smiled warmly. "Nobody doubts the efficiency of the King's Legion. It's just that by moving a second company, you also send that much more of your personal protective force away from you. Surely Garyd's troops and the company you already have in the province are enough."

"Garyd's troops are beleaguered and demoralised, and I don't think they have faith in him as a leader anymore. When the next company arrives, I'm putting it and Garyd's troops under the command of Primus Carro, who will lead an all-out assault on the rebels, crushing them once and for all."

"A sound idea. Carro is an excellent officer." The duty should have gone to Captain Vox, but everyone knew the man preferred the comforts of Launceston to the necessities of the battlefield. A waste of a man.

Eero nodded in agreement, happy that Johl agreed with his decision.

"But the situation at home—here, in Launceston. You will have fewer legionaries here." *Trap set.*

"I'm not bothered. If the rebellion spreads to Launceston— which I highly doubt—half the Legion can defend the palace well enough. Plus, we have the entire Launceston Garrison and a very capable governor to lead them." He gestured at Johl.

And trapped, Johl thought with an inward smile. *Easier than expected.* "Your confidence in me and my army is much appreciated, Your Majesty. We will defend you to the last man if need be."

"It will never come to that. But knowing that I have a loyal, capable governor by my side helps me to sleep better at night."

Johl smiled. *Trapped, indeed.*

24

KNOW THY ENEMY

In the gallery of trust hang portraits of duplicity. Only the discerning eye unveils their artistry.

—Unknown
Tasmanian proverb

Nahla had much on her mind. Her investigation had come to a standstill, Myel was still unconscious, there was suspicious activity within the palace, and now war was on the horizon.

She leaned against the palace wall overlooking the temple courtyard, watching Second Company undergo the Litany of Water. The whole unit, including their cavalry detachment, was arrayed in perfect lines. From her vantage point, a breeze tempered the warm afternoon sun. It would be hotter down in the courtyard, with a day's worth of stored heat slowly being released from the pavers.

When the water carriages started going into the temple, she licked her lips, suddenly thirsty, sympathising with the legionaries and their horses standing at parade rest. Guardian acolytes passed through the ranks, offering sips from water pouches. Nahla couldn't remember that happening when Primus Carro had First Company formed up for their rite. Maybe it was each primus' prerogative to allow their troops to partake of water while waiting for their carriages to be filled. Perhaps Primus Marcle of Second Company was more lenient.

Questions about water still gnawed at Nahla every day. Lately, those questions seemed paltry compared to the larger issues affecting the kingdom, but it was still a logical problem that she could not fathom. How was Launceston so well supplied with water? Why were the Guardians the only ones allowed to source and distribute it? Why did they need to convene with God to request water *every single time*? Who was this God who supposedly provided an endless supply of water that nobody else could access? Why did the Guardians feel the need to protect the temples day and night with security details of Divine Guards? The questions puzzled her, but she couldn't devote enough time to find the answers. There were bigger problems to deal with, and, deep down, her conscience told her it would be dangerous to investigate.

She rested a hand on the pommel of her preceptor's sword, frowning at its unfamiliar shape. King Eero had guaranteed her a new sword and armour to go along with her promotion to lieutenant, but what she really wanted was *her* sword, the one she brought from Melbourne. Johl had it, or at least she hoped he still had it. If he'd smelted it to make something else, there would be hell to pay. She wouldn't put it past him to do something so spiteful. Not wanting to think of the worst-case scenario, Nahla instead imagined Johl mounting the sword to a wall and laughing at her every time he saw it. That way, at least she had a chance of recovering it.

The first water carriage exited the temple, wet and dripping, and another entered. Like last time, a Guardian led the donkeys into the dark interior, and the doors closed behind them. *What is happening in there?*

While watching the event, she spotted Lieutenant Barrin at the head of one of the platoon columns. Such a serious man, but an excellent officer. It would be such a waste if he lost his life fighting rebels. The same could be said for all the legionaries. How much sway did Eero have with the provincial garrisons? It didn't make sense to send his own elite force to Scottsdale when one of the neighbouring garrisons could reinforce Garyd's troops. Couldn't Eero just demand that his lords support each other? Maybe his powers as king were limited, either legally or socially.

As she contemplated the kingdom's power dynamics, she heard a soft footstep on the stonework behind her. At first, she thought someone might have been sneaking up on her, but it was only Chamberlain Hayla. Sometimes that woman moved too quietly, and Nahla berated herself for letting her get so close.

"What can I do for you, Chamberlain?" Nahla asked, giving the hooded woman a sideways glance.

Hayla carried a scroll of paper and a small sack. "I have your official promotion document, plus some ribbons that were hurriedly made by the Legion's tailor. The ribbons are identifications for you and your Protectors."

Nahla put the scroll in the wall's crenel and pulled out a black ribbon from the sack. It was a calligraphic swirl of the letter *P*, all using one length of material, but sewed and bunched together to form the right shape. It had a pin on the reverse side. Nahla thought the design was too decorative.

"Unfortunately, Captain Vox cannot officialise the change in assignment for your legionaries," Hayla continued. "He is otherwise engaged with war preparations. You will have to pin these on your soldiers yourself."

"That's fine by me." Nahla's tone was sour, and even she felt she was being passive aggressive. Something about the way Hayla stared from under the hood was putting her off.

The chamberlain broke eye contact and surveyed Second Company below. "I know you were not in favour of war in Scottsdale. In truth, it's not really a war. But you would know that, considering your background."

Nahla didn't reply immediately. That this woman knew something of her past made her uneasy. She regretted opening up to her the first time they'd met. It was a critical error, a slip in judgement probably borne out of a desire to forge a bond with the only respectable woman she'd met in Launceston until that point.

"What about my background?" Nahla asked.

"I have been unsuccessful in verifying your story, but your skills lend weight to it. So I am inclined to believe you, even though I have no hard evidence."

And you'll never have hard evidence, Nahla thought. So, she embellished with some half-truths, just to throw Hayla off the scent. "I am not proud of my past, but I do tell the truth when I say that I have military experience. I hope you can accept that I do not wish to speak about it."

"Of course." Something in Hayla's tone said that the topic would be raised again.

They observed the litany for a while before Nahla spoke again. "If the war is not really a war, then why are we calling it a war?"

Hayla shrugged. "To make Eero happy. To make him feel like he's going to battle with his enemies. A short, victorious war in the north will renew his courage to fight the Kingdom of Hobart in the south, if it should ever come to that."

"Is it a possibility?"

"It has been a possibility for over twenty years. Eero has lived half his reign with the threat of a major war looming on his southern border. I imagine the prospect of war excites you at some primal level."

"Anyone who enjoys war is a fool."

Hayla laughed. "Then there are plenty of fools in Tasmania. This will be a war between kingdoms. I am certain war will come eventually. At that time, the people must rally around the king." Hayla paused, and Nahla could almost hear the gears turning in the chamberlain's mind. "You told me that you fought for your king during your civil war. Do you believe a king should be supported, no matter what?"

"My loyalty was unquestioned."

"But your king was challenged by others. How did you discern which side to support?"

Where is she going with this? Nahla's mind raced to figure out Hayla's game, but the chamberlain had a sneaky way of weaving multiple topics into one conversation, going off on tangents and coming back when it suited her.

"There are many factors to consider," Nahla said. She was going to leave it at that, but added, "Ultimately, you choose the side that is morally right."

Hayla laughed again, sardonically. "Morals. Who sets the morals of our world? The only moral everyone understands is the Decree of Water."

There, once again, water took centre stage in society. Everything revolved around the demand, supply, and distribution of the all-important liquid. Nahla still couldn't see where Hayla was going with her questioning. Fortunately, she didn't have to endure it any longer. Rhos approached them.

The legionary stood at a respectful distance and waited for Nahla's signal to interrupt, which Nahla promptly provided.

"Lieutenant," Rhos said crisply, "Prince Myel is awake. He is asking for you."

Maybe the non-existent God of Launceston has answered me, Nahla thought sarcastically. She faced Hayla. "Chamberlain, it has been a pleasure, as always, but I must take my leave."

"The pleasure was all mine, Nahla. We must continue our conversation sometime."

"We shall." A promise she never intended to fulfill.

Someone barked a command in the courtyard and Second Company stomped their sandals. Then, as one, the unit about-faced and platoon columns began marching away from the temple.

Nahla collected her promotion scroll and bag of ribbons. "Lead the way, Private Rhos," she said, and left Hayla behind.

As much as Matriarch Anurak hated Prince Myel, the Guardians had set up Myel with everything he needed to recuperate. He'd transferred to his residence earlier in the day. Nahla found him propped up in bed, benefitting from a cross-breeze through two open windows. A servant busied himself with various items in the room, while the legionaries Jaymen and Brande stood like sentinels. In fact, Nahla found the house well guarded. The Protectors were taking their jobs seriously.

"Nahla!" Myel called, then winced and put a hand to his head.

"Got a headache, Your Highness?"

"I guess so. Feels like I've been hit in the head with a mace. And it's Myel. Remember?"

Nahla allowed herself a short, nasal laugh. Maybe it wouldn't be so bad for Jaymen and Brande to see how friendly the prince really was.

"What have you been up to while I was napping?"

"Well, while you were *knocked out*, a lot of problems took shape." Myel gestured at a chair and Nahla dragged it closer, sitting. "For a start, your father is sending Second Company to Scottsdale. They're going to join the First and crush the rebels."

Myel put his head back against his pillows and frowned. "The complete opposite of what I wanted. Something tells me that's not the worst news."

"An assassin got to Daxton."

"He's dead!?"

"No, he lives, but there's a very good chance he'll die soon. He's unconscious."

The news made Myel close his eyes and sigh. "Did they at least catch the assassin?"

Nahla told him about the gong farmer—how he'd attacked Daxton in his cell, then was detained in Launceston Prison, and then slaughtered in the prison carriage on the way to the palace.

"Our enemy, whoever it may be, is getting desperate," Myel said. "But they are still at least one step ahead of us."

"Your father's chamberlain was not very upset that the assassin was killed. Makes me wonder."

"Hayla has always been a hard nut to crack. An emotionless woman, unless she's disappointed with someone." He glanced at Jaymen and Brande, and that jogged Nahla's memory.

"Well, murders and assassinations aside, you now have your very own personal guard of eight legionaries, with me in command. I am now a lieutenant."

He smiled. "Ah, so it's not all bad news. Congratulations!"

"You had to get knocked off your horse for me to get promoted."

Myel shrugged. "Let's take the good with the bad. But now, the bad. It sounds like our investigation has ended prematurely."

"Not quite. The wine that poisoned Governor Ibeza—it had to come from somewhere." Myel's strained nodding convinced Nahla she was on the right track. "Who would be the best person for me to talk to about that?"

"You can see the Royal Apothecary."

Someone grunted in the room.

"You have something to say, Private Jaymen?" Myel asked.

Jaymen straightened his back. "Permission to speak freely, Your Highness?"

"Always."

"The apothecary is a cranky old bastard."

That made Myel smile, which made Nahla smile. She dropped her chin and looked away to hide it.

"Thank you, Private Jaymen," Myel said.

"This apothecary—do you think he'll help us?" Nahla asked.

"Depends what we ask. What did you have in mind?"

To be frank, Nahla wasn't sure how the apothecary could help. "I just want to ask him some questions."

Jaymen cleared his throat.

"Would you like to come with me, Jaymen?"

"Me? No. The apothecary hates me."

"When are you going?" Myel asked.

"I'll go tomorrow. It's getting late now."

Myel nodded, then shifted his gaze to the end of his bed.

"What are you thinking?" Nahla asked.

"Have Second Company left yet?"

"They're leaving the city as we speak."

He sighed. "That means we have about twelve hours before they link up with Carro's company. That's twelve hours to find some hard evidence so we can stop this conflict."

"It will take them longer than that to reach Carro. A company moves only as fast as their supplies. Then, when they link up, they need to send a message to Lord Garyd, and he's to attach his garrison to the Legion. We probably have two days before they begin the offensive against the rebels."

"Okay. That's better. It's not ideal, but at least we have more time." He blinked tiredly. "We need Daxton to survive."

Nahla nodded. "Yeah. And to wake up."

25

THE SNIPPET

Even the faintest whisper of truth can rattle the keys of curiosity and unlock doors to a boundless realm of understanding.

—**Cass the Blasphemer**
The Truth

Nahla was so eager to speak to the Royal Apothecary that she arrived before he'd opened his shop. While waiting outside, she tried to calculate if Second Company had reached their destination. They had left Launceston at around five in the afternoon, which meant they still had a few hours to go, assuming Primus Carro was still in Springfield, and assuming Primus Marcle hadn't force-marched the entire way.

The Royal Apothecary occupied one section of a long building filled with support services, such as the Royal Tailor, the Royal Cobbler, and the shared offices of the Royal Chronicler and the Royal Archivist. Nahla waited next to a door marked with a mortar and pestle, the universal symbol of the herbal and medicinal services provided within.

A bearded man about half Nahla's height and twice her age approached the store. He stopped at the front door, looked Nahla up and down without greeting her, then unlocked it and stepped inside. He slammed it shut before Nahla could speak or follow. The palace's bell had not yet sounded the seventh, and since that was when the apothecary officially opened his place of business, she decided it would be polite to wait for the bell.

The clicks and screeches of locks and latches emanated from the wooden shutters. They swung open, and again the apothecary stared at Nahla. It was awkward, and Nahla wished they could just get on with their business interaction, but the man shuffled away into the bellows of his shop.

A few minutes later, the bell struck seven o'clock, and Nahla entered the shop. She'd barely closed the door before the apothecary gave her a less-than-friendly greeting.

"What do you want?" he asked.

"I'm Lieutenant Nahla of the King's Legion."

"I know who you are. Wherever you go, trouble follows you. What do you want?"

"I would like to learn about wine." So far, she hadn't taken two steps away from the door, sensing that she'd be kicked out any moment.

"Lieutenant, you are in the wrong place to enquire about wines. I suggest you visit the wine steward or the cupbearer. Better yet, try Jaruk Easton in Devonport."

"My apologies, sir." Nahla stepped forwards and lowered her voice. "I am more interested in the poisoning of wines. How it can be done, how long it takes for a poison to do its work, and if a poison can be detected."

The apothecary nodded slowly. "You're talking about the prison governor?"

"Precisely."

"Do you have a sample?"

"Unfortunately not."

"Then I'm afraid we cannot proceed."

Nahla continued undeterred. "Do you make poisons?"

He scoffed. "Lieutenant! A self-respecting apothecary does *not* dabble in poisons."

"Perhaps I was too blunt. *Could* you make poisons? Is it possible?"

"Well, of course it's possible. But it should not be done."

"I agree. But let's assume that someone is going to make a poison, and that this person will add it to wine. What would be required?"

He looked about his store as if the answer was obvious. Then he pointed at different items. "You'd need the right ingredients, and the brewing station, fire, water—"

"So not just anybody could make a poison if they had the knowledge and ingredients?"

Appearing to be at the end of his tether, the apothecary shrugged. "Can you murder somebody with just your finger?"

At first, Nahla didn't understand, but then it hit her: technically, it was possible to create a poison if one had the right knowledge and ingredients. But it could be done more efficiently with the right tools.

So she had learned that somebody, somewhere, had brewed a poison and sent it to Launceston Prison. That was nothing exciting, because it was an obvious fact. The all-important double-barrelled question was: Who and why? Unfortunately, she was getting nowhere with the apothecary, so she called it quits.

"I'll take my leave. Thank you for your time." The apothecary grunted as Nahla turned, but she stopped as she reached for the door. She had a thought. "Could you brew something that restores life?"

"That, Lieutenant, is my business. Well, not to restore life from death. No, the dead are dead. But my medicines can nurse a dying person to better health."

"The person in question lost a lot of blood and is recovering under the care of the Guardians."

The apothecary scoffed. "They don't know a thing about healing. There is more to life than water." He picked up a leather-bound book from the bench behind him and started thumbing through it. "Blood loss, you say?"

"Yes."

He licked a finger and turned pages faster until finding the one he wanted. "Here. Just as I thought. Sanguine Thirst." He eyed a shelf at the other end of the room. "We have none in stock, so I will need to make it. I assume you want it immediately?"

"Yes, please."

"One bottle?"

"How much in one bottle? Would one bottle be enough?"

He picked up a conical glass. "About that much. How nearly dead is your patient? Never mind, I'll make you two bottles. Give one to the patient as soon as possible, and then the second one tonight. Come back in an hour and they should be ready."

Nahla was about to agree to that, but a thought occurred to her—a big thought that she should have considered much earlier. The poisoned wine arrived at the prison in a shipment from the palace. The Royal Apothecary was within the palace walls. And the wine itself was a high-quality variety consumed by the nobility. There was a very real chance that this grumpy apothecary was the one who poisoned the wine in the first place. That certainly explained his gruff manner and the way he shut down Nahla's questions. If he was, in fact, the poisoner, Nahla wondered if he had put two-and-two together and realised he was making medicine for his original target. The webs of suspicion and deceit were spinning thicker by the day.

"I'll stay here," Nahla said. "I'd like to watch the master at work."

"That is highly irregular."

"I have a great fascination and appreciation for people who are at the height of their professions. I would consider it an honour and a privilege if you allowed me to stay." Perhaps flattery would soften this old man's attitude.

Her efforts made no visible impact. The apothecary remained impassive, but then frowned, raised his eyebrows, and allowed her to stay.

She studied the ingredients in the book, which he'd left open by the bellows. The brief description said of the medicine: *Restores life*. Nothing more, but it was enough for Nahla. Then, as the apothecary collected the ingredients—fresh fruits from bowls and various plants from his garden outside, she made sure he'd collected everything and wasn't adding anything else. No doubt a medicine that restored life could be corrupted by adding ingredients that did quite the opposite.

She felt way out of her league here and wished that Jaymen had come along with her. According to her limited understanding of the human body, Daxton had lost enough blood to put his body into shock. She didn't know what part of the body made blood, or how quickly it was produced, so this medicine was her only chance to revive Daxton as soon as possible. It was a gamble, but she really didn't have much time left, nor any better ideas.

The process took an hour because the apothecary first had to heat water, then grind ingredients, do some mixing and cooking, then allow the medicine to cool before filtering it into two glass bottles, which he promptly sealed with corks. Throughout the process, Nahla asked about the ingredients and the method, trying to understand the science behind everything.

"If this doesn't work, I'm afraid your friend was never going to survive," the apothecary said. Solemn words, indeed.

"Understood," Nahla replied. "And thank you for doing this on short notice."

"In life-threatening situations, everything is short notice. Hurry along, Lieutenant."

THE DIVINE GUARDS AT the Royal Infirmary stopped Nahla and Jaymen at the front door. They questioned her about the bottles.

"It is medicine from the Royal Apothecary," she told them.

"You would dare to bring such unblessed concoctions in here?" one of them asked. She was a tall woman with piercing blue eyes that complemented the colour of her armour.

"And I suppose your medicines have the blessing of God? And all the patients here walk out in good health? Don't waste my time."

She barged through without further incident, because that was all the Divine Guards were doing—arguing for the sake of it. Jaymen grinned victoriously, enjoying the moment.

Inside, the building was teeming with priestesses, but they gave Nahla a wide berth. It could have been the determination on her face, or her reputation, or that she had the scarred and grey-haired Jaymen in tow. The place was busier than usual. Jaymen told her it was probably to prepare for the hostilities in Scottsdale. The badly wounded would be sent to the infirmary for treatment and recuperation if the Guardians' infirmary in Scottsdale was full or inaccessible.

As expected, there were two legionaries and two Divine Guards near Daxton's door. The legionaries saluted.

"Has anyone come to see Daxton?" she asked.

"Just the Guardians, Preceptor," one legionary replied. Nahla hadn't been outfitted as a lieutenant yet. Since she didn't look the part, she didn't bother correcting him. "Make this a standing order if nobody has told you already: send a messenger to Prince Myel's house as soon as anyone other than the Guardians, Prince Myel, or I enter this room. Understood?"

The legionaries responded affirmatively. Then Nahla and Jaymen entered. A priestess sat beside Daxton's bed, folding clean bandages in her lap, and a Divine Guard stood a few paces away. She was not the same one who had challenged her last time.

"You're not allowed in here," she said with a stern voice, standing.

"Why is there no legionary in this room?" Nahla asked.

"The priestess said you are not allowed in here," the Divine Guard said.

"On the contrary," Nahla replied. "I am one of the few people who *are* allowed in here. Now answer my question. Why is there no legionary in this room?"

"Your legionaries are not required to be in here," the priestess answered. "They are becoming a hindrance."

"Your inability to coexist with my legionaries is the only hindrance I can see. Now, please leave us."

"I must attend to the patient."

Nahla glared at the priestess. "I will care for him for the time being."

Nahla refused to make the request again, instead using her piercing eyes to whittle the other woman's resolve. The priestess glanced at the Divine Guard for assistance. When Jaymen and Nahla faced the guard, she must have decided two against one were unfavourable odds.

"Come, priestess," the Divine Guard said. "Let us give these pigs what they want."

The priestess glanced at the light-orange medicine in Nahla's hand, offered one last defiant stare, and stormed off in a huff, Divine Guard in tow.

The room stank, so the first thing Nahla did was open a window.

"He's in a bad way, isn't he?" Jaymen said. "All our troubles in Scottsdale, all because of this guy?"

"I'm pretty sure he's a puppet," Nahla said. "There's a bigger enemy in the shadows."

She popped the cork off one bottle and froze as she wondered how to feed it to Daxton. How does an unconscious person swallow medicine?

"Would you like me to do it, Lieutenant?" Jaymen asked. "It needs to be done slowly. They can sip unconsciously, but very slowly."

Jaymen administered the medicine, pouring tiny amounts onto Daxton's lips, which dripped into the mouth. Daxton, even while sleeping, licked and swallowed automatically. Nahla paced the room while she waited, cursing the slow process. The room's only window overlooked an extensive herb garden tended by half a dozen priestesses. She wondered why they hadn't fed him this miracle concoction already. Maybe it was a recipe invented by the Royal Apothecary and he hadn't shared it. Despite the central role the Guardians played in everyday society, they sure had a lot of enemies.

After Jaymen emptied the first bottle, he and Nahla stood back and waited. Nahla didn't know how long it would take or even if it would work. Before too long, Daxton breathed deeper and grunted at an involuntary movement, but his eyes remained closed.

"Have you ever saved anyone's life before?" Jaymen asked.

Nahla thought back to her countless battles and skirmishes. "I've saved many." *But not enough*, she thought as the memory of her king flashed in her mind. "But not like this. You?"

"Only one person, before they busted me down to private. Remember I said I did something stupid and got demoted?"

"Yeah."

"Well, I got a bunch of people killed, and then I saved the wrong person."

Nahla sighed, knowing the feeling all too well, but she didn't want to share her experience. It would lead to too many questions, and she wasn't ready to have that conversation yet. "What happened?"

Daxton stirred. Nahla and Jaymen momentarily shifted their attention to him, but then he settled again.

"A barbarian tribe ambushed us while we explored beyond the kingdom's western border. Remember I said I'd fought in the nude?" He chuckled. "Yeah, they attacked at dawn while we were encamped. I slept in the nude when I was young and reckless. Didn't matter where we were or who might see me. So I jumped out of my tent naked with . . . well, *two* swords, if you count . . ." He grinned and shrugged. "Anyway, we beat them, but our lieutenant didn't want to pursue, even though we could have followed them back to their camp. We had an ambitious sergeant, and I convinced him to quietly break off from our unit and hunt down the barbarians who'd fled, or at least scout in the direction they went. He secretly recruited some others and, short story long, our little band was surrounded in the forest and slaughtered. I saved a private's life instead of the sergeant's."

Having been a commander at various levels of seniority, Nahla could think of several reasons to praise *and* condemn the sergeant for agreeing to pursue the barbarians. But there were obviously more details to the story. "Why was it the wrong decision to save the private? What made you choose the private instead of the sergeant?"

"The private was closer and easier to carry, and I just wanted to get out of there. We disappeared into the forest, and it was hilly country, so the barbarians quickly lost us. I treated the private's wounds, and we somehow found our section again, but by that time, they had rejoined the rest of the company. That's when everything got worse."

Jaymen shook his head. "The sergeant I abandoned was the son of the company's primus. Can you believe that? It wasn't very well known, but if I knew that, I would have never let him die in the forest."

"You would have let the private die instead? There was no way of saving both?"

"You know what it's like. Everything happens so fast. In that moment, my mind saw two options: save the private and escape, or *try* to save the sergeant and maybe get killed. I picked the easier option. I didn't know it was the wrong one. The primus ended my training as a medic and demoted me to a private. Then he whipped me himself—more lashes than anyone had received in the history of the King's Legion. My back was so torn up that King Eero passed a law banning the whipping of legionaries."

Now if only the same law could apply to the Guardians, Nahla thought. She imagined what her back looked like after the punishment they had inflicted on her. "What about the private?"

"The private received only a few floggings, since he had agreed to join the unsanctioned mission. But he was not responsible for the whole affair."

"I bet he was thankful that you saved him."

"He was, and still is. Private Barrin is now Lieutenant Barrin, and he is probably the best lieutenant in the Legion. Maybe the situation taught him something."

Nahla smiled. "I've met him. He's a good—"

From the hallway outside, they could hear muffled commands and defiant retorts through the thick stone wall and timber door. Nahla started for the door, but after a final shout from outside, someone flung it open and Matriarch Anurak marched in, wearing a blue robe with a high, stiff collar.

"What are you doing here, Nahla?" she croaked. "You have no right to dismiss my Guardians. Get out of here at once!" A stream of Divine Guards and legionaries followed her in.

"I'm sorry, Preceptor," one of the legionaries at the door said. "She would not take no for an answer."

"You will address me as Her Eminence!" Anurak bellowed. "And why should I accept orders from you? This is the Royal Infirmary, which the Guardians oversee. You are invading my jurisdiction."

Nahla drew herself up before the tall religious leader. "With respect, Matriarch, I am providing Daxton with medicine to aid his recovery. I must speak to him about recent crimes and the growing hostilities in the north."

"Medicine?" Anurak asked. She scrunched her face in disgust.

"From the Royal Apothecary."

"You dare to usurp the Guardians' divine right to care for this man on his deathbed?"

"I am ensuring he lives."

"He is a criminal!"

Daxton murmured, and all eyes fell on him.

Anurak spun around. "We must fetch someone to attend to him."

"No!" Nahla said. "I need to speak with him."

"He is our patient, and we must care for him," Anurak replied.

"Well, he's my last lead in an investigation that affects the entire kingdom. When I'm done with him, he's all yours." When Anurak opened her mouth and stepped forwards, Nahla spoke to Jaymen. "Draw your sword and keep them back."

Jaymen did so, which was met by a half-dozen other swords being drawn as Divine Guards and legionaries responded in kind. The house of healing was on the verge of being painted red.

"Enough!" Anurak bellowed. "Put your weapons away and everyone get out! That includes you, Private."

Jaymen looked to Nahla for permission. She nodded. Everyone sheathed their weapons and filed out with only mumbled protests before the door closed.

Anurak, now alone with Nahla, muttered something under her breath. Nahla ignored her as she knelt next to Daxton. The man was blinking awake and grimacing with pain when he moved his neck.

"Easy, Daxton," Nahla said calmly. "You have a bad throat wound. Try not to move."

He settled his head on the pillow, looking at her sideways with bloodshot eyes. He tried to speak, but his voice was croaky. He coughed, then whimpered as the movement hurt his wound.

"Keep him steady," Anurak said, but Nahla ignored the obvious statement.

Daxton tried speaking again, quieter and slower. "Who?"

"Who attacked you?" Nahla asked. When Daxton gave just an inkling of a nod, Nahla answered. "It was a gong farmer employed by the prison. But we don't know why he did it, or if someone put him up to it."

He tried mouthing something, but he was either struggling to vocalise the words, or he had too many questions to ask at once.

"Somebody killed the assassin before I could speak to him. I still don't know who's trying to kill you. First poison, now an assassin. Why does someone want to kill you? Do you know who it is? Is it the same one who was helping you in Scottsdale?"

He breathed heavily and blinked as if he was drifting off to sleep again . . . or worse.

"Stay with me, Daxton. I need answers. What did you want to tell Prince Myel before the assassin got you?"

As he spoke, his throat was too congested and he spluttered. After some more laboured breathing and throat clearing, he looked her in the eye and spoke one word, though it came out almost as a whisper.

Nahla's eyes widened. Anurak stared, dumfounded.

"Thank you, Daxton," Nahla said. "Thank you." Then she stood and swept past Anurak, rushing to tell Myel the news.

26

IDENTIFIED

When the torch of truth illuminates the darkness, creatures of the night scurry for shelter. But once seen, they are easily found again.

—Cass the Blasphemer
The Truth

M<small>YEL WAS WELL ENOUGH</small> to be moved to his garden, but he reclined in the shade on a day bed. A Guardian hung nearby, watching for signs of regression, and several servants toiled the earth to keep the fruits and vegetables neat and fresh. A third of the garden was being replanted with new seeds under Myel's watchful direction.

He spotted Nahla as she entered the spacious backyard. "There's my trusty companion," he said. "What did you discover?" When he read her face, he dropped his smile. "Oh. That bad?"

She stopped by his side and remained standing. "We need to speak. Alone."

He regarded her for a moment, saw the seriousness on her face, and then turned to the priestess. "May I return to my quarters without you?"

"I would feel more comfortable if I were with you," the priestess replied.

223

"The prince will be fine for the moment," Nahla told her. "I'll send for you if needed."

The Guardian humbly bowed. The prince was unsteady on his feet, even with Nahla's support. They moved at a gentle pace, and he commented several times about how the world spun. "I hope I get over this quickly. But they say it could take up to two weeks."

Nahla set him down on his bed, making sure to gently support his head against the plush pillows. He sighed deeply and reached for a cup of water while Nahla brought a chair closer.

"I got no leads from the apothecary," Nahla said. "But I had him prepare a reviving medicine for Daxton. It worked!"

"Really?" Myel's eyes sparked at the news. "Then why are you so gloomy?"

"Daxton struggled to speak, and he could barely move. But I asked him where his support came from in Scottsdale and who might be trying to have him assassinated. He gave me one name: *Johl.*"

Myel's head sunk into his pillows. He stared at the ceiling. "I'm surprised and not surprised at the same time. This changes everything."

"Do you think the mercenaries who attacked us are linked to Johl?"

"Something tells me that's what you think."

Nahla nodded. "Never has a puzzle so neatly fit together. I'm glad you have a personal guard now, because if Johl can target us once, he can do it again."

"The balls on him! I just don't understand why he would do it! Supporting Daxton, I mean. What does he gain? Are you sure Daxton wasn't just throwing you off the scent?"

"The man was very nearly killed. It wasn't some random prison yard attack. Even he has to admit it was an assassination attempt. I see no reason for him to protect his handler anymore."

"True." He thought for a moment. "I know there is tension between my father's lords. But this sort of clandestine undermining was more than I anticipated. It's outright treason."

"But like you asked: What does Johl have to gain from it? What's in Scottsdale that isn't in Launceston?"

Myel pulled a face and shrugged. "The province is rich in raw materials, but they're not fully exploited. Apart from that, there isn't much difference between the two provinces. Scottsdale is bigger, but that wouldn't account for much."

"So he might want access to raw materials?" Nahla wondered. In her homeland, people got rich through money. It was her civilisation's way of assigning value to people, land, materials, produce, services, and products. If people had more than enough, they were wealthy. But in Tasmania—or at least in the Kingdom of Launceston—it was different. There was no money. Wealth was derived from the control and exchange of resources and production, much in the same way as Melbourne, but with the money element removed. Of the two, Nahla felt the Launceston model was better, because money had caused too much conflict back home. But now it seemed like even the lack of money couldn't stop an ambitious lord from trying to climb higher.

"I don't understand how Johl would get the land and resources, though," Nahla said. "He can't be the lord of two provinces, can he?"

"I suppose anything is possible. All it needs is my father's approval, but the other lords might not like it, and I think it would be a foolish thing to do anyway."

"Why do you say that?" Nahla knew why it was foolish, but she wanted to see if Myel understood the situation. This was an excellent opportunity for him to think critically about real-world politics.

"If Johl controls two provinces, the power and status quo between him and the other lords becomes even more unbalanced. He's already considered the first among equals because he's the governor of the capital province, but if he is also Lord of Scottsdale, then that will give him too much sway at court, and it will weaken my father's position as king."

"Excellent analysis," Nahla said. "You've progressed well."

"None too soon, by the looks of it."

"Have you noticed that Johl is awfully close to Vimarr?"

"Yes, they've been close for a long time," Myel said, stroking his stubbly jaw. "I think they spent a lot of time together as kids."

"They're about the same age as us."

"I hated when he visited the palace as a kid. Vimarr was all right then, but he changed as he grew older."

"What about Garyd and Alden?"

Myel raised his eyebrows. "You already know that Garyd and Johl don't like each other. It's even worse with Alden."

"Why?" Of the four lords of the kingdom, Nahla had seen Alden the least.

"Alden controls Campbell Province. It's less prestigious than Launceston, but whoever controls Campbell must be the most capable military governor because it borders the Kingdom of Hobart. Campbell's garrison is twice the size of Launceston's for exactly that reason. And because the southern border must remain the strongest, Alden receives the most resources for fortifications and the most labourers. He even gets extra water sometimes, usually sent from the Launceston Temple."

Water, Nahla thought. "Hmm."

"What is it?"

"Would Johl see the Scottsdale Temple as a prize?"

"I don't follow."

"Water is the most valuable resource in the kingdom. It's supplied from the city temples. If Johl controls the two temples in Launceston and the one in Scottsdale, and has Vimarr's support in Devonport, he can nearly dictate the total supply of water throughout the kingdom."

"He wouldn't dare," Myel said, but his words lacked conviction.

Nahla spread her hands. "Who's stopping him? A clueless matriarch? Your father? Garyd? It seems like we're the only ones who suspect his plans, if he truly harbours those ambitions."

Myel scratched his jaw.

"If we're right," Nahla continued, "then the rebellion in Scottsdale is just a diversion, or a reason for Johl to assume control of the province. He'll kill tens of thousands of people just to get what he wants." She let the words sink in.

Myel bit his lip. "Did you get a written statement from Daxton?"

Nahla shook her head. "He could barely speak, and had no energy to move. Even moving his head was problematic. But Matriarch Anurak was present. Two witnesses should be enough." Right then, she regretted allowing Anurak to eject Jaymen from the room.

"You must take this information to my father immediately. You and Anurak. Present it together."

She stood. "Understood. But I think we should send a message to Scottsdale first. If we hurry, we can prevent a bloodbath in the province."

"Get me some paper and my seal. There's some on the desk over there. And fetch a rider."

Nahla called for one of the Protectors outside Myel's room. The strongly built young legionary named Sheph entered. He had repeatedly impressed Nahla during training sessions. "Bring us the fastest cavalry trooper you can find."

"At once, Lieutenant!"

While the legionary went searching, Myel and Nahla drafted a short but stern letter to Primus Carro. They scrunched several sheets of valuable paper before settling on the right wording. It was direct, but did not reveal too much, because the ultimate order to halt the attack would come from King Eero:

Primus Carro, CO, 1C, King's Legion,

Incriminating details concerning the planned attack against the rebels have surfaced here in Launceston. Pause all military action until you receive further instructions from the king. New orders will soon follow this letter.

Myel

There was no need to add his title, or even the commonly used *P* after his name to denote his princely status. His name alone would carry enough weight, and the wax seal would be his official signature.

By this time, a cavalry trooper entered the room, following Private Sheph. He bowed to the bed-ridden prince and did his best to stop his eyes from wandering. It was probably the first time he'd been inside Myel's residence, let alone the prince's bedroom.

"I see you're already kitted out for a ride," Myel said. "Good. You have a long ride ahead of you." He sealed the letter and waved it in the air so the wax would cool faster. "Take this letter to Primus Carro in Scottsdale Province. He should be encamped at Springfield. If you encounter Second Company along the way, bypass them and go straight to Carro. Understood?"

"Yes, Your Highness," the trooper replied.

"Then be on your way." He handed him the letter. "Time is of the essence."

The trooper saluted and left in a hurry.

"I'll take Anurak to your father," Nahla said. "With any luck, Johl will be detained, and the Legion recalled from Scottsdale before the end of the day."

She smelled victory and justice, the perfect combination for all the trouble Johl had given her. Finally, she could topple her mortal enemy from his perch.

27

STONEWALLED

Beware the enemies in plain sight. Our true adversaries
may be the ones we least suspect.

—Hayla the Sage
Lessons in Government

Nʜʟᴀ ᴡᴀɪᴛᴇᴅ ɪɴ ᴛʜᴇ palace's throne room. Matriarch Anurak had
not wanted to leave the cool confines of her Guardians' administrative building, but Nahla refused to back down. Now Anurak
paced along the windows of the shady side of the palace, catching
the intermittent breezes that wafted in.

Finally, King Eero arrived, shadowed by his ever-present
chamberlain. Hayla took her position beside the throne as Eero
dropped into it.

"This better be important, Nahla," Eero said.

Nahla could hear the strain in his voice. The impending military action in Scottsdale was already wearing him down. It was
a good thing they'd sent a message to stall the offensive. Who
knew how Eero would feel once the blood started flowing? But he
needn't worry about that now. She told him straight.

"Your Majesty," she began with a bow, "I come bearing grave
news that affects the campaign in Scottsdale and the integrity of
your court."

Eero leaned forwards. "Speak." Hayla's ears had pricked up and Anurak edged closer to the conversation.

"Lord Johl supplied the rebels in Scottsdale." Despite the quietest gasp from Hayla, Nahla pressed on. "Because of this, I believe the assassination attempt on Daxton, the murder of the gong farmer, the poisoning of Governor Ibeza, and the attack on your son were all instigated by Johl to hide the truth."

The king sat back, rested his head on the cushioned headrest, and stared at the other end of the room.

"With what evidence do you support these accusations?" Hayla asked.

"Oral testimony from Daxton, who has survived the assassination attempt."

Hayla's eyes went wide. "You have this testimony in writing?"

"There was hardly a need to record it. I asked him who was responsible for the troubles in Scottsdale, who was supporting him. He said Johl. Anurak heard him too." Nahla gestured at the matriarch.

"Just 'Johl'? That's all he said?" Hayla asked. She stepped forwards. "You realise that hardly counts as a testimony? A single-word answer could be misconstrued to mean anything."

Eero looked down at them. "The accusation still warrants investigation."

"Your Majesty," Hayla replied. "The man's a rebel. His sole purpose is to break the kingdom. We cannot take his word."

Again, Hayla was shredding Nahla's efforts. She knew it was the chamberlain's job to advise the sovereign, to be the voice of reason and clear-sightedness. They didn't call her the Sage for nothing. But Hayla was developing a nasty habit of challenging Nahla at almost every opportunity.

"I agree," Eero said. "Hence the investigation. Send for Johl. He should have a chance to defend himself."

Nahla's heart pumped. To face Johl in this epic standoff was the icing on the cake.

"Here and now, Your Majesty?" Hayla asked. "You don't wish to question him in private?"

"Not at all! He must face his accuser and defend himself. Bring him here."

After a moment's pause, Hayla nodded. "At once, Your Majesty." She disappeared through a back door.

"Somebody bring me a pear!" Eero bellowed, then he smiled at Nahla as if the shocking news of Johl's potential treason meant nothing to him.

Nahla put her hands behind her back and paced. Anurak had returned to the windows and stood with her back to everyone, watching the goings-on outside. She hadn't said a word since leaving her office.

A tray of pears arrived. Eero hastily bit into one before offering to share. Nahla respectfully declined. Anurak ignored the offer.

They waited in silence for Johl.

LORD JOHL MADE IT a point to stay in peak physical shape. If he demanded strength and stamina from his soldiers, then it was his duty to set the example. He wrestled with Jugg outside under the hot sun where his soldiers could see him. So far, he had bested Jugg several times, though the larger man had brought him down with unexpected moves more times than Johl was happy to admit. He expected Jugg to defeat him every time, due to the sheer size of the brute, but maybe Johl's skills and finesse gave him the upper hand. That, or Jugg didn't want to make his master appear weak.

He was grimy from the dirt and sand in the wrestling ring. A large fist swung towards him, and he dodged deftly, grappling Jugg's arm and twisting. He was about to perform a finishing move to immobilise the giant when he spotted Hayla approaching. She wasn't a beautiful woman by his standards, but wearing her colourful robes amid the dark-clad, sweating, dirty soldiers, she was refreshing to look at. He called for timeout and released Jugg.

"Chamberlain," he said, wiping at his forehead. "To what do I owe the pleasure?"

Hayla came right up to the wall of the ring and stared Johl in the eye, her expression grim. "The king requests your presence."

She watched him, and he felt unnerved. "You'll allow me a moment to clean myself?"

"I think you had better come at once, Lord Johl." A slight nudge of her head brought him closer to her, so close that he could smell her fruity breath and the flowery fragrance of her privileged status at court. She spoke so quietly that he barely heard her. "You have been accused of treason."

The words made his heart race. He felt like falling backwards or turning around to hide his face. But he maintained control and tried to breathe evenly, hoping nothing in his facial expression betrayed his feelings or the desperate thoughts that were racing through his mind.

"Then I shall follow you back," he said.

She nodded. "The sooner the better." She half-turned, then added, "Come alone."

As she returned to her carriage, Jugg stepped beside him. "What did *she* want?"

The question didn't register, for Johl's mind was spinning. He wondered where he had gone wrong, what loose end he hadn't tied. Daxton was pretty much dead, if not dead already. Any soldier or agent involved in the cover-up was also dead, except for the few in his inner circle, such as Jugg and Ermi, his poison maker. He debated fleeing, but quickly decided that it would confirm his guilt. No, speaking to the king would give him a chance to defend himself. Eero was malleable. He'd twisted his mind enough to know that.

"I need to see the king," Johl said. He hopped the wall of the wrestling ring and pointed to the first soldier he saw. "Get my carriage ready." He donned his sword, which his own chamberlain had kept safe during the wrestling match.

"I will come with you, my lord," Jugg said.

"No," Johl replied. He held up a finger. "I'll go alone. I shouldn't be long."

With that, Johl marched to his carriage, fully prepared to fight for his life.

HAYLA ANNOUNCED LORD JOHL'S arrival without breaking her step. Then she returned to her place next to the king.

Johl followed her into the throne room, looking like a hot mess. Nahla had never seen him so dishevelled. It was as if he had just been wandering in the wild for days on end.

"Lord Johl," Eero said. "Has Hayla told you why you are here?"

"No, Your Majesty," he answered. If the king's tone had shaken him, he hid it well. He frowned and stepped in front of Nahla. "I was told to come as soon as possible. I apologise for my appearance."

Eero waved away the last sentence. "You are here because Nahla accuses you of collusion with the kingdom's enemies. Sedition, Johl! Treason! Listen to her statement."

Johl spun around to face her. Though he looked about ready to strangle her, Nahla stood firm. She re-positioned herself so that she and Johl stood an equal distance from Eero. It was a minor correction, but it showed that right now, with all that was at stake, Johl was no longer safe in his superior position. It was a subtle jab, showing that she was closer to the king than she had ever been.

"My lord," Nahla began, "I am accusing you of several crimes, but I will start from the beginning. Prince Myel and I have been investigating the situation in Scottsdale, and evidence has finally surfaced that points to you as the instigator and cultivator of the rebellion."

She put her hands on her hips and stood straight, a power move that always had worked in the court of King Vasylis of Melbourne.

Johl eyed her suspiciously. "No amount of evidence could possibly support such a ridiculous assertion."

"On the contrary. We have oral testimony from the leader of the rebellion, a man whom you have been trying to assassinate since he arrived in Launceston." She caught the flash of terror in his eyes. "Yes, Daxton. He's alive. He survived the brazen attempt on his life and named *you* as the one who supplied his forces and kept him informed about Lord Garyd's troop movements. You must have panicked when he was captured, because several disturbing incidents followed. First, you visited him with your lackey, Jugg. Then, the poisoned wine intended for Daxton was intercepted by Governor Ibeza, who drank it and died the same night. After that, the lowest employee of the prison, a gong farmer, infiltrated Daxton's cell and horrifically attacked him. Finally, when being brought to the palace for questioning, the gong farmer was murdered in the prison carriage, along with several other prisoners unconnected to your plot."

Johl's chest rose and fell. While he was stunned into a staring silence, Nahla continued. "But worst of all, you organised an ambush against the king's own son. Mercenaries on the road between Scottsdale and Launceston. He was getting too close to the truth, wasn't he? You had to dispose of him. And since your enmity for me is so strong, why not eliminate me along with the prince?"

Johl licked his lips. "You've put a lot of thought into this. Daxton told you all that, did he?"

"It doesn't take much to connect the dots. And I think an audit of your records and interrogating your court should provide evidence."

He straightened his back. "You dare to question the loyalty of a Lord of Launceston? You, a nobody who has weaselled her way into the king's good graces and poked her nose where it doesn't belong?" He scoffed. "And I think you may be poking somewhere else too. I imagine there is a reason you and Myel are so close."

She felt her blood boil and grabbed her sword handle.

"Nahla!" Eero roared. "Calm yourself. And you, Johl, you have not addressed Nahla's accusations. Stop attacking her honour and that of my son. Defend your honour instead."

"Oh, but Your Majesty," Johl said in the politest way possible, "Nahla's honour is highly questionable. She accuses me of treason, which is a complete lie. Meanwhile, Nahla is not who she says she is. Chamberlain Hayla, perhaps you should tell the king what you have learned about our esteemed Legion lieutenant?"

Now it was Nahla's turn to feel worried. Hayla, the snake, had twisted their conversations like a corkscrew, and now she was going to open the bottle of Nahla's past and pour it out for everyone.

Hayla moved so she could face the king. "Your Majesty, I have spoken to Nahla on several occasions, and she has confided in me about her supposed origins. Her words were most concerning. Nahla Northborn, if that is even her real name, states that she is not from Tasmania at all."

That made the ponderous Eero sit upright. "What?"

Johl smiled victoriously.

"Nahla is a woman from a distant land," Hayla continued. "An outsider, an exile. She came to us from a kingdom called Melbourne, far to the north, where she served closely under her sovereign."

Eero stood on his dais and stared down at Nahla. Meanwhile, Johl moved next to Hayla, clearly showing who he sided with.

"Now I have two trusted agents accusing each other's integrity." Eero cast his eyes between Johl and Nahla, as if deciding who he should skewer first. "Nahla, is it true? Are you a foreigner in our land?"

She squared her jaw as she contemplated the right words. "Yes. I am from a kingdom so far away that we never knew Launceston existed. In fact, it is so far away, I have no hope of ever returning." Maybe the context might help Eero see she was not a threat.

"Then why are you here?" he asked. "Are you a spy?"

Her heart pumped madly. She felt all control of the situation slipping through her hands. Eero, Hayla, and Johl gazed upon her with venomous eyes. Even Anurak had returned from her window and stood on the sideline. She must have finally understood Nahla's ignorance of religious laws.

Nahla imagined the thoughts that must have been running through Eero's mind. Potentially hostile forces now surrounded him on nearly all sides: Melbourne to the north, the wild tribes to the west, and Hobart to the south. Only his eastern borders remained safe, but only because there was nothing past them. However, even Nahla agreed that if a kingdom could spring up in the north, then it was possible that one existed to the east as well. She could see Eero fretting, imagining his realm crumbling with internal strife and external pressures.

"Your Majesty," Nahla said. "I am not a spy. I fought valiantly for my king, but we lost a civil war, and they gave me a warrior's punishment. They exiled me. My kingdom sends exiles into the Endless Land to die. Your people call that land the Barren Waste. The Endless Land was supposed to claim my life, but through sheer force of will, I kept walking and reached civilisation again—Tasmania. Here, I found a new king to serve and a new people to protect. And I believe my actions have shown that I serve you without reservations. I am certainly not conspiring against you or supporting your enemies." She glanced at Johl, who winced. "On the contrary, I am trying to protect your sovereignty and the lives of your subjects."

Eero stared at her for a long time. His eyes met hers, and it was as though he peered right through them, seeking truth, searching for the emotion behind Nahla's words. He returned to his throne and propped his chin on a fist. "Have you met others from your homeland since you arrived?"

"None, Your Majesty. I saw a lot of skeletons on the way here."

"Could you or someone else make the return trip?"

She sensed his worries, even though she had already answered the question. "It is a long walk with extreme heat, terrible winds, and no shelter. I would not want to try it, and I would not wish the journey on anyone else."

Eero took a deep breath. Perhaps his fears had subsided. "We will speak about this another time. Your kingdom must be investigated, but right now we have a more present accusation to settle." He turned to Johl and scowled—the first truly negative reaction Nahla had seen him give to Johl. "Your defence, Johl."

"Your Majesty," Johl started, "I am very surprised that you believe this nonsense. You have known me since my birth. How long have I served as your closest and most trusted provincial lord? How hard have I worked to improve my province and thus benefit the rest of the kingdom? How many troops have I trained and supplied to the southern and western borders?"

"How many troops have you sent to Scottsdale Province?" Nahla interjected.

Johl glared at her. "His Majesty insisted on sending the King's Legion. But I appeal to you, Your Majesty, not to let the accusations of this outsider weaken your trust in me. I have *not* colluded with the rebels. I have *not* targeted your son. I was *not* responsible for the death of Governor Ibeza or the man who attacked Daxton. And I have *never* been responsible for any assassination attempts on Daxton's life. Have I advocated for his execution? Absolutely! The man is a criminal, and we need to make an example of him.

"Contrary to Nahla's accusations, haven't I always advocated a firm hand in the Scottsdale rebellion? Even before we knew they were rebels—when we just thought of them as bandits—I was encouraging a harsh response. Frankly, I am surprised that similar bandit or rebel activity has not grown to the same alarming size elsewhere in the kingdom. It is a credit to you, Your Majesty, in your efforts to keep the kingdom safe and the problem contained to one province."

Eero smiled and waved away the flattery. "Your record as governor is impeccable, which is why Nahla's accusation was so alarming."

"My accusation stems from Daxton's testimony," Nahla said. She'd be damned if she let Johl play to Eero's heart. "Johl's governorship means nothing if he cannot absolve himself. We need to see *evidence* that contradicts Daxton's testimony."

Hayla cleared her throat with the most quiet and delicate sound. "Nahla is right, Your Majesty."

Hearing those words gave Nahla hope again. She really couldn't understand Hayla. On the one hand, she had challenged every word from Nahla's mouth and even tried to discredit Daxton's testimony, short as it was. But now she spoke in favour of Nahla, and rightly so. Johl must provide evidence, but she knew he was a shifty bastard, and he would tamper with any evidence he supplied.

Johl spread his hands out. "My records are open to you, Your Majesty. I am more than willing to allow your chamberlain to inspect every page of my books. She will see that nothing is out of order."

"I would like to interrogate people under your employ too," Nahla said. Records may be fudged, but people talk. Johl had an unlikeable personality, so she was counting on many people to speak up—soldiers, smiths, cargo handlers.

"That is unnecessary," Johl replied. "My chamberlain keeps impeccable records on everything that happens in my province."

"No," Eero said, "I think interrogations are a good idea." When Johl shot the king a wide-eyed face, Eero shook his head. "But Nahla will not lead them."

"Your Majesty?" Nahla asked.

"Until we have sufficiently investigated your past, I cannot allow you to be involved in such delicate matters."

"Then may I suggest Lord Alden audit Johl's records and interviews his officials? He is a neutral third party." The suggestion was brilliant, as evidenced by the half-second of nervous twitching in Johl's eye.

But Eero shot her down. "I will not drag Alden into this," Eero said. "He has his hands full already." He paused and regarded the

Launceston governor again. "Don't worry, Johl. If you are innocent, then your books and your people will prove it. I'm actually wondering if there is someone in your court who is using you as a scapegoat."

"An interesting thought, Your Majesty," Hayla said.

The grubby governor sighed deeply. "In that case, I would like to question Daxton myself, to determine why he named me and *only* me."

"Daxton did not say 'Johl'!" Anurak boomed from behind. Her strong voice, which belied her age, echoed in the throne room.

Nahla clenched her fists and fought desperately to control herself. *What is Anurak doing!?*

"This frivolous discussion has gone on for long enough," Anurak said. "Daxton was speaking nonsense. In fact, he could barely speak at all. The only sounds he could vocalise were pure babble, the sounds of a man recovering from near-death. He didn't say 'Johl' at all."

The seconds of silence that followed felt like hours. Nahla wanted to respond. She wanted to give the old hag a firm back-hand across the face, but she was too stunned by Anurak's outright lie. *Daxton had named Johl, damn it! Why is she destroying my case?*

Finally, Nahla summoned the inner strength to speak before the others. "You were in the room, Matriarch. You heard him just as well as I did."

"I heard the babblings of a semi-conscious man recovering from severe blood loss. There was a reason why the Guardians were nursing him back to health slowly. Who knows what damage you did with that potion?"

"What potion?" Johl asked. Now he had seized upon something else to discredit her.

"The Royal Apothecary—a master of healing in his own right—created an elixir of rejuvenation for Daxton. It was powerful enough to drag him back to consciousness and give him the strength to speak to me."

"The Royal Apothecary had no business creating that potion," Anurak muttered.

"Your Majesty," Johl said, "you see the efforts Nahla goes to in order to stain my reputation. Forcing a criminal to regain consciousness, and then imagining that he speaks my name?"

"He said it loud and clear," Nahla replied.

"Who should we believe, Your Majesty?" Hayla asked. "Your appointed Matriarch of the Guardians? Or a recent addition to the King's Legion, who just so happens to be an outsider?"

Eero rolled his eyes. "Nahla, are you sure Daxton named Johl?"

Nahla did her best to reply politely. "I heard what I heard, Your Majesty."

"Can you get a signed testimony from him?"

Before Nahla could speak, the crisp voice of Anurak cut her off. "Daxton is not in any condition to participate in this investigation. He is not of sound mind, and he needs his rest."

"What he needs is the hangman's noose," Johl murmured.

Hayla inched closer to Eero's ear. "While he may still be of some use to us, I don't think we will lose much if we execute him."

"Agreed," Anurak said, "but after he has recovered. Executing a man with his full mental faculties sends a better message to your enemies."

"I would still like to get a signed testimony," Nahla said.

"Forget it, Nahla," Anurak retorted. "The man has lost all sense. Stop trying to look for evidence where there is none."

And just like that, they'd discredited her argument and were now making nefarious plans. Eero regarded her with a sad frown, as if he felt sorry that she had made a fool of herself. "Then it is settled. The Guardians will nurse Daxton back to good health, after which he will be publicly executed. We spread the message far and wide, which will demoralise his supporters in Scottsdale."

"An excellent plan, if I may say so, Your Majesty," Johl said, and it made Nahla sick.

Eero took the kind words in stride. "However, I am still some-what suspicious of how the rebels became so well equipped. Hayla, I'd like to audit every craftsman and merchant in the kingdom, as well as the court records from Scottsdale and Launceston. If there is a plot afoot, I want to uncover it."

Despite her disastrous political defeat, Eero's words gave Nahla a glimmer of hope. Surely *some* evidence would surface!

Hayla furrowed her brow and studied the stone floor. "That will take time, Your Majesty, but it shall be done."

"Good. Dependable as always." Eero faced Anurak. "See to it that Daxton recovers quickly. The sooner he's dead, the better." Then, to Johl, he gave an almost apologetic smile. "I suggest you get your affairs in order. Hayla will audit all governors' records personally."

Johl straightened his back and puffed out his chest, once again a proud man. No longer did he need to grovel and flatter the king in a presumption of innocence. Nahla hated him even more for it.

"I eagerly await Hayla's company at Castle Trevallyn," Johl said. "You will find all my records at your disposal, and my word intact. Rest assured, if we find any rebel sympathisers in my province, I will deal with them swiftly and painfully."

"I expect nothing less, Johl," Eero said. "I am sorry for dragging you here and subjecting you to this embarrassment."

"I have thick skin, Your Majesty. I hope that once this investigation is over, our dear Nahla can finally put aside her dislike for me and we can get on with governing the kingdom."

Nahla felt her blood boil. The fact that everyone smiled at the sentiment without chastising him made it even worse.

Eero waved. "Indeed. Until we meet again, Governor."

"Your Majesty." Johl bowed more deeply than Nahla had seen before. Then he swept his bitter eyes over her one last time before leaving the throne room.

"Nahla, you stay here. Everyone else," Eero said loudly so the guards at the far end could hear, "leave us."

Once all doors had closed, Eero beckoned Nahla to come close. She went right up to his dais, so close that it was bordering on impropriety. She was fuming about losing Johl. She really thought she had him this time, but he had wiggled expertly through the cracks and pounced on the opportunities opened by Hayla and Anurak. *Damn them! Damn all three of them!*

"Keep your voice low," he whispered. "Hayla has a secret room from which she can eavesdrop. She thinks I don't know about it." He laughed. For a man who had just condemned another to death and promised similar fates for any involved in the rebellion, he was rather jovial. "What you did today was right. You had a suspicion, and you came to me. You acted like a true officer of the Legion."

"I was the Captain of the Royal Guard in my old kingdom."

"Indeed?" He raised his eyebrows. "So you're another Captain Vox? I can see the benefit of having two highly experienced military officers in my court, especially if our relations with Hobart go south—pardon the pun." He laughed again. "But your past requires investigation too. I'm sure you understand."

"I do, and I apologise for keeping it a secret. I was concerned for my life."

"I can appreciate your fears." He paused and looked Nahla up and down. Standing this close, she could see the silvery-white strands of his wild, curly hair. "Knowing about your past has certainly answered a lot of questions already. I thought it strange that a woman of your abilities had gone unnoticed in the kingdom until now." He paused again. "We will speak more of your past. I am keenly interested in your kingdom. For now, though, a simple question: Are your people an immediate threat to me?"

"No, Your Majesty. Nobody knows about Tasmania. Even if they did, any forces they might send to invade you would suffer horrible casualties while crossing the Endless Land. It's far too hot."

She purposefully left out that if an invasion force was sent, they'd be abundantly supplied with water for the journey and would take many tents for shelter. But the heat would still be unbearable for many. She had never known such heat before, and the wind was ferocious.

Eero nodded, apparently satisfied. "Good." Then he changed the topic. "This problem you have with Johl. It ends now. I know you hate each other, but I cannot have my best people bickering and plotting each other's downfall while there is so much at stake. If war comes to Launceston, either through a full-scale rebellion or an attack from Hobart, or, God forbid, *both* a civil war and a war of kingdoms, I need you and Johl united by my side. Understood?"

Nahla nodded. She had lost one king already. She had no plans to lose another. "You have my heart and my sword, Your Majesty. Your wish is my command." She hoped that would be enough. To some degree, she meant it, but no order, even if it came from royalty, would stop her from bringing justice to Johl.

"I'm glad to hear it. Now, return to my son and tell him his investigation is over. Hayla and I have taken over."

"As you wish, Your Majesty." Nahla bowed.

She remembered about the rider Myel had dispatched to First Company asking Primus Carro to wait for further orders. Without missing a step, she turned and left the king, already deciding not to mention it. A few days' delay wouldn't be too bad. Carro would be confused, and he would probably send a letter back asking for orders once he grew impatient. That would then confuse Eero and probably get Myel in trouble, but nothing that Myel didn't already expect. It might just give her and Myel enough time to enact a plan from the broken pieces of their investigation. Maybe free Daxton and send a message to his people to scatter. It was that or bloodshed. Now, with Johl off the hook, the potential for slaughter in Scottsdale grew immensely.

Nahla had much to discuss with Myel, and they both had to keep watch even more vigilantly. She'd taken a calculated risk in calling out Johl so publicly. But he'd beaten it, and he'd want revenge. More revenge than he'd ever wanted before.

Nahla would be ready for him.

28

BATTLE TO BATTLE

*In the shadows, the cat licks its wounds, gathering strength
to leap once more, for its spirit knows no defeat.*

—Unknown
Tasmanian proverb

Lord Johl, Governor of Launceston Province, the first among
equals, could not walk fast enough to his carriage. When he
entered and slammed the door shut, his hands shook and he felt
the sweat trickling down his neck.

That was too close, he thought worriedly. Nahla was painfully
accurate with her allegations, and that frightened him beyond
measure. He had only survived the onslaught in the throne room
because some key people challenged his nemesis at the right
moments. As much as he hated to admit it, he would be forever
indebted to Matriarch Anurak and Chamberlain Hayla.

He took a few deep breaths, then told his driver to take him
back to Castle Trevallyn. The driver must have sensed the anger in
the order, for Johl heard two loud cracks of the whip and felt the
carriage jolt.

Right now, Johl regretted many things. He regretted not
having bested Nahla during their first meeting; he regretted that

Nahla had survived when forced to compete as a gladiator; and he regretted that the damned woman had stubbornly survived an ambush by one of the kingdom's most dangerous mercenary gangs. He regretted not warning Daxton that Eero had sent Nahla to spy on him for her test of loyalty—he'd learned of her mission too late. Then, when Daxton was captured, Johl regretted how difficult it was to get to him. In fact, through no fault of his own—and, for once, without the involvement of Nahla—several of his assassination attempts had failed.

But he had come out on top. It had raised King Eero's suspicions, but at least he was leaving the palace alive. Now he had to make sure his records were adjusted so cleanly that nobody could possibly question them. He had moved supplies out of his province, and none of it was accounted for in his books. The records of producers and craftsman had to be triple-checked and adjusted to ensure they matched the master record managed by his chamberlain. That snake Hayla was good with numbers. She would examine everything with a fine-toothed comb, but not even she would find the holes in the province's inventories.

Falsifying—or, rather, improving the falsification of—the records was the easy task. The harder part was speeding up his plan now that Nahla knew part of what he was up to. But that meant drastic decisions that had to be made as soon as possible, and then enacted even faster. His mind spun at everything that needed to be done: war, slaughter, public executions, heavy proclamations. He'd wanted to ease into those troublesome matters, but now they would need to happen in rapid succession. The longer he waited, the more dangerous Nahla became. The sooner he moved ahead with his plans, the sooner he'd be in a more favourable position to deal with that damnable woman. Then nothing could stop him from crushing her once and for all.

His mind raced with dark ideas as his carriage sped through Launceston.

W<small>HEN</small> N<small>AHLA</small> <small>LEFT</small> <small>THE</small> throne room, anger and frustration bubbled within her and painted her face red. Outside, a cluster of legionaries hushed into silence the moment she appeared. They took one look at Nahla and averted their eyes. Except for the legionaries posted *outside* the throne room the whole time, these men and women had heard Nahla's accusations against Johl—accusations which made perfect sense—and also witnessed how badly Nahla failed. They let the lieutenant seethe in her defeat, but what had transpired would no doubt spread to the barracks once their shift was over. Nahla took some consolation in that.

She walked across a courtyard to Myel's residence. Sergeant Garrus and Private Brande flanked the front door. She ignored their inquisitive faces and barged inside. The house was cool, as always, and she marched straight to Myel's room, not bothering to knock.

Myel drifted quickly to his bed like a child who was caught red-handed.

"What are you doing up?" Nahla asked, closing the door behind her.

He plonked himself on the mattress. "Nahla! Two things: Since when did you stop knocking, and since when did you start talking to me like a nurse?"

Nahla pulled a chair close to his bed. In her grumpiness, she frowned at how she needed to do this simple act every time she entered the room. The damn priestesses kept moving it back. "We have a big problem, Myel."

He grinned slightly when she said his name without the title, but her tone checked him and his face fell flat. "Tell me everything."

She related every detail of what had happened in the throne room. With each sentence, Myel's brow furrowed deeper and deeper.

Myel closed his eyes and shook his head. "My father has no idea what he's just swept under the carpet. I hope you're not giving up because of this."

"Not a chance."

"Then what are our next steps?"

"Be on the lookout for Johl's retaliation."

He shook his head. "No. That's *defensive*. I want to go on the *offence*. Dig deeper, strike while Johl is scrambling to recover, cut him down while he's still climbing back up."

Nahla felt her face flush with delight. Not just at the thought of going after Johl more fiercely, but also because Myel had correctly identified an opportunity and wanted to exploit it. He was learning well and progressing fast.

"We can't stick our noses anywhere near Johl at the moment," Nahla said. "Your father has told me to stay away from him."

"Then we adjust our strategy." Myel grinned like he had a dirty secret to tell. "Shift our attention. I'm thinking of Anurak. She supported Johl. Why? She heard Daxton's testimony, so why did she deny it?"

"I'd like to know." Nahla cracked her fingers, imagining herself running amok in the Guardians' administrative building. "There must be a link between them. Tomorrow, I'll go to their headquarters and do some snooping."

Myel grinned wider. "I have a better idea." He did a "come hither" motion with his finger. She leaned in and he spoke softly into her ear. His manly whisper and hot breath sent a shiver down her spine, but his idea startled her even more.

"No," she said. It intrigued her, but it was too dangerous. "No way. You're not even fully recovered yet."

"I'm well enough. And I can see it in your eyes—you want to try it."

As much as she wanted to deny it, she couldn't. The thought had tantalised her for a while, and now that Myel suggested it, she really wanted to give it a go. But it was terribly dangerous.

"I do. But if we try it, I should go alone."

"Absolutely not. We go together, or not at all."

"More people will make it more dangerous."

"Having me there is exactly what you will need if we find anything useful. Who would dare refute the eyewitness testimony of a prince?"

He had a point. "Fine. But you follow my lead and do everything I say. I mean it. We could land ourselves in so much trouble that not even your princely status could save us."

"I know, and I agree you should take the lead. The question is, how do we do it?"

They fell silent for some time. Nahla did what she normally did when faced with a sensitive mission. She pulled it apart, examined it, thought of everything that could go wrong, and tried to figure out how to make more than one thing go right. This one was tricky, but she was no stranger to complexity. What would make it harder was Myel's presence. If only there was some way to hide him . . .

Nahla raised an eyebrow. "I think I know how."

They plotted for the rest of the day and well into the night, making sure they covered everything several times. They only had one chance to get it right.

"We need help," Myel said after a yawn. "And backup."

"I don't like the word backup, but I agree that we need help."

Nahla rounded up the Protectors. Some were on guard duty, and the others were sleeping blissfully in their recently converted quarters on the ground floor of Myel's home. They lined up in Myel's bedroom, fully dressed in their uniforms. Nahla insisted the uniforms were not required, but the legionaries she had awoken insisted on presenting themselves properly.

With the door and windows closed, Myel sat up in his bed and nodded for Nahla to begin.

"If we give you a command that goes against everything you've believed in, would you do it?" Nahla asked. It was a big question. Answers were not immediately forthcoming, so Nahla pressed them. "Some difficult times may be upon us. I need to know if you will do what's necessary for Myel's safety and for the good of the kingdom."

This time, Sergeant Tullius raised his chin and nodded seriously. "Jaymen told us what Daxton said—that Johl is the one supplying the rebels. Whatever happens now, you have my loyalty."

"And mine," Jaymen said.

Then the rest nodded and expressed the same.

"Permission to speak freely, Lieutenant?" Garrus asked.

"Go ahead."

"What happened when you met the king today?"

Nahla and Myel shared a glance.

"My father dismissed Nahla's case," Myel replied. "Matriarch Anurak denied Daxton's testimony. Lord Johl has not been arrested, but he has been ordered to provide his records to my father's chamberlain."

A wave of mild grumbles and scowls swept through the eight Protectors.

That feedback gave Nahla confidence. "I have called you in here because Prince Myel and I have not given up. We have a plan. A very dangerous plan. Our mission may reveal nothing. In which case, we all forget that it happened. But if we discover something incriminating, every one of you will share the same accountability as the prince and me. And if something goes wrong, all our lives will be at stake. Before we tell you about it, I am giving each of you an opportunity to step away and avoid the risk. You may leave now if you wish. We won't judge you."

Eight proud faces stared back at her.

"Very well," Nahla continued. "From this point on, there is no turning back."

Nahla and Myel outlined the plan. The Protectors listened with interest, glad to be finally taking some action that might yield hard results. The threat of death hung over everyone, but Nahla kept emphasising the big picture—the kingdom. After all, in protecting the prince, weren't they also protecting the kingdom?

29

ONE FATEFUL NIGHT

Throughout history, few have received the dual blessing and curse of being the instigators of change. There are pivotal moments when the threads of fate converge, and we find ourselves standing at the precipice of choice. Yet, as we tread the intricate paths of life, it is often in hindsight that we come to comprehend the magnitude of these moments. Our decisions, like ripples in a fountain, extend far beyond our own reflection, touching the lives of others and reshaping our very existence. It is in these sacred instances, where the weight of our choices becomes apparent, that we grasp the profound interconnectedness of all things. For within the quiet depths of each decision lies the potential to transform destinies, to unravel the knowledge that has been so carefully woven by those before us, and to reveal a new landscape, forever altered by the choices we dared to make.

—**Nahla Northborn**
Journal of Penance

IN THE COURTYARD OF the Guardians, Nahla led a water cart towards the looming temple. She wore a white robe stolen from the priestess who was living with Myel during his convalescence. Earlier in the day, she'd sewn blue stripes onto the robe's shoulders. Tucked under the robe's hood was a blonde wig she had borrowed from Myel's steward. She covered every strand of her black hair with the blonde imitation. The Protectors followed behind the water cart, mounted on horseback in two columns. They neglected to wear their insignia, and they also wore capes and hoods and kept their heads low.

Nahla had picked a late hour because Matriarch Anurak would most likely be in bed and the Divine Guards watching the temple would be drowsy. As luck would have it, the night was cloudy, so an especially dark shadow blanketed the courtyard. She pulled her hood as far forwards as it could go and cast her eyes to the ground as she approached the Divine Guards by the temple entrance. She bowed, mimicking the slow movements she had observed so many times before.

"A royal mission to Campbell Province," Nahla said to the guards. "I am to perform the Litany of Water and accompany them on their journey." She handed them a sheet of paper signed with King Eero's name and seal. Myel's father had given him a stamp to help with the administrative load of the kingdom. It came in handy.

One Divine Guard examined the letter under a single fiery torch-light. Nahla stepped back to get away from the torch's luminescence. Fake hair or not, Nahla had a popular face. She couldn't risk these guards recognising her.

"Proceed, sister."

Nahla felt it would be more believable if she performed the litany herself, if only to convince the other priestesses that she was one of them. From her observations, she'd found out that the litany was not a word-for-word prayer; rather, it followed a series of predetermined topics which a priestess could speak about in her own words. Nahla had spent most of the day practicing what she would say to get it just right. She faced the Protectors.

"God of Launceston," she said with just enough volume that the small group could hear her. She didn't want her voice to carry over the courtyard to Matriarch Anurak's open window and wake the beast. "We thank you immeasurably for the supply of your life-sustaining water, for without it, the world would stop, and life would perish. We respect this divine provision and the channel through which you provide it, and we respect the sacredness of its use in everyday life. *Fiat*."

"*Fiat*," the Protectors softly intoned. Since hearing it for the first time, Nahla had learned that it loosely meant "Let it be".

"We pray for that gift once again tonight," Nahla continued. "Our valiant soldiers are embarking on a long journey. Your water will help them arrive in good health. What is not used on their journey will be donated to the poor and needy of Campbell, because water unites us all. Please, if you will, provide us with your sustenance. We remain your servants forever and always. *Fiat*."

"*Fiat*."

The burning torches crackled in the ensuing silence. Nahla turned and waited, fearing that her prayer was not good enough, and that she had aroused the suspicions of the Divine Guards. But they stepped aside, gesturing for Nahla to enter.

Nahla swallowed hard as relief washed over her. She kept her head down and led the mule-drawn water cart towards the temple door and into the dark interior. A coolness enveloped her, and she found the experience refreshing. After several steps, the doors closed behind her with a thud.

She was in utter darkness, and she worried that if she moved, she'd lose her sense of direction and walk into something. The mule screeched, and then the temple was suddenly as bright as day.

"Oh, my goodness," she whispered as her eyes surveyed the most forbidden place in the entire kingdom. Then she shook the sense back into herself and got to work. She went to one of the barrels on the cart and quickly opened it.

Myel shot up, taking a deep breath. "Why did you say such a long prayer?"

"I had to make it sound convincing," Nahla snapped. She threw back her hood, catching the blonde wig before it fell. "And it worked. We made it."

"So we . . . did." Myel's eyes scanned the room and his voice trailed off. He stepped down from the carriage wearing nothing but an old shirt and pants. For a moment, he stood transfixed at the temple's guts, wearing a face of childlike wonder.

It was like nothing Nahla had ever seen, and judging by Myel's expression, the experience was mutual. The temple was one cavernous room with innumerable light sources that glowed with other-worldly brilliance. Their shine was constant and focused, completely unlike the flaming torches and braziers used by kings and commoners alike.

Gigantic cylinders stretched up to the tiered ceiling. Many pipes criss-crossed from cylinder to cylinder in perfectly straight lines and a variety of clean angles. Every pipe eventually found its way back to a single master pipe as wide as Nahla's torso that went into the ground in the middle of the temple.

"Don't tell me . . ." Myel said to himself.

He knelt next to the main pipe. Next to it was a large red wheel and a cubiform contraption with strange markings. Some had numbers and lines, similar to a carpenter's measuring stick. There were also coloured circular protrusions of a strange glass-like material. More markings beneath them identified what the protrusions were, but neither Nahla nor Myel knew all the words. They identified the words ON and OFF, but the other words made no sense to them.

"This must be a lost ancient language," Myel said. "Or maybe an earlier version of English."

Myel and Nahla tried sounding out the words, but they had no way of knowing if their pronunciation was correct. Myel wrote everything he saw—strange words like PRIME, BOOST, WARNING, and FLOW RATE. The characters looked similar to their language, and they were easy to copy, but their meaning was anyone's guess. Another set of protrusions, square this time, were numbered one to four in standard numeral characters. The entire contraption was made with an assortment of materials that Nahla had never encountered. It looked like metal, but felt like something else.

"What is it?" Nahla asked.

"I think this is what I've imagined for so long. It's a device for sucking water out of the ground."

"Is that why our world is so dry?"

"Maybe." He ran his fingers over the strange box. "This raises more questions, but I think it says a lot about the Guardians." He looked up at the giant cylinders and pointed. "Let's go up there."

A flight of metal steps went up to a landing that wrapped around the temple. More flights led higher and higher to other landings at every tier of the temple's ziggurat design. Nahla and Myel ascended to the first level, inspecting the pipes and cylinders along the way.

"I bet these are water tanks," Myel said. He knocked on one of them. "I reckon the water is summoned from the ground and kept in these. Then, when the Guardians come to get water 'from God', they just source it from these storage tanks."

"If that's the truth, then your people have been lied to for how long?" Nahla asked.

She was careful to frame the question objectively, though she already knew it to be true. Her own people in Melbourne sourced water from wells; however, their method of doing so was vastly different to what she was seeing here, and religion also had nothing to do with it.

"The decree about water has been with my people for generations. It is ingrained in our society." He paused and put a hand on a pipe. "So cold." He looked upwards, and Nahla knew he wanted to continue exploring.

"We should finish here. It doesn't take long to fill up a single water cart. The Divine Guards might get suspicious."

"Do you think they have the authority to come inside? I've only ever seen priestesses enter, and only the ones with blue stripes on their robes."

"Still, we shouldn't linger."

His face sagged. "Okay. But I swear on my dear mother's life we'll come back here, and we'll open it for all to see."

Myel rarely spoke about his mother, who had passed away while giving birth to him. If he made an oath on her name, he must have been serious.

They went down to ground level and Nahla broached the topic. "What are you thinking?"

"I'm going to confront my father about this. There's no way he doesn't know about it."

"And if he truly doesn't?"

"Then the lies of the Guardians are the next biggest problem after Johl."

Nahla bit her lip anxiously. "And if they're in league with Johl?"

"Then we're in all sorts of trouble."

They stopped by the water carriage and Nahla gave the mule a pat. "We should think about this first."

"No. We're running out of time. I'm going to speak to him." When he made a decision, he could be so headstrong.

Nahla, aware that time was quickly passing, pushed Myel unceremoniously against the water cart. "We'll talk about this later. Get in so we can get out."

As he climbed the carriage, Nahla gently pushed against his firm bottom to stop him from falling backwards. "It is an absolute joy to be woman-handled by you." He flashed her a cheeky grin and slid into one of the dank barrels.

Nahla rolled her eyes and sealed the top, stifling a smile. Even in the most crucial moments, Myel had a way of making her smile with only a few words or a suggestive facial expression. But she didn't let those thoughts distract her, because now she had to figure out how to douse the cart with water to make it seem like it was full.

A flexible pipe sat neatly coiled around a purpose-built stand. Nahla had never seen or felt a pipe that was so flexible. One end was already attached to a water tank. She unravelled some of it and brought it to the carriage, then wondered how to summon the water. Back home, they used a pumping device with a long lever. Some pumps were big enough to require two people to use in a see-saw action. But there were no pumps like that in the temple.

Next to the rest of the still-coiled pipe was a handle similar to the one on Myel's water tank in his garden. Nahla turned it and water began pouring out of the pipe. She doused the barrels and some of the cart's wooden framework. As a last-minute thought, she put some water in a few barrels, just so they would make a sloshing sound as the cart rolled across the courtyard outside. Then, when the job was done, she cut the water flow and did her best to wrap the pipe up like she'd found it.

Her next challenge was leaving the temple like a normal priestess. This part she hadn't seen. How were the torches turned off? She supposed the same way they were activated, but they had shone automatically when she'd entered.

Every passing second brought her closer to being discovered, so she pulled the hood over her head, ensuring her wig stayed in place, and turned the mule around. As she approached the door, she spotted a lonely switch on the wall. Did it control the lighting? She bit her lip and flicked it. The surreal torches shut off, casting the temple into darkness again. Then the doors opened and she could see a small area of illumination outside, lit by the fires of handheld torches.

She led the mule out, pausing only to reach for her torch, which one of the Divine Guards returned to her.

"A safe journey to you and the King's Legion, sister."

"Thank you," was all Nahla said, because she couldn't wait to leave.

Garrus, leading the Protectors, barked an order and the others swung their horses and moved into convoy formation, accompanying the water cart out of the courtyard.

Nahla's heart thudded harder than ever before. She could not believe what she had just done, what truths she had learned, and that their mission was a success. But she was also worried about what would happen next.

THEY DITCHED THE WATER cart in an out-of-the-way spot among some trees just outside of the city. Nahla and Myel dressed themselves in their armour, which the Protectors had safely stored in their travel packs. Then they mounted the horse of the lowest-ranking Protector, Marston, who hopped on with Sheph. The entire group rode back into Launceston via a different road, entering the palace grounds via the military gate.

The Protectors were professional. They didn't ask questions, but even in the torchlight, Nahla could see in their faces how eager they were to hear about the temple. Once they were safely inside Myel's house, they crowded into his study and locked the door and windows.

"The Guardians have lied to us," Myel said. "No Divine Being provides us with water. It does not appear miraculously. It is pulled from below the ground. I presume there is an inexhaustible supply, because we haven't run out after all this time."

This news shocked the Protectors. From the stalwart sergeants to the lowliest privates, they vocalised their feelings of betrayal and demanded to know what would be done about it. They questioned their service as legionaries. Nahla, sensing the risks of such talk, gave them a stern reminder that they served the king, not the Guardians, and to remember who they were speaking to.

Perhaps fearing to speak out further, the Protectors fell into disciplined silence. Everyone waited for Myel.

"I am going to my father about this," he said plainly. It seemed to go down well with his soldiers.

"You have our support, Your Highness," Garrus replied. Though he shared the same rank as Tullius, he had held the rank of sergeant longer, so he was the most senior Protector after Nahla.

"I want everyone on duty tonight, inside and out," Nahla said. "The next few days will be critical. Dismissed."

Eight military-grade sandals stomped on the smooth stone floor and eight fists saluted, then the Protectors filed out. Nahla regarded Myel from across the room.

"I urge you to reconsider," she said. "Let's make a plan and do some more digging before we go to your father."

He furrowed his brow. "Absolutely not. What more is there to investigate? We've uncovered the greatest lie in the kingdom's history. Once people learn about this, there will be chaos. I *must* talk to my father about it, and I'll go tonight. I don't care if he is asleep."

They argued about it for hours—their first proper argument, with icy voices and clenched fists. Nahla worried about the repercussions of taking another wild accusation to Eero without developing a solid plan against everyone and everything that stood against them, especially now that their enemies seemed to include more than just Johl. Moreover, in bringing this news to Eero, they would admit their crime of entering the temple. Myel didn't care about that. Instead, he feared that the longer they waited, the more damage Johl would cause. No, he had to confront his father, and he would do it alone.

"You demanded to come with me to the temple," Nahla said. "Now I demand to go with you to your father."

Myel gave her a warm smile tinged with sadness. Such a change from the wildly passionate man he had been moments ago. He knew what he was about to do, knew the risks, and knew that he was dragging Nahla into it. But that smile melted Nahla's heart. "I knew I could count on you. Let's go."

So off they went to ignite a flame that could very well consume the entire kingdom.

30

CONFRONTATION

Faced with a deep, fundamental truth, the reactions of men diverge like a flock of sheep at an intersection. Some cannot bear the weight of truth's revelation and flutter away into the comforting embrace of denial. Others resist with fierce determination, clinging to their convictions and twisted reasonings, despite the piercing clarity before them. And there are those who embrace truth's majestic presence, their hearts expanding with newfound wisdom and understanding, motivating them to action. Truth is a potent force that unveils the hidden layers of existence and has the power to illuminate, shatter, or elevate the human spirit. How we respond to its call reveals the depths of our character and the trajectory of our journey.

—Cass the Blasphemer
The Truth

WHEN NAHLA MARCHED INTO the palace, she felt an inkling of the power, passion, and confidence that coursed through Myel's veins. Right then, Nahla had nothing but admiration for the man. She'd seen him grow from a timid introvert to a force to be reckoned with in such a short time, and through no small part of her own. Now he was going to confront his father about something that could completely destabilise the kingdom. Though Nahla wanted more time to prepare, she still gave him her full support. It was her sworn duty to do so, but her own moral sense and her growing friendship played a part too.

261

Even at this late hour, they came across Chamberlain Hayla prowling the corridors. Or perhaps the chamberlain had heard of Myel's presence and had come to intercept him. Nahla stood close to the prince, wary of the mysterious woman with her concealed dagger and duplicitous agendas.

"Prince Myel," Hayla said as courteously as possible, "what brings you to the palace of night?"

"I must speak with my father," Myel said. He didn't stop for her. Hayla hurried to keep up with him, and Nahla smiled mischievously at the spectacle.

"The king is busy in his war room," Hayla said.

That made Myel stop. "Doing what? My father is never awake."

"Ensuring that the invasion of Scottsdale will be successful."

Nahla and Myel shared a glance. Myel pressed his lips, which told Nahla all she needed to know—that coming to the palace tonight was not a hasty mistake. He stormed off in a different direction. Nahla followed, but Hayla took a different route. She probably knew all the secret passages.

By the time they burst into the war room, Hayla was already present; however, it looked as though she hadn't had much time to warn Eero. The king stooped over a large table, on which was an incredibly detailed map. With him were Captain Vox and Nahla's nemesis, Lord Johl.

This should be interesting, Nahla thought.

Eero straightened and levelled a finger at his son. "You, boy. *You* have delayed the assault against the rebels. Carro sent me a message. He is *not* happy."

"I am not a *boy* anymore, Father. I understand more that you think I do. Your invasion is unnecessary and unwarranted, but I'm here for a different reason."

"Then spit it out! I have plans to make."

The parties faced each other in the dim candlelight. It was entirely fitting that Eero, Johl, and Vox stood on one side of the table, Myel and Nahla on the other, and between them a map of Scottsdale—the province that had divided father and son ever since Myel got himself involved in the rebellion. Curiously, Hayla stood next to both groups, as if she was sitting on the fence.

Myel took a deep breath. "I've been inside the temple."

Eero gasped. "You what?"

"You heard me. I went inside the temple tonight. I've seen everything. I know water isn't from God. I know the prayers are useless. I know the Guardians are useless. I think I know how water is sourced. But I know you've been promoting an age-old lie to your subjects."

Nahla cleared her throat. "I was there too."

"Of course you were," Johl said with a scoff. "You probably put him up to it."

"It was my idea," Myel said. "Why, Father? Why lie to your people like this?"

Eero dropped his gaze to the map. "You wouldn't understand."

"But I was supposed to understand eventually, right? When were you going to tell me? On your deathbed? When I became king?"

Eero sighed. "The day before your coronation, you would have been led into the temple in secret and told the truth. If you accepted it and swore an oath to maintain the secret, the Guardians would have crowned you the following day. If not, they'd have executed you on the spot. The people would be told that God did not accept you as the new king. This is how the monarchy has functioned for as long as recorded history."

It was fleeting, but Nahla caught just a glimmer of sadness in Eero's eyes. Had he felt comfortable accepting the lie when he was proclaimed king? Did he swear the oath just to stay alive? It all made sense to her now. King Eero and Matriarch Anurak were so close because that was the ruling structure of the kingdom—religion and politics, rulership by religious appointment. Except that, too, was a lie.

"So the Guardians would have killed me?" Myel asked quietly.

"You would not have accepted the oath?" Eero countered.

"Don't you know me by now?"

They spoke as if they were the only two people in the room. Father and son were obviously sharing a bittersweet moment, but Nahla had to break it. Too much was at stake. "It sounds to me like Lord Johl already knows the secret."

"I have a privileged position in this kingdom," Johl replied. "I am one of King Eero's closest confidants."

"The Lord of Launceston always knows the truth," Hayla explained. "That is why he is considered first among equals and keeps his office until death."

"And you, Hayla?" Myel asked.

"It is my job to know everything."

"Who else knows?" Myel asked his father.

Eero received an approving nod from Hayla. "Anurak and a special group of senior Guardians." He faced Vox. "And now my Captain of the King's Legion."

Vox stood straight-backed and held his chin high. "I will take this secret to my grave."

"I know you will," Eero told him, though that could have meant immediately or at the full term of his natural life.

What Nahla really wanted to know was how the secret was kept so tight when so many people knew about it. If there were five Guardians at every temple in the kingdom who were allowed inside, then that was already twenty-five people. She couldn't be sure how many Guardians knew, but twenty-five was a conservative number, and it was already too many for such a profound secret. It was no wonder that a woman like Cass, whom she had met in Launceston Prison, was so easily accused of blasphemy and sentenced to death. She wondered if the poor woman was still alive.

"What you have told us is the worst imaginable crime," Johl said. He wore a wicked smile, and his eyes glowed in the candlelight.

"Nahla, of course, cannot be allowed to live. I'm sure you understand, Your Majesty."

Eero didn't reply, but he regarded Nahla with a regretful scorn. Nahla's blood pumped harder. She was on full alert now that Johl's machinations were out in the open.

Johl continued. "His Royal Highness must be given the opportunity to swear his oath. After all, he is your heir, and I am sure we can put him under oath before he is ready to ascend the throne."

Eero's eyes lingered on Nahla. Then he sighed deeply and turned his attention to Myel. "It will have to be done officially by Anurak, but I will ask you now for my peace of mind. Do you agree to uphold the Water Oath? Do you agree to maintain the secret that has kept the monarchy strong for as long as time can remember? Do you accept the price of blood if you cannot agree to the price of water?"

Even before he finished speaking, Nahla knew how Myel would answer. Without thinking twice, Myel gave his firm response.

"No."

Nahla had never been a mother, and she had never known her real parents. But she had seen enough fathers lose their sons, and the pain in Eero's eyes spoke of just the same loss.

"Then I have no choice," Eero whispered. "I must put you to death."

Hayla drew her dagger in silence, but Nahla saw the movement of her robes and the glint of steel in the candlelight. As Hayla thrust the dagger towards Myel's throat, Nahla unsheathed her sword and whipped the sharp blade up against Hayla's hand. The chamberlain shrieked. The dagger clattered harmlessly against Myel's cuirass, then dropped to the stone floor.

"Get out of here!" Nahla barked at Myel.

Eero and Hayla backed away while Vox and Johl rounded the table, swords drawn.

Myel also drew his. "What about you?" But a guttural growl

from Johl, who came at Nahla with full force, drowned out his question. Their swords clashed.

"I said get out!" she repeated while parrying. "Get as far away from here as you can."

"Guards!" Hayla shouted. "Guards!"

Nahla battled against Johl and Vox. Fortunately, the size and furnishings of the war room did not provide enough opportunity for them to encircle her.

"Go!" Nahla bellowed, and Myel finally left. As he passed through the door, two legionaries bustled in. They stood back as Nahla parried her dual attackers.

"Capture Prince Myel," Hayla ordered the legionaries. "Do not let him escape!" They hesitated. "Run, you fools!"

Nahla tried for the door, but Vox thwarted her movements with some skilful lunges. When she defended against them, Johl used the opportunity to strike devastating blows. But she had modified her armour, closing the gaps and joints with sections of her special brigandine garment that she'd brought from Melbourne. Hence, she shrugged off the attacks. Johl clenched his teeth in frustration.

Deciding enough was enough, Nahla swept her sword low against Vox's leg. The man was twice her age and not nearly as nimble, and he failed to jump in time. The sword sliced deep into his calf and he collapsed in a wail of screams and curses.

Johl swung hard against Nahla. She deflected the attack, but her footing was wrong and it sent her stumbling past Vox towards Hayla and Eero. She tried to escape by rounding the table, but a hand grasped her ankle and she tripped, falling to her knee. The hand felt small and bony. She cursed Hayla's quick response as she spun around, ready for Johl's inevitable strike. Even before she could get to her feet, she saw Johl's sword coming down and she instinctively raised her own to stop it. The clash of metal on metal nearly pushed her sword against her forehead. Using all the power she could muster in her legs, she pushed herself up, forcing Johl backwards into Eero's soft, portly frame.

While Johl chased her around the table, Nahla bolted for the door. Just as she approached it, Hayla's dagger embedded itself in the wooden frame, missing Nahla's face by a hand width and stopping her in her tracks. The slimy chamberlain had thrown it from a crouched position across the room, using her unwounded hand. Nahla contemplated pulling it out as a second weapon, but there was no time. Her pause in momentum was enough for Johl to catch up.

The governor fought Nahla once again. Their fight was long overdue, and Nahla relished the opportunity, but bemoaned the circumstances. They were terribly close to one another. There just wasn't enough room to fight properly. Eventually, Nahla found herself in an armlock with Johl, wrestling to get her sword arm free while simultaneously holding his sword out of the way.

"Any help would be appreciated," Johl barked, and Nahla knew it irked him to ask for support.

Vox, useless on the floor with his wound, failed to come to Johl's aid, so Hayla grabbed the captain's gilded sword and pressed it against Nahla's throat.

"Cease your resistance, Nahla," the chamberlain ordered. She'd thrown back her hood in the madness, revealing a crop of short, auburn hair. "It's over."

Nahla and Johl locked eyes and held each other in their death grip. She was unwilling to let go, to let the threat loose again.

Johl smiled that evil smile again. "Let go of me, Nahla. You've lost."

Finally, against her will, she released him and threw her sword on the polished stonework. Hayla kept her weapon close to Nahla's throat. Eero stepped closer to the now former King's Legion lieutenant—the woman he once valued so highly. Bitterness and contempt had washed away his jovial spirit. Nahla knew this was the end of the line for her. If they were willing to kill Myel here and now, then her death was just around the corner.

31

FAMILIAR WALLS

In the labyrinth of life, familiarity often becomes a beacon
of solace. I am comforted by familiarity's embrace. It whis-
pers tales of known patterns, predictable outcomes, and a
sense of control in the face of uncertainty.

—**Nahla Northborn**
Monologues

NAHLA RELIVED THE PAST. Lord Johl's black-clad soldiers dragged her
through Launceston Prison's dark corridors. She'd been stripped of
her officer's sword, and her valuable armour was violently pulled
from her body. Now she wore only a white undergarment. It did
nothing to vent the furious heat boiling within her.

She'd been bested again by Johl, but the situation was now
more dire than ever before. Johl stood closer to the king, united in
their goal to protect their unholy lie about water. Myel had fled, but
Nahla didn't know if he even made it out of the palace grounds.
If he'd been captured, he could be standing before his father
right now with a sword at his throat. Or he could be dead already.
As for herself . . . well, she felt her end swiftly approaching. She
was neither sad nor regretful, just angry. Angry that she had let it
come to this. Angry that Johl still roamed free while she had been
condemned.

Angry that she had failed to protect another kingdom of innocent people.

Keys clanked in a heavy lock and an even heavier metal door screeched open. Then the soldiers pushed Nahla in so hard she fell to her knees. The door banged behind her, the echo ringing in her ears.

"Fresh meat," came a sinister voice.

Nahla stood and scanned the collection of dirty, haggard faces. A man approached her. He was roughly her size, shirtless, and covered in grime. But he froze a few paces away, then took a step backwards.

"Touch me, and you're dead," Nahla told him. He shrank back, defeated by her recognisable face and her authoritative warning.

"Nahla!" The owner of a soft voice ran past the retreating man and caught Nahla in a hug. Nahla thought she'd never see the fair-skinned, fair-haired woman again.

"Cass?" Nahla hugged back. She only spent one night by her side, but she welcomed seeing a familiar face in this grim moment. "You're still alive." She wanted it to be a question, but she was so happy to see Cass that it came out more like a statement.

Cass stepped away. "They think I'm dead already," she said with a devilish grin. She had such a youthful vigour despite her predicament. Nahla wondered how old she was.

"I've found some of your writings in hidden corners of the world. You didn't tell me how active you were."

The young woman shrugged. "People need to know. Words are my weapon."

"We'll be needing a lot more than words soon. The kingdom will soon be at war."

"What do you mean? Why are you here? Last I heard, you became a legionary."

Nahla put her hand on Cass' shoulder. "I'm a blasphemer, like you."

They stared at each other like twin sisters who had been separated at birth.

"What did you do?" Cass asked, smiling.

Nahla smiled back. "I snuck into the temple."

Cass' eyes widened. She mouthed the words as if trying to make sense of them. Other prisoners moved closer. Nahla surveyed their expressions. Some appeared shocked, others had their faces scrunched in disbelief, still others listened with keen interest.

"I snuck into the temple," she repeated. "So did Prince Myel. I disguised myself as a Guardian, and he hid in a barrel on a water cart. We learned a terrible secret, and now we're paying for it."

"What did you learn?" someone shouted from the back.

"What was inside?"

"Were you discovered?"

"Why was the prince there?"

"Calm down, everyone," Cass shouted. They actually listened to her. "Let Nahla speak."

Cass evidently had some kind of sway over these people, which Nahla used to her advantage. With two fellow prisoners branded as blasphemers, she could ignite something that would catch Johl's attention. He may have imprisoned her, and though she had accepted her death, she wasn't prepared to go down without a fight.

She related everything that had happened earlier that night. How she'd petitioned God, how she'd entered the temple under false pretences, and how she and Myel explored the innards of the mysterious building. She explained Myel's suspicions about how water was sourced and stored and then used to control the people. She explained how Myel brought the truth to his father, and how the king admitted to the lie that had governed the lives of the citizens of Launceston for innumerable generations.

A murmur of anger swept through the cramped cell. She related how the king ordered the immediate execution of his son.

When she mentioned how close Chamberlain Hayla had come to ending Myel's life, a few prisoners gasped. They crowded closer to her, smothering her with their body heat and foul odours.

"Myel fled at my order, but he wanted to stay and fight," she explained.

"He's a good man," a voice shouted out of sight.

"I then fought Lord Johl," she continued.

"That bastard!"

"Murderer!"

"Tyrant!"

It was a cell of like-minded prisoners. All she needed to do was incite them into an unstoppable fury.

"Johl is the reason I'm here," Nahla shouted back. She wanted the surrounding cells to hear too. "Who put you in prison?"

"Johl!" several people yelled at once.

"What were your crimes?"

"Being poor."

"Being too crippled to work."

"Disturbing the peace."

Nahla was not naive. She knew they were euphemisms for real crimes, but she also suspected those were crimes of desperation— thieving just to stay alive.

"How many gladiator contests has he organised?" she asked. Various numbers flew back at her. "You see, Johl murders you all for the mere entertainment of the people. Do you know what it is? It's a distraction! He's keeping the people happy while he commits crimes far worse than all of ours put together. Do you know he tried to kill Prince Myel on the road from Scottsdale?"

A wave of scoffs swept the cell. Some prisoners even spat on the filthy floor in disgust.

"It's true. The prince and I were getting too close to the truth, and he tried to have us killed. He hired mercenaries to ambush us."

"How did you escape?" a young man asked. He couldn't have been older than twenty.

"We fought bravely. He had a King's Legion escort, but two legionaries lost their lives. That's two more victims of Johl's evil plans. Fourteen, if you add the mercenaries we killed in self-defence. But that's not all. You've all heard of the inmate named Daxton? They held him in a tower in this very prison. Johl tried to assassinate him several times. That's why Governor Ibeza died—drinking poisoned wine meant for Daxton. Why? So Johl could hide his connection with the rebellion in Scottsdale."

"What rebellion?" Cass asked.

Nahla had been so caught up in the momentum of her speech that the question didn't register at first. Of course, these prisoners must not have heard that the bandits in Scottsdale were actually an organised rebellion. She updated them.

"Johl has been supporting the rebellion in direct opposition to Lord Garyd, right under King Eero's nose. As we speak, there are two companies of the King's Legion in Scottsdale. A war is brewing, and Johl is behind all of it. He has big plans, and he's going to slaughter tens of thousands of people for his own gain."

An old woman raised her hand politely. Nahla wondered what she could have possibly done to end up in the dark walls of Launceston Prison. "What does Johl want?"

All eyes fell on Nahla again. That was the one thing she and Myel couldn't figure out. What would motivate a man to spill so much blood? Was it water? Land? Resources? It could have been one or all of those things, or others. Right now, though, she needed to give these inmates another reason to hate Johl—a reason to follow her lead. A reason that might not be far from the truth.

"We think Johl is trying to seize Scottsdale for himself," she said. "There's a temple in the province. More water means more power. He knows the lie of the temples, and he has vowed to keep it a secret. The more control he has over the kingdom's water, the more power he has to influence people. Then nobody can stop him." She let that sink in. "He hasn't obtained that power yet, but he's close. He's driven Prince Myel into hiding. He's locked me up to prepare for an execution, and he has the king in his pocket. He's labelled me a blasphemer, but I'm not going down without a fight. Will you stand with me?"

Of all the crimes Nahla had heard of in Launceston, being labelled a blasphemer was the worst of the worst. The crowd of inmates went quiet, suddenly wary of admitting out loud that they supported her. That was how ingrained the Guardians' teachings were in Launceston society. If they followed Nahla, they would automatically become the worst criminals in the prison. Would they willingly sign their own death warrants when the executioner was barely a stone's throw away?

"I stand with you," Cass said. She faced the crowd. "How long have I advocated for truth and action? Well, we have the truth. Now we need to take action! Are you going to let them step on us forever? Or will you do something about it?"

A tall, skinny man with greying hair pushed through the crowd. He towered over Nahla and Cass, but he seemed kindly and unthreatening. "I'm with you."

Then came a woman with a deep scar along her cheek. "Me too."

One by one, the prisoners pledged their support. It was hard to count in the shadowy cell, but Nahla figured she had about fifty inmates swearing their allegiance to her.

"Down with Lord Johl!" Nahla shouted. The inmates repeated it with a roar. "Open the temples!" Again, they echoed with fervour.

The cell thundered with the relentless repeating of these brief cries. Eventually, the surrounding cells joined, creating a deafening taunt against any who opposed. Nahla watched their cell door, saw one of the prison guards peer inside, his face a contorted mix of fear and horror. He locked eyes with her, and she stared with such a determination that he backed up and disappeared.

Nahla smiled at the small victory, hoping it would be the first of many—hoping that this was not, in fact, the beginning of her demise.

32

DESPERATE REPLY

Provoke the wasps, and their flight becomes a tempest of fury.

—Unknown
Tasmanian proverb

IN THE DEEPEST PART of the night, Johl tossed and turned in his bed. His sheets and pillows were slick with sweat. The dampness on his neck only made his slumber even more uncomfortable. He usually spent the hours of darkness frolicking with a woman— one of the innumerable peasant girls or townswomen from in and around Launceston. But tonight, when his thoughts assaulted his mind, he just wanted to be alone.

He'd successfully defeated Nahla and Myel together, and in the presence of King Eero, no less. He should have been happy. Soon after the altercation, Eero had quit the war preparations for the evening, and Johl had retired to his castle. Sleep should have come easily, knowing that his two greatest enemies were out of the picture. But too many secrets were revealed lately. The future suddenly seemed foggy. How would Myel and Nahla's revelations affect his plans? How soon could he have Nahla executed? Would the Legion catch Myel and bring him to justice? So many questions.

But the worst question of all kept playing on his mind: How would Eero handle the situation? Even now, Johl worried that Eero would turn against him. If that happened at this point in Johl's plans, he could not hope to save himself. The next days and weeks would be critical.

A harsh knocking on his door jolted him. His fatigue slipped away instantly, replaced by alertness . . . and fear. He threw off his thin bed sheet and grabbed the sword leaning against his bedside table. If Eero had changed his mind and ordered Johl's arrest, he'd be ready to fight. The door shook as someone pounded harder. Johl gulped.

"Enter!"

In came Jugg, discernible even in the bedroom's darkness.

"My lord," Jugg said. His voice rumbled like an avalanche of boulders. "I bring dire news."

Johl breathed a little slower, but he kept a firm grip on his sword. "What is it, Jugg?"

"Nahla is spreading dissension in the prison." He closed the door behind him. "The inmates are shouting for your downfall, and they're ordering that we open the temples. What does all this mean?"

Even locked away from society, Nahla is still causing me trouble! He sighed, cursing his stupidity. After the mind-spinning episode at the palace, he'd hastily ordered Nahla's incarceration, sending her to the prison's general population. He should have known better. He cursed himself again. He should have put her in isolation or sent her to the palace's dungeon where she would be truly alone. Better yet, he should have run his sword through her right there in the war room.

"My lord?" Jugg asked. He laboured on the last word, sounding impatient.

"What?"

"Why is Nahla inciting the prisoners like this? What does it mean?"

"This problem is above your head."

"Is it a problem I can fix?"

Oh, how Jugg wanted to skewer Nahla! But Johl wouldn't give him the satisfaction. Before he could reply, he heard his chamberlain frantically speaking to someone outside. Many hurried footsteps sounded from the hallway, renewing Johl's fears.

"To me, Jugg!"

The large man crossed the room before the door burst open. Johl's chamberlain entered, carrying a small lamp, adding much-needed light to the bedroom. Trailing him was a retinue of important people: King Eero in royal robes, Captain Vox limping with a bandaged leg, Hayla with a bandaged hand, and Matriarch Anurak with groggy eyes. Johl readied himself for a fight.

"Johl!" Eero barked. "There is madness in the prison. Inmates are on the verge of rioting. We must do something."

Johl relaxed. His king had not come to arrest him. He was seeking help. In fact, by coming to Johl, Eero showed that he was coming to his *only* source of help at a time like this. That put Johl at ease.

"We need to act fast, Your Majesty," Johl said. "Quell this problem before sunrise."

"The problem goes beyond the inmates," Hayla said. Eero stepped aside so she could be seen. "The prison guards have heard everything. They must be dealt with too."

"Hayla has already silenced the legionaries who may have overheard our scuffle with Nahla at the palace," Eero told him. He ran a finger across his neck.

Johl flinched, imagining the quiet woman doing such dirty work. She seemed completely unaffected. But she was right to question the prison guards as well.

"The entire shift must be killed," Johl said. It was amazing how casually and quickly he could order executions when pushed into a corner. "We must kill them before they go home and tell their families. I will have Jugg round them up and take them outside the city."

"Take them to the Tamar Valley," Hayla said. "As far north as you can go."

"A long way to travel just to dump bodies," Jugg mumbled.

"You won't be killing them here," Hayla snapped. Johl sensed the big man bristle at the rebuke. "You herd them into carriages before the next shift arrives. Then you take them out to the valley and kill them there. Burn them alive in the carriages so nobody can identify them."

Eero swallowed hard and looked at the floor, clearly uneasy about hearing such talk. Johl found an extra reason to be wary of Hayla. She was displaying a ruthlessness he hadn't seen before. Johl's chamberlain turned pale.

Jugg looked to his master for approval. When Johl nodded, he turned back to Hayla. "It shall be done."

"As for the inmates," Johl said, "I'll send a force into the prison to slaughter them. Every last one of them."

"The whole prison?" Eero asked.

"Nahla's cell block, at least. It will be hard to know how far her treason has spread." He paused. "But I have no qualms about cleaning out the entire population. I can always refill it."

The king sighed with his eyes closed and rubbed his face. This was a desperate time, but he was uncomfortable with the necessary response. "What about the new prison governor? What's his name?"

"Yoshi," Hayla said. "If he has been informed about the revolt, he goes too. Yoshi does not live in the governor's cottage in the prison, so he may know nothing yet. But if his guards are professionals, they would have informed him by now. Be prepared to eliminate him and his entire household."

Johl nodded soberly. "Jugg, round up your most trustworthy soldiers. Take five carriages to the prison and get rid of the guards. Find out if somebody told Yoshi." Then, facing his chamberlain, "Gatlin, find Lieutenant Devlan and send him to the prison with orders to slaughter Nahla's cell block. By the time he is done, I will have arrived to assess the situation and will issue further orders about the rest of the prison."

Jugg and Gatlin departed. The room fell silent once Gatlin closed the door. Johl's mind still ran through contingencies for this bloodthirsty dilemma.

"We can use the assault on the prisoners to explain the deaths of the prison guards," Johl said. Some part of Hayla's emotionless plotting had rubbed off on him. "We say the prisoners overran the prison and killed all the guards. Before we notify their families, we burn all the prisoners' bodies in the courtyard and pretend the guards were included."

"With that story, you'll have to kill the entire inmate population," Eero noted.

He had a point. Because of it, the decision came easy to Johl. "What must be done will be done."

33

ASSAULT

And so we rushed the mob of defenceless criminals, confident that their soft skin and hard heads would be no match for our sharp blades.

—Private Penna, Ravenswood Company,
Launceston Provincial Garrison
Personal communication with the company medic

Hɪɢʜ ᴜᴘ ɪɴ ᴛʜᴇ gatehouse, Lieutenant Killo of Launceston Prison wiped sweat from his brow as he surveyed the prison courtyard below. The rising sun cast shadows on the ground, but the tower's bricks still released captured heat from the previous day. He had just completed his morning tour of the prison's perimeter wall, a task which the Officer of the Day did every morning. When Governor Ibeza was alive, he liked to join his lieutenants as they toured the facility, but the new overseer was different. Yoshi insisted on living in his private residence with his family rather than the modest governor's cottage within the prison's walls. Killo could not blame him for that, but it meant Yoshi was never present for the morning inspection. He frowned at Yoshi's apparent disinterest.

"Provincial garrison's on the move again," the tower guard said.

Killo followed where she pointed. True enough, a column of Launceston soldiers quick-marched along the road approaching the prison.

"They've got somewhere to go, by the looks of it," the guard continued.

Killo watched them closely, estimating at least a hundred troops. He had never been a soldier, but he'd been around enough to know their differences. The bulk of them carried swords, but the front and rear ranks gripped polearms. An officer rode on horseback alongside the unit.

They came to a fork in the road. If they'd kept going straight, they would have headed towards the centre of Launceston. Instead, they veered off towards the prison.

"They're coming here," the guard said. "Were we expecting them, sir?"

As the unit marched menacingly towards the high walls of the prison, Killo squinted and tried to remember the day's orders. There had been no mention of a visit from the Launceston Garrison, and certainly not by a hundred of them. However, the night officer reported some alarming activity among the prisoners—nonsense about temples and water and bringing Lord Johl to justice. Perhaps Johl had heard about it and sent this force to silence them.

"I'll see what they want," Killo said. He stepped out of the tower and positioned himself on the walkway above the portcullis. When the soldiers halted in front of the prison, he shouted down at the commander. "State your business."

The man on the horse cocked his head to one side. "To whom am I speaking?"

"Lieutenant Killo, Officer of the Day."

"I am Lieutenant Devlan. Lord Johl has instructed us to assault the block where the prisoner named Nahla is held."

His assumption was correct, Killo noted. Except the truth was harsher than he'd imagined. "Just what do you mean by *assault*?"

"We are to execute every prisoner in the block. I'm told we may experience some resistance. I don't think we will drag them out to the executioner's platform, so we will have to slaughter them in their cells."

Killo's stomach churned at the talk of such bloodshed this early in the morning. "I would like to speak with them first. This is a prison matter, after all."

"I'm afraid my orders are explicit," Devlan insisted. "We are to go to the prison block and begin the executions at once."

Damn it! Why couldn't Yoshi be here to handle this? Killo forced his face to stay neutral. "Open the gatehouse!"

The portcullis rose and the double gates creaked open. Killo returned to the tower so he could descend the spiral staircase. Inside, the guard stared at him wide-eyed, but he ignored her. Down in the courtyard, half the soldiers had already marched in and were forming up into three ranks. Killo approached Devlan, looking up at the officer sitting high and proud on his horse. "Must you go through with this?"

"My orders are explicit." Devlan stared down at him. "They say nothing about the prison guards assisting us, so you can stand aside if you wish. All I ask is that you show us the way."

Killo bit his tongue and called for a nearby guard. "Take these soldiers to X Wing, A Block."

"All right," Devlan shouted. "Polearms in front, swords following. Leave no inmate alive!"

The guard gulped and led the soldiers to the prison's main building. They entered two-by-two, like ants marching into an enemy nest.

Killo sidled over to a guard by the gate. "Go to Governor Yoshi's house. Bring him here immediately. Run!"

Nₐₕₗₐ ₕₑₐᵣₐ ₜₕₑ fₐₘᵢₗᵢₐᵣ sound of sandals stomping on stone-work. There were too many to be just a handful of guards. No, this was something bigger. She smelled trouble.

"Soldiers!" someone yelled from another cell.

"This is it, everyone," Nahla announced. The cell huddled around her. "They've heard our taunts."

Keys jingled at the cell door.

"Fight back!" Nahla shouted. She faced the door. "Don't let them silence you!"

The door burst open and long polearms were pushed inside, but they found no victims because everyone had assembled against the opposite wall. Then came a trickle of soldiers clad in the black of Johl's garrison.

"If the other cells can hear me," Nahla yelled, "remember what happened today! Down with Lord Johl! Open the temples!"

Her fellow inmates repeated the war cry and charged the soldiers. Cass stayed by Nahla's side for the moment, assuming the role of Nahla's second-in-command. The first line of prisoners bore the brunt of the polearms. Several were impaled—one polearm being pushed through two inmates at once. A burly fellow grabbed the weapon as its wielder jabbed it towards him, raising it out of harm's way.

The initial attack stalled because the soldiers took too long to pull the long polearms out of the dead and dying bodies. The next line of inmates approached them too fast, and the following line of sword-wielding soldiers filled the space behind the pikemen. Nahla quickly saw the mistake the soldiers had made and capital-ised on the opportunity.

"Rush them! Beat them down." She moved with her defending force, seeking a weapon of her own.

The prisoners swarmed against the soldiers, who were now bottlenecked at the door. The pikemen went down under a barrage of fists, but swords quickly came to their defence. The cramped cell didn't allow room to swing and slice, so the soldiers stabbed mercilessly in a well-disciplined formation, stomping forwards with each thrust. Within moments, at least ten inmates had fallen under the unstoppable advance. But the soldiers were still outnumbered, and she noticed one had stumbled on the left side.

"Push forwards!" she bellowed. "Grab their arms!"

The inmates roared with rage and screamed in pain as they faced the onslaught. A soldier shouted orders from the corridor outside, encouraging the troops not to slow down and to hold on to their weapons. But the left side continued to crumble. The gap from the first fallen soldier had not been filled, and prisoners soon exploited it, flanking the front rank and fighting off the next. In less than a minute, the front line of soldiers slowed and stopped as they tried to secure their flank. This opened a gap in the middle, which more prisoners rushed through.

Nahla pressed ahead and grabbed a soldier who was trying to strike a screaming woman. She brought the man down and stomped on his face, knocking the lights out of him. She held his sword arm while she did so and felt his grip slacken when he went unconscious. Now she had a weapon of her own. Other inmates had armed themselves too, including with the polearms from their dead cell buddies.

The yelling and metal clashing increased as the larger inmate force grew stronger and the soldiers tried desperately to hold their ground. Nahla cursed the confines of the cell. She was literally fighting shoulder to shoulder with the other prisoners and didn't have much room to use the sword, but she managed to drive it into one soldier's belly, then another, and another. Each soldier that fell to the ground meant another sword for her raging band of criminals, and each sword meant a better chance at success.

The soldiers were backing up to the doorway.

"Push harder!" Nahla yelled above the din. "We almost have them."

The prisoners responded with gusto, using the soldiers' tactics against them. They formed a line and stabbed. Nahla saw what they were doing, smiled proudly, and counted the movements for them so they could all attack and move together. The soldiers brought no shields, perhaps feeling that they would be unnecessary against unarmed criminals, so all they could do was batter the prisoners away as they retreated through the doorway. Their commander berated them as cowards. Then, seeing that the prisoners were advancing with weapons, he rallied the troops to make a new stand in the corridor.

If the cell was bad, the corridor was worse. The cell was wide and deep enough to hold at least fifty prisoners, but the corridor was long and incredibly narrow. While it limited the ability of the soldiers to defend themselves, it also prevented Nahla's prisoners from mounting an overwhelming attack.

Then Nahla saw her opportunity. The sergeant commanding the assault stood just two ranks behind the front of the Launceston troops, and next to him was the prison guard who unlocked the cell door. That guard would have the keys to the other cells in the block. There had to be at least three hundred prisoners in this block alone, and possibly five times that number in the entire wing, maybe more. She *needed* those keys.

Nahla raised her sword. "Charge!"

Strong-armed men carrying the polearms took the lead, thrusting with all their might. It put fear into the eyes of the soldiers in the front ranks, followed by the emptiness of death. The inmates rushed them with such speed and huddled together so tightly in the narrow passage that there was no avoiding the attack. The soldiers cried out in pain as the metal-tipped weapons slid through them. The inmates kept pushing, firmly lodging the polearms into the bodies. Then the sword-bearing prisoners took over, swarming the next rank of soldiers.

Nahla moved with her people, her eyes trained on the prison guard. She didn't want to kill him, because this was not his fight.

But if he fought back, then she had no choice. Those keys ensured her success.

The sergeant identified her, growled her name, and moved to attack. Nahla pushed his sword aside. It clanked against the stone wall. Then she punched him square in the face and he fell back with a bloodied nose. She finished the dazed man with her sword, running him through with a quick motion. Behind the dead sergeant, the prison guard watched on with a pale face.

"The keys," Nahla demanded above the sound of battle. "Keys! Now!"

He handed her the keychain and stumbled backwards, disappearing into the throng of dead and dying troops. The keys came to her just in time. Her followers were thinning out, especially now that a larger body of soldiers had met them in the corridor.

She found Cass by her side and handed her the keys. "As we pass each cell door, open it and tell the prisoners to fight with us."

Cass nodded. The neighbouring cell was already behind them, so she wasted no time obeying the order. Reinforcements swarmed out, picking up swords from dead soldiers and prisoners alike.

As Nahla continued to fight, she noticed a plumed helmet at the rear of the dwindling garrison unit. An officer! That told Nahla two things: first, if the officer was leading from the rear, then this paltry force was all they had to face; second, their battle was nearly over.

"Remember," Nahla shouted at the top of her lungs, "water flows freely in the temples! Down with Johl! Open the temples!"

That psychological tactic worked. The unexpected words slowed the soldiers so much that their officer had to yell at them to keep fighting. But the damage was done. Nahla's words were right now making inroads into their minds, causing them to question what exactly they were fighting for.

Their pause in defence gave the prisoners a critical advantage. Six or seven soldiers were cut down in a matter of seconds. Cass opened another cell, and another fifty prisoners joined the fight. The soldiers were now vastly outnumbered and facing certain death.

Then came the words every officer hated to utter—the order to retreat. It was a useless order to give in such a situation, because the soldiers had been retreating ever since they left Nahla's cell. But now they did it with official permission and moved much faster, which made Nahla grin with delight. The officer with the plumed helmet disappeared and the soldiers who had stood near him followed. The ones closest to the prisoners swung madly to protect their retreating comrades.

Cass opened yet another cell, and now the corridor was crowded with hot, stinking, sweating prisoners with a taste for blood. There was a mad rush for the cell block's exit. A few inmates slipped through, but the Launceston troops had formed a defensive line in the much larger room outside. Prison guards quickly sealed off the cell block with a huge, barred gate. The inmates who had made it through were quickly sliced up and left on the floor to bleed to death.

X Wing now belonged to Nahla. She watched the remnants of the Launceston Garrison run out of sight while the prison guards remained on the other side of the barred gate. They gripped swords and shook in fear as the inmates laughed and mocked them.

A cheer swept through the prisoners and many clapped Nahla on the shoulder or shook her hand. Some even hugged her. She cheered with them, astonished that they had actually beaten a trained and disciplined unit of provincial soldiers. Then she examined the carnage they had left behind. Bodies littered the corridor and blood painted the floor and walls red. They had won this fight through sheer force of will, but Johl's troops would be back with a vengeance. She had to prepare her people for the next attack.

34

THE SCOURGE OF NECESSITY

In difficult times, an iron hand is absolutely necessary to achieve the desired results. What some view as reprehensible, others identify as justified. Such is the weight of public office.

—**Hayla the Sage**
Lessons in Government

FROM HIS VANTAGE POINT at Castle Trevallyn, Lord Johl watched a line of black horse-drawn carriages heading to Launceston Prison, escorted by foot soldiers and led by the fearsome Lieutenant Jugg. Right then, he'd realised a critical error had been made and rushed out alone on his speedy horse to confront Jugg.

As Johl galloped along the road, the sound of his horse's hooves must have alerted the big man. Jugg looked over his shoulder but kept his horse going forwards.

"Where is Lieutenant Devlan?" Johl asked even before he slowed his horse to walk alongside Jugg's.

"Haven't seen him," Jugg mumbled. "The fool takes too long to prepare."

"*You* are the fool!" Johl barked. "He was on this road thirty minutes ago. I thought you had already preceded him. But now I see *you* are the one running late."

Jugg stared at him, his mouth open. "That means—"

"That's right," Johl cut him off. He could feel himself boiling over, and he didn't care that he was berating his favourite lieutenant in front of the lower ranks. "You were supposed to get to the prison *before* Devlan to get the guards out of the way. Now the bloody fool has probably stormed the prison and every damn guard will know about the slaughter."

"I had to organise all these carriages!" Jugg snapped.

"I don't care for excuses." Johl pulled off to the side and stood in his stirrups to address the convoy. "Get to the prison, on the double!"

The foot soldiers grabbed onto whatever handholds and foot-steps they could find on the carriages, then the drivers whipped their horses to speed. Those who couldn't hitch a ride ran with their full complement of arms and armour. Johl returned to the front and ordered Jugg to follow him. They rode on ahead.

When he arrived at the prison gates, Johl found one guard patrolling above. The poor woman was already running to admit the provincial governor when Johl demanded to be let in. As the gates opened and Johl and Jugg trotted inside, the sight that greeted them made Johl's anger blaze even hotter.

A line of tired, bloodied soldiers streamed out of the prison's main building, led by none other than Lieutenant Devlan. Johl squinted when he saw the man, but first he had to deal with Governor Yoshi. The tall, thin man saw Johl and stomped over, waving his hands in confusion.

"My lord, what is happening here?" Yoshi asked. "Your soldiers have started a war in my prison!"

"Watch your tone, Governor," Johl warned. He stepped down from his horse. "My soldiers came here to quell an insurrection that was beyond your powers to prevent."

"Your troops seem unsuccessful." He gestured at the ragged soldiers who were assembling in the courtyard.

You don't know how lucky you are, Johl thought. If Jugg had gotten his act together sooner, then all the guards, and possibly Yoshi as well, would be on their way to a death sentence. He inspected the troops from afar and found a new reason to hate Devlan. If that was how many soldiers Devlan organised for the execution, then it was doomed to fail even before they'd left the castle.

Jugg's carriages rolled into the courtyard, and the big man yelled at the drivers to line up.

"What are they for?" Yoshi asked.

Johl had to think on his feet. "For the dead prisoners. Unless you want to cart them away yourself?"

The governor didn't take the bait. That, or he was too smart to question Johl further. "My lord, I really must protest. Surely you could have consulted me first."

"This is out of your hands now. Don't worry, you'll get your prison back soon."

Johl left the governor before he could say anything else. He called Jugg and Devlan to him for a private conference.

"You have a lot of explaining to do," Johl said to Devlan. "Tell me why I shouldn't kill you right now."

Whatever confidence Devlan may have felt disappeared in an instant. "We assaulted the prisoners as ordered, my lord. But they fought back. They pushed us out of their cells, found some keys, and unlocked more cells. They overran us."

"You didn't fight hard enough," Jugg said menacingly.

Johl looked Devlan up and down. He had not a speck of blood on him, while most of the men and women under his command looked as though they had bathed in it. "You got here too fast. The guards were supposed to be taken away first. That's your first mistake."

Devlan glanced at Jugg. Maybe Jugg hadn't relayed the mission's instructions correctly. Or perhaps Devlan wanted to one-up Jugg by beating him to the prison.

"Your second mistake," Johl continued, "was bringing too few troops with you." He pointed at the remnant of Devlan's force. "It's no wonder you were organised so fast."

The young lieutenant gulped. "My lord, I brought a hundred soldiers."

Johl's eyes went wide, and he looked at Devlan's troops again. Closer to fifty stood in the morning sun. He stepped right up to the lieutenant and lowered his voice. "You are lying to me, or you are admitting incompetence. Tell me again how many soldiers you brought to the prison."

Devlan took a step back, but Johl grabbed him by the neck of his cuirass. He went pale. "One hundred, m-m-my lord."

"Then you are incompetent! How could you lose half your force against unarmed prisoners?" He breathed heavily and stared into the frightened lieutenant's eyes, searching for answers.

"It was Nahla, my lord. She kept encouraging the prisoners to attack. They were chanting something about water in the temples and demanding your life." He swallowed hard. "They just kept coming."

"Shut up!" Johl pushed Devlan away as he released the man's cuirass, and Devlan lost his balance and fell back onto the paved courtyard. Johl stood over him, and when Jugg did the same, he cast a shadow over Devlan's pallid face. "Do not repeat what Nahla said, and discourage your soldiers from talking about it. Did you at least kill Nahla?"

Devlan looked at the stone pavers.

"Was Nahla killed?" Johl yelled.

"I . . . I don't know. I think she lives."

Johl took two heavy breaths before pointing vehemently at the man. "You're going back in there."

"My lord," Jugg said, "if you send me, I will do it right."

"No, Devlan will redeem himself. And this time you'll lead from the front, you coward." Johl was a firm believer in doing something himself if he wanted it done right. That much had been proved repeatedly in the recent past. But even he was not mad enough to storm a prison full of angry criminals by himself just to kill Nahla. And he certainly wouldn't send Jugg. He wouldn't give the burly man the pleasure of ending Nahla's life.

"If you can, bring Nahla to me," Johl told Devlan. "I will slit her throat myself." He turned to Jugg. "How many soldiers did you bring?"

"Twenty, plus drivers."

"It's not enough." Then he faced Devlan again. "Get up. You look like a fool down there. What's the situation like inside?"

He stood and brushed the dust off his uniform. "In the prison? They're locked in X Wing. The corridors are narrow, and the cell doorways are narrower still."

"How many inmates?"

"At least two hundred."

Johl wasn't the most experienced military leader among Launceston's governors—that title went to Lord Alden. Johl also chose not to have a captain in his provincial army, as was customary in the other provinces. Instead, he saved that role for himself. He usually left tactical decisions to his lieutenants, but this time he needed to assume direct control of the units assaulting the prison. That said, he knew a thing or two about command. For example, he knew that if he was attacking a difficult position, he needed at least twice as many soldiers as the defenders. "Jugg, go back to the castle and bring four hundred troops."

Devlan whistled. "With respect, my lord, you won't fit four hundred in that prison."

The look Johl gave him would have set a haystack alight. "You're not making the decisions here. Go and see to your survivors."

Lieutenant Devlan saluted and marched away with his tail between his legs. Jugg confirmed the order for four hundred extra soldiers, then returned to his horse and galloped away.

Seeing that Johl was alone again, Governor Yoshi approached once more. "My lord, may I know what you intend to do now?"

Johl sighed and examined the governor. He looked clueless, which was exactly why he approved the appointment. This prison would see much use in the near future, and he needed a governor who could be walked over. But now Yoshi would be dead by the end of the day, for he had heard about Nahla's blasphemous speech.

"We will assault again."

"But why, my lord? Why kill everyone?"

"You've heard the reports of blasphemy. Don't we execute blasphemers?"

"Yes, we *execute*, not *slaughter.*"

"It must be done."

"But it's within *my* prison."

"And who gave you this prison?"

Yoshi went silent.

"Exactly. This prison is in my province. I appointed you to oversee it. Nearly every inmate has been condemned by me. If I must execute a whole cell block, I will. Do you have a problem with that, Governor Yoshi?"

"No, my lord."

"Good. Now get me some food. I haven't eaten breakfast yet."

JOHL ATE HIS BREAKFAST in the onsite governor's cottage. As he chewed some fresh bread, he realised that Governor Ibeza most likely died in the same chair in which he now sat. Ibeza, the man Johl inadvertently killed while trying to poison Daxton. He used poison because Nahla and Myel had barred him from entering Daxton's cell.

He threw the rest of the bread onto his plate. That damn Nahla was at the centre of everything! He cursed the day she appeared in his life. From their very first encounter, she had been nothing but trouble. Who knew how different the world would be if they had never met? He looked back on their interactions to see where he'd gone wrong.

At their first meeting, he had opened the interaction by accusing her of water theft—his first mistake. If he had simply ignored the dirty woman drinking from a water tank, his life would have been much simpler. But then he'd fought her, and she'd defeated him, and because she had bruised his ego, he'd sent her to prison and arranged for her to die in the gladiatorial contest—his second mistake. How was he to know that Nahla would be such a superb fighter in a large free-for-all against gladiators? How was he to know that King Eero would notice her and immediately recruit her into his Legion?

Johl downed half a cup of water. But of course, the troubles didn't stop there. His third mistake was failing to convince Eero to give Nahla a different test of loyalty. Instead, he'd allowed Nahla to go right to the secret fulcrum of his dealings in Scottsdale Province. Nahla had defied orders and plucked his most important asset, Daxton, out of Scottsdale and brought him back to Launceston. That was when everything started going downhill fast.

His fourth mistake was not pushing hard enough to get Daxton into a position where he could be murdered easily. That led to his fifth mistake, which was going to kill Daxton personally, arousing Nahla and Myel's suspicions. How could he have known that at the exact moment he and Jugg went to the isolation tower in the prison, Nahla and Myel would be there too?

The downhill run got worse after that. He had a great idea to poison Daxton, but mistake number six was not ensuring the poisoned wine would definitely make it to Daxton's cell. Instead, Governor Ibeza had confiscated it, consumed it, and died. That lead to more scrutiny around Daxton, more suspicion towards Johl, and a further tightening of security in the prison's isolation tower.

Johl remembered the feeling of jubilance when he heard that Nahla and Myel were leaving for Scottsdale. It gave him room to breathe and opened up possibilities. Hiring the gong farmer as an amateur assassin was an enormous risk, but one that nearly went perfectly. The seventh mistake was not giving the gong farmer the right tool for the job. He was given a dagger, but it would have been much more effective to poison the blade. Everything was much clearer in hindsight. That seventh mistake was a two-edged sword. Not only did the gong farmer fail to kill Daxton, but Daxton's wounds required him to be moved into the palace grounds to the headquarters of the Guardians. While he had relative freedom of movement in the palace, visiting the Guardians was not something he did regularly, and Daxton was still under guard, anyway. He drew comfort from the fact that Daxton was unconscious and would probably die from his wounds. Thankfully, his palace spy had arranged for the gong farmer to be killed before questioning.

That left Nahla and Myel. To kill a prince is no small task, but Johl was determined to see it through. He shook his head as he thought about the daring nature of his plan. But there again he made a mistake—his eighth—namely, not hiring enough mercenaries to deal with Myel, Nahla, and the prince's guards. Surely being ambushed by a numerically superior force would have been enough to cut their lives short! But no, they'd killed all the mercenaries at the expense of only two legionaries. Again, Nahla was central to the failure of his plan.

But the biggest mistake he had made in this tumultuous story was not killing Nahla when she attacked him the previous night. He rubbed his eyes. It seemed so long ago, and yet it had been less than twelve hours since Nahla and Myel announced their infiltration of the temple. Right then, he should have summarily executed Nahla on the spot. It took the combined efforts of Hayla, Vox, and himself to subdue her. If he had killed her, he wouldn't be here after a sleepless night trying to slaughter an entire prison block. He wouldn't have the truth of the temples spreading among the inmates, prison guards, and provincial troops.

He glanced out the window of the cottage. Every person in the prison courtyard and every soldier Jugg brought with him would have to be murdered to hide the truth. Nahla's prisoners were chanting about the temples and water and how the Launceston governor was complicit in the whole lie. He couldn't afford any prison guard or provincial soldier taking that information home. Now his mind raced to think of how to accomplish that terrible task. He supposed Jugg would be central to seeing it done. Jugg would be the only survivor.

The man himself rode into the prison courtyard again, followed by a mass of jogging soldiers. Johl watched them form up into neat rows and shook his head. These men and women had the worst luck. They'd been pulled from their barracks to fight prisoners, but each of them was already dead. Or . . . maybe not all of them. No, he would keep fifty alive by not sending them into the prison, by not exposing them to Nahla's blasphemy. Those fifty could also help him with another task.

Johl drank another glass of water before heading outside, a plan already formulating in his mind. Lieutenants Jugg and Devlan stood in front of the assembled soldiers, as well as another lieutenant who must have come with the new unit. He motioned for Jugg to come to him so they could speak privately. They huddled off to the side, far away from everyone else.

"Choose fifty of these new soldiers who don't deserve to die and set them aside. I need them for something else." He spotted an important face. "Why is Kessia here?"

"She insisted on coming along because I pulled some of her troops into this mess and because she has a vendetta against Nahla."

Johl frowned. *Another one who wants Nahla dead.* Lieutenant Kessia was an exemplary officer. He didn't want her to die, and he certainly wouldn't give her the honour of taking Nahla's life if she was so lucky to reach the woman inside. "Pick Kessia and fifty of Kessia's soldiers and set them aside. There will be some . . . killing out here while Devlan is inside."

Jugg cocked his head.

"Trust me. I will give an order once Devlan and his soldiers are inside. My order *must* be followed. Understood?"

Jugg squinted and nodded carefully. "Who is dying?"

"Too many."

They returned to the main body and Johl gave Jugg time to do his restructuring. Johl had a few words with Devlan and Kessia. For this operation, Devlan would re-assault the prison—and succeed this time. Kessia was temporarily under Jugg's command. She was warned that an unexpected order would come her way soon and that she must follow it to the letter. She didn't like the temporary hierarchy, but she had no choice. Still, she made a point of turning the earless side of her face to Jugg whenever the brute spoke.

Once Jugg had reorganised the troops, Johl climbed on top of one of the black carriages. There were three groups of soldiers— the remnant of Devlan's original attacking force, the larger force that Jugg brought, and the fortunate fifty who were being saved for a special job.

"Soldiers of the Launceston Garrison," Johl began. His voice echoed in the courtyard. "I have brought you here to mete out divine justice. Within this prison is a growing horde of blasphemous criminals, led by none other than Nahla Northborn. Do not listen to her nonsense. Do not let it taint the purity of your souls. Instead, channel your righteous anger and give these prisoners the punishment they deserve. No blasphemy goes unpunished. Slaughter them all. Leave no prisoner alive. Whoever drags Nahla to me will be promoted to a lieutenant and will have no more want in life. Now go, see that justice is served!"

The soldiers roared in support of their lord's stirring words. Then the lieutenants took over. Jugg growled for his fifty to stay put. Devlan found his voice again and corralled his four hundred towards the prison's only front entrance. Kessia snarled at not being allowed to join the fight.

Johl called for Governor Yoshi. "Bring every prison guard in the facility to this courtyard, including the ones on the wall."

"And leave the inmates unwatched?" Yoshi asked.

"They're in cells, aren't they? Make sure all cells are locked and get your staff out here. It's for their safety, and to prove a point when Nahla is brought to me. Don't waste time!"

Yoshi jumped to it, relaying the order to other guards, who then ran off to gather their colleagues.

There would be much killing today, Johl noted. Indeed, there had already been much killing inside, but that was nothing compared to what would soon happen. And Johl had ordered every drop of blood. But, he supposed, the real person responsible for that blood was Nahla. Even after she was dead, he'd make sure the world never forgot it.

35

REPRISAL

When the enemy returns with allies, know that the hourglass of fate is emptying its final grains.

—Unknown
Tasmanian proverb

Nahla was surprised at how long the soldiers stayed away. She used that time to strengthen the resolve of her inmate army and kit them out with armour from the dead soldiers. Then she planned some defensive tactics. She wanted to get out of the cell block, which meant getting the large, barred gate opened. That would let a flood of soldiers into the corridor again. Therefore, she positioned a few rows of weaker prisoners with less formidable weapons right in front of the gate to entice the enemy soldiers into the corridor. Hidden either side of the gate were sizeable groups of stronger prisoners with polearms and swords. She hoped the flank attacks would stall the enemy advance enough for the weaker inmates to withdraw and for stronger ones to rush the soldiers head-on and push them back out into the common area.

For the last hour, the prisoners who were unfit to fight were chipping away at the stone wall in one cell, using the metal tips of some broken polearms. If they could break through the sandstone, then they could breach the adjoining cell in the next block, adding to their numbers. Cass was overseeing the work.

Someone with a loud voice had been hollering from a nearby wing, his voice carrying through the stone corridors. An inmate in Nahla's area, a man with an operatic voice who apparently knew the other one, bellowed back at him. They relayed questions and answers about what had transpired in X Wing. This news was then carried to the other wings in A Block. When Nahla demanded affirmations of support, the entire wing erupted in cheers. All Nahla had to do was get keys to doors. The keychain Cass held had more keys than cells in X Wing, which meant they probably had all the keys for the entire block.

Heavy footsteps pounded nearby. A door squeaked open and the footsteps grew louder. Then a gravelly voice barked orders. The soldiers had returned.

"This is it," Nahla warned. "Get ready."

A mass of soldiers appeared in the common area and paused in full view. Two rows of pikemen headed the force. They lowered their six-foot-long polearms, aimed directly at the gate. An officer, the one who had brought up the rear last time, pushed to the front and jingled keys in his hand. He and Nahla faced off.

"Do you surrender?" the officer asked. He had a hint of fear in his voice.

"Never," Nahla replied firmly. Surrender would mean death. She'd rather die fighting.

The officer frowned and gulped. He looked at the barred gate, then at the keys. He gave the keys to a junior and ordered the man to unlock the gate. This junior, possibly a sergeant, looked more experienced than the officer. He approached cautiously, but with enough confidence that Nahla actually admired him. Nahla could hear every eager breath, every shuffling sandal, every rustle of armour. The sergeant unlocked the gate and rushed back to his place.

So now the unlocked gate was the only obstacle between the trained military force and the ragtag mob of inmates. Nobody moved. Nobody wanted to be the ones to open it and admit the enemy to their side.

Nahla knew she had to let the soldiers come to her, but she worried about the pikemen. She hoped her decoys would retreat quickly.

"Open the gate," Nahla said quietly.

One man—a hero—stepped forwards and pulled with all his might. The moment the gate moved, the pikemen charged. Thankfully, Nahla's decoys had time to slip out of harm's way. The pikemen screamed into the corridor, chasing them towards the sea of better-armed prisoners.

Then the flankers struck. A soldier saw the movement just a moment too late. He only had time to yelp before a sword found its way into the side of this torso. Now forced to turn and face the unexpected foe, the polearms were useless in the narrow corridor—too long to swing around and fight sideways. This vanguard unit fell quickly and mercilessly.

"Forwards!" Nahla shouted. "Push them out!"

As one, the inmates roared, tasting victory. Elsewhere in the wing, the other prisoners chanted in support, knowing that freedom was moments away. The mass of prisoners clashed with the stalled soldiers, Nahla in the thick of it.

The Launceston officer was leading from the front this time. He was very brave or very stupid—possibly both. Nahla didn't give him enough time to contemplate either choice. She kicked him off the end of her blade and he tumbled backwards into the cluster of soldiers behind him.

They made it out of the cell block and into the more spacious common area. There, runners dashed to the other wings to free their fellow inmates. Protected by a determined line of armoured allies, these runners unlocked gates and disappeared down a maze of corridors that spiralled away from the block's central common area. The shouts from the other wings reached new heights as freedom approached.

The common area quickly overflowed with hot, sweaty bodies as soldiers poured in from one way and prisoners flooded in from every other entrance. Nahla barely had any room to defend herself, much less to strike against the nearest foes. It felt like they were fighting more troops than last time.

"Push!" Nahla shouted. "Push harder!"

A group of large male inmates bellowed and charged, swarming past Nahla and crashing into the head of the enemy force. Their swords broke down the initial resistance.

"Keep going," Nahla encouraged. She joined the effort as others came to her aid. Together, they formed an impenetrable wall that pressed the soldiers back through the door from which they came.

As the prisoners flooded the common area, Nahla had a sudden realisation: they controlled X Wing! There was still much fighting to be done, but if they could seize control of one wing, they could take them all.

"We've done it!" Nahla called above the clashing swords and shouts of battle. "On to the next wing."

The armed and armoured prisoners rushed through the wing's main entrance to continue the fight. Meanwhile, Nahla stayed back to give the fresh inmates some directions. They had to strip the dead and dying of their weapons and armour before they joined the fight, otherwise they would be nothing more than sheep against wolves.

The next hurdle was finding keys to the next wings. This assault had been curiously devoid of any prison guards, but Nahla was sure they'd find keys somewhere. If they could push the soldiers out of the prison entirely, then at least they would have some breathing room to find some means of freeing their compatriots.

She shook her head as she returned to the fighting. How did she go from being a respected captain of a king's personal guard in Melbourne to a criminal leading a bloody riot?

She knew the corridor from X Wing led to the prison's main building. This was a large, multi-storey structure housing the remand centre, the guards' cafeteria, several storage rooms, and the prison's armoury. The more inmates she could arm, the better.

The corridor between the main building and X Wing was wider than the other corridors, which only meant the prisoners and the soldiers could fight in rows of six instead of three. It was clear neither side wanted to be stuck in the short passage. Someone threw a wooden chair, flattening a group of soldiers. In retaliation, the soldiers threw it back, as well as more dangerous objects like spiked balls and knives. Without shields, the prisoners succumbed to these aerial attacks.

Nahla spotted a sergeant in the middle of the sea of soldiers. Her distinctly plumed helmet turned in every direction as she shouted orders to close ranks and push back. Nahla told the inmates who were behind the front line to toss back everything the soldiers threw at them, but to aim for the sergeant. Then she turned her attention to more immediate threats.

It was unclear how many soldiers were in the prison, but Nahla knew her force still outnumbered them, especially now that all of X Wing was free. Because of this disparity, the inmates gradually pushed the soldiers down the corridor and into the more confusing network of hallways, stairways, and rooms of the main building. Now Nahla couldn't direct all her prisoners at once. They separated of their own accord, with clusters of fighters out of sight and earshot.

Some soldiers tried to close the heavy double-door to the X Wing corridor. They jammed prisoners between the cracks and lopped off limbs before finally sealing it shut.

"Get those doors open!" Nahla yelled to anyone nearby. While several inmates rushed to complete the order, she continued fighting her way through the building's ground floor.

In the madness of battle, she struggled to remember what room and what corridor led to another. She had not explored the prison while she was a free woman. With the bulk of her force now cut off, she had to get to another wing and release the next few hundred prisoners to swell her numbers.

"Follow me," Nahla called. At once, over twenty prisoners rallied to her side.

They ran toward Z Wing, but met a heavy collection of pikemen. Nahla retreated down another hallway, this time to Y Wing, but yet another determined unit of pikemen stood guard. They levelled their long weapons and waited, content to hold their ground. Nahla gulped. The soldiers had gotten wise to her plans. She didn't have enough people to risk storming those polearms. She would lose half her force before their swords even reached the pikemen. Even if she won, she had no keys, and she'd be left without enough inmates to storm the doors to the next wing.

She had to get outside, so she took her ragtag group of prisoners back the way they came and ended up in the prison's reception area. There, a shockingly low number of inmates battled against a superior enemy. They were relieved when they saw Nahla, but it didn't make the fight any easier.

"Batter down those doors," Nahla said to the strongest men. "We'll cover you."

She kept the area in front of the doors clear as some prisoners used whatever solid objects they could find. They grunted and yelled with each thrust. The rhythmic thuds punctuated the sound of battle like a marching drum, and that reminded Nahla of the military band from her homeland. She fought harder to keep the soldiers away from her breaching party. As swords clashed and mistakes were made, soldiers and inmates met their deaths.

Then came the merciful sound of a lock breaking and wooden splinters tearing. Daylight flooded the reception area.

"Outside, now!" Nahla shouted. Her allies rushed through the exit, some feeling the sun's rays for the first time in months.

Nahla slipped through the opening and scanned her surroundings, squinting against the bright morning light. She spotted some disconcerting details. The Launceston troops had fresh reinforcements waiting for them. That nearly stopped her heart. But more troubling was the bloody pile of prison guards by the far wall. Such a horrific sight, despite the fighting and killing over the last few hours! Questions flooded her mind: *Is this assault part of a larger purge of the prison? Is Johl taking control of Launceston? Are his troops engaging in similar attacks throughout the city?*

Within moments, soldiers surrounded her small unit of inmates, piercing and slashing from all sides. Nahla could feel the situation slipping from her control, wishing, begging, praying that the rest of her prisoners would break out and come to her aid. But as her allies dropped and lay motionless in the courtyard, the soldiers sealed the doorway to the prison's main building, hammering the last nail in Nahla's coffin.

The man responsible for it all sat atop his horse, far from Nahla. In the shortest moment between breaths, Nahla spotted him in the distance. He watched with interest from the shady side of a wall. Lord Johl had his arms folded, observing the bloodthirsty struggle like nothing more than a spectator at a gladiatorial contest. Next to him, on his own horse, sat Jugg.

In her last-ditch effort to throw off her enemies, she issued a challenge directly to Johl.

"Come and fight me like the man you'll never be!" she screamed above the din of battle. "Come and do your own dirty work!"

She actually heard his laughter. She felled three more soldiers in a red-hot surge of anger. Then she slipped through the fighters, taking down more soldiers as she made a beeline for Johl.

It was madness charging towards two armed men on horses. She could be cut down in seconds. Her legs burned as she ran. Her hair fluttered in the wind like a jet-black fire. Johl smiled as she approached. He drew his sword—*her sword!*

Then Jugg jumped off his horse and ran towards her.

"Jugg!" Johl shouted. "Stop!"

Nahla and Jugg began their long-awaited fight with the loud clash of steel on steel. Their momentum carried them into each other and they bounced and spun away in an almost dance-like manoeuvre. Nahla, being lighter, recovered faster and lunged at Jugg's back, but the beast turned just in time to knock her sword away. They faced off in their own unique defensive stances.

"I've dreamed about this moment, Nahla," Jugg said. "I'm going to enjoy carving you up."

Nahla's eyes watched all three threats around her—Jugg in front, ready to pounce; Johl to the left, approaching on his horse; and the innumerable soldiers to the right, slaying the remnant of her fellow prisoners. At any moment, an attack could come from either side.

"I'll kill you, and then I'll kill Johl," Nahla replied. "Save the best for last."

"*I* am stronger than Johl!"

With that, Jugg swung heavily across Nahla's shoulder, but she stepped back. While Jugg's sword scraped the stone pavers, Nahla brought the pommel of her sword into Jugg's nose. The big man growled and stumbled, already bleeding and dazed. Nahla saw her opportunity and plunged her sword into Jugg's belly, but the tip of the blade caught on some metal plates hidden beneath his leather armour. *So, he's wearing a brigandine*, she thought—a style of armour she had inadvertently introduced to the kingdom. She knew the weak spots.

Realising how close he'd come to death, Jugg fought back with even more tenacity. Man became animal as Jugg swung, stabbed, punched, and kicked in every effort to dominate Nahla. She'd fought him before, but he had never attacked like this. He seemed detached, speaking words that made no sense, foaming at the mouth, growling and grunting like a beast. Nahla stepped backwards in a desperate defence.

With the leather outer facing of Jugg's armour suit, Nahla couldn't see how the metal plates were joined beneath. She was tempted to strike into his chest again and hope that her sword would find a gap in the plates, but the risk was too great, and Jugg wasn't giving her any chances. Her only other options were to strike up into his armpits, to slash his exposed arms or legs, or to aim for the face or neck. Again, Jugg swung too fast and too erratically for Nahla to even try. Her every move was either a dodge or a parry.

Any man, no matter his strength, could only sustain such heavy-duty fighting for so long. Jugg, being stronger than most, lasted longer, but Nahla noticed him slowing. His strikes were weaker, his movements sluggish. She had held her ground, as her sword master had taught her years ago, and now it was her turn to fight back.

Nahla went on the attack. She swung up, battering Jugg's sword. The flesh on his arm rippled, no longer hard as a rock because he had no more strength to flex muscles. He failed to bring the sword down in time, and Nahla slashed at his wrist, slicing at a tendon. Jugg dropped his sword, swore, and rolled away from Nahla's next move. He moved with a speed that betrayed his size, and despite being tired and wounded, he was dextrous enough to retrieve his sword with his unwounded hand.

But it was too late. Jugg struggled to fight left-handed, and Nahla quickly outmanoeuvred him. She struck low, cutting behind his knee. He staggered, swung madly, missed, and then collapsed completely as he tried to spin around on his knees. He tried to get up, but accidentally put all his weight on his wounded wrist and fell again with a raging shout. Nahla brought her sword down on him, aiming for his head, but he raised his sword to block. The blow from Nahla knocked his sword backwards so far that his blade sliced his forehead. Nahla hacked down on his left wrist, cutting his hand off, rendering him useless. He screamed in agony. Then she put the tip of her sword to his neck and faced Johl.

"Shall I fight you now?" she taunted.

"Don't be a fool," Johl replied with a smirk. "You've already lost." He gestured at the rest of the battle. Only three prisoners still fought, and one went down at that moment.

"The fight doesn't end until one of us dies," Nahla said.

Johl tightened his grip on the reins. "So be it." He spurred his horse and aimed Nahla's sword at her in a typical cavalry charge.

Nahla kicked Jugg in the face and stepped away, ready to face Johl's attack. She was at a supreme disadvantage. Spare polearms were on the ground nearby, but she could not reach them in time. The courtyard was flat and featureless, so she could not use terrain to her advantage. That left her with one choice.

As Johl's horse approached, Nahla had to make a snap decision: roll to the left or roll to the right. It was a common cavalry tactic to pretend to strike an opponent on the side that the sword was positioned, encouraging a defenceless soldier to dodge on the unarmed side. But at the last moment, a skilled rider would alter course and bring the sword down on the other side, striking the unsuspecting soldier on the head or across the back or shoulder. Johl definitely knew how to fight on horseback. The correct defence was unclear.

She feinted right, on Johl's unarmed side. The agile governor reacted quickly, swinging the sword to attack, but Nahla spun at the last moment, narrowly missing the wide-eyed horse. Johl, however, had a special move which Nahla felt rather than saw. The horse kicked back, grazing her arm. The metal horseshoe tore through flesh and Nahla hollered in pain.

As Johl slowed his steed and tried to turn around on the slippery pavers, Nahla bolted for Jugg's horse. The muscular animal snorted as Nahla approached, clearly disliking the scent of a frenzied stranger, but Nahla climbed into the saddle. Her eyes snapped to the prison gates, but they were closed and guarded. She would not have time to cross the courtyard, dispatch the soldiers, and open the gates before Johl caught her. He was charging back already, so she spurred Jugg's horse to meet him.

She gripped the rein with her wounded arm and readied her sword arm. Her sword—the one held by Johl—glistened in the morning sun. Johl held it high, poised to strike. Their horses passed each other. Nahla swung, Johl parried. Then they lost momentum and spun at the waist to watch where the other was going. They stabbed, swung, elbowed, and punched near each other.

For some frustrating reason, Jugg's horse spun opposite to Johl's, precariously exposing Nahla's back. She turned in her saddle, ready to deflect any attacks. Johl lunged, but he was just too far away to reach her. Instead, he stabbed at the rump of Jugg's horse. The animal shrieked and reared. Nahla held on for dear life, but the rearing brought her closer to Johl, who was already prepared to attack again. She was now seconds away from death.

She used the same tactic against him. While holding onto the rein for dear life, Nahla swiped down against Johl's horse, cutting deep into the beast's neck, a move that froze her heart. The blow was devastating and the horse dropped instantly, throwing Johl off. He hit the stonework with a thud. Nahla prepared for the fatal strike, aiming down where the neck joined the shoulder.

Before he stood, Johl swung sideways and sliced the front legs of Jugg's horse. Nahla quickly removed her feet from the stirrups and jumped clear as the animal went down. The last thing she needed was to be pinned under a horse.

"You bastard!" Jugg growled. He hobbled to Johl, shouting

obscenities about his horse and pushing Johl over before he could stand properly.

"Shut up and get off me!" Johl yelled back. He battered the larger man away, which was easy because of Jugg's wounds.

Nahla charged towards Johl while he was distracted, but Johl must have heard her footsteps. He blocked her sword strike like a wall. She'd bested him on foot before, but this was different. She'd been fighting for some time already, whereas he was still relatively fresh. Back then, she had her sword too, whereas now Johl wielded it, no doubt feeling its superior balance.

By this time, the remaining prisoners had been killed, and a great number of Launceston soldiers were gathering in a wide circle to watch their governor fight his mortal enemy. They cheered him on, which distracted Nahla. She tried not to let it dampen her spirit, but she knew that even if she defeated Johl, she was still a dead woman. There was no way she could fight against at least two hundred soldiers. So, if she must die, then there were two things she resolved to do: one, kill Johl; and two, retrieve her sword and die with it in her hand. Then at least she would perish while grasping her last treasured memory of home.

The realisation of impending death gave her renewed energy. She fought harder, faster, knocking back Johl with more strikes. He defended expertly and surprised her with a few good attacks. But her surge of vitality wore thin. Before too long, after having fought twice in the prison and long enough outside, Nahla suffered the same fatigue as Jugg. The human body just wasn't made for prolonged battle with heavy implements of war.

Johl bested her, knocking her sword from her grip and then cracking her across the jaw with his sword hilt. The brute attack knocked her aside and she stumbled a few steps towards the prison wall. There, panting, she spat blood, angry that she had been defeated, but glad that she had fought to her last breath and would die a warrior's death. And, by some cruel twist of fate, the sword she had commissioned in Melbourne, and which had felled innumerable foes by her hand, would be the same sword that took her life now. Johl, breathing heavily, smiled.

"You've won," Nahla said.

"So it would seem," Johl replied. They spoke as if they were the only two people in the world, as if there weren't an audience watching them.

"Well, go on then. Get it over and done with." She dropped to her knees, accepting her fate. She dropped her head, presenting her neck to him.

She heard the sword slide gently into its sheath. The sound made her looked up with a mixture of disappointment and confusion.

"I've already defeated you in one-on-one combat," Johl said. He straightened his back and stared down at her, suddenly looking composed and snobbish. "I've wanted to kill you myself, but now I've realised it wasn't your blood on my hands that I wanted. No, it was the feeling of victory, to know that I had bested you. Now I can use you for a much better purpose."

Nahla glared at him. His words shook her to her core. At that moment, if she had a weapon, she would have slit her own throat instead of letting Johl use her in his own wicked schemes. Her end was coming, but now it wasn't coming soon enough.

"Lieutenant Devlan!" Johl shouted without taking his eyes off her.

"Devlan is dead, my lord," Lieutenant Kessia replied. She wiped at some drying blood on her cheek. She stepped up to Johl, who hadn't flinched at the news that one of his officers had been killed.

"Kessia, take Nahla into custody," Johl said. "Lock her in the governor's cottage."

Kessia's cheek twitched when she glared at Nahla. She delegated the task to several soldiers and they stormed over to Nahla, lifting her by the shoulders. As they carried her away, she heard the rest of Johl's orders.

"Call off the executions in the prison," Johl continued. "We'll continue tomorrow. Pile the dead inmates in the middle of the courtyard and burn them. All the prison guards are dead, so we can send their bodies to their families and say that they died when the prisoners rioted. Take our dead and wounded back to . . ."

Nahla's stomach felt empty as the soldiers dragged her away. Johl had won, and hearing the way he was cleaning up his mess made her sick to the core. There would be more executions the next day. She wondered if she would be one of the victims, or if Johl was keeping her alive for something more sinister. Whatever the case, she had failed to stop him. For that, she felt she deserved nothing better than a swift execution. It's what she deserved when she failed her old king in Melbourne, and now she deserved the same for failing Myel.

As the soldiers threw her into the prison governor's cottage and locked the door, she curled up on the floor and cried. She cried because Myel was left without her protection in the wilderness. She cried because she could not defeat a wicked man. And she cried because that wicked man would now kill many thousands of innocents throughout the kingdom. In her misery, all she could think of was the welcoming embrace of death that Johl would surely provide in his own time.

36

KISSING THE SWORD

The darkness of life, or the darkness of death? At least one is more peaceful than the other.

—Unknown

Graffiti on a cell wall in Launceston Prison

Lord Johl, Governor of Launceston Province, first among equals, stood in the gatehouse of Launceston Prison. He breathed evenly, calm now that the storm had subsided. He'd emerged victorious. Now there were just a few loose ends that needed tying.

"Must we go through with this?" King Eero asked. He stood by one of the narrow windows in the gatehouse, looking down on the road in front of the prison.

"It is absolutely necessary, Your Majesty," Johl replied. "Difficult times are upon us, and you must display strength now to show your people that you are ready for what lies ahead."

Below, outside the prison's walls, citizens crowded around an elaborate public execution platform. While they waited for as many people as possible to arrive, Johl's troops were systematically hanging and beheading prisoners. Their crimes: involvement in the prison riot and the murders of prison guards.

"It just seems like overkill," Eero continued after one particularly gruesome beheading that required two chops.

313

"The people demand retribution, particularly the families of the deceased guards. By doing this, you ensure their support."

Eero stepped closer and whispered. "Who really killed the guards?"

Johl faced him and frowned. "It was the night previous."

Eero raised his eyebrows and returned to the window. "Events have transpired differently."

"Your Majesty, the deed is done. Yesterday and today are a black mark in Launceston's history, but you are responding in the best possible way by executing the entire prison population."

"All for one woman." Eero scoffed.

Yes, exactly. About three thousand people would be dead by the time the executions were over. That number included all the prison guards, Launceston soldiers, and inmates killed during the two assaults, plus the inmates to be executed publicly. He hoped they got through them all in one day.

All for one woman. Johl could not believe that he had lost two hundred and thirty-six soldiers, including one officer and several sergeants. After the executions, the remaining troops would be marched back to Castle Trevallyn to be whipped for their poor performance. The soldiers who weren't involved would be forced to watch so they could learn the lesson too—Lord Johl expected a top-notch military force, not a band of weak, incompetent cowards.

Even Jugg had been badly wounded. Soon after Nahla was locked away, Johl had Jugg whisked away for treatment. He visited him overnight, berating him for defying his orders. If Jugg had killed Nahla, Johl supposed he would have murdered the brute himself. But the man deserved every wound Nahla inflicted on him. The ligament behind his knee had been severed, just like the tendon on his right wrist. Both wounds were firmly patched up by Johl's resident team of Guardians at the castle. But the worst wound, the severed left hand, was nothing but a red, bandaged stump. Nahla had felled a giant, and he had the scars to show it. To add insult to injury, Johl kept Jugg under medical care while they dealt with the executions, so he would not see Nahla meet justice. Kessia, on the other hand, would see the spectacle and relish the death of the woman who had cut off her ear.

They were saving the worst criminal for the largest audience. The road and adjoining field were swarming with townsfolk, farmers, craftspeople, children, and the elderly. The King's Legion mingled under the gatehouse and on the fringes of the assembled throng. A large cluster of Divine Guards and priestesses, along with Matriarch Anurak, perched themselves on a higher point in the field. Scattered among the people were groups of Johl's own troops. They all needed to see the kingdom's most dangerous enemy executed before their eyes. They needed to understand why she was being killed, why they needed to trust their king, and that Nahla's blasphemies were lies and were not to be tolerated. Of course, the "blasphemies" in question were exposing actual lies, but those lies were necessary to maintain order in the kingdom.

Control was vitally important. There would be changes in the kingdom—changes that might upset some people. To keep them placated, Johl needed water. The people survived on water. They required it for drinking, bathing, crafting, and farming. The only place to get it was from the temples, or the extremely rare occasion it drizzled from the sky during a "miraculous act of divine kindness". Johl could not have the people believing Nahla's revelations about the temples. If they believed water was freely available, that there was no God who supplied it after receiving heartfelt supplications, then there would be anarchy in the kingdom. Frankly, he was glad he stopped Nahla not a moment too soon.

Satisfied that there were enough people congregated below, Johl crossed to the other side of the gatehouse and looked down on the groups of inmates and soldiers in the prison courtyard.

"Kessia?" he called.

The lieutenant came into view, apparently from a shady spot under the gatehouse. "My lord?"

"Bring Nahla and her crony. Their time has come."

THEY LED NAHLA AND Cass out through the prison's tall front gate. The moment the crowd saw them, they booed and hurled the vilest verbal abuse. I had announced them as blasphemers and the instigators of the riot. In the eyes of the crowd, the prisoners before them were the worst of the worst.

A tight cloth covered Nahla's mouth, so she could not speak in her defence. Her hands were also bound. She had never felt so helpless in her life, not even when she had been captured by the enemy of her homeland and exiled. At least back then they had accorded her the honour that a respected warrior deserved.

As they approached the execution platform, Nahla saw the mound of bloodied heads that had been swept off. From the courtyard, she'd heard the crowd roar every time one of her fellow inmates perished. She felt a pang of distress every time, for she was responsible for all of their deaths. She incited them to riot. However, when she actually saw the disembodied heads staring into oblivion, she felt a new kind of agony and sickness rise within her gut. Which method would they use against her? The chopping block, or the noose? Or would they do both—hang her first, then lop her head off as a final measure?

She exchanged a glance with Cass. The pale woman looked tired, but she bit down on her gag with a fierce determination. Her hands fidgeted under their bindings. Seeing Cass' resolve gave Nahla strength.

The soldiers pushed them up the steps to the execution platform. There were two executioners. One checked the knot on the noose and re-positioned a wooden stool, the other cleaned and sharpened a big, heavy sword. Both wore masks. It was strange that in a kingdom where people were executed or assassinated so frequently, the executioners still wore masks to protect their identities.

The hangman grabbed Cass with such force that she lost her balance. He dragged her to the noose. Meanwhile, the other executioner still sharpened his sword on a grinding wheel. Two soldiers pushed Nahla towards the chopping block and forced her down by the shoulders.

This was it. The end. The illustrious military commander from Melbourne had fallen, and now she was being executed as a criminal in a foreign land.

Suddenly, the crowd quietened. She heard Johl's voice.

"Before you are two of the kingdom's worst criminals." He was full of assurance and sincerity. "Nahla Northborn and Cass the Blasphemer are responsible for hundreds of deaths. The lives of your friends and family members were cut short yesterday because of these two disgusting individuals. Do they deserve their punishment?"

The people howled their response—a resounding affirmative. Nahla turned her neck and looked at the gatehouse sideways. She could see Johl in one of the windows. In the next window was King Eero, an unwitting participant in the beginning of the end of his reign. He stared blankly at Nahla.

"But these women are much more than murderers," Johl continued. "They are blasphemers. They spread lies about our God. They desecrate the sanctity of our temples. They belittle the sacred duties of our beloved Guardians of Life. For this, there can be no greater punishment than death. We shall remove their memory from our histories. We shall never utter their names again. Once their blood has seeped from their bodies, it will be as though Nahla and Cass never existed."

Another roar of support from the crowd. Oh, they were being led like sheep, Nahla thought dismally.

"One more blasphemer remains at large—a man you once loved, a man close to the heart of our very own king. It is none other than Prince Myel, formerly the heir apparent of our great kingdom. He is a wanted man, and we will bring him to justice in the same way as the two women before you. Not even the king's own son can escape the punishment reserved for blasphemers. Such is the seriousness of our worship and the importance we place on the age-old Decree of Water."

The crowd cheered again, but it was somewhat quieter.

"Executioners! You may proceed."

Nahla heard Cass struggling against the grip of the hangman. She imagined him hoisting her up to the noose, because she would be too fidgety and defiant to stand on the stool and slip her head in herself. Then the ominous grinding sound of metal on stone ceased, and Nahla knew her executioner was ready to deal the fatal blow. She felt the man's heavy footsteps as he moved into position. Out of the corner of her eye, she saw the tip of the sword before he raised it.

She closed her eyes, imagining Myel roaming the wilderness and gathering support so he could save the kingdom before it was too late. Myel would have to fight without her.

The trapdoor burst open and Nahla imagined Cass struggling in the noose. Everything went quiet as reality set in.

Nahla, warrior of the north, knew that this was the end.

APPENDIX A

CHARACTERS

PROTAGONIST

Nahla – Exiled warrior from the Kingdom of Melbourne.

ROYAL HOUSEHOLD OF THE KINGDOM OF LAUNCESTON

Eero – King Eero; Ruler of the Kingdom of Launceston.

Hayla – King Eero's court chamberlain.

Myel – Prince Myel; son of King Eero.

KING'S LEGION

Barrin – Lieutenant in the King's Legion.

Brande – Private in the King's Legion.

Carro – Primus Carro; commanding officer of the First Company of the King's Legion.

Dehra – Lieutenant Dehra; commanding officer of the Special Company of the King's Legion.

Garrus – Sergeant in the King's Legion.

Jaymen – Private in the King's Legion.

Marcle – Primus Marcle; commanding officer of the Second Company of the King's Legion.

Marston – Private in the King's Legion.

Ragh – Corporal in the King's Legion; male twin to Rhos.

Rhos – Corporal in the King's Legion; female twin to Ragh.

Sheph – Private in the King's Legion.

Tullius – Sergeant in the King's Legion.

Vox – Captain Vox; commander of the King's Legion.

LAUNCESTON PROVINCE

Devlan – Lieutenant in the Launceston Provincial Garrison.

Ermi – Lord Johl's physician.

Gatlin – Lord Johl's court chamberlain.

Ibeza – Governor of Launceston Prison.

Johl – Lord Johl; Governor of Launceston Province in the Kingdom of Launceston.

Jugg – Dangerous criminal, later a lieutenant in the Launceston Provincial Garrison.

Kessia – Lieutenant in the Launceston Provincial Garrison.

Yoshi – Governor of Launceston Prison, successor to Ibeza.

SCOTTSDALE PROVINCE

Garyd – Lord Garyd; Governor of Scottsdale Province in the Kingdom of Launceston.

Ziva – Captain Ziva; commander of the Scottsdale Provincial

Garrison.

DEVONPORT PROVINCE

Jaruk Easton – Wealthy wine merchant based in Devonport Province.

Vimarr – Lord Vimarr; Governor of Devonport Province in the Kingdom of Launceston.

CAMPBELL PROVINCE

Alden – Lord Alden; Governor of Campbell Province in the Kingdom of Launceston.

GUARDIANS OF LIFE

Anurak – Matriarch Anurak; leader of the Guardians of Life.

Tish – Priestess.

MISCELLANEOUS

Cass the Blasphemer – Inmate in Launceston Prison.

Daxton – Bandit leader.

Deeno – Cargo wagon driver.

Jin – Royal Apothecary of the Kingdom of Launceston.

Killo – Launceston Prison lieutenant.

Vasylis – King of Melbourne.

APPENDIX B

GLOSSARY

Ceremony of Divine Discipline – The penitential, corporal punishment issued by the Guardians of Life for the most serious crimes against the Water Decree that do not deserve execution. The ceremony involves the recipient of the punishment being whipped while reading aloud the Water Tenets.

Divine Guard – The security arm of the Guardians of Life, responsible for protecting temples and other religious property and personages.

Endless Land – The term used by the Kingdom of Melbourne to describe the great empty expanse south of their domain. They are unaware that a land called Tasmania is on the other side. In the Kingdom of Launceston, the Endless Land is known as the Barren Waste.

Eternity's Void – The term used by the Kingdom of Launceston to describe the great empty expanse east of their domain.

Fiat – An ancient word of unfamiliar origin, meaning "let it be".

God's Eye – The Launceston term for the sun, linked to the teachings of the Guardians of Life.

Guardians of Life – The official religious institution of the Kingdom of Launceston.

King's Legion – The elite military force based at Launceston Palace, sworn to protect the sovereign and their household. The

King's Legion are also sometimes deployed in wartime to assist the provincial armies.

Litany of Water – The religious ceremony during which a priestess of the Guardians of Life petitions God for water on behalf of a worshipper or group of worshippers.

Matriarch – The leader of the Guardians of Life.

Preceptor – A non-commissioned officer in a training role in the King's Legion of the Kingdom of Launceston, passing on their specialised knowledge and skills to other legionaries.

Primus – The commanding officer of a company of the King's Legion of the Kingdom of Launceston.

Provincial Garrison – Any of the armies serving each provincial lord of the Kingdom of Launceston.

Water Decree – The royal law governing the supply, distributon, and consumption of water in the Kingdom of Launceston. Also referred to as the Decree of Water.

APPENDIX C

THE KING'S LEGION

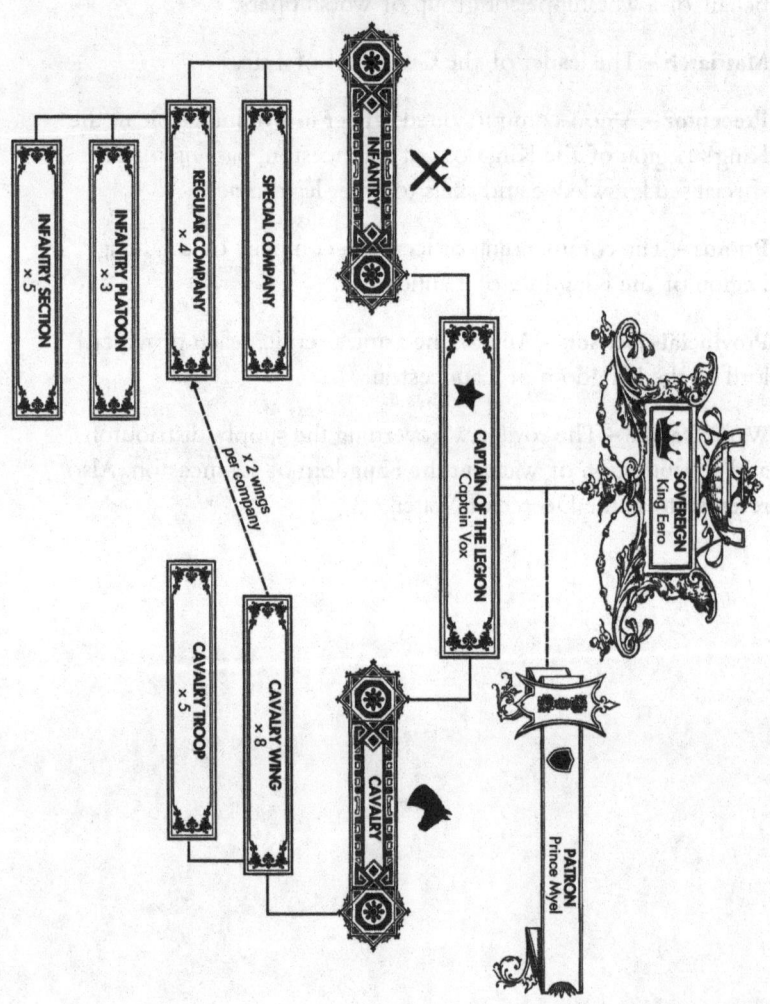

ACKNOWLEDGEMENTS

A book is rarely the product of one writer's sole efforts. I am indebted to the hard work of Emily Brain, Promita Guha, Melissa Hattingh, Shayla Olsen, Lynette Hanlon-Nix, and Carla Scott for the preparation of *Nahla*. Many hours went into assessing the manuscript, editing, proofreading, developing marketing and promotional plans, and coordinating the publishing project.

Thanks also goes to the many Wattpad readers who followed the story as a new draft chapter was published every week. The Wattpad first-draft serialisation experiment was a resounding success, and I owe it all to the many unnamed readers whose thirst for the story kept me writing until the entire book was done.

SPREAD THE WORD

If you liked *Nahla: Warrior of the North*, please leave a rating and/or review on Goodreads. This helps other readers find the book. Word-of-mouth is also very helpful. If you think your friends, family, or social media followers would enjoy *Nahla*, please tell them about it. I greatly appreciate your support.

ABOUT THE AUTHOR

Nick Marone grew up in Sydney, Australia before eventually moving south towards Canberra. He developed an interest in science fiction in his teens and has been hooked ever since. His first book, the novella *Fire Over Troubled Water*, was released in 2019, which was later followed by novels in the Space Trip Universe and now the Nahla Chronicles. Over the years, he has worked for *Aurealis* and *Andromeda Spaceways Magazine*.

You can follow Nick at **nickmarone.com**.

NAHLA: ENEMY OF THE KINGDOM

NAHLA CHRONICLES: BOOK 2

The fight has just begun. Launceston is tearing itself apart. The King's Legion and provincial garrisons fight to contain a growing rebellion. King Eero struggles to maintain his iron hold on the populace. Faith in the Guardians of Life has been shaken, threatening to undo the status quo that has been so carefully nurtured for as long as recorded history. Nahla's legacy spreads far and wide, fuelling the discontent among the people.

Lord Johl, Governor of Launceston Province, has plans of his own, now made all the more difficult by the secrets uncovered by Nahla and Prince Myel. But he has the upper hand. His enemies are on the run, and he has overwhelming forces on his side, some of which have been kept in the shadows until now.

Pursued by Johl's army, Nahla's band of rebels flee until they can flee no more. Inevitably, they must face the cruel lord in one decisive battle. When that happens, it won't just be a battle for survival. Rather, it will be a monumental clash for the kingdom, a fight for truth and peace against the oppressive grip of lies and tyranny.

Scan with phone to go to
Nahla: Enemy of the Kingdom

THE GREEN REBELLION: A SPACE TRIP STORY

SPACE TRIP UNIVERSE: BOOK 0.1

Ichika Sato is an overworked and underpaid human resources officer. All she wants is a relaxing holiday enjoying the beaches and jungle walks of Paradise. The resort planet is touted as the hidden gem of the Centaurus Arm, and it is exactly what she needs to reset her mind.

When Ichika arrives at her long-awaited holiday destination, however, she finds a resort filled with people, contrary to the advertisements. But there is something more unsettling at play. The rough surf, the rustling trees, the rumbling wind—all speak to an impending disaster. Everyone sees the signs, but nobody knows what they mean.

Paradise is caught off guard. Instead of sunbathing peacefully on the beach, Ichika is trapped on the planet along with the rest of the tourists, at the mercy of Paradise's wrath. It's a fight for survival and a quest for understanding as Ichika teams up with tourists and resort workers to stop Paradise from destroying itself.

Scan with phone to go to
The Green Rebellion

SPACE TRIP

SPACE TRIP UNIVERSE: BOOK 1

Four friends—Dave, Eddie, Jimmy, and Chuck—are fed up with their boring lives. So when Eddie builds a personal interstellar spacecraft, the obvious thing is to go somewhere. Little do the guys know that simply going somewhere is never quite that easy. The galaxy is a big place, full of complex worlds, people of ill repute, and unexpected events popping up at the wrong time.

Join our woefully underprepared friends as they try desperately to get to the tourist world known as Paradise. Climb aboard *Liberty*, Eddie's oddly-shaped but perfectly functional ship, and share in their pains and joys as they press on to their goal and maybe learn a bit about themselves along the way. You deserve a break, too, and what better way to do so than to spend time with four misfits who clearly need help?

Chuck says to bring coffee when you meet them at the spaceport—don't forget!

Scan with phone to go to
Space Trip

SPACE TRIP II: THE JOURNEY TO FIND THE SECRET OF THE THING IN THE BOX

SPACE TRIP UNIVERSE: BOOK 2

Following their wild maiden voyage aboard *Liberty* and their impulsive purchase of an abandoned resort city, Dave, Eddie, Jimmy, and Chuck haphazardly embark on a new adventure.

Jimmy buys a mysterious box from a small, unassuming antique shop. When he finally gets it open, the secrets it contains will pull him and his friends into a galaxy-spanning hunt for answers and, hopefully, treasure. All Jimmy wants is a few pots of gold.

But the guys are not the only ones interested in the box and its mesmerising contents. A wealthy collector is on their tail—he cares less about treasure and wants more than just answers.

What's in the box? Why are four hopeless treasure hunters scouring the galaxy to unlock its secrets? Who is their pursuer, why is he after Jimmy's bargain box, and what tricks will he play to get what he wants?

Scan with phone to go to
Space Trip II

ESCAPE VELOCITY:
THE WORLDS OF NICK MARONE

This collection holds all seventeen short stories written by Nick Marone up to December 2023. Seven have been published by Delta-V Press, *Aurealis Magazine*, *Etherea Magazine*, *Science Write Now*, *Space and Time Magazine*, and a Deadset Press anthology called *Journeys: Aussie Speculative Fiction*. Rounding out the collection are ten more never-before-seen stories.

From soft science fiction to cyberpunk, humour to near-future, space western to portal fantasy, Nick Marone shows the breadth of his interests and his ability to cross subgenres with ease. Aliens, robots, and artificial intelligence feature heavily in these stories, but at the heart of them all are raw explorations of human emotions and motivations. Nick Marone escapes into science fiction, and he invites you to join him in a variety of worlds, alongside a mix of relatable characters.

Scan with phone to go to
Escape Velocity